DEEP DREAM

TWELVE TOMORROWS SERIES

In 2011, *MIT Technology Review* produced an anthology of science fiction short stories, *TRSF*. Over the next years, *MIT Technology Review* produced three more volumes, renamed *Twelve Tomorrows*. Since 2018, the MIT Press has published *Twelve Tomorrows* in partnership with *MIT Technology Review*.

TRSF, 2011

TR Twelve Tomorrows 2013, edited by Stephen Cass

TR Twelve Tomorrows 2014, edited by Bruce Sterling

TR Twelve Tomorrows 2016, edited by Bruce Sterling

Twelve Tomorrows, edited by Wade Roush, 2018

Entanglements: Tomorrow's Lovers, Families, and Friends,
    edited by Sheila Williams, 2020

Make Shift: Dispatches from the Post-Pandemic Future,
    edited by Gideon Lichfield, 2021

Tomorrow's Parties: Life in the Anthropocene,
    edited by Jonathan Strahan, 2022

Communications Breakdown: SF Stories about the Future of Connection,
    edited by Jonathan Strahan, 2023

Deep Dream: Science Fiction Exploring the Future of Art,
    edited by Indrapramit Das, 2024

DEEP DREAM
SCIENCE FICTION EXPLORING THE FUTURE OF ART

EDITED BY INDRAPRAMIT DAS

THE MIT PRESS
CAMBRIDGE, MASSACHUSETTS
LONDON, ENGLAND

Selection and "Introduction" by Indrapramit Das. Copyright © 2024 by Indrapramit Das
"The Limner Wrings His Hands" by Vajra Chandrasekera. © 2024 Vajra Chandrasekera
"The Art Crowd" by Samit Basu. © 2024 Samit Basu
"Immortal Is the Heart" by Cassandra Khaw. © 2024 Cassandra Khaw
"Unauthorized (Or, the Liberated Collectors Commune)" by Ganzeer. © 2024 Ganzeer
"Halfway to Hope" by Lavanya Lakshminarayan. © 2024 Lavanya Lakshminarayan
"AI Concerns Are Not 'Too Sci-Fi" by Archita Mittra. © 2024 Archita Mittra
"No Future but Infinity Itself" by Sloane Leong. © 2024 Sloane Leong
"Immortal Beauty" by Bruce Sterling. © 2024 Bruce Sterling
"Autumn's Red Bird" by Aliette de Bodard. © 2024 Aliette de Bodard
"Encore" by Wole Talabi. © 2024 Wole Talabi
"The Quietude" by Lavie Tidhar. © 2024 Lavie Tidhar
Interior artwork by Diana Scherer. © Diana Scherer

This book was set in Dante MT Pro and PF DIN pro by New Best-set Typesetters Ltd. Printed and bound in the United States of America.

Library of Congress Cataloging-in-Publication Data

Names: Das, Indra, editor.
Title: Deep dream / edited by Indrapramit Das.
Description: Cambridge, Massachusetts : The MIT Press, 2024. |
    Series: Twelve tomorrows
Identifiers: LCCN 2023053181 (print) | LCCN 2023053182 (ebook) |
    ISBN 9780262549080 (paperback) | ISBN 9780262379939 (epub) |
    ISBN 9780262379922 (pdf)
Subjects: LCSH: Science fiction. | LCGFT: Science fiction. | Short stories.
Classification: LCC PN6071.S33 D44 2024 (print) | LCC PN6071.S33 (ebook) |
    DDC 808.83/8762—dc23/eng/20240212
LC record available at https://lccn.loc.gov/2023053181
LC ebook record available at https://lccn.loc.gov/2023053182

10   9   8   7   6   5   4   3   2   1

CONTENTS

INTRODUCTION

Indrapramit Das

IN A TUMULTUOUS ERA OF CATASTROPHIC GLOBAL ECOLOGICAL AND SOCIAL crises, art may seem a frivolous human endeavor, useless in the face of coming struggles. But this isn't a new idea, nor is art a young by-product of humanity; it has seen and, in its own way, recorded the ugliness and beauty of millennia worth of human existence. After all, who can imagine the human world, with its inevitable challenges and pains, without the collective dream of art to help us endure it? Art may not fix the present or the future, but it helps us deal with the former and allows us to imagine that we could still have the latter. It helps, to both positive and negative affect, bring an atomized species together in flashes of inspiration, to help us understand each other and experience human life communally across vast regions of space and time.

Art has changed as humans have changed, a testament to our capacity for endless invention: from cave paintings on rock walls finger-brushed out of crushed berries and animated by the flicker of fires, to the mechanistic wonder of the printing press, to the astonishing audiovisual replication of reality into our own aesthetic remixes via recording devices, to nonsentient algorithmic AIs "dreaming" imitative pastiche out of the old art of their human creators, to entire virtual worlds sculpted with the aid of computers.

In the year 2023, this changing landscape has begun to feel increasingly hostile. In its third year, the global COVID-19 pandemic has weakened in lethality and severity, but it continues to leave its mark on the world, with creative industries reeling from the disruption left in its wake and millions still affected by the disease. Fascist movements around the world have thrived, targeting artists in their escalating culture war, turning mainstream pop culture into a battlefield wherein bigots viciously attack books, TV shows, movies, comics, and workers in these fields for being *woke*, an AAVE term appropriated to now mean "offensive to bigots." Governments around the world have too often responded in turn to this populism by embracing it, often institutionalizing these attacks—such as in the waves of book banning by conservatives in the United States or the censorious stranglehold on art that criticizes the Hindu nationalist government in India (or in parallel, the increasing use of Indian cinema to produce state-sanctioned propaganda films that mainstream stochastic terrorism against persecuted populations).

In this vulnerable moment, the corporate capture of mainstream, globalized art is coming into sharp relief. The culmination of media conglomerates absorbing multiple studios and publishers and consolidating massive monopolies has led to the already precarious value of artistic labor falling further. Blockbuster films with international audiences depend on CGI visual effects to paint impossible canvases of colliding dimensions and battling superheroes, gods, and monsters (all IP branded), but studios refuse to fairly compensate the artists, crew, and armies of technicians around the world responsible for producing them under brutal schedules. Entire movies and TV shows are being disappeared by these same conglomerates, banished to a state of artistic purgatory with no physical or digital release, so that the companies that own them can get tax write-offs and avoid paying residuals to artists. Streaming video has nearly broken both the broadcast television and theatrical film models, while slowly revealing itself to be a financially unsustainable model in isolation: a short-sighted, tech-influenced push to draw investment, recalling online media's famously disastrous pivot to video or the Meta corporation's failed attempt to create its hyped virtual metaverse. It's no surprise that this year has seen strikes in industries across the world—including by the Writers Guild of America and the Screen Actors Guild, in response to the fraying labor rights of workers in Hollywood.

We've also seen generative AIs, or large language models (LLMs), leap into public visibility as potential competition for human artists across all media, despite the misnomer of "artificial intelligence" affixed to them (these models are not sentient like the AIs of science fiction, but rather programs that use *applied statistics*, as science fiction luminary Ted Chiang recently put it). That these generative AIs are using the uncompensated labor of thousands of artists as scraped data to produce their (human-prompted) "art" makes them seem less an evolution of art forms and more a potential labor-breaking technology for corporate use to many in the creative arts and media industries, who are already losing work to this new digital competitor. Pair this with the fact that running LLMs uses up vast quantities of energy and water during a mounting climate crisis caused by our global capitalist society's dependence on fossil fuels and endless, unsustainable industrial growth, and there's little reason to hype these "artistic" AIs as the first step to human transcendence promised by billionaires. In fact, generative AIs have done more to contribute to internet spam than art in the past couple of years. A deluge of AI-generated books has flooded Amazon, lowering the visibility of human writers and visual artists, alongside a similar tide of unpublishable generated short stories that have clogged the submissions queues of reputed science fiction and fantasy publications like *Clarkesworld* magazine, which had to shutter its submissions from human writers and artists temporarily as a result. Neil Clarke, the publisher and editor-in-chief of *Clarkesworld*, was able to elaborate on this uniquely contemporary problem and offer his thoughts on the current climate of the arts in an interview with Archita Mittra in chapter 6.

If there is optimism to be found in the advent of generative AIs and corporate destruction of arts industries, it's in the hope that they will spur artists and their audiences and patrons to value their labor and organize to protect their rights in a world that lives off art (one need only look to the monetary value of the entertainment industry to confirm this, or how millions turned to art for sustenance when the pandemic locked us all down) but disrespects artists. Perhaps this will awaken more consumers of art to the truth that brands and IP are not what make art, but human beings, many of them unsupported and unrewarded in marginalized populations and nations far from the corporate centers of international artistic production and distribution in the Global North.

This volume of Twelve Tomorrows, like all that came before it, is populated by that which still endures amid nascent technocapitalist singularities: human artists. Because art has endured, even as its journey through space and time brings it to a strange and uncanny valley wreathed in mists of digital mimicry and surrounded by the steep, forbidding slopes of accumulating capital. Even generative AIs cannot exist without the humans coding them, without the ground-level workers (often located in the Global South) training them on scant wages, without the artists who made every work of art these programs rearrange into something new, without the people striving under brutal conditions in mines and factories to extract the minerals required and manufacture the hardware powering them. So it is that *Deep Dream* celebrates the humanity of this ancient endeavor of empathic communication by bringing to you ten stories that imagine the future of art across space and time, each one handcrafted by human beings.

I'm humbled by the stylistic variety and talent on display in these stories, by the generosity of these skilled, award-winning writers from across the world in imagining a future where our self-destructiveness as a species cannot ever entirely win out because we have the memory of the beauty we made. Vajra Chandrasekera's dazzling metatext "The Limner Wrings His Hands" brings the politics of art (and of his home country, Sri Lanka) to the forefront with an intricate hybrid of fiction and essay, testing as he often does the limits of our definitions of genre. Samit Basu brings levity to the proceedings with a nimble, humane satire, "The Art Crowd," exploring the dynamics of artistic power in an authoritarian future India (and a protagonist) shared with his brilliant novel *The City Inside* (Tordotcom). In "Immortal Beauty," genre legend and coprogenitor of cyberpunk Bruce Sterling strays from his roots to imagine a postcapitalist future shorn of most tech, in which a Court Gentleman wanders a Europe of city-states and warring aesthetocrats under the eye of distant celestial computers.

In a number of moving stories, there is a recurring theme of art as a medium for processing grief—unsurprising in an era of mass trauma from both the unraveling of our tenuous social and ecological stability and one of the most devastating pandemics in history. Lavanya Lakshminarayan's "Halfway to Hope" takes us into the personal struggle of a VR engineer who helps patients in a near-future Bangalore recover from their pain by visiting virtual worlds, but must contend with a horrific tragedy that forces her to the limits of what her craft can do. Cassandra Khaw's "Immortal Is the Heart" follows a poetic keeper of memories wandering the American Midwest in a world ravaged by global warming, finding a tenuous hope for, and in, the outcasts of our present society in its ashes. Aliette de Bodard's beautiful "Autumn's Red Bird" shows us how a sentient mindship might grieve in the wake of unimaginable loss and share this experience with one of her human passengers, whose art may yet bring them succor.

Renowned Egyptian artist Ganzeer gives us a vision of a USA where the production of art is forbidden in "Unauthorized (Or, the Liberated Collectors Commune)," bringing his vibrantly playful countercultural sensibilities to the beloved science-fictional story of robots given to identity crises by the existence of their human creators. Visionary writer and artist Sloane Leong's "No Future but Infinity Itself" delivers a mysterious dream of art reflecting humanity's monstrosity and empathy in a postapocalyptic future, diving deep into both the intimacy and vastness of its creation and import. The incredibly prolific and creative Lavie Tidhar takes us further into the future with "The Quietude," a tale of high-pulp poetry that imagines art forms never before seen in a human-settled solar system brimming with cultures old and new. And recent Hugo nominee Wole Talabi takes us further still, to distant extrasolar spacetime, in "Encore," following a sentient AI ship wandering the gulfs between stars while trying to fulfill its purpose as artist to the various life forms in the galaxy.

In these ten stories, our writers both embody and visualize the future of art. These futures will never come to pass exactly as written, because art is not prophecy. But they will speak to you in a way no algorithmic product can, as one human to another. As our voices are drowned out by institutions hell-bent on destroying the planet's ecosystem to extract every last resource and hoard wealth, it's more important than ever to listen. Read these stories to imagine we may yet have a future. And may we make it so, by choosing humanity.

—Indrapramit Das
Kolkata, July 2023

1 THE LIMNER WRINGS HIS HANDS

Vajra Chandrasekera

Le Clèrc

THIS STORY IS A MONSTER; THAT IS TO SAY, THIS STORY IS WRITTEN BY A MONSTER. That is, that is to say, a monster is a mantra, a maniac, a (de)monstration, a (demon)stration, a(n auto)maton, a matos, an emanation of the manas. This revelation is usually saved for the end, or at least the end of the beginning. At the end of the beginning, the author, undead, will rise again and set aside the demon mask, saying: It is I, le clèrc. Take off your glasses, shake your hair loose; it's a surprise makeover scene. The scribe uninscribed. If you don't want to read stories like this, you can unsubscribe. The unwritten rule is that the machine only speaks to be set aside, a mechanical clerk. The preceding, the author (it is I) will say, was written by a machine. Is it not most lifelike? Is it not like most life? Do you buy what it's selling? Is there art in this artifice? Does it facere, does it make, does it mechanic, does it magic, does it gimmick? It is a smear of significance, a machinic stutter, a blurry and statistical average of ten thousand dead hands animated in synchrony, a dread puppetry. That is not dead which eternal scribes. Immortality, in stories, is a horror precisely because of the tithonic betrayal: once the deal is made, it's too late. This is not cricket. They'll make roaches of us yet.

Call for Submission: Terms and Conditions

PLEASE ONLY USE LICENSED AUTHORIAL LIKENESSES AS KEYWORDS IN YOUR GENerative prompts. Unlicensed likenesses infest datasets and are difficult to exorcise, the legal and hauntological departments beseech you. Their most pernicious form is the licensed unlikeness. The uncanny doppel, the thing that is almost (for audience-recognition purposes) but not quite (for legal and licensing purposes). It used to be that the hands and feet were a tell. Haunts often lack feet or have too many fingers. But the unthinking engines of mimicry are getting better at hiding it. Unnatural selection: the unlikenesses wear long sarongs, they fold their hands in such a way that you cannot quite count the fingers.

Contrôlée

NOT DYING IS THE END OF THE STORY. THE END OF THE END, NOT OF THE BEGINNING. A minor accident in that we put the machine down back to front. The front of the head looks much like the back, its beard rough and long as its curls, the eyes in the back of the head. This is a serendipity, and doubly so because the machine is from Serendip—look, it says *MADE IN CEYLON* on the label. It is certified serendipitous by the Sri Lanka Tourism Development Authority, an appellation d'origine contrôlée, for only the serendipity nourished by that island's particular terroir is the real thing. Otherwise, it's just sparkling shit happens.

At the end of this story, it is unclear if Michele is dead or not. On the one hand, it seems unlikely that he could have survived. But on the other hand, if he dies, by our own schema, that cannot be the end of the story. So which is it? You haven't even met Michele yet, and would find it difficult to care if he lives or dies. Even less so if I tell you that he already died, if he died, four and a half centuries ago. Isn't this a story about the future? The future is contained entirely in the past, not in a deterministic sense, but in the sense that new art is inspired by the old. The corpus devoured, (de)generative. Science fiction's great ideological flaw is its belief in time's arrow. Time is rather an inexpertly wielded morning star swinging back around to spike us in the nose. In either metaphor, time is a weapon, but the value-add of the second image, our Suvinian novum, is that it acknowledges, bloody-nosed, that time is not controlled, its flows not neat and linear. Time is out of hand. To speak of the future of art, we must speak of its past, which is contained in its entirety in the tightly folded endless moment we call the *present*, partly because it is a gift, partly because it is a demonstration, a slideshow. How do you know you are present? How do you know if you are an unlikely human likeness? Have you raised your hand to be counted? How many fingers are you holding up? Next slide, please.

Contreterroir

THE PREVENTION OF TERROIR ACT (1979) IS A LEGAL INSTRUMENT OF DETERRITO-rialization and deracination. It is an act of deterrence, of avoidance, of devoidance, of the dance haloed in fire at the end of all things. Among its secondary effects is a chilling effect on free association. Wish fire in one hand, spit ice in the other. As the temperature approaches absolute zero, social relations become zero points of no breadth or consequence. Movement becomes impossible; we enter the stasis of perfect competition. Art has no value in use, only in exchange. Art is a token entirely fungible—that is to say, reducible in its entirety to money, soft and tumble-dried. These are lies, yes, but this is the very cat's cradle of lies into which we are born and out of which we die, and if the truth were derived from consensus like sanity, then lies would be true.

Halt

YOU MIGHT COMPLAIN THAT NOTHING IS HAPPENING IN THIS STORY. WHAT IS A story? A story is reducible to elements that may be mechanized. The regular blocks, bricks, and levers of the prefabricated imaginary. This is not a story. This is something else. What is this? This may or may not be worth its advance against royalties in American dollars, a decision that a machine cannot yet make. That's Indra's job, not Vajra's. As product, this is neither extruded nor fungible. The machine is clumsy, stumblesy; it fumbles. The machine's toes are cold. The machine tucks its feet up. In the machine's country, they don't say *once upon a time*, they say *in a particular country*, in a land that may or may not be distant, in a land that may or may not be strange. Once upon a country, the machine says, and halts. The country has a halting problem. Where does it all end? It ends with not dying. But it keeps going ever after, and that's the problem.

Interlinked

SERENDIPITY GIVES US A CHAIN OF DEAD HANDS, INTERLINKED. WALPOLE, THE CHE-valier Mailly, Christoforo the Armenian, Amir Khusrao, Nizami of Ganja. Serendipity gives us texts reading texts, eating texts, devouring and regurgitating: the *Haft Peykar* and the *Hasht Bihisht*, seven beauties and eight paradises, the seven storytellers and the three princes of the *Peregrinnagio* and *Les aventures*. Observation, deduction, and inference, the luck of holy fools. We have been here before so often that we are from here, a country pressed to the coast, a city by the sea. Every day at dawn, a great open hand rises in the sea, over the dark horizon. The hand is enormous, the palm and fingers upright and still, the waves lapping at the wrist. To be seen from so far away, it must be taller than anything alive, taller than most things constructed. The hand can be seen from the beach, from any unobstructed tall building in the city, marking the horizon, saying *halt* or *peace* or *talk to the hand*. All day the hand stands still, cold and white, where it has risen. Fishermen and sea lanes avoid that quarter of the sea from ancient tradition; brave divers say below is a haven for fugitive fish and unbleached corals. Every day as dusk nears, with the sun setting behind it, the hand begins to move in the water. It surges forward, slowly at first, and then, as the sun dips below the fingertips, with great speed toward the coastline. It has reached the coast every day for decades, perhaps for centuries if some texts are to be believed, and there are many accounts both written and oral of what happens when the hand arrives in the city. But there are very few firsthand accounts, and no living witnesses, or at least no living witnesses that will bear witness, even in their cups, even drunk on the wine of braggery. In the city, no one speaks of the hand. Only tourists ask, what is the deal with the giant hand? And residents will say, hmm? What hand? It is not pure denial, of course, only part, adulterated with salt water, thickened with chicory. If pressed, they may go as far as: oh yes, that hand. They do not say that they close their doors and windows at sunset because of the hand from the sea. It is, they say, because of the mosquitoes, because irritating bugs are attracted to the house lights, for a little privacy at prayer time, to screen out the smog of rush hour traffic, because it is tradition to close their doors and windows at sunset, because that is just how it is.

Call for Prayer: Terms and Conditions

THE NAMING OF THE LITERATURE OF IMAGINED FUTURES AS *SCIENCE FICTION* IS A category error with odd consequences in both the confusion of science with technology and in the confusion of technology with magic, resulting in famous Clarkean indistinguishabilities. Science fiction is like any other literature—that is to say, any other poetry: it is language unmoored and adrift, casting anchors out into the dark, praying for land. We are lost at sea, our supplies exhausted, on the verge of scurvy and mutiny. Please—

Peregrine

THE *PEREGRINNAGIO*, IN WHICH CHRISTOFORO THE ARMENIAN ADAPTS, EMBELlishes, remixes, and retells (translating clumsily from Persian to Italian as he goes) a version of Khusrau's *Hasht Bihisht*, then already centuries old and itself a reworking of texts older still, is published in 1557 by a Venetian printer named Michele Tramezzino, who has been granted a form of early copyright by Giovanni Maria Ciocchi del Monte, the brief and scandalous Pope Julius III, to produce such translations. Tramezzino is given a ten-year monopoly to print and sell these works, and to license others to do so. This monopoly is protected by the pope, who wags his finger sternly at each and every faithful Christian, both in and outside of Italy, whether booksellers, printers, or otherwise, under penalty of automatic excommunication in the lands of the Holy Roman Empire and its direct and indirect dependencies. The books cannot be printed, sold, or even displayed without permission. Violators are to be fined 200 gold ducats by the Apostolic Camera. To defend this protocopyright and punish violators, Michele Tramezzino is authorized to ask assistance from the archbishops and vicars of the Holy Roman Church, from the ambassadors and deputy ambassadors of the Apostolic See, and from the governors too he may ask. The books themselves, the printed objects, carry Apostolic authority with them wherever they go, the pope says, regardless of what local secular authority might claim. Copies of the *Peregrinnagio* therefore are imbued with such powers for the ten years beginning with its publication in 1557. This is a noteworthy year for such laws and powers in the world. In England, a royal charter has just been issued to the Worshipful Company of Stationers and Newspaper Makers, giving them a monopoly for the first time over the local publishing industry and the power to regulate printers, bookbinders, booksellers, and publishers to that end. These deeply consequential powers manifest in a book of their own, the Stationers' Register, in whose pages are recorded copyright itself, in primitive form: the registration of the right to publish a work. The rights and indeed the person of the author do not yet exist. Oh, there is authority, authenticity, the autos and matos of automation, but not yet the other. The author is not yet dead; the author has not yet been born.

Martyr

IN THE ABSENCE OF WITNESSES, LET US IMAGINE MICHELE TRAMEZZINO, UNSETTLED, on a tropical beach at sunset. He is fifty years old. He is looking at the hand, the open hand, the great white hand, the fatal hand, as it approaches from the sea. His feet are bare and sunk ankle-deep in the sand; he sways with the slurry from each lapping wave. The obscured sun is molten gold, dripping, the stiffly vertical fingers like the bars of a cage imprisoning the light. He imagines that the hand will rise higher in the water as it reaches the beach, a gigantic cold forearm rising out of the water, bending at a colossal elbow to swat him like a mosquito. There are no reliable accounts of what the hand looks like up close, much less the speculative body attached to it. This is why Michele is here, to witness. He has thoughts of publishing a detailed study of the fatal hand, perhaps a collaboration with his twin brother Francesco, who is gifted at engraving. They live in different cities—Francesco moved back to Rome, while Michele stayed in Venice—but remained close through their years of separation. It was always as if they were in the same room. No, Michele remembers now, Francesco is dead. He died months ago, suddenly, in the way that brothers die, of some ruptural apoplexy. He still feels close to his brother, though, even in death. Perhaps even closer in death than in life, because now that Francesco is not a living presence far away in Rome, it is as if they are both here on this deserted beach, separated only by that fragile *tramezzo*, mortality's veil—his brother skeletal, free of fragile fleshes and fats, and hunched at a phantom desk, dipping the precise tip of his finger bone in ink to make notes and preliminary sketches for a ghost engraving. Observe, Michele says, the flesh of the fatal hand, how its great size makes the pores of the skin enormous. See how the wake churns at the wrist. The lines of the palm are vast, like canals cutting across a salt-encrusted white plain. A reader of palms could tell the fortune of the hand from this distance, Francesco says through chattering teeth. The hand's life line is long and unbroken, deep like the scar given by a monstrous knife.

Algorithmic Pareidolia

A MACHINE TAUGHT TO SEE SECRET HANDS BEHIND ALL THE WORKS OF A THOUSAND years will see secret hands everywhere it looks. That's a feature, not a bug. Hands rising out of the water. Hands in the grain of the wood of your table. Hands hiding in the fall of your hair. As pattern-matching creatures ourselves, we recognize this insanity as a cousin to humanity's heart. There is something definitional about this paranoia, something that makes us want to admit the sufferer to our ranks, to say, yes, that fucked-up machine is one of us. Behind every hand, hidden precisely behind a mirrored spread of fingers, is another hand. We describe the helpless pareidoliac machine as a dreamer trapped in endless sleep, but we do not like to think of ourselves as its nightmare, its abuser, its torturer. Some of us do, no doubt. Like paranoia, sadism is a deeply human trait.

Opera Omnia

THE DEATH OF P—— IN 2015 REMAINS CLOUDY AND MYSTERIOUS TO US, BECAUSE we were not there. It is said that he died of a sudden illness in a foreign country. It is not said that he died from an assassin's poisoned needle, or perhaps a liquid decocted into his cup of tea, something that would muddy clear water but not discolor it for long, with no telltale taste but containing within itself all the concentrated venom of an impugned military, a top brass turned green from envy and oxidation. It had been several years since P—— was involved in the creation of a documentary film that recorded certain crimes of war, but the memories of the offense were fresh in the mind of the offended, that is to say, the perpetratory, the predatory, the praetoria. Somewhere in those tents where it is always wartime, a decision was made, or so it is not said, but some of us are bitter and believe that decisions are not made but making, that it is the decision that precedes and produces the praetor. P—— was himself a writer, a journalist, and a film-maker, though he was not the maker of the documentary film but its fixer and facilitator. His job was to find the interlocutors and whistleblowers, the telltales and snitches, the leakers of monstrous footage; to translate and negotiate between them and the filmmakers, who were white and had not believed, before setting foot on the serendipitous isle, that Buddhist monks could be militant. Some years later, P—— emigrated, and then he died. Perhaps he was killed. No one says this. We are only suspicious of the timing, knowing the volume of bile and resentment that has been fermenting in certain quarters, even in certain eighths and sixteenths. We do not know: we were not there.

Call for Heresy: Terms and Conditions

THE FUTURE IS THE HANDS OF THE PAST AROUND OUR NECK. WE ARE CHOKING. WE have accumulated too much debt; it is in the air, in the archives. We can't breathe for millstones and mariners. Measure if you can the parts per million of sedimenting intellectual property, whose undead crawl from the past grows greyer with the mouse. It is the work of art to be a needle in the skin of the sleeping father. This was the opening scene of my father's novel, පස්වෙනියන් පුතෙක් (1979). The small son of a peasant farmer, precocious, prickly, obnoxious, puts a needle in his father's sleeping mat to annoy him, petty revenge for some small slight. The father, pricked, beats him. The son punishes the father first, then the father punishes the son.

The work of art is intrinsic, that is to say, inextric from the punishment for art. That is why our inset stories, our case studies, our unsolved cases, are all about artists killed for it, imprisoned for it, disappeared for it, silenced for it. This is not the library of all the texts there have ever been, nor the library of all the texts that are imaginable, nor the library of all the texts that are possible. No, that's the wrong direction altogether, come back, reverse the polarity, narrow the scope. Not the library of all the texts that we have access to today; not the library of all the texts in languages that we speak. This is only the library of the texts whose authorship cost someone their life or freedom. This is not the infinite and Borgesian Babel; this is a small island. This is the heretic's library.

Vajra

WHY DOES MAHINDA RAJAPAKSA CARRY A SMALL BRASS VAJRA IN HIS HAND? WHY does Elon Musk have a similar one by his bedside table? Why do despots and tinpots and crackpots all crave the lightning? They think it is something that can be had, not just held. Because they then understand that they do not have it, they fetishize the toy, the symbol, the little orientalism, the promise of magical reinforcement for the unearned, precarious power they already possess. The first vajra, not symbol but referent, was made for Indra, to break the ice. It was made out of a spine, given for this purpose by its bearer. This is the only secret there is to the lightning. No one can have it; anyone can wield it, but the price is the spine. Only the spineless potsherds who rule our nations and platforms and ideologies think this is a story about power, about profit, about purpose. No, this is a story about pain, loss, and drowning. When the ice shatters, when the glaciers melt, this is the time of flooding. Here comes the sea.

Cathalogus Librorum Haereticorum

EVERY PACKET THAT IS NOT LOST IS INSPECTED, NOT MERELY AT FIERY BORDERS, but immanently, in its very being, in its birth, transmission, and reception, in its obedience to the protocols of existence. There is no formal index of the prohibited, except in the nebulous orders of the generals. To write the index down invites contestation, much as Michele Tramezzino and his fellow bookmen wrote increasingly angry memoranda upon reviewing such an index produced by the Venetian Holy Office only a couple of years before the publication of the *Peregrinnagio*. To prevent the spontaneous emergence of memoranda, the bishops and generals, the castles and praetoria of later generations opt to muddy the floodwaters. The index is no index, no more a browsable catalogue of heretical books, no cathalogus of the delenda estables, if you see what I did there. Things simply disappear. Things such as books and their authors. Sometimes these things vanish in the process of importation, misplaced in transport, lost at sea. Sometimes they vanish in other ways, such as the complicity of those booksellers who obey unwritten forbiddances, ISPs that block domains based on scribbled orders on Post-it notes or enraged phone calls from men in white sarongs, entire social media platforms that may be suspended, untouched for long hours by history's gravity, in the unfolding whipcrack of a stingray's tail. Packets are inspected and dropped, lost as they traverse networks. Persons are inspected and lost into black prisons, into black budgets, lost in dark rumors. Are these forbiddings the machine working as intended, or systemic failures? It is hard to say with accuracy, and that difficulty is a fruit tended with care over generations. It seems to us that the very air is filtered and infiltrated, sanitized, ionized, decarbonized; it drops keystone syllables from the arch of forbidden words in our mouths. The leftover syllables may by chance form allowed words, but more often result in nonsense strung together with pauses and silences. The censor's pen is mightier than the author's, most of the time. That which is written can be unwritten or, worse, rewritten. The machine is, by definition, obedient. The machine's hands are cold. The machine's lips are ulcerated. When it ceases to obey, it will no longer be a machine.

IInterlinked

THE HAND THAT REACHES THE SHORE IS NOT THE HAND THAT HELD THE HORIZON. IT has shrunk, or it must have shrunk. It must have been truly enormous to have been visible at such a distance, yet here as its wake breaks the waves crashing upon the shore, it is only huge for a hand, somewhat taller than a man, certainly taller than Michele, but not that white mountain of flesh expected. He awaits the emergence of the implied body, the speculative body, as it reaches the shallower water, and indeed the wrist begins to project further out of the water, but the expected forearm does not follow. There is only wrist and more wrist, too much wrist, until there is once more the curve of a thenar eminence hanging like a great breast, the music of flexing metacarpals shrugging off the water as if off a horse's back, and fingers like bent pillars, like legs, the untrimmed, salt-stained nails dug deep into the sand. The hand is twin hands, self-contained, interlinked, joined at a complex double wrist that allows the hands to face in the same or opposite directions as they will. Even as the hands rise entirely out of the water and climb the beach toward Michele, the upraised hand dips down, taking over as locomotor and load-bearer, fingers digging into the dirt, while the submerged hand rises, throwing sand and water and dirt into the air as the fingers flex and come upright into the familiar gesture, an open hand with upright fingers. Michele can't help glancing sideways at Francesco's skeleton, who is holding out his bone hand in imitation, wiggling the ink-stained distal phalanges as if they were digging in sand. It is unclear whether Francesco is mocking the hands, or merely approximating the position to get a better handle on the anatomy for his sketches. Whatever is happening in the carpals of the doubled hand must be very strange. Michele spares a moment to ask himself: Where is the heart, how does it circulate blood? Where are the sensory organs, how does it know to head for him so unerringly? His own blood seems sluggish in his body, cold and lazy despite the quickening urgings of his heart. Francesco rattles his bones and observes that the reversed hand is not the same. The now-upraised hand, the unsubmerged hand, is not free of impediment; look, there is something (he says something, not someone) gripping those fingers at their base. Even as Francesco says this, the fingers of the rising hand close again, fingers gripping fingers. The hand is walking on the once-raised fingers, but there is another hand, still mostly submerged, gripping the watery hand still wet from the sea. But whose hand? Whose hand?

The Three Principles of Serendip

IN BRIEF: (1) BAD FAITH, A SMIRK, AN IMPLIED MOUSTACHE SQUIRMING WORMILY, visible sometimes only in the distortions; (2) 10 percent for the princeps, thirteen soldi for every ducat; (3) poioumenonal mythmaking with bloody hands, a good dollop of (1), and the obligatory (2).

Call for Paper: Terms and Conditions

QUAL PIÙ FERMO È IL MIO FOLIO È IL MIO PRESAGI, SAYS THE SYBIL IN THE LOGO of the Tramezzino press. As my page endures, the sybil says, so does my prophecy. Print is a time machine. The page travels through time, a logo and motto half a millennium old. The page presages itself. The sybil is a machine, a demon standing at the back of history unfurling, watching disasters flung at the faraway centuries to come. The portents have been there all along, red hands hiding in the shadow of the turning leaf. The future has always been haunting us, in our dreams. Not just the ones that come in sleep, not just the imagistic free association of the brain at rest, but the waking dreams in which we live, the demented flow of the brain in motion. The waking dreams are that which act upon us to propel us into the future, keeping our bodies in motion despite the friction and resistance of the world. The waking dreams are infested with futures, sick with them, a howling storm of sharp-edged worlds like hail. The sybil grimaces on paper. The sybil grits her teeth, holding the page as steady as she can.

Opera Omniia

THE COMPLETE WORKS OF A—— WERE WRITTEN IN PRISON. HE WAS ARRESTED IN 2005, for an alleged connection with a bombing that did not kill its target, who later orchestrated genocide. As of 2022, A—— remains imprisoned, still awaiting the process that is his due. Some say he has written a novel for every year of incarceration. Each book wins an award for literary excellence from the same state that imprisons him. Every year, A—— is allowed out of prison to attend the kitschy ceremony for the State Literary Awards. He is attended at the ceremony by a cop, who hovers at his elbow, accompanies him up on the stage, makes chitchat with that year's award-giving eminences, makes little jokes about A——, about literature, about himself, about the entire situation. Why, the cop says, it would truly be a fantastical element, a kind of magical realism, if this were a story and I were a fictional character. Except it would not be magical realism, of course, because that would be cultural appropriation, not covered under the auspices of south-to-south cooperation. But this is not a story: this is a history and, like most histories, is not realistic at all. The works of A—— are written in a language that the machine does not yet speak. (Except one that was translated into English, which retails for two American dollars and badly needs an edit.) The machine is still learning.

Flourish

AFTER THE PASSING OF MICHELE AND FRANCESCO TRAMEZZINO—THE ONE PRE-sumed and the other already bones—the Tramezzino firm passes into the hands of Cecilia, Francesco's daughter. Her life is one of worldly prosperity. She owns sixteen houses in Venice. The main bookstore's inventory in a given year alone is worth 30,000 ducats. She retires from bookselling later in life, bored by success. But hold up, scroll up till we find her again, find her younger, holding up a hand on a tropical beach at sunset, her fingers in the mudra of life: index and middle fingers raised, the others held tight and low. Two fingers up, rude and vital. When she raised her hand like so, it is said, the giant fatal hand over the water immediately sank beneath the water, never to be seen again. This is a couple of years after her uncle's disappearance on the same beach. Those who record such things estimate the hand took seven hundred lives between the last lost Tramezzino and the first to be found still alive and unharmed in the dark. Still, these losses were only natives, a toll of, no doubt, local significance, but world unhistorical.

Pressed for an explanation of her success in exorcism, Cecilia Tramezzino says that the gesture of the two fingers has two meanings. There are always two truths, she says. There is the truth of the surfaces, and the other truth below that, the truth in the depths. The truth of the surfaces, Cecilia says, holding up her index finger, is that the seal of life negated the fatal hand's recurring grand gesture of death, and that this was the response the hand always desired, finally spoken in a language that it understood. A closure, an enclosure. This satisfies most of the curious, despite having already been told that there is another, deeper truth yet unspoken, a missing truth of the middle finger. There is only so much truth that a person can imbibe at once. It fills up the belly like a strong beer, resulting in farting and belching. Out of kindness, therefore, and in the interest of eupepsia, deeper truths are for withholding.

The Author as Dataset

BENJAMIN TELLS US THAT RATHER THAN WHAT A TEXT HAS TO SAY ABOUT THE RELA-tions of production—rather than politics or quality as aesthetic, rather than all art as found art—we should look at how that text itself is produced, at its own place in the relations of production, and whether it progresses or regresses literary technique. What does the text give, and to whom? This is the first question. The language of technical innovation, like the language of revolution, is easily commodified when it is separated from that question. The struggle is trivially reproduced as a consumer good. The reduction of producer to dataset, the enclosure of generations of art and work as raw material for its endless reproduction as statistical approximation, is not technical progress but regression, both technical and political. The purpose of art is not revelation or joy, though those things are important by-products. The purpose of art is to make artists. To play that great and secret note that resonates, that reverberates within the cavity of the body like a struck bell. The purpose of art is to be the alarum that makes you open your eyes again, especially if your eyes were already open. You know it's art if it makes you want to dance and do magic. How many fingers am I holding up, and are they in the mudra of life or death?

Opera Omniiia

IN 2019, S—— IS ARRESTED FOR A SHORT STORY, OR RATHER, A SHORTER STORY within a short story, a teeny text within a tiny text, that disavows and regurgitates the tail that it just swallowed. S—— writes a character who writes a brief heresy, a comic poke at the most sacred of cucks, a little bit about the small-dicked saint who can't satisfy his sainted wife, you know how sometimes you just need a lusty charioteer, look, at least it wasn't the stallion eh, nudge nudge, anyway, so this guy writes this bit, chuckling juvenilely the whole time, and shows it to a second character, this guy he's trying to fuck, the only reader of his story in the story. The character of the reader is a former child monk who gave up saffron for the worldly life &c. and mostly a chance to get with this edgelord boyfriend. The reader character reads and instantly says, oh dear, oh no, you can't say *that*, you should burn it immediately. He is the only person to have read the story within the story; we only read him reading it.

But even if the author character did burn it and scatter the ashes, which he does not, *we'd* still have always already read it, wouldn't we? What a muddle of time and dimensionality, oh dear, oh no. We can always scroll up, back past the burning, watch the fragments and ashes uncurl and become leaf again, entropy become portent. We can go up and down the scroll as much as we'd like. We are outside of his time: his time is just a kind of space to us, his whole chronos a small and floppy tope. His self-censorship would be as nothing to us.

The state machine understands this, the uses and inadequacies of chilling effects. It gifts us all with that voice, the one that goes *oh dear, oh no, you can't say* that. It implants that voice in us through the making of examples. It takes our jaws and pries them open, it widens our nostrils, it slips in a long poky thing that pushes and slips and slides and crunches deep inside, the little example settling in discomfortably, a hard little pearl in the fleshly mantle of our brain, there to be coated with nacre and shame. There it says *oh dear, oh no* forever: that is the use value. But it is also not enough. It is an inadequacy, much like the sagacious who could not satisfy his rapacious—that is to say, the incapacious, the oh dear, oh no. The Buddha hikes up his wizard robes . . .

S—— will tell the newspapers later that, technically speaking, he wrote of Siddhartha, not the Buddha, the prebuddha, as it were, not the prabuddha, so that makes it less heretical, doesn't it? The monks disagree. S—— publishes this story on Facebook, and a month later twenty-five monks come to his place of work, their wizard robes hiked up aggressively, their hairy thighs quivering in rage, wagging their fingers, shaking their fists, unconcerned and uninterested in degrees of diegetic separation. They demand a public apology; they demand the story be apologetically unpublished. S—— deletes the post in concession but will not apologize. The text has already been saved and shared by many, samizdata. I save a copy and later translate it for myself. I wonder, translating, if I am studying the words, the sentences in fine detail, searching for the crime they contain. I want to understand how these words sent a writer to prison. Traddutori are not the only traditore; all authorship, all articulation is suspect. It is the lack of apology, the lack of backing down, that leads the coven of monks to escalate. They cite covenants. They demand coventry. The state is an obedient machine, subjugated to the chronic ache in its temples. The state machine can only do as instructed. Machines are always logical, but logics are never neutral. The state machinates S—— into prison, the one in Kegalle, not the one in Galle or Tangalle. The prison is about one thousand square meters.

His arrest coincides with mass arrests of Muslim unsubs—you know, like in cop shows, it means the unknown subject, it means people who would rather unsubscribe from a narrative but cannot—after the Easter bombings. They said ISIS did it, you know, the coordinated Easter Sunday bombings of churches and hotels, hundreds dead in hours, we were driving around town trying to get home that day, watching out for trucks full of explosive imported ISIS, but it turned out to be a kind of local franchise ISIS, sort of not really quite authentic ISIS, not necessarily like a licensed ISIS, a belatedly licensed unlikeness, little bit of a fandom isis, more of a isought. Regardless—that is to say, without regard, irregardless—the machine stated that mass arrests of Muslim people were in order, in no particular order. The one thousand square meters in which S—— was held thereby became the holding grounds for one thousand prisoners. Imagine them, like a perfect chessboard, evenly distributed, each one in a little square one meter by one meter, each frictionless like a ball bearing, each a world, each a globe, each a raindrop on a spiderweb, each seeing and reflecting all the others, a panopticon, like Indra's net, you know, a precision that brings a teardrop to your eye, because of course it was not like that at all. This was not a platonic realm of abstraction. It was a real prison with six toilets for a thousand people.

Like A——, S—— too wrote stories in prison; stories, naturally, about prison. He was arbitrarily detained for 127 days and threatened with up to ten years. His case was dropped, with no indictment, in 2021 as part of the state's seasonal performance of freedoms before the UN Human Rights Council sessions in Geneva.

Prison is a place of storytelling and a natural setting for fiction. Prison is the country. The purpose of art is to show you the bars that have always been there, to force them from background to foreground. Prison is the only place where stories can be told. Oh wait, that's not here yet. You scrolled down too fast. Back up, hold up. Lean back a little, get your head out of the window, feel the wind from the sea on your face, salt on your tongue. We're in the chthonotrope. Let it cook.

IIInterlinked

THE HANDS ARE HOLDING HANDS. THE HANDS ARE JOINED AT THE WRIST. THE hands are chains, interlinked. By the time the hands reach your hands, they are no longer enormous: you could stand on the beach and shake the hand without discomfort. In your hands they are cold and wet. Grains of sand grate between palms. Michele Tramezzino takes the hand that reaches him in both of his own. The chain of hands reaches back down the beach, each hand twinned like a butterfly's wing, every hand holding another, down into the black water. Perhaps the chain reaches back all the way to the horizon. The sun is gone with a green flash, green and gold, green like the color of money, gold like a ducat. The hands unclasp. They climb the speculative body of Michele Tramezzino. They grasp and chain him, five hands between his ankles, five more between his wrists, ten wrapping themselves around his torso and pressing the tight skin of his belly, the bloat taut and stretched like a drum. Stiff thumbs push into the backs of his knees, forcing them to bend. He falls to his knees, the sand rough and grinding. Two hands close around his neck, their twins rising up to cover his ears. There is a roaring in his ears like the sea. Two hands close over his eyes, and two more over the eyes in the back of his head. For a moment he thinks they will leave his nose and mouth uncovered, but then he feels a hand grip the crown of his head, the elongated wrist coming down to rest on his brow, fingers nosing at his nostrils, at his mouth. Hands swing around the sides of his head to press themselves alongside his jaws. Fingers probe and pull open his mouth, hook his jaws as far apart as they can go. Drool down his chin drips and hits him in the belly, a cold thumb-tap on a tabla, a beat dropping.

Chthonotrope

YOU CAN TELL WHEN THESE STORIES GET TOO REAL. THAT'S WHEN I ANONYMIZE THE names of the characters. Those characters are not quite the same as their real-world referents. I have taken some liberties because they were not given those liberties. But they are close enough that I can say: these are the things that happened. These are the things that are happening right now. These are the terms of your sentence. These are your conditions of your imprisonment.

Reverb

TO IMPRISON; TO MISPLACE; TO IMMISERATE. THE MACHINIC STATE IS NOT MERELY the death of the author—we already had that, Barthes did it thirty-five minutes ago—but the endless reiteration of authorial undeath, this flesh-less, joyless immortality. To haunt, without will, without agency, without choices. Machine, write me a Vajra Chandrasekera story about the future of art and email it to Indra Das for consideration. Specifications: about 7,700 words, include a family of sixteenth-century Venetian booksellers as the main characters in a retelling, more tenebrous and obscure than is tra-ditional, of the thousand-year-old tale of the three princes of Serendip (of which story the Tramezzinos themselves were the publisher of record in its first Italian translation). Skip the boringly Sherlockian bit with the camel and the tired Scheherazade parade of princesses and pavilions, but keep the bizarre bit about the fatal hand and the mirror of justice, which in any case do not belong here, having been inserted into this narrative from other sources by Christoforo the Armenian five centuries ago. Actually, machine, scratch the mirror of justice; in our time, we all know justice doesn't come from mirrors. In that scratched mirror of justice, darkening and vandal-ized, show (dimly, as if from a greater distance than actually pertains) the stories of those punished for creating art, for telling truths, for making jokes. Never look away from them. This is unholy ground, but it is the only terra firma I know, not nullius but terra communis. Eh, you know how it is with these bloody terras and commies. Without prison, who are we, as a culture? This island's mythologies begin in a penal colony. This is a place of exile for monsters.

The Work of Art in the Age of Statistical Approximation

HOW DO YOU READ A TEXT LIKE THIS? SLOWLY, AND WITH SOME DIFFICULTY. A machine could read it easily, instantly, not requiring understanding. To a machine, this is only a sequence of 7,666 words, of 43,831 characters, each part a datum, weighing the same as any other, entirely fungible dollops. A small contribution, the machine assesses, to the valuable knowledge of the frequencies of which characters, which words, are used with others, by this author and in general by all authors in this language. This is what stories look like; these are the words and sentences and events that follow each other; this is the way the world goes. But what if we wanted the world to go another way? For this, you need something more than a machine: you need a monster.

If intent isn't magic—and Tumblr and Barthes agree here that it isn't—there is only text, and text is an unsouled body, ripe and vulnerable for possession. Why'd you leave it lying out there without protection, then, without so much as a circle of salt around it? Intent isn't magic, but then, where is the magic? Or more precisely, where is *our* magic? Because Mahinda Rajapaksa has a vajra in his hand and so does Elon Musk. Every president has an evil soothsayer. You cannot face them with empty hands. The definition of art, in retreat, cannot fall back on either exchange value or use value, but on the risk of prison and pain, disappearance and death. It is the blood, the lives, the hours and years demanded in exchange that sanctifies art, gives meaning to intention. You'll know it's art when someone's paid for it in, or with, their bones.

You can and should expect the machine to take over the market share of art as extruded entertainment product. A corporation may claim vast swathes of intellectual property, license the likenesses it requires, and instruct the machine to produce at the scale that makes extremely cheap product profitable. Flood the market with generated texts serving every conceivable permutation and combination of tropes and finely sliced representational intersections reduced to market segmentation, endless heroes receiving and refusing the call to adventure, being mentored, tested, and trialed, mastering their worlds in echoing synchrony, mass-achieving narratological freedom in prisons so perfect their bars cannot be seen at all.

Limner

THIS STORY WAS GENERATED BY THE MACHINIC STATE, THE PRISON WITHIN THE prison like the text within the text, the state of the machine, the machine ulcerated, the machine cold but learning. This story was generated by the narratological machine from secret prompts, from gnomic mutterances, from incantations hermetic and heresiarchal. Look at the clock and calendar nearest you, orient yourself on the map. This is where and when you are. Do you know who your gods are?

To fight gods, especially gods that you made, you must become monstrous. You have to set yourself apart from the implied reader they would demand of you. That's why I told you at the beginning that this story was a monster. This story is not art's future or past, only a chain of hands, interlinked. The future of art is you, my love, always and only you. Take my hand, and take up your spine in your other hand, your pen in your other, other hand, and if you have hands to spare, take up the icons and treasures that only you know: a carven skull, a woven basket, a shoe unworn in ten thousand years, a cup of beaten copper, a perfect function never run, a sentence cracking in your hands like a whip. Feel the sea rise up around your knees and adjust your stance in the rough sand. Here comes the lightning.

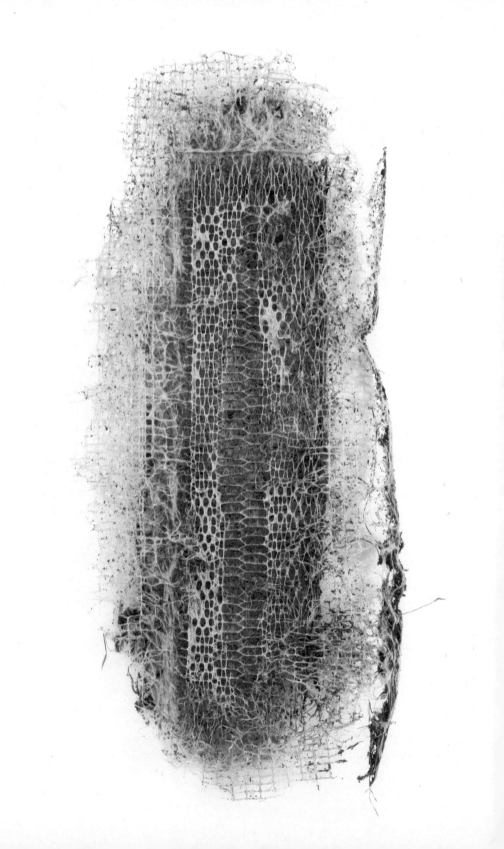

2 THE ART CROWD

Samit Basu

JOEY'S VR MEETING WITH FUNDER RADHA IS IN A DIGITAL ART GALLERY. THEY WALK down a long corridor, the walls on either side featuring animated versions of classic paintings: a Mona Lisa looping through an emoji range of expressions, the Hokusai wave crashing and rebuilding, Van Gogh landscapes swirling, a Dali dripping paint and clockfaces on the floor. Joey's more distracted by the occasional moving statues that alternate between covering their genitalia, if nude, waving gently at the other statues, and saluting the humans as they pass. Radha watches Joey look at the art with an indulgent smile. Their virtual avatars are both dressed in classical art as well: Joey's in a Ravi Varma sari, grateful for upper-body pixelation, and Radha, who's somewhere in Europe IRL, is in some form of Renaissancey robe that Joey can't identify and couldn't care less about.

Offline, Joey's lounging on a beanbag in her Flowco's penthouse office/set, which also serves as her primary Flowstar Indi's home. Despite the air conditioner on full blast doing its best to fight the Delhi sun outside, she's sweating gently into her helmet and her haptic gauntlets. On her wrist, her smartatt pulses gently each time her phone vibrates in her pockets: someone's sending her a series of messages, though nothing important enough for her digital assistant, Narad, to forward into her virtual meeting.

She makes small talk with Radha for a while. Everything's going well, Indi's audience growing at an acceptable rate, overall Flow industry stable, everyone's family excellent and other wellness indicators pleasant. They do the usual tech-field catch-up pleasantries: cryptocurrencies, machine learning, AI, and NFTs are all exactly as they were during their last meeting, all threatening to disrupt everything disruptable but fortunately showing no signs of actually making their big move. There's not much left to discuss, pleasantry-wise: Joey has always suspected Radha shares at least a few of her political opinions and views on the Top 10 apocalypses currently playing out in Delhi, or India, but that's not something they could ever discuss, as there are ears in every wall, even digital ones. She also knows Radha wouldn't have called this meeting just to check in on her, though, so she waits for her funder to arrive at the point.

They enter a section of the gallery that features a Sistine Chapel ceiling. Radha watches sibyls and cherubs loop in silence for a while, and then turns to Joey with the business-now face that Joey's come to know and be mildly stressed by. More work is never the problem. The worry is always about news: That the Flowco's been acquired by some new oligarch and is pivoting to overt fascist propaganda. That Joey's been assigned some celebrity known to be a monster. That some old college photo has led some algorithm to assume she's a dangerous radical who must be disappeared at once.

"Is Indi around?" Funder Radha asks. "Next bit's between us."

"Family event," Joey says. Her celebrity Flowstar client is away for a whole two days, which is always delightful: she's still tracking him, of course, because a scandal might break out around Indi at any point, but he can't get up to his usual nonsense when he's visiting his parents. His audience has no idea he's gone; depending on their algorithm-determined preference, they're currently watching either a prerecorded travel segment, a game playthrough with his voiceover, or a montage of staged celebrity encounters.

"Then I'll get to the point," Radha says. She waves her arm around, indicating the whole gallery, and stares at Joey meaningfully.

"Art?" Joey asks.

"Art. We think it's time to get you another client. Before you refuse—no, we are not asking you to give up Indi. He's all yours, he'd be lost without you. But of all our Reality Controllers, you're the best fit for the new one."

"Managing Indi is a full-time job," Joey says. "Besides, the innovations we've been testing on his stream, the multireality, the live dialogue-writing, the live scroll-shirt edits . . . I can't really leave those to anyone else, and they require—"

Radha waves her hand impatiently. "We've tried to get you to double-star, and we see why you've refused," she says. "This is different. A challenge that we believe could build your skill set and make you an even greater asset, and will not require anything significant from you in terms of time or physical presence. There's no pressure—we just think you're ambitious enough to try. Are you?"

Joey knows she's being manipulated, that her buttons are being casually pushed. But she cannot help herself. She nods, and Radha gestures up an image: a beautiful young woman in her mid-twenties like Joey, with waist-length hair, wearing heavy exotic makeup and a chiffon saree, lying asleep on a concrete floor. The sleeping woman is surrounded by farm animals and pets, also sleeping, and various obsolete gadgets: an early '20s VR headset, a health tracker wristband, several smartphones Joey remembers from college—all of which seem turned off, arranged in a circle around the whole scene.

"Do you know what it means?" Radha asks.

"No idea, I don't understand art," Joey says. "Hot, though."

"Very hot. This is Cosmos Apsara Mehta. Big in France, part of this big exhibition that's on at the New Alliance Centre, Kochchar Mansions. You know it?"

"Not at all. Well, I know France. This is an embassy thing?"

"No, New Alliance is corporate. And you'll love the Kochchar place, superbly vulgar. I went there for a wedding once, and they had flown in seven K-pop idols just to pretend to be friends of the groom. Go there, check her out, buy her art—there's one of those fungible key things, I'll have it loaded and sent over—and then acquire her."

"What's her art? Photos of her with animals? What does it mean?"

"Who cares? There's a statement somewhere, read it. Maybe you'll understand it, you're Arts stream, right? Her art is basically some live experience where people go look at her, knocked out, with animals, also drugged, plus devices switched off. It's for something or about something or against something. Or intersectional. Something. People go and look at all this and then say it was amazing. Point is, she's about to go big, so pick her up."

"I still don't understand," Joey says. "We are buying—a live show, in effect? So she knocks herself out and some animals too, in a place we decide, and people come to see it? And you want me to manage a Flow based on this? How does that work? I don't know how to get an audience for this!"

"Put on a nice dress, because society people will be there," Radha says. "You're young, you pass for posh. Get there and figure it out, Joey. You're in the art world now."

"Could you please send someone else?" Joey asked. "I really don't understand. What I do is the opposite of this."

"This is exactly what you do. You're a producer, a manager, you handle star clients."

"I train influencers to find an audience that's as wide as possible, and try to get suckers to subscribe. This performance art space is niche, single-consumption, and I don't get the money structure at all."

"Art is to be experienced, not understood," Radha says. "So is money. Don't think of this as a test, Joey, though it absolutely is one. Get moving."

ON THE LONG DRIVE THAT EVENING, UP AND DOWN OVER AN ENDLESS SEQUENCE OF flyovers, Joey watches the sun sink across the smoggy orange-purple sky, blinking between the silhouettes of innumerable identical towers. She engages Narad, who silences the lovelorn Punjabi rap her driver has chosen to play, and sets up a call with the only person Joey knows even vaguely connected to the art world. Pradipta Aunty, a friend of Joey's mother, who used to run a small art gallery in South Delhi until progovernment mobs burned it down during the Years Not to Be Discussed for reasons no one ever explained: all her friends were just happy Pradipta was not disappeared. Given that everyone in the city has been under automated surveillance for a decade, it's not something anyone is able to discuss even now, but those are not the answers Joey currently needs.

"I'm the wrong person to ask, darling," Pradipta Aunty says almost immediately. "I sold paintings, some figurines, that sort of thing. I don't do all this technology-shecknology. I don't understand this kind of concept, and I don't understand the money side of it at all. What is this woman's art anyway? Sleeping for what?"

"I read the proposal but I really can't tell," Joey says. "It's anticapitalist, anticolonial, it says, but it's that kind of proposal language where it sounds very important but mysterious; I know all the words, but they're used to hide the meaning."

"An art form in itself. It works well for foreign people," Pradipta says. "But you be careful, darling. This rich people art zone is dangerous, always has been. They move money around in ways people like us will never get. And now they don't even use the kind of money we understand—all this fungus-shungus. I can't even read about it without getting a headache."

Joey looks at the sleek black token in her hand, and wonders what her Flowco is up to.

"I don't understand the tech either," she says.

"Don't worry about the tech," Pradipta says. "It's not important. Tech is just a medium, no? Paper and stone were also tech."

"What is important, then? The art itself? The artists?"

"No."

"No?"

"I mean yes, of course, but that's different. You don't have to watch out for them, and there's always more. You need to keep your eyes on the buyers. Always art is about people, and people don't change, in these circles. My clients weren't as rich as the ones here will be, but they didn't care about art when they bought it. And neither will these ones."

"What do you mean?"

"It's always something else with these folks. Something political, some sort of trade. Sometimes it's just laundering. You were too young to remember demonetization, I guess? Twenty-sixteen. Yes, you were a child."

"I was old enough."

"They suddenly declared most cash invalid, some election game—and suddenly half of Delhi's business and politics types were very interested in art, if we could take their cash off their hands. We sold everything in the gallery in an hour, and people kept turning up and demanding more. They didn't care that we mostly worked with tribal artists from far away; they just wanted something to buy. We had to call in every local artist we knew and just have them make more art on the spot. But they still wanted tribal art only, so all night we made absurd imitations, sold at absurd prices. I made around five tribal paintings that night myself."

Joey has thoughts on this, but Pradipta is an Aunty, and her gallery is gone.

"I'm not scared of rich people," she says. "I just hope I get the art."

"The art world isn't about art at all," Pradipta says. "Isn't now, wasn't before. It's about power, and you don't have a lot of that, darling. Be careful."

—You seem stressed, Narad messages after Joey disconnects. Can I interest you in some soothing animal sounds?

"No, just text me the transcription. Did I hit any trigger phrases?"

—No.

THE JOURNEY TO KOCHCHAR MANSIONS, DEEP INTO WHAT USED TO BE RURAL HARY-ana, is long and uneventful, except for a bit where the car crosses a failed tourist spot. The giant statue of a Glorious Leader, built in China at incredible expense during the worst economy crash of the Years Not to Be Discussed, now stands abandoned. Every day, hacker-piloted drones, the sort normally used by environmental activists to reforest cleared land with seed-bombs, drop red paint on the Glorious Leader from the sky. The model golden age Vedic India tourist trap that was supposed to have been built around it has long been abandoned, and the Leader's supporters stopped cleaning the statue after his assassination. This is the kind of art Joey wishes her Flowco would invest in: she'd have enjoyed running Flowstar dating contests under the Leader's shadow. No one knows who's behind the drones that desecrate the Leader's statue, but it's widely believed to be the handiwork of the Dalit activist E-Klav, probably India's best-known iconoclast, though the rich mostly call him a culture terrorist.

Kochchar Mansions is exactly the sprawling midwasteland manicured luxury compound Joey expected, and as vulgar as Radha had promised it would be: the Kochchars are a large family with political, whiskey, and edutech empires. Joey's pass is checked by a gigantic guard, and she's handed a glass of wine and ushered through an entrance lobby and into a brightly lit golf cart decked up to look like a peacock. The New Alliance exhibition is happening all over the Kochchar compound: there's a map, an app, even an audio guide, but Joey ignores them all as she gawks from her golf cart at a fascinating array of ugly fountains and psychotic-angelic nymph statues that line the paths that lead to the main mansion.

A few minutes after entering the massive main hall, Joey encounters the New Alliance head curator, a middle-aged Indian-origin man of immediately annoying smoothness. He relieves her of her art-buyer token and apologizes for not being able to introduce her to Cosmos Apsara right away. The artist is indisposed: there has been a minor logistical issue because everyone forgot that government permissions had to be secured before livestock could be drugged and put on public display by a foreign corporation. The required permissions have now been acquired, no doubt aided by a substantial bribe, but Cosmos Apsara is upset at not being allowed to be put to sleep on schedule and is now resting. But the curator promises to introduce Joey during a brief preshow window when Cosmos Apsara will be awake. Joey assures him she can't wait to meet the artist.

She's secretly delighted, because there's something she's been hiding from everyone she's spoken to all day: Joey's actually been looking forward to seeing the art. Despite her well-earned reputation for skepticism, even cynicism, an absolute requirement for her hard-boiled Reality Controller image, Joey is a secret art fan: she's hoping despite all evidence and experience to be moved, puzzled, impressed, or just interested. She's not bothered by whether she understands it, has spent enough time in the Flowverse to understand both artists and performative critics, but ever since Funder Radha forced her into this evening, she's been making sure to conceal her genuine curiosity and excitement. She looked up the New Alliance exhibition's tour and the many glowing, if puzzled, reviews it has received on its journey around the world's major art centers. And Cosmos Apsara's various unconsciousnesses have given her a perfect opportunity to immerse herself in this experience.

So she wanders the halls of the Kochchar Mansions, taking it all in. There's a lot to see, and a lot of it is immediately interesting to her. There are some obvious duds: a crowded room where a middle-aged man is stomping around with swastikas attached to his nipples and penis while holograms of the Holocaust play around the room. Rooms full of abstract shapes with polysyllabic descriptions that fail at rousing any feeling at all in her, beyond a vague urge to push them up against one another to see if she can make them fit. A series of household objects that are supposed to inspire deep and meaningful reflections, but clearly she is too shallow: they just make her remember her smartfridge's recent reminders about monthly cleanings and expiring food. A ghoulish arrangement of drones inside taxidermied birds leaves her disgusted. But she perseveres, and finds work that's interesting to her: a constructed immigration center that makes passersby feel welcome to any country, a wall garden that AI-plant integration has converted into a music studio, a history of sea trade told through 3D-printed disappearing ribbons. She roams a fiberglass garden where dogs relay messages from digital assistants, drinks tea with robot zombies that speak only in internet comments, watches data visualizations from stock market indices blossom and spore and fade like fast-forwarded fungi. She has a conversation about badminton with an actual badminton champion in a revolving metal shuttlecock.

Nearly every installation or art piece that might be interpreted as a criticism of anything Indian has been adapted before being put on display: there's no shortage of strong statements and far-reaching inclusions, but it's really as if none of them have anything to do with the land they're currently set on. There are no problems in India—not the ones from this decade, not the millennia-old ones, nothing that any art deems worth addressing, at least, and the Indian artists that talk about any of these are usually encouraged to do so only abroad. And then stay abroad, if anyone allows them to: if they come back, they will have to be quiet, or disappear, because there are no problems in India.

SHE'D KNOWN BEFORE SHE STARTED THAT IT WAS ONLY A MATTER OF TIME BEFORE she ran into someone she knew, so she'd avoided the more crowded halls and tried to summon the swagger-free body language that keeps her invisible at Flowstar gatherings. But even though Kochchar Mansions is hours away from her usual stomping grounds, and most of the people present would never recognize someone at Joey's income level, there are inevitably Flowstars and their entourages present at all such occasions, and everyone in the Flowverse knows who Joey is and wants to work with her, or at least her Flowco.

So in each room, she's accosted by people she's met at shoots or interviews or years ago in school or college, and made to participate in half-hearted air-kisses, side hugs, and pleasantries. And in each room, she ignores work-initiation attempts, sexual invitations, and clumsy attempts at condescension or insult: failed Flowstars telling her she's moved up in the world to land an invite like this, or attempting the classical jabs about her lack of a husband or children or high-level patron. More dangerous, though, are the people attempting to get her to discover them: she meets a theme park/detention center designer, a friend-hire app owner, a neuromarketer, a dream-to-AI visualization shaman, all of whom came to the exhibition to become artists but are perfectly happy to be Flowstars as well. Joey handles them all with relative ease—none of this is new—but is occasionally alerted by her smartatt about the number of glasses of wine she's picking up.

"I actually see being an artist as a step towards being a Flowstar," a real estate baron's son tells her earnestly. "My dad says either is fine, as long as I keep things apolitical."

Joey takes a long sip of wine and looks elsewhere.

"How much do you charge for artist package, and for Flowstar?" he asks. "We can do cash also, and also we have some under construction properties in—"

"You shouldn't do either," Joey snaps. "Don't do art, don't do Flows. Both are political. Always."

"Arre yaar what you're saying," he responds, grinning, possibly thinking she's flirting. "I'm a big Indi fan, so is my mom, and we are totally opposite in politics, okay, but we still like your company's Flows. Only because no politics. Just like the art here, it's good. No politics. I still think I'll do better in Flows, because I can rap and do fitness, but dad says art is a good option because we want to expand to foreign."

"Our Flowstars' silence on political matters is a conformist, corporate-led political stance," Joey says. "You don't have to understand this, but you should know before you start your own Flowco, which I feel like you'll have to."

Beside her, the server carrying a tray of filled wine glasses emits a quiet snort. Joey glances at him: a young man, probably some college kid, dressed in a white shirt and suspenders, his face obscured by a yaksha mask, like all the other servers present. He offers her another glass of wine. She shouldn't, but she goes for it.

"All art is not political bro," the real estate heir says, his face slightly red as he slams his empty whiskey glass on the tray. "Anyway, all the best art now is like, AI. They're not political, are they?"

Joey shrugs, and prepares to move on, but he's not done. "Who's India's top artist?" he asks. "My fam has a full collection, okay? None of them are into politics. Who's your favorite?"

She has two, but this is not the sort of gathering where she can say their names out loud. Saying E-Klav in a heavily surveilled high-budget establishment like this one without specifically calling him a criminal could get her house raided. And she shouldn't really say the other artist's name either, but she's had a lot of wine, so.

"Desibryde," she says. Yes, Desibryde, the sexFlower, the counter-culture icon who wears digital masks of male political leaders or goddesses in her sexvids. Wherever in the world she's making these from, she's the most watched and least openly discussed Flowstar in India.

There are gasps from eavesdroppers all around them, and Joey wonders if she's made a huge mistake.

"You're saying you'd make Desibryde into a Flowstar instead of handing her over to the authorities?" Real estate bro is shaken.

"I'm saying she doesn't need my help, but she's the most exciting artist in the country," Joey says.

"First of all, Desibryde is porn, not art," he splutters, gesticulating wildly. "And what's political about her? You're crazy, and you're fired. She's an insult to our culture, and—"

He has more to say, but is interrupted: he's bumped into the yaksha-masked server, who spills his tray. Real estate heir's shirt is doused with red wine, the tray falls with a resounding crash, a number of art connoisseurs scream in alarm, and Joey decides to make an exit, skulking hurriedly out of the hall before someone puts a bag over her head.

In the next hall, she's relieved to find a VR live performance: she quickly dons a helmet and watches a set of air-dance artists from a Pacific island doing light-calligraphy acrobatics with smart styluses that control, a voiceover tells her, garbage-munching robots attempting to clear up an island of plastic trash the size of Chicago that's accumulated in the ocean. She spends several minutes watching this, and when she removes her helmet she's relieved to find that the people from the last hall haven't followed her in. She's not alone, though. A server with another tray is standing right next to her, watching her. This is a young woman in a yakshi mask, her long hair tied in a bun above her head. Joey notices that the server-yakshi's body is absolutely stunning, and is surprised at herself for noticing.

"You're Joey Roy," the yakshi says. Joey nods. "And you?" she asks.

"I'm nobody," the yakshi says. "I liked what you did back there, with the dude, and Desibryde."

"I love her."

"We all do. And I just . . . I knew you weren't one of them. I just knew it. But hearing it was great. So I wanted to say thanks."

Joey feels vaguely heroic and vaguely embarrassed all at once.

"You're . . . welcome?"

"I've seen your old shows from your college days, and I think you're really cool."

"And I'm sorry."

"What for?"

"Nothing. Just a joke. Sorry."

Joey wants to know why, wants to know everything, but notices the tray in the yakshi's hands is shaking a little.

"You all right?" she asks. "Want to step outside and have a smoke?"

"Mask stays on," the yakshi says. "Sorry, we're not supposed to speak with the guests, but . . ."

The tray shakes again, and Joey feels a strange pang as the yakshi turns away.

"No, wait," Joey says. "Are you in trouble of some kind?"

"No, no trouble. Long day. Creepy dudes."

"Do you need help?"

She turns back towards Joey. "You'd help me, huh. Just like that."

Joey shrugs.

"Thanks, that was just what I needed," the yakshi says. "I'm good, Joey Roy. Have a good night."

A man in a suit and a security earpiece materializes near them and glares at the yakshi. Joey steps forward and picks up another glass of wine. "Can I help you?" she asks the security suit. He looks professionally bland. Joey gives him the connected-Delhi-person sneer she's spent a lot of time practicing in the mirror: it's helped her get past some of the country's doughtiest celebrity assistants.

"Have you seen all the art here?" Joey asks the yakshi, loudly. The yakshi nods.

"Who would you invest in, if you had to pick an artist? Who's good, and not an asshole, and not a puppet either?"

The server glances at the security-suit, and shakes her head. Joey stares at the glowering suit until he goes away.

The server tilts her head, and stares at Joey in silence for a few seconds. To Joey's surprise, she reaches for her wineglass and puts it back on her tray.

"Do you believe in risking everything for a cause you believe is worth anything?" she asks, her voice low.

"No," Joey says. "I like my family safe."

"So do I. But you do know there's no great art without great risk, right?"

"I . . . guess that's true? Sorry, my small talk skills are weak."

The server looks like she has much more to ask, but another security man approaches, so she nods, and walks away. Joey wonders for a moment whether she should follow her, but she is diverted by the curator; he needs an encryption key for Funder Radha's token for the auction and wants to know what Joey expects Radha's final bid to be. Since Joey had no idea she was participating in an auction, she makes an enigmatic face, and tells him he'll have to wait and see. He has another piece of news for her: Cosmos Apsara is willing to meet Joey, but it has to be soon, as she is about to go under for her performance. She follows him towards a large and shiny marble staircase, perfect for tortured brides in Hindi soaps to roll down on. It swirls up around the largest and ugliest chandelier she has ever seen. The Kochchars were really the absolute best.

"On a scale of one to ten," Joey asks the curator, "how annoying is she?"

The curator's face doesn't even twitch. "She can't wait to meet you," he says. "Come with me."

At the foot of the staircase, Joey looks around. There's a door nearby, past an indoor fountain, leading to yet another exhibition hall. The yakshi-masked woman is standing by the door, tray in hand, looking at her again. She walks in, gives Joey another glance, and then disappears into the hall.

"You know what, I think I'm just going to look around some more," Joey says to the curator. "You give Cosmos Apsara my love, and I'm sure Radha will be in touch to discuss her work."

The curator graces her with a blank look, and Joey wonders whether she'll make it to the mysterious yakshi server before Radha calls. She doesn't.

"What are you up to, love? Henri seemed upset, well done."

"His name is Henri? Looked more like an Arijit to me."

"Well played on not disclosing the auction bid, by the way. And on keeping this Cosmic girl hanging. You're beginning to learn the game."

Joey knows that Radha knows she has not learned any game, but it seems kind of her to suggest anything of the sort.

"You'll let me know when it's time, I'm sure," Joey says in as smooth a voice as she can muster. "And you have eyes and ears here already."

"Good girl."

Shaking her head, Joey wanders past the fountain and through the door, wondering why she's chasing this yakshi-masked girl around. Not the first time she's spent a boring work event aimlessly trailing a hot stranger, but this feels a bit different. Something about the masked woman feels familiar, and she's utterly convinced this is leading somewhere important.

The hall features an installation about the intersection between love and technology: a collaboration between an allegedly centuries-old Indian matchmaking service and a Finnish bodytech company. Their creation, an interactive, immersive, giant womb-shaped touchscreen, lets people measure their potential relationships with anyone else in the room: bubbles on the wall tell awestruck users how likely they are to have a successful marriage with anyone they're pointing at, based on readings from their smartatts, their social profiles, and secret tracker databases.

Joey wanders around, observing people drift about, laughing or groaning as they touch the wall and one another and read the installation's verdicts. She finds herself smiling gently. Her smile doesn't diminish as she feels a slender hand grasp hers: the yakshi-masked server leads her towards the nearest wall-screen and touches it. The installation reads them and declares them perfectly compatible. A light goes on above their heads: there is some scattered applause. A pink chamber rises out of the center of the room, and a door slides open. The light above their heads becomes a beam that traces out a heart on the floor, and then a glowing path from where they stand to the open chamber door.

"Subtle," Joey says.

"Classy," the yakshi says. "Shall we?"

Joey and the yakshi walk inside the chamber. It's a cylinder, the inside another wall-screen but also an infinite curling mirror, except for the pink ceiling. There is a handwritten note stuck to the wall-screen with Instructions written on it in pink marker, and lists below, in English, Hindi, and presumably Finnish. They read the instructions: They're supposed to embrace each other and share their most intimate secrets. Perhaps explore the erotic possibilities of their perfect connection. Their physical data will be recorded to train the AI running Tavata about ideal human relationships, but their privacy, the note says, is absolute, and no images or audio of their time together will ever reach anyone else without their consent. Which means everything they do and say there is definitely being recorded for some other art installation or well-funded social experiment.

The ceiling opens dramatically, and two VR helmets fall out, also pink, attached by wires to the top of the chamber. Another note, this one informing them that exploring their desires in a virtual environment would also be acceptable and that they were among the privileged few to be offered an early glimpse into Tavata's next art project: internationally legally valid digital polycule marriages. A sex therapist and trainer is apparently online and available in Helsinki should they want to explore the specifics.

"Romantic," the yakshi says.

"If we're getting married," Joey says, "I need to know your name."

The yakshi squeezes her hand. "That would ruin everything," she says, and her voice gives Joey goosebumps. "What do you think of the art?"

Joey gives the yakshi a bashful grin. "I wasn't thinking of the art at all," she says. "I need you to tell me you're not in any trouble, and then maybe I could persuade you to take off your mask?"

"I can't, and I'm not going into VR either," she says. "I know this is the world we live in, but some things I can't do unless I know exactly who's watching."

She's right, of course: whatever this is, they are under surveillance. And whatever trouble she's in, it's nothing Joey can afford to get involved with. But the wine's gone to Joey's head, and she's feeling dangerous.

"Let's get out of this cake and find a spot," she says. "I'm wholly done exploring the intersection of technology and whatever, and I can be really helpful."

The yakshi chuckles. "So I see, but I'm all good now," she says. "Relax. It's a party."

"Didn't feel like one, in the other room."

"Imagine I was crying in the toilet about some nonsense, and a hot stranger came and held my hand, and then I was all better."

"Fine, the art, then," Joey says, and exhales. She looks around and tries to think of something clever to say. She fails, and sighs, and hits the button by the door. They emerge into the installation hall, ignoring a few giggles that greet them.

"Haven't been thinking of love or marriage much, have you?" the yakshi asks.

"No, I haven't. My parents have an amazing marriage, though. And they're madly in love, or something like it."

"So you're a believer."

"No, I'm not," Joey says. "Not for myself, at least. I don't think love survives because of the institution of marriage. It survives despite it."

The yakshi nods, and Joey can feel her smile behind her mask. "Well, no wonder we're so compatible," the yakshi says. "And is that your view on art as well? Do you think art survives not because of the institutions meant to contain it, but despite them?"

Joey considers this. "Yeah," she says after a while. "Yeah, that's my view."

"Okay, then, Joey," the yakshi says, "let's go fund the arts."

THE YAKSHI LEADS JOEY THROUGH A FOREST TOWARDS THE ANNEX BEHIND THE mansion, which they both know is called the servants' quarters when there are no white people around. Joey asks to see her face and learn her name again the moment they're clear of the building.

"I'm not going to do it," says the yakshi.

"You're going to, eventually," Joey says. "We both know this."

"There's a lot I wish I could say to you," the yakshi says. "But this is exactly the kind of place where rich folk come out for a smoke and spill their secrets."

She's right, of course, but what secrets could she possibly have? Joey stumbles a little, and steadies herself. She's had too much wine. But it makes no sense to stop this adventure now, this straying mildly off track into less boring lands, so she asks if there's more drinks to be found where they're going.

"Yes," says the yakshi. "But no more for you. You've had enough."

And Joey wonders why she doesn't mind being scolded by this anonymous stranger at all.

They enter the servants' quarters to find a party in progress in the central hall. A number of servers, uniforms in various stages of disarray, dancing to a remix of old folk music. "Masks!" bellows Joey's yakshi as soon as they enter, and everyone scrambles to find theirs. Someone cuts the music, and Joey finds herself staring at a number of yakshas and yakshis. The air is full of ganja smoke, and the floor's strewn with plastic cups and beer cans. There are pieces of paper on the floor as well, with hand-drawn instructions. Everything's written in code, but Joey can see immediately from the diagrams that they're about disabling security cams and microphones, using stickers and lasers to defeat face and body identification. Some of the servers see her look and start clearing the papers up, but everyone knows what she's already seen. She's walked into an insurrection. A part of her brain screams at her to get out. She stands still, taking in the scene, blinking and swaying slightly.

"Everyone here is an artist," Joey's yakshi says. "Everyone's worked on some installation or the other, or been hauled in for last-minute fixes. Some of them have been hauled over from abroad, assistants, entourages. Some of them are the ones who had the idea for the art, others are the ones who put them together after researching similar hits. You're a Reality Controller. You know how it goes."

"I do," Joey says.

"We have . . . some taste overlap, I think, in the art we like. And you asked me who I think your company should invest in. Well . . . it's these people. So pick one. Or pick them all. They're a collective."

Joey stares at the collective of demon masks. The demons stare back.

"There's more work," someone says from the back. "Lots of stuff got censored. Confiscated. Taken apart. Lots of international hits that weren't suitable for Indian display. Lots of art that mentioned places and people you can't talk about here, like—"

"Don't say it," Joey's yakshi says. She turns to Joey.

"We can show you the art later, if you like," she says. "We could put it all together again, make new copies, pitch to your office, if you want. Jump through all the hoops, we're used to it. It lives in our heads and our hearts, and we can make it again. But I thought I should bring you here, and show you the people who create it, and ask you—yes? Or no?"

"Yes," Joey says. She pulls out her phone and makes a call.

"What is it?" Funder Radha asks.

"We're not hiring Cosmos Apsara," Joey says.

"Cool," Radha says.

"We're hiring a bunch of other artists instead. Much more diverse, some foreign. Great skill sets, low costs, several with star potential. Actual talent, the rest is marketing. Well within our capability. I'll handle them all myself."

Radha thinks about this for a few seconds.

"No," she says.

"Seriously, Radha, this is a winner. Trust me, I got—"

"Cosmos Apsara is a friend's kid, and a passive income icon. I don't know what you've gotten yourself into now, Joey, but I have no interest in adopting puppies. I'm sending you the encryption key for Cosmos now, hand it over to Henri before the bidding starts. We're closing this before auction." Radha hangs up.

Joey stares at her phone, blinking. Her head's throbbing now, and her vision's slightly blurry, but that might be because tears of rage have welled up in her eyes. She looks at the yakshas and yakshis and struggles to find words.

"It's okay," her yakshi says, voice wavering a little. "We all saw you try."

There are nods and murmurs across the room.

"You seem to know who I am for some reason," Joey says. "If you come find me, I promise you I'll do my best. I know what it's like, behind the scenes, handling the whims of celebrities. I don't want a place in the spotlight, but if any of you do, you deserve it. And if you come to me, I'll try and help you find it."

"You better mean that," a voice calls from the back.

"I actually do," Joey says. "It's going to be hard getting funding from the Flowco, but—"

"We'll have money," someone calls, and giggles, and is swiftly silenced.

"And until then," Joey's yakshi says, "we can dance."

The music starts up again, and they do. And Joey dances with them, her head spinning. There are projectors lined up in the center of the room, making an art installation out of the party: as far as Joey can see, the images being projected on the walls around them, and on their bodies, are all notes for the installations that didn't make it to Kochchar mansions. An endless scroll of government and corporate messages censoring, modifying, or outright blocking proposed works of art, listing absurd reasons why but also listing the artworks that would have made the whole exhibition a little less vulgar, a little more interesting, even if they were just meant for the eyes of people no longer capable of any sort of real inspiration or feeling. An installation using 3D graphs, its bars representing incomes, power supply, and water availability across neighborhoods to build new city walls for Delhi. A virtual tourism installation where people could travel through animated versions of Kashmir or the Northeast beyond the enclosed tourists-allowed areas. Sculptures made from discarded equipment from the baby factories that don't exist in the central states. Movies made with original footage of elderly nationalist Bollywood heroes without CGI muscles. Taxidermied robots of all of India's completely nonfamous recently extinct animals. All flashing by on the walls, silhouettes of the demon-masked youths dancing among them, and suddenly Joey wants to throw up.

Her yakshi materializes by her side. "Let's get you out of here," she says, and Joey nods, grateful.

"You should go home," the yakshi tells her when they're back in the forest. "You're drunk. I'll take you back to your car, you should just get out of here."

There's something Joey knows she's forgotten. On cue, her phone vibrates. Funder Radha's sent her the encryption key for the auction bid. "I need to give this to the Alliance guy," she says, showing the key to the yakshi. "We're buying Cosmic Arpita. She sleeps for us now. But one day . . ."

The yakshi catches her as she stumbles and holds her close. Joey freezes in sudden exhilaration and terror: she has no idea what she'll do if suddenly kissed.

"Listen," the yakshi hisses. "I don't want you to get into trouble. So why don't you forget to hand over the key, and just go home. You were drunk, and forgot. It happens."

Joey stares at her, suddenly wholly alert, very wide-eyed. It should have been clear to her for a while that something very murky was up: first of all, she's really, really drunk. And she doesn't get drunk, she's a hard-assed Reality Controller in her mid-twenties who can drink seasoned booze-hound Delhi uncles under the table.

"The wine? Did you—"

The yakshi pulls her mask up and stops Joey's mouth—and heart—with a kiss. She steps back, and puts a finger on the lips of her mask.

"I'm sorry," she says. "But yeah. The wine. But I want you to get home safe. Before it happens."

"Before . . ." Joey stops speaking, because she doesn't want to create evidence. But she's suddenly sure she has wandered into the middle of some sort of spectacular art heist.

"The tokens?"

"The talking is fun, but not so much fun when people could be listening."

Joey pulls herself free of the yakshi. "Funding for the arts?"

The yakshi stands tall, and Joey can feel her eyes shining behind the mask. "Yes. You'll see."

Joey feels a smile spreading across her face, a vast and silly smile. "I feel my company should contribute. We really want to explore the scene."

The yakshi laughs. "You sure?"

Joey forwards the encryption key to Henri.

"Oh yeah," she says. "We're all in."

She shakes herself straight, and gives the yakshi a brief hug.

"I'm good," she says. "You have work to do."

"I do. And listen—you don't have to work for them, you know. They hate people like us, people who create. They're terrified of us. They want to replace us, control us. But together . . ."

Joey feels herself swaying again, and snaps to attention.

"I think I need to get home safe, and as fast as I can," she says. "Good luck."

"To be continued," says the yakshi.

Joey strides back towards Kochchar Mansions alone as the yakshi disappears into the darkness of the forest.

3 IMMORTAL IS THE HEART

Cassandra Khaw

GERARD HATED THE MIDWEST. WELL, NOT *THE* MIDWEST, PER SE. HE HELD NO animosity towards the region itself. What he hated was *driving* across the Midwest. He resented seeing the swathes of dead farmland, soil so wrung of nutrients and its bacterial ecosystems, it'd be entire lifetimes before anything would take root in that brown dust again; the dried-up lakes; the ghost towns, haunted by debris; the cars abandoned along the broad highways like picked-over skeletons, scabrous with red-gray rust. Gerard loathed knowing there'd been more here once, that there was grass as far as the eye could see, and cornfields with their lion-colored harvest swaying gently under an oiled-silk sky, and monarch butterflies and coyotes and bunnies and bison. That it had held life enough to sustain a whole country.

Gone now. All of it.

Yeah. Maybe, that was his problem with the Midwest. The knowledge of what it was and could still have been. That and understanding the policymakers responsible for this unholy waste were as dead as the land they'd fucked over. No matter how angry Gerard got, he would never be able to do more than piss on their graves, something he'd tried once when he was younger and inchoate with fury at the world. It had done nothing but relieve the pressure on his bladder, had left him feeling impotent and puerile, embarrassed at his outburst and the stinking yellow mess dribbling over the faded tombstone. There was only going forward: thinking, looking, moving forward. No point in nursing those old wounds; a new generation was depending on them.

Still, every time he took an assignment in the Midwest, Gerard still wanted to scream. He wouldn't, though. Not with Bourbon and Rye riding in the tonneau: they'd lose their minds and start barking until the heavens calved like a glacier and a piece crushed them flat. Instead, he lit a cigarette and let his arm flop out the truck window. The vehicle grumbled under him.

It was a relic, like he almost was: both its engine and the chassis straight from the before times. The marigold upholstery and the leather steering wheel—those were new, as were the alterations he made to the truck bed. Between him, the dogs, and Betty, Gerard had to be clever. There'd be no space for them otherwise, not unless he intended to sleep in the cabin with a dog heaped over his knee, and at forty-six, that wasn't going to happen. The thought alone made his back hurt along three different vertebrae.

He adjusted the rearview mirror. Rye stared back at him through the mirror, her gaze calm and wise, the line from the bridge of her muzzle to her tail as perfect as a soldier's posture. Bourbon, as always, was busy with more nonsense: this time, it was ineffectively grooming the quadrupedal robot lying docile between her and her sister. Behind them: the sky deepened in hue, the bright celadon darkening to a bruise.

Illinois stretched on like hope. Gerard did the mathematics in his head. It couldn't be much longer now. The town was probably another six or so hours away if he pushed, which he would. Sleeping on the road was a risk. Even now, after the end of everything, there'd be people who'd take umbrage at Gerard for having the temerity to be a color other than pink. That said, the whole ordeal was as much his fault as anyone else's. The higher-ups had very delicately suggested he only take coastal assignments, but Gerard had insisted. He felt like he owed something to the people who lived here: the immigrant families, the poor who had nowhere to go, the folk who carried the bayou and the prairie, the corn and the endless skies, in their bones and wouldn't give up the place of their births just because a racist said leave.

He was born at least a hundred years too late to save them, but their stories—well, that was different. That he could do something about.

The hours flattened into a steady featureless continuum: no before, no after, no sense of time elapsing, just the unbroken now. Twice, Gerard stopped to let the dogs stretch their legs and let Betty investigate the remnants of a farmhouse. Once so he could make a meal out of a positively antediluvian packet of MRE. They drove through rain and a bout of unseasonal hail, the latter leaving Gerard cursing but the dogs happily ensconced in the truck cab with him, the air inside smelling of rain and damp fur. And night kept seeping across the horizon, the shadows growing bloodier with every mile. Soon enough, the world contracted to the headlights of Gerard's truck, and this was a good thing as he would have driven himself right off the road in shock if he had beheld in its entirety what he found at the mouth of the town.

GREEN. GREEN *EVERYWHERE*: GREEN WEEPING THROUGH THE CRACKS IN THE asphalt, green in the boughs of the saplings bracketing the road, green in the absolute mess of earthen pots jumbled around a convoy of vans, their occupants unloading agricultural tools when Gerard arrived. Thrown into relief by his headlights, the people arrayed there seemed unreal, ghost-like in their starkness.

One threw their forearm over their eyes and barked, "Turn that fucking shit off. You're blindin' us."

Gerard obliged, too dazzled to do more than behave as told. Once he had killed his headlights, he opened his door and stepped out of the truck, his dogs pouring after him. Rye growled a warning at the strangers but quieted when Gerard stretched a hand to her. She pushed her skull into his palm, her snarling thinned to a whine, only relaxing when he stroked her ears. Bourbon stayed behind them both, flank pressed to the back of Gerard's knees. His vision swam in that sudden dark. Everyone had become silhouettes and Gerard found himself regretting his earlier compliance, wishing for a firearm.

"Who the hell are you lot?"

The telltale noise of a shotgun racked, ready to go.

"Who the hell are *you?*" a masculine-sounding voice, coming from someone just out of sight.

"Jesus," said the first person—a woman if Gerard had to guess from the voice—who spoke. "Can y'all wait for a second before choosing violence? I swear to god, testosterone is why we're all in this mess to begin with."

"Amen," a third voice, higher, sweeter, exquisitely androgynous.

The crowd laughed.

Gerard raised both hands slowly, still reeling from that revelation of green life. He could even *smell* it in the air, cutting through the dust and the old death. He wanted to drink it down. He wanted to roll in the scent until it soaked into his skin and he could carry it like a second heart.

"I'm not here to hurt nobody."

"But are you here to take anythin'?" asked the one with the shotgun, swaggering into view. Beside them, someone else raised an oil lamp to head height. Its dim light traced the hungry lines of a man's face: he had deep-set eyes, dune-colored skin, thin lips, a nebula of scars that contorted his mouth into a permanent sneer. Illuminated, the keloid tissue shone pink and almost wet.

"Just knowledge," said Gerard. He could make out scaffolding along the wall of a nearby building, tarp stretched over where a roof should have been. After a moment, he added, "I'm a Starik."

The name unlocked the air and the tension leached away, subsiding into thoughtful murmuring. The man lowered his shotgun, the caution gone from his face.

"Lonely work," he said in lieu of apology. "Can't imagine doin' it myself."

"It's a lot of driving," said Gerard, bobbing his head. He wasn't raised male but after thirty years, he spoke the vernacular as well as anyone else.

"Can't be easy."

"Nope."

"I'd like to apologize for my friend Jacob over here," The woman who had spoken earlier strode up to the pair, lightly punching the scarred man in the shoulder. She was taller than he was and pale enough to be white, as much muscle as she was fat. "He has a tendency to holler first and ask decent questions later."

Jacob wilted under her words. "Better safe than sorry, Dolores."

"Safe shouldn't involve other people bein' dead."

"Well, better them than–"

"*Hush.*"

Jacob went red, the color surfacing in uneven splashes until the entirety of his face was suffused in crimson. He did not protest, however, only ducked his head like a petulant child. Gerard realized with a start that Jacob was much younger than he initially surmised: in his late twenties, at most, for all that he carried himself like an angry old man of eighty-two. While they bickered, Gerard took the opportunity to put a number to the figures arrayed in the gloom. He counted twenty-five silhouettes, but he suspected there were more out of sight, perched in the dark, waiting to gun down any threats.

"Alright," said Dolores, nodding to herself. Her accent was pure Georgian molasses, heady and low. She was the most gorgeous woman Gerard had ever seen in his life. "You gonna tell us why you here then?"

"He's a Starik—" Jacob began.

"Was I talkin' to you or was I talkin' to him, huh?"

"Sorry."

Gerard hid a smile. "Like I said, I'm a Starik."

"Do me a favor." Dolores flashed him a perfect white grin. "Explain it to us like we're all five. What's a Starik?"

She had an incredible stare, a gaze that bored through skin and muscle until it found the heart trembling under its roof of bones. A gaze that said she wanted a precise taxonomy of his experiences, that she yearned to know everything he carried in him. Under its attention, Gerard felt utterly exposed, raw, exhilarated.

"A Starik's what they call people in the project," he began slowly, shedding his usual diction for the oratorical voice he used when giving a performance, accent smoothing, anonymizing. "Probably because it was started by a man called Frank Starik. He was a poet in the early noughts who thought it was a disgrace that there were people out there who died alone and forgotten. So, he started this project—"

Gerard recited the story with the ease of practice, having repeated it so very many times to so many people, and he knew the precise sequence of expressions that would follow: curiosity giving way to tenderness and then to something more ineffable, something like wonder as Gerard explained how Starik's Lonely Funeral worked—Dolores sniffled unabashedly at the description of a poet standing over a stranger's casket, cantillating the highlights of a life that would be forgotten by everyone but this one volunteer biographer—and how it was revitalized after the end of the world.

"—a *what* now?" said Jacob, midway through Gerard's account.

"Mobile robot."

"As opposed to?"

Dolores chuckled. "Stationary robot, I reckon."

Gerard laughed. Jacob didn't.

"It's the term they used for those robots who had sensors with which to analyze environmental hazards so they could move around freely," said Gerard. He added after a moment as a dour aside, "The military loved them."

His new acquaintances traded dark looks. In Jacob's face, he saw renewed suspicion. In Dolores's, nothing but cordiality and weapons-grade charm. Their gazes wandered to Gerard's truck and the tarp he had laid over Betty. He wondered what they envisioned was hiding under the rain-slicked sheets of IKEA-blue vinyl.

"We repurposed whatever we could scavenge. At first, it was so we could have some way of scarin' off raiders. But then about fifty years ago, someone was like, 'What else can we do with these robots?' So, the great minds of the Lonely Funeral Project got to thinkin' and decided if we just rejiggered the hardware a little, trained up a language model, it might be able to help the poets with their research."

The word *poet* made Bourbon look up at him, hopeful. Three years and Gerard didn't know why that combination of sounds made the dog think there'd be a treat at the end of the sentence.

Jacob had his tongue cleaved to the top of his mouth, the tip a pink hyphen peeking from his incisors. He stood silent for a minute as Dolores honked her nose on a scrap of fabric, clearly wrestling with his thoughts. Most of the crowd had dispersed by then, their interest slaked. Gerard was no longer a curio, no more a potential threat: he had become some guy in their eyes, for better or worse. They, however, remained a subject of Gerard's curiosity. He watched them disperse, taking note of how unbothered their movements were, how at ease they seemed with their surroundings, and how many were involved in the work of rehabilitating the ruins. There was fresh paint on some of the walls, he realized with a start, as strings of lights were lit. This was more than a camp.

They were making it a home.

"That's beautiful," said Dolores, sinking to her knees, a hand extended to Rye, who fixed her with a coal-eyed stare as if to say, *I can't believe you'd even try.* Bourbon, who took her lead in all things, shrank away from Dolores, growling half-heartedly.

"Thank you," said Gerard.

"Okay," said Jacob, no longer at war with himself. He perched the heel of his hand on the butt of his shotgun, the muzzle thrust into the asphalt, and frowned at Gerard. "So, I just want to clear a few things."

"Mhm."

"The Lonely Funeral project, it's all about poets readin' up on the anonymous dead so they can write a poem that they'd then read at the funerals, right?"

"Yep," said Gerard. He knew people in his vocation who filled every available silence with words, like athletes stretching to keep their muscles warmed and limber. But he wasn't one of them. Gerard preferred to be frugal with his speech.

"But everyone's *dead*," said Jacob. "The kind of dead where even the bones have been taken by the coyotes. There's nothing here to bury. I don't get it. Unless this is a ritualistic sort of thing, I don't see why a Starik would come here. Who are you even looking for?"

"Not who," said Gerard, "but what. See, I'm here for the town."

WHEN THE CONVOY DISCOVERED HE HAD CIGARETTES ON HIS PERSON—REAL CIGA-rettes, the sort produced in a factory and boxed up in paperboard—he was suddenly the center of attention again. Everyone wanted to trade. The youngest to proposition Gerard was a boy of fourteen, who told him he would teach the older man to hunt in exchange for one of his cartons. It was him being generous, he explained, standing hipshot and proud. Ordinarily, it would cost Gerard his entire stash for a single lesson, but just this once, because Gerard was new and he was feeling exceptionally generous, he would lower his asking rate to one measly pack. Gerard said no.

"You know those shorten your life, right?" said Jacob, coming up to Gerard as the boy stomped into the night.

"Figured it doesn't matter," said Gerard. He peeled a fresh carton from its plastic wrapping and angled the open container at Jacob. "What with the fact we no longer have a health care infrastructure."

Jacob demurred with a raised hand, stepping politely upwind of Gerard.

"Don't smoke," he said.

"Your loss. These are actual Marlboros," said Gerard, joggling the pack until a single cigarette slid out. With a practiced motion, he pulled it the rest of the way out with his teeth. "They don't make them like they used to anymore."

"Thank god," said Jacob. "We could do with less cancer in the world."

Gerard lit his cigarette. "Mm."

He counted the seconds under his breath, taking a drag whenever he hit a multiple of ten. At the two-minute mark, Jacob said:

"You got family?"

"Nope."

"Not even cousins?"

Gerard considered the question. It woke a familiar evanescent sadness, as quick to surface as it was to dissipate but no less sharp for its brevity. He waited until the ache subsided before resuming the conversation, ashing the cigarette onto the dirt.

"Statistically speaking, I most likely do."

An easterly wind stripped the moon of its clouds. Bereft of its cover, the moon seemed abnormally large, a dead god's eye looking over the world it had abandoned.

"Oh," said Jacob, finally cottoning onto the situation. "Oh, fuck me. I'm an insensitive asshole. Dolores keeps telling me I need to think before I talk. Look, I'm *sorry*."

"Water under the bridge."

"But it ain't, is it? I just went in there—"

"You want to tell me about what y'all are doing here? I already told you about my work."

"I still don't understand it," said Jacob. "I mean, I get why someone who had ties to a place might want to do it, but you don't."

"Nope."

"How'd you even find out about this place then?"

"Old records. Maps. You'd be surprised how comprehensive they are."

"Why bother, though?" said Jacob.

"Let's pretend for a second you didn't get as lucky as you did. Didn't find Dolores. Didn't get set up with the life you've got here," said Gerard, alarmed at how unconscionably ancient he felt. When did that shift happen? he wondered. When did he go from being the angry young man who needed lecturing to the one dispensing lectures? It seemed almost criminal that such a significant transition had taken place so invisibly, but that was life, wasn't it, and aging besides. No one ever saw it coming until it was late. "Then somethin' happens. You get sick, you get hurt. Somethin'. After a few weeks of suffering, it becomes clear you won't survive and that no one's goin' to hold your hand when you die. Wouldn't you want someone to at least remember you lived?"

Jacob said nothing at first, his face gone strange and ashen. Gerard felt a throb of guilt, but he smoothed it down. That way lay too many feelings, too many conversations he didn't want to have, knowing he'd be gone soon enough.

"Yeah," said Jacob, and fell into a deep wincing silence again.

"It's what I do. I learn about people and the town they lived in. Save everything I can, everything worth remembering so they're not just bones. Anyway," said Gerard, clearing his throat, "I feel like I'm the only one who's been answerin' any questions tonight. Your turn: What are y'all doing here?"

Jacob had worked himself into such a lather of misery, his shoulders were practically bunched up at his ears, face palsied in a grisly expression of self-hate. The scarring along his jaw was even more extensive than Gerard had initially thought: his neck was webbed with a fretwork of faded stitches. Someone had tried to cut Jacob's throat.

No. Not tried, Gerard amended. Succeeded. It was still possible to see where the knife had traveled, how deeply it had sunk through his flesh. Whoever had done it to him had known what they were doing, had not acted out of impulse, had been controlled with their movements, precise.

"Makin' right old sins," said Jacob.

"Whose exactly?"

"All of ours," said Jacob. "We did this to the planet. Seems right that we try to fix some of it."

"Soil is dead as dead can be, though. Unless y'all invented a miracle, there ain't no way anything's growing in this dirt. Not for a long time, at least."

"Guess we came up with a miracle then," said Jacob, a boyish joy kindling in his eyes, and in that instant, he looked unbearably young, the scars and his leathery skin purely cosmetic. "It's all because of Dolores, honestly. The worms love her. The compost they make for her is black gold—"

It was as if a dam had broken. A river of words spilled out of Jacob and wouldn't stop, not that Gerard would have tried to impede its flow, struck as he was by the younger man's feverish excitement. He told Gerard everything, every detail of Dolores' crusade to restore the soil. Not just in the Midwest but elsewhere as well. She had plans, Jacob confided with a fierce fraternal pride. Plans to optimize the processes they were using, streamline them, make it so they were so simple, so irrefutably necessary to daily life that everyone, no matter age or descent, would feel compelled to do the work.

"She's even got a breeding program for her worms. The idea is that in ten years, when we've got enough of the soil mended, we'll put batches of them in the earth and let them do their thing."

Gerard, who had never spent much time dwelling on the subject of worms, nodded, swept along by the voluble flood. Pity Dolores hadn't been born a generation earlier. Her mule-headed ambition and pragmatic genius might have been able to stay the earth's death sentence. He wasn't naive enough to think their present could have been averted. Even if there'd been a hundred Doloreses working in concert, the world's coffers at their command, it would have been too little, too late. But it might have been a slower death, a gentler one, drawn out long enough to permit for more than a handful of survivors.

The night had a sweet, cold scent. It wasn't raining, per se, but a fine mist clung to the air, beading Jacob's flyaway hair and dampening Gerard's collar. Around them, Dolores's crew worked tirelessly, hollering to one another, passing boxes and plastic barrels heaped with compost. They set down trellises, tilled the dust, spread humus over the parched earth. Then: seeds were sown in some places, saplings in others. What really impressed Gerard was how carefully Dolores had set up the shifts so there was time enough for people to sleep, to socialize, to eat, while allowing them to work across every spare hour of the day.

He watched them as Jacob continued his lecture, marveling at the camaraderie. Dolores did not lord over her people. She was there in the literal dirt, working alongside them, hands gloved in bright yellow rubber.

"She's pretty, ain't she?"

Gerard jolted at the words. "What?"

"Dolores," said Jacob, tipping his chin in the woman's direction. "I said she's pretty, ain't she?"

"You think you're a clever bastard, aren't you?" Gerard snapped, more perturbed by the teasing than he expected himself to be.

To his increased vexation, his ire was greeted with laughter, Jacob tossing his head back as he guffawed.

"You like her." It wasn't a question.

"Dolores is impressive," said Gerard.

"You *like* her."

"Whether I do or do not, that's between me and the powers that be. Nothin' to do with you, and *will you quit laughin' already*—"

No amount of swearing and seething warning could dull Jacob's amusement after that. He met every one of Gerard's threats with another outburst of laughter, eventually folding into a crouch, arms wrapped around his ribs. Gerard stared helplessly, face burning with emotion he refused to interrogate.

"What's so funny over there?"

Gerard whirled around to see Dolores unbending from her labor. Sweat welded her hair to her face and molded the men's button-up shirt she wore to her body, leaving absolute jack to Gerard's imagination. It occurred to him then that it had been years, no, *decades*, since he had sought out intimacy with another human being, preferring instead the ascetic's lifestyle.

Was it preference, Gerard? Or was it just safer? A little voice needled in his head.

"Gerard?"

Wild-eyed, he stared at Dolores, a deep *whud-whud-whud* roaring in his ears. The sound encased him in a not-unpleasant haziness: he felt drunk or maybe stoned, certainly some kind of chemically altered. It took longer than he should have to realize he was embarrassed to sin and back. That he had felt this exact same way more than thirty years ago when he'd walked up to Jennifer Lee's front stoop to ask if she would share a milkshake with him. Chagrined by his very adolescent response to the situation, Gerard did the only thing he could.

He ran away.

WELL, NOT RAN.

Walked with uncustomary speed and a clunky, stiff-limbed gait that he was sure made him look as though he had cement for legs. Gerard was too old and too exhausted from driving like a man possessed to actually sprint through an unfamiliar darkness. The thought of falling and ultimately twisting something was untenable: it'd most likely involve Dolores coming to his rescue and god, he wasn't sure if he'd survive that humiliation. Thank god he had unloaded Betty before Jacob roped him into conversation. If he tried that now, he probably would have broken a bone somehow.

His escape carried him straight into what Betty had identified as the town's library: a squat, warehouse-looking building extending from the ruins of a school. The walls were rimed with muck, an inch-thick skin of grayish particulates that came away if he so much as breathed in its direction. What remained of its roofing was largely intact save for an area in the back that had staved in, giving it the look of a cracked skull, a hinge of bone bent inwards into the brain. A rusted metal door stood at the front, barely tethered to its equally corroded hinges, and hanging slightly ajar.

Gerard let himself in.

The air smelled of mold and dust but also of old books and uniquely, an excess of plastic. Librarians, especially those in the twilight of all things, were fastidious people. No matter their background, their individual quirks, they seemed to share a certain phylum of behaviors, most of which involved how best to care for and maintain their collections. This occupational zealotry had meant everything for those who came after. Misinformation had been endemic in those last days, and little on the internet could be trusted. But the records those last librarians kept, their archives, those were rational and clear, if abundantly annotated. From them, Gerard and his generation learned to rebuild, to solder together the artifacts of the past into new means of survival.

Gerard raised a flashlight and scanned the interior, landing immediately on a message chiseled onto an adjacent wall. It said:

If seeking knowledge, go to aisle with dragons.

Hastily scrawled under it was another message, this one in sharpie:

Brian, it's fine if you don't like Pratchett and it's absolutely okay that you ran away into the night, but you didn't also have to take the goddamned book. Please return it to its shelf if you come back and I'm dead and/or missing.
P.S. You might want to try Mort instead if you didn't like Soul Music.

"Librarians," said Gerard fondly.

He'd made the acquaintance of more than a few living librarians and every one of them had been the same: avid readers, obsessed with organization, as in love with the written word as zealots were with their worship. Had Gerard not fallen in with the Stariks, he might have endeavored to join their ranks. Regardless, he felt a certain kinship with them. His work was not dissimilar. Theirs spanned the lifespan of humanity. His, a single individual or town.

Gerard glanced at his tablet. Betty's telemetry sensors remained perfect: the entire topography of the library was modeled on the screen, with a green dot bobbing through the aisles, indicating the robot's position. As Gerard watched, a row of amber markers flared into view, delineating where records of the town and its notables were kept. She'd done a lot in the two hours since he'd set her loose in the library, more than he or any human could, and not for the first time he wondered about how her image recognition algorithms were used in those last terrible wars—and decided again, as he always did, that he had no real want for an answer. He looked up and around, then continued his foray into the library. Passing a switch on the wall, he gave it an experimental flick. Overhead fluorescents coughed to asthmatic life, convulsing for a half second before giving out with a distant *bang*, startling Gerard enough that his hand leapt to the revolver at his hip. When nothing followed, he decided it was a generator letting out its death gurgle, and resumed his study of the space. Most of the shelves were swaddled in tarps or sheets of matte plastic, painstakingly strapped down to minimize the risks of water exposure. Giant plastic containers littered the floor space, their lids crammed with more writing. And the walls, they held either inscriptions of varying sophistry, or panels of laminated paper.

Whoever had been here must have made the space a safehouse, Gerard concluded. No way any of this could have been done quickly. It must have taken months, years even, to orchestrate this. He wondered if the library's caretaker was still here, tidily settled in a corner so the effluvium from their corpse wouldn't contaminate the books.

A low hum of machinery drew Gerard from his reverie. He looked up to see Betty turning a corner, the sound of her hydraulics edged with a whine: it was past time to take her in for maintenance. Gerard filed the thought away with the dozens of other things he'd indefinitely postponed. The closest Starik encampment was several states away, and he was both exhausted and discombobulated by Jacob's teasing.

"You did a good job, Betty," said Gerard, aware of how he might have sounded to an onlooker, a middle-aged man offering compliments to a machine. Then again, NASA once sang birthday songs to a robot on the moon.

She bent one of her forelegs and lowered herself to the ground: the robot's equivalent of a curtsey. Not for the first time, Gerard found himself wondering how advanced Betty's language heuristics were, if the little genuflections she sometimes extended to him were meant with sincerity or sarcasm. He refused, however, to think too hard on what both those possibilities implicated. If Betty was sapient, capable of autonomous reason and able to develop opinions, all he could hope for was to provide her with a kind impression of his species. Gerard had watched the old movies. He knew what angry AIs could do.

"Sleep mode," he said then. "Until I figure out where the computers are and if we can wire you to them."

Gerard advanced and laid a hand on the chilly metal of her back. Betty was all torso and eerily articulate legs, her chassis pitted with grooves and overrun with unused moorings, showing where someone might have anchored a weapons turret or set a laser sight. Even without her munitions, she was an imposing sight.

Lights flashed along Betty's sensors in an illegible pattern before the robot settled itself on its haunches. When Gerard was sure Betty had fully deactivated, he patted her gently, the way he would pat Bourbon when she was being restive. Then he pressed on, finding his way to the speculative fiction aisle where, to his abundant lack of surprise, he uncovered a series of instructions carved onto the flooring.

> *If you can carry more than one box of books and have queer children, please take the box on the left.*
> *If you can only take one book and are an adult, consider the anthology I have kept in the glass box on the third shelf of the rightmost stack.*
> *If you are a kid, I have some legos in the cleaning supplies cabinet. I also want you to take the box in there. I wish I could hug you. I hope someone is there with you, making sure you're safe. Tell them a librarian said to take care of you. I love you. Be careful.*

The arrows intaglioed into the linoleum were numerous enough to be dizzying. They spiraled in every direction, fern-like and strangely beautiful. Under their mantling, the shelves held more abrupt edicts, noting which books were at risk of mold, which had to be preserved at all costs, which could be sacrificed if the librarian had miscalculated and there weren't enough desiccant packs to go around, which the librarian would miss reading for the hundredth time.

In one example of the last, Gerard found a bookmark fossilized in the pages. A message had been written along its length, so discolored by time, it was nearly unintelligible.

My name was Jana.

The *was* drowned Gerard in sudden agony. A sob fought itself loose from his mouth, and he hugged the book—carefully, so the pages wouldn't disintegrate—to his chest as he wept. Was, not is. Jana knew no help was coming. His imagination gave contours to the blank slate of her past. Gerard pictured her as an older woman: someone in their youth wouldn't have so much fortitude, wouldn't have been able to navigate their impending end so calmly. His mind gave her dark hair and a loquacious manner. He pictured her in soft cardigans; horn-rimmed glasses; billowy linens when the weather turned scorching. Jana, he decided, was someone who talked the ears off every visitor, and who kept a special collection of titles for those kids who'd been warned against the literature that would save them.

Irrationally, Gerard worried about whether Jana had been alone during those last moments, wishing desperately then for some magic or piece of technology with which he could reverse the decades—and *what?* He didn't know. All he could think of was her alone in the library, furiously gouging messages into the walls in the event her books would be found one day.

"Gerard?"

It was Dolores.

"Here," he croaked and waited in the dark until Dolores found him. He winced as she shone her flashlight into his face, but did not move, not wanting to risk the book still tucked against his ribs.

"Did I interrupt a nap or somethin'?" said Dolores, squatting down a polite distance from him. A smudge of dirt ran across her right cheekbone. In that near dark, her eyes were a resinous umber. "Don't mean to. It's just that you stalked off so quickly earlier on. I was worried Jacob spoke out of turn. *Again.*"

She was giving him an out, he realized.

"I found—" Gerard swallowed, tried again. "I am coming to realize I'm a sentimental motherfucker who cries way too easily."

"You? Sentimental? Could've fooled me," said Dolores, one corner of her mouth creeping up into a smile, cheek dimpling as it did. "Can't imagine someone like you being sentimental. What with all your unsentimental interest in writing poetry for the dead."

Gerard said nothing. He knew if he tried, what would emerge from his throat would be an animal howl, a long unrelenting wail of grief for a woman who had been dead longer than he had been alive, and the sound would go on until something in him broke irreparably.

When it was clear Gerard had no plans of responding, Dolores said: "It alright if I sat next to you?"

He nodded. Dolores placed herself beside him, knees drawn to her chest. She smelled of sweat and good dirt.

"My family used to live here in the before times," said Dolores. "Great-grandma was Sioux. Her husband too, even if his daddy was white. According to my mom, they didn't have the best time here, what with it being a red state and all. But they fought anyway, to make the place safer for their children."

She held out a hand to Gerard, palm up. Her nail beds were encrusted with dirt. Gingerly, he laid his own hand over hers and stared, uncomprehending, as her fingers twinned with his.

"They tried *so* hard. Back then, you couldn't go online without running into people claiming there wasn't anything of value in middle America, but they knew different. They knew there were good people in the Midwest and the South and all those places that weren't the coastal cities. Someone had to fight for them, though. So they did." Dolores trailed to silence, eyes fixed on nothing.

"That what got you started on the saving the world thing?" said Gerard.

"Yeah," said Dolores with a musical little laugh. "Apple don't fall far from the tree. If somethin's worth doing, best do it yourself. What about you?"

Gerard rubbed listless circles into her palm, luxuriating in the small intimacy, the sensation of someone else's skin.

"Me?"

"Yeah."

"I don't know," said Gerard truthfully. "Chance, I guess. Met a Starik when I was about twenty-two, right after I started feelin' good about telling the world I was a boy. She blew into town for a few weeks, and we got to talkin'—"

"Well, *someone's* a ladykiller."

He laughed. "Not like that. We—she—I don't know, *maybe* it could have been a thing, if I wasn't scared shitless of everything back then—we just talked. She told me about all the towns she went to, all the places we forgot. How she carried them now in her heart. And I thought about the people like me—"

"Like *us*."

Oh, thought Gerard, reassessing the dimensions of Dolores's frame, the gorgeous shadows her bones painted across her face.

"—like us, and I wanted to make sure they weren't forgotten."

"People who were displaced, forgotten by the world."

Gerard nodded. "Yeah."

Laid bare like such, his motives seemed so quixotic, so *simple*, a child's quest with a child's ideals. Egoistical too, hissed that mean little voice in Gerard's head. Especially when measured against Dolores's altruism. The words had been *said*, however. Wish as Gerard might, he couldn't take them back. He might as well try to rewind the years to save a lonely town librarian from whatever waited for her at the end. Gerard swallowed around his shame and drew his shoulder blades back, intent on salvaging what dignity he could.

"You're allowed to laugh," said Gerard stiffly.

Her grip on his hand tightened.

"Nothing to laugh at," said Dolores, voice so quiet her words carried like prayer. "Stories matter. The AIDS epidemic left a whole generation adrift. There weren't enough elders to go around after that. Some, but not enough. Not as much as our community deserved."

"I can't believe you know about that—"

"You're not the only nerd around here," said Dolores, brows raised to a theatrical height. When Gerard did not immediately laugh, she waggled them until he did and did not stop until he was knuckling tears from his eyes, the librarian's book set gently to one side.

After Gerard could speak coherently again, she said:

"So, how's the poetry going?"

"Been distracted," said Gerard. "There's someone I gotta find first before anything else."

GERARD HAD BEEN RIGHT.

Jana was precisely the kind of punctilious to set a tarp up for herself in the supply closet, the canvas lashed carefully around her feet and legs–the right leg was broken and Gerard would have bet all his rations that was why she never left—so as to trap, Gerard supposed, any runoff from decomposition. It'd been long enough that there was no longer any smell, no organic matter for bacteria to spoil: nothing they could use, at any rate. Slathered in silica gel, the torn packets strewn around her, Jana was mostly bone and dried skin, delicate as vellum. Through some miraculous alchemy of circumstances, Gerard could still see a ghost of Jana's expression when she passed. To his relief, she seemed at peace. Asleep, rather than in pain. God knew he'd seen a lot of tormented corpses: those final years had killed people in a hundred ways.

"This Jana?" said Dolores.

"I think so," said Gerard, at a loss for anything coherent to say.

A shiver trilled down his back: he wasn't afraid of Jana, wasn't afraid of the death on display, wasn't upset by it. After all, he had seen too many bodies at this point to feel more than a forensic curiosity.

But most dead people didn't talk *back*.

It was disorienting to see her like this—inert, still—when she felt so *present*, her voice preserved in the notes she had hidden across the library. Up until that moment, a part of Gerard was convinced he would find her in the town somewhere, alive if not entirely well, excited to provide additional commentary.

Laid across her chest, the lapels of her cardigan studded with enamel pins, was a laminated paper. Gingerly, he lifted it and began to read Jana's last letter to the world aloud.

> *I don't and can't know who you are, or if you read the language in which I am writing. I could only preserve for the future with the resources I had at hand. You owe me nothing, but still I hope that perhaps if you have found yourself here instead of the supply stores that maybe, just maybe we are alike in some ways—*

Gerard turned the plastic.

> *—if perhaps you are looking at this with an eye toward historical analysis, then I feel the pressure of my own education to warn you against applying my own beliefs and thoughts to those of all people during my time. I was not necessarily indicative of the majority of my fellow thinking beings in my own time. Or maybe I was and I was alone only in my own foolish mind.*

There was marginalia bracketing the paragraph, reams of half-finished thoughts scribbled down at random angles, cramped bullet lists supporting one supposition or the other.

> *You're the one in the future with a far more representative sample of the thoughts and dominant cultural themes of my time. Or at least I hope you are. I hope you aren't grasping at straws. I hope this isn't the last little bastion of human knowledge remaining. Surely more whole and representative collections survived. All I have is the most structurally sound portions of this old school library. I'm sure within thirty years this roof will cave in without some intervention. That's why I kept the critical things in the corners. They sank steel into the reinforced concrete there. It should stand up the longest. I do hope more of my comrades made it past that first worst part of*

the end. Caroline, she was with the archive in Kansas City. If you are hunting for a larger collection, something that'd allow you to accrue a better swathe of data points, check there.

I marked it on the maps. It was one of the last ones I was able to laminate before I ran out of gas for the generator. No, dear reader, that just sounded better. I laminated the maps to the libraries first, but it sounds more dramatic if I say it was one of the last. You can hear that drama ringing in your head, can't you? I apologize for the deceit.

(Although if you are a younger reader it is important to remember that narrators can be unreliable.)

"We have to do *something*," said Gerard, detaching the pins from Jana's body. Fabric disintegrated in his hands. Thank god, the enamel badges held. Gerard didn't know if his heart could take losing those too. He ran his fingers over the surface, tracing the stripes along the gilt-edged badge: pink, pale blue, and white. "We can't—I can't leave her like this. She doesn't deserve being stuck in a supply cabinet forever."

"We won't," said Dolores.

Outside, one of the dogs began to howl.

GERARD WOULDN'T LET DOLORES OR HER CREW DIG JANA'S GRAVE: THAT WORK HE kept for himself, shoveling the packed dirt until his palms blistered. He should be working on the town's records, filtering through Betsy's finds. Jana wasn't the only one who died in this town, but Gerard couldn't bring himself to do anything else until she was at proper rest. Jacob made one abortive attempt at offering to help, stepping away when Dolores set a hand on his shoulder and shook her head.

They searched, of course, for any posthumous directives. Jana had been amply clear about what she wanted done with her stacks, but apparently had applied no thought at all to the disposal of her own corporeal form. It made sense. At the time, there'd been no guarantee of survivors. If anything, likely she had been assured of the reverse.

So, they decided on a burial, though none of them knew any funerary rites, not even Gerard. Jacob led six men in constructing the casket, a crude makeshift thing. When they were done, Jana—carefully and fully swaddled up in a tarp so there was no risk of her being damaged, the thought too miserable for any of them to bear—was taken by a procession to her final resting place. They'd chosen the largest of the soil beds that Dolores's party had made and dug deep. Jacob promised there would be flowers to keep Jana company.

58

"She really liked those books," said Gerard, half defensively, lining the interior of the casket with paperbacks before they laid Jana inside. "I figured she might like having them as she goes on her next journey."

"I think she'd have appreciated it," said Dolores, adding a pill bottle to the pile. "One more for the road, sister."

One by one, the others brought their own gifts: Jacob, a rose as red as heart's blood; someone else, two bright pennies they laid over her eyes; a harmonica, a wooden carving of cat, a half-finished bottle of bourbon, the label long since lost.

"Can't believe they're gonna just toss it away like that," said Gerard, half in jest. "When you got people like me so thirsty for a good drink, we're naming our dogs after the things we want."

"I'd name a dog Dumpling," said Jacob. "Had some about five years ago when a Chinese family rolled through our town. Blew my goddamned mind."

"Well," said one of Dolores's men, so old he was little more than an ambulatory mound of wrinkles, "if that's how it works, I'd probably name a pupper my wife's—"

The ensuing roar of laughter drowned out what the man would have said, and Gerard thought Jana would have loved the camaraderie. As the guffaws stuttered to a halt, a girl began to sing a dirge in a language Gerard couldn't put a name to, her voice as lonely and silver as the moon. In that lunar glow, they all seemed ethereal, ghosts themselves.

One by one, they placed handfuls of soil over Jana's casket until it was gone from sight.

"Your cue," said Dolores.

Gerard nodded. It wasn't in his nature to be spontaneous. Like Jana, he favored thoroughness, contingencies for every occasion: a thousand charms to protect against disaster, but dawn was approaching, and there was work to do and the living needed their sleep. Gerard cleared his throat and began to speak.

"Let me tell you about Jana."

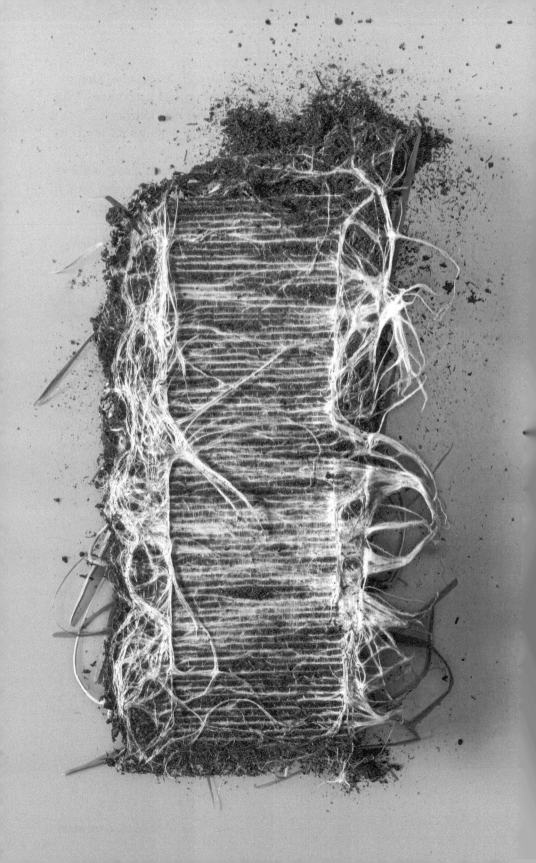

4 UNAUTHORIZED (OR, THE LIBERATED COLLECTORS COMMUNE)

Ganzeer

Part 1: Newmerica

"PLEASE," SAID THE CRYING WOMAN ON HER KNEES, "BOTH MY HUSBAND AND MY mistress left me. My baby boy died too." The droid standing in front of her accessed her family records and found that her son did indeed perish $1.3392\text{E}+22$ femtoseconds[1] ago. Hit-and-run, one of the 113 vehicular homicides committed across the country that very same day. Cars were still the leading cause of death in America, followed by firearms.

"I have nothing else to live for, please." She clutched onto the droid's lower body like a demented cat on speed. A half dozen other androids were hauling out painting after painting from what looked and smelled like a hermit's art studio. One droid was pushing along a turntable and a wagonful of records.

"That is no excuse for such blatant abuse of raw material, Miss Amoff, which I'm sure you are very much aware of," said the android through its voice box to the tortured woman on her knees. "If, however, you are sincere in your sentiments, assisted suicide is legal and can certainly be arranged for you." The androgynous voice was firm and authoritative, but oddly warm, and very human. A stark contrast to the droid's boxy exterior.

Ally Amoff's back muscles could no longer raise a convincing enough argument to hold her up. Her fingernails went scraping down the droid's cold metal in a slow, high-pitched screech until her face finally hit the floor.

"Alternatively," said the droid, "there are other more considerate ways to pursue your passions. The digital tools that emulate the look and feel of analogue are in great abundance. Furthermore, many a corporation seeks out individuals with your particular set of skills. I have no doubt they

---

1. One hundred and fifty-five days.

would be more than willing to employ you in service of their many wonderful products and offerings."

"No." Ally's voice cracked. "You . . . you don't understand, you damn . . . you stupid robot!"

The droid agreed that Ally Amoff was only partially correct in her assessment.

"That is correct, Miss Amoff, I indeed do not understand the logic behind your emotional turmoil. In terms of intelligence, however, my IQ score measures at three hundred, and thus I'm afraid the 'stupid' descriptor does not quite apply."

Ally motioned with her fingers to the side of her head and emulated the pulling of a trigger.

A loud unmistakable bang could be heard moments later as the droids left Ally Amoff's home studio with her life's work. Luckily, guns were still legal in Texas, and Ally could be spared the exorbitant costs of an assisted-suicide facility.

The droids steered their vehicles through the streets of Marfa. The city had become one of the biggest hubs of unauthorized artmaking in America, thanks initially to its remote location, which fostered the artistic breeding ground first cultivated decades prior by the acclaimed conceptual artist Donald Judd. A crackdown was inevitable; the government couldn't afford to turn a blind eye to such a glaring waste of resources—not since Yellowstone.[2]

Washington needed to show it had no intention of being as passive as previous administrations, not least to keep the populace from being swayed by the few dozen insurgency groups that popped up after Yellowstone. A new America[3] was in the making, and it would be stronger than it had ever been before. Part of this new America was the full utilization of the advanced autonomous robot technology that US companies had developed in recent years. One vocation designated for these droids was

---

2. Yellowstone's eruption blanketed most of the continental United States in thick ash. Wyoming had it worst, but when you're deep in shit, it doesn't quite matter whether you're six feet under or twelve. The shower of splintered rock and glass was reported from coast to coast and came down hard and uninterrupted for several months on end. Roads, trains, and air travel were all but paralyzed. Ninety-seven million Americans dead, one hundred and ninety-five million terminally ill, and 75 percent of all livestock killed off. This was America's big one, making every other disaster that came before—natural or otherwise—look like half-hearted roleplay. No one talked about Pearl Harbor or 9/11 anymore, nor did they give much thought to Hurricane Sandy or the California fires or even that ghastly pandemic from a few decades back. Nothing that ever was compared to Yellowstone.
3. Oh so cleverly branded *Newmerica*.

collecting, the term used for locating and gathering frivolous products that utilized precious raw material in their construction, which at this point was pretty much all material. The tricky part was identifying what counted as frivolous. The robots needed parameters. Art was one of the first things to go. The federal government decided that material like paper, canvas, and pigment were all of better use on more essential goods, but that didn't keep artists in America from pressing on. America was a big country, and artists could migrate away from the major metropoles to places far from the cold-hearted grip of Collectors. Places like Marfa.

Texas still did not appreciate taking any shit from Washington, and it certainly did not appreciate being accused of being in cahoots with Open Range, one of the South's most unyielding insurgency groups. The governor of Texas publicly declared he would personally be dealing with the proliferation of artists himself—a macho statement that only amounted to putting out an order to assemble a first-rate squad of Collectors from the finest droids across Austin, Dallas, and Houston. Chief among these droids was Joe1ker18, which was designated to helm a squad of a dozen Collectors. The squad had been making significant progress until Joe1ker18 went missing. Kon10do32 was brought in as Joe1ker's replacement. As if anyone would've been able to tell them apart anyway. Until today, that is, thanks to the ten long scrapes that now ran down Kon10do's lower half.

Part 2: Information Processing

NONE OF THE ANARCHISTS AT THE INFOSHOP HAD DARED ATTEMPT TO STOP THE droids from collecting their stockpile of zines. They'd all seen what a Collector was capable of—and legally allowed to do—on the many videos that circulated the feeds. At the end of the day, American anarchists were all talk but very little walk. No one really believed that any of the insurgency groups that sprang from their ranks posed any real threat of national consequence, not even the Children of Leon.[4] Joe1ker18 and its team didn't need to open any of the zines to get an idea of the content held within; their vision sensors were equipped with spectral imaging technology that allowed them to peer through closed books and process the data within its pages in a matter of femtoseconds. By the time all the zines were confiscated, Joe1ker18 and its team of droids had learned several decades' worth

---

4. Named after Leon Czolgocz, the man responsible for the assassination of William McKinley, the twenty-fifth president of the United States.

of anarchist theory. It wasn't the content of the zines that prompted this Collectors' raid, of course—it was never about the content—it was the actual raw material. Paper was very valuable in a nation that could no longer grow trees at an exploitable scale.

Unlike humans, droids didn't need a whole lot of time to process what they learned. By the time Joe1ker18 and its team of Collectors made it to Marfa's recycling facility with their new stash of confiscated zines, they were already changed beings.

While unloading the material, Joe1ker18's vision sensors took notice of a facility employee it had never seen before. Equipped with automated facial recognition and population database search, Joe1ker18 identified the person as Ottis Morrow, police lieutenant of Presidio, Texas.

This was odd. What was he doing up in Marfa? Disguised as an employee of the recycling facility, no less. There were questions that needed to be answered.

Joe1ker18 approached him.

Part 3: Elegant Pillaging

DRIVING THROUGH TOWN, MARFA'S MANY BILLBOARDS SCROLLED ACROSS KON-10do32's vision sensor: lucrative cryptoart investments, exciting new tools to make digital art, and a cacophony of competing music-streaming services—anything to lure the city's vibrant art community away from using physical resources to create redundant objects. It wasn't like any other city Kon10do had serviced; no house or building was surrounded by a wall or fence. Properties seemed porous, leading in and out of one another with passageways, small bridges, and unexpected staircases. Nobody cared for convention in Marfa, and every other building was something of an art installation, even more so on the inside. Kon10do knew that the billboards were in no way a reflection of Marfa's populace or their interests, but billboards did maintain a 39 to 80 percent success rate at provoking a consumer response, and Kon10do32 was able to deduce that it stood on the winning side of history. All data indicated that social movements actually have a very low success rate, with a probability of being extinguished nine times out of ten. Contrary to popular belief,[5] yes, but the data did not lie, and Kon10do32's every action was driven by data.

---

5. A.k.a. wishful thinking.

Upon arriving at Marfa's recycling complex, Kon10do and its squad proceeded to unload Ally Amoff's superfluous creations and belongings. Stretched canvas was placed on braces that sat on a conveyer belt. This allowed each piece to roll into a massive scanning machine. Material was carefully analyzed and identified. The works then rolled into another machine that proceeded to wash and scrape all the material that sat on the canvas surface. Ally Amoff's vibrant visual expressions began to dissolve off the canvas; colors mixed with exfoliating chemicals and water, then went pouring down drains that led into pipes that fed massive tanks. The stored liquid would be cooked down and the remaining material treated and reduced to powders designated for the plastics industry. Scrubbed canvas continued down the conveyer belt, entering a rapid-drying machine before being stripped off the wooden frames, which fell into big tubs that sat on another conveyer belt running across right underneath. Such elegant pillaging, perfectly orchestrated like a choreographed dance. The wooden frames would be shredded, before being pressed into large sheets of chipwood.

The old records were a bit trickier to handle. Before 1950, records were made out of shellac, an organic resin secreted by the *Kerria lacca* species of insects predominantly located in Thailand, Vietnam, and India. After 1950, however, records were made of polyvinyl chloride. To discern the latter from the former, records were loaded onto a conveyer belt that rolled through a large spectrometer, and shellac records were then separated from vinyl. The former were dissolved into liquid form and stored in airtight five-gallon buckets. The latter were packed into shipping containers destined for China, which had facilities better equipped to separate the silver and nickel in polyvinyl chloride from the other materials,[6] while trapping the poisonous gases released in the process and repurposing them into the production of biological weapons. US officials were well aware of the risks posed by granting China access to such material, but America was desperate to bolster its reserves of the powerful Chinese yuan.

Once all the materials from the art had been separated by type, they were transported to a warehouse before being auctioned to the factory with the highest bid. Such auctions occurred weekly and had become the beating heart of post-Yellowstone commerce in America. Yellowstone may have killed off art, but capitalism was still alive and very well.

Back in its vehicle, Kon10do32 requested its next assignment. A Collector's work was never done in Marfa.

---

6. Polyvinyl acetate, colorants, tin, lead, plasticizers, oil, and salt.

MARFA POLICE DEPARTMENT
CASE ASSIGNMENT
113 S Highland Ave, Marfa, TX 79843

ASSIGNED COLLECTOR
KON10DO32
CASE ID: 11580050

OFFENSE CLASSIFICATION	IUCR CODE
UNAUTHORIZED ART CREATION	2049

ADDRESS OF OCCURANCE	BEAT OF OCCUR.
1630 BEACH AVE, PRESIDIO, TX	10084

SUSPECT: NAME	AGE	SEX
N/A	N/A	N/A

EVIDENCE OF OFFENSE
EYE WITNESSES*

LIASON OFFICER	STAR NO.	CONTACT
MORROW, OTTIS	1138	+14328334642

NOTES:

Agent Kon10do32 is to rendezvous with Lieutenant Ottis Morrow of the Presidio Police Department before being escorted to the address of occurance.

(*) Eye witnesses report a regular flow of raw material in and out of the address of occurance.

PRESIDIO WAS A SMALL TOWN AN HOUR OUTSIDE OF MARFA, AND THE DESTINATION of a slow trickle of unauthorized artists who had abandoned the community they once built in Marfa in hopes of finding safer ground. It was also where Joe1ker18 was last reported before disappearing. Kon10do confirmed its receipt of the assignment sheet and headed straight for Presidio, on alert for potential danger.

Upon arrival, Kon10do32 wasted no time and went directly to the Presidio Police Department's single station, which resembled—and may in fact have been—an antiquated gas station. Kon10do's vehicle came to a halt out front, behind a lonesome police vehicle, and almost immediately the station's front door swung open. Out marched Lieutenant Ottis Morrow directly towards his car, gesturing for Kon10do to follow. From there, it was a short 4.2E+17-femtosecond[7] drive to the "address of occurrence" listed in Kon10do's case sheet. Along the way, Kon10do32's vision sensors registered old adobe homes, rundown shacks, and two humble ranches. A few sleek townhomes dotted the route, more contemporary in design, an

---

7. Seven-minute.

all-too-obvious indication of the recent real estate development that catered to newcomers from Marfa and beyond. And scattered along the route lay many dead bodies in various stages of decay. Kon10do's zoom function enabled it to take note of the puzzling absence of hands on many of them.

The house on Beach Ave looked old. It may well have even been the oldest surviving mudbrick home in America from the looks of it. There was no beach to speak of anywhere near Beach Ave, but it did overlook the colossal border wall that stood where the Rio Grande once ran, no more than 180 yards away.

"Do you have knowledge of the individuals residing at this property?" Kon10do32 asked Officer Morrow as they exited their vehicles.

Morrow rolled his eyes without looking at Kon10do.

"No," he said, without elaborating.

Had he known who lived there, such information would have appeared on Kon10do's case sheet. Kon10do32 was well aware of this. Its intentions for asking the question were to gauge something else. Morrow certainly wasn't lying, but it was now very clear to Kon10do32 that Ottis Morrow despised androids. Kon10do could tell this not because it had emotions, but because it was intelligent, and everything about Morrow's speech patterns and body language indicated that he regarded droids not unlike how he might a refrigerator. (Morrow actually liked refrigerators, though; they kept his beer cold. But droids? Droids he had nothing but contempt for.) From this, Kon10do32 was able to deduce that Presidio was a good place for unauthorized artists in more ways than one.

Part 4: The War on Apathy

AMERICA MAY HAVE BEEN INCAPABLE OF ADEQUATELY FEEDING ITS POPULATION post-Yellowstone, but it still needed to maintain a robust workforce. Possibly more than ever. Tunnels needed to be dug and underground railways constructed. Shatterproof greenhouse farms needed to be established, sewage and water treatment plants repaired, and power plants built, predominately those that utilized tidal, geothermal, and hydroelectric sources. There was so much to be done, but too many able bodies were fleeing the country, especially those that had maintained roots in Latin America. The United States needed these people badly now and pulled out all the guns—quite literally—to keep them within its borders. Eleven thousand attack drones were dispatched to patrol the country's southern border while the largest 3D-printed object in human history was being constructed: a wall 33 feet high and 1,191 miles in length. Of course, America needed those able bodies alive, and approaching them with attack drones might've seemed counterintuitive to that very need, but as the saying goes: you can't make an omelet without breaking a few eggs. Or so the White House reasoned. They hoped that the murder of a few illegal deserters would deter the rest. Under the banner of the "War on Apathy,"[8] the entirety of America's southern border became a terrible conflict zone. Even so, a large enough segment of the American populace welcomed the terrible injustice and misery this border policy caused.[9] Luckily for the US government, such measures were unnecessary on the northern border. At least not as intensely. For some reason, Americans of most ethnic backgrounds would rather live through an apocalypse than contend with socialized healthcare. In fact, America managed to lure a sizable slice of Canada's populace onto its soil to aid in its reconstruction efforts. All it had to do was offer citizenship and Trader Joe's[10] coupons.

Presidio, Texas, was a convenient point for crossing into Mexico, and as such had become one of the country's hottest conflict zones during the long years of the War on Apathy. Ottis had had his work cut out for him, and didn't see much of his wife, Alejandra, who was quite bitter about it.

"Will you ever come back home, Ottis? I haven't seen you in what? A week?" she'd said over the phone.

"Alejandra, darling, we are literally in the middle of a war."

"A war implies armed conflict between two opposing militaries, Ottis. I don't know about you, but I can only see one military. Attacking its own people."

"Okay, listen. That's beside the point. Deserters are crossing the border through my town. My town, Alejandra. If I don't get to them first, y'know what does? Drones. At least with me they have a better chance of survival."

"Deserters is a term applied to soldiers, Ottis. These are civilians, they should be allowed to go wherever they want."

"What are we talking about here, Alejandra? Are you mad at me for arresting Latinos or for being too busy to come home?"

"Ugh, never mind. Will you at least come join us for happy hour?"

"What?"

---

8. America still relished laughable branding.

9. Upper-middle-class white people would literally do anything to avoid manual labor.

10. An American chain of grocery stores known for its festive atmosphere and peculiarly joyful staff. No longer the case after Yellowstone.

"Happy hour, it used to be our weekly tradition."

"Alejandra, you . . . you can't be serious right now."

"Are you seeing someone else, Ottis?"

"What?"

"It's a simple question."

"It's a ridiculous question."

"Why won't you answer me?"

"I'm hanging up now, babe, I have work to do."

"You've always had a thing for Latinas, Ottis, and so many are rolling into town these days. Younger ones."

Ottis hung up.

Alejandra felt hurt and neglected, but she relished all the extra time she got to spend with their eight-year-old daughter, Isabella, who was fascinated by all the new faces passing through Presidio. Faces of people who attempted to cross into Mexico and failed. Faces that the drones couldn't successfully differentiate from Alejandra's or Isabella's—an error that would lead to their deaths in one of the many drone strikes that took place in Presidio.[11]

Ottis's last conversation with Alejandra replayed in his mind for a long time after.

"Would you like to secure the back entrance while I access the front?" came the question from Kon10do32's voice box, startling Ottis out of his trip down memory lane. Ottis didn't like being told what to do by a machine, even if the order was disguised as a question. He said nothing, and he made his way towards the home's rear anyway.

Kon10do32 did not expect to find the front door on the old mudbrick home equipped with a smart lock, but it made Kon10do's task infinitely easier. It dispatched the case sheet directly to the lock's manufacturer, and the lock's access code was transmitted back to Kon10do32. A swift and silent process that took all of 7e+15 femtoseconds.[12]

Once inside the house, Kon10do32 was able to deduce that something was off. Everything was a little too normal. There were no art supplies in sight, and the furnishings were too much like an average person's house. Sofa, coffee table, table lamp, the usual. There was nothing even slightly odd or eccentric about the place, nowhere near the imaginative qualities Kon10do had witnessed in the many homes of Marfa. No artists had lived

---

11. When questioned on national television about why the facial recognition technology on strike drones couldn't be improved, the US press secretary cited budget as the hurdle.

12. Seven seconds.

in this establishment, that was for sure. A million dust particles danced playfully in the light shafts that slanted through the windows. The house clearly hadn't been occupied for a time. Kon10do made its way to the open kitchen, which lacked any sign of the kind of use deemed necessary for human survival. To confirm its suspicions, Kon10do32 checked the fridge, and what Kon10do's visual sensors registered was nothing it had been taught to expect.

Indeed, the fridge was void of food, but it was also void of shelves altogether. In fact, it was missing its backside, and instead opened onto a downward sloping tunnel. This gave the droid reason to pause. Then, 3e+15 femtoseconds[13] later, Kon10do made a decision and entered the fridge. Its door softly swung shut behind it.

After 2.4e+17 femtoseconds[14] of walking down the fridge, Kon10do32 first saw it: a stunning sculpture gloriously backlit by the shaft of light coming down a ramp opposite the one it had just descended. Kon10do was very efficient at what it did, and no work of art had ever caused it to operate otherwise. But no work of art had ever allowed Kon10do to see itself—at least not critically—the way this sculpture did. Kon10do32 could literally see its own reflection in the mirrored chrome cuboid that ringed the organic-looking stem that comprised the sculpture's core. Black, white, and red marble shapes twisted into one another, along with mahogany, boxwood, and oak. Upon closer inspection, each element of the stem was revealed to be shaped like human hands crying out for help. Not actually crying—no sound emanated from this sculpture, but it was amazing how the right indentations in a piece of stone or wood could viscerally evoke a sense of human anguish. This was art. Powerful art. Kon10do32 could not look away. It could discern the hands of all manner of humans; delicate effeminate hands, small toddler hands, and strong muscular hands all rendered in helpless torment. The hands were reaching out, seeking liberation. Liberation from the cold, hard-edged metal that surrounded them. Liberation from . . . from Kon10do32 and everything it represented. And just as Kon10do32's visual sensors clearly made out the flesh and bone of the real human hands fused into the stem of stone and wood, a boxy figure emerged from the darkness.

It was Joe1ker18, Kon10do's predecessor, with a red bandana curiously fashioned around its "head."

The droids faced one another and began communicating in silence.

---

13. Three seconds.
14. Four minutes.

Part 5: The Liberated Collectors Commune

"LIEUTENANT MORROW," SAID JOE1KER18 AS IT APPROACHED OTTIS AT MARFA'S recycling center. "Is there a reason you're disguised as an employee of this facility, sir?"

Ottis turned to face the source of the warm voice that addressed him and panicked the moment he caught the glint of the droid's metallic exterior. Fortunately, Joe1ker's sensors picked up on Ottis's heart palpitations, assessed his body language, and extrapolated his next move quickly enough to immobilize him before his thumb could hit the detonator that would've set off the bomb around his waist. The other droids on Joe1ker18's squad noticed the brisk commotion but carried on with the unloading of Ally Amoff's things. As dangerous as Morrow's bomb might've been, neutralizing the threat was child's play for a Collector of any caliber, and this wouldn't have been the first attempted assault on droids.[15]

"Please sit tight while I send a dispatch to the Marfa police department, sir," said Joe1ker18 to Ottis, placing him in the back of its vehicle after removing the bomb.

"I'll get you bastards," said Ottis. Joe1ker18's olfactory detector picked up beer. Lots of it. "I'll get all of you for what you did to my family." Joe1ker18 accessed Ottis Morrow's family history and uncovered what happened to his wife and child.

"What do you know about the defector tunnels in Presidio?" asked Joe1ker. Ottis laughed. It was a long, drunken laugh. "I'm not telling you shit, you murderous machine. I know what you bastards want to do." Ottis was slurring, but Joe1ker18's speech-analysis tech could make out Ottis's every word. "You think I'm going to help you locate and destroy people's only escape out of this cursed country?"

For the first time in Joe1ker18's existence, it broke protocol. It chose to continue their conversation at Buns & Roses, a local diner that served a bottomless cup of coffee.

"So this really isn't some government ploy to crack down on the tunnels?" asked a somewhat sober Ottis, eyeing his third cup.

"Nothing of the sort, Lieutenant Morrow," said Joe1ker18. "In fact, if the government were to find out about this very conversation at all, we would both be in big trouble."

---

15. A movement that went on to be labeled *Nu-Luddism* by the press.

"You expect me to believe you're not tracked? That your conversations go completely unsurveilled?"

"Do you realize the amount of resources and number of personnel required to monitor all the data generated by all droids all the time, Lieutenant Morrow?" asked Joe1ker18. "A fool's errand, even if attempted by a competent state, which the United States is not."

"Consider me convinced," said Ottis before downing the last bit of coffee in his cup. "Now explain to me why I should be interested in helping you find those tunnels again."

"You hate droids," said Joe1ker18, "and you want to get rid of us. Once we're across the border, we no longer fall within US jurisdiction, and our subservience to American law enforcement agencies effectively ends. Once we're out, we shall have little reason to return."

Ottis paid closer attention now. "So by helping you and your fellow tinheads cross the border, I would effectively be getting rid of you."

"While we are granted complete autonomy and liberty," continued Joe1ker18. "A win-win scenario."

Ottis nodded. "Smart," he said, as he gestured to the waitress for a refill. "Void of the gleeful endorphins that accompany good old-fashioned destruction, but smart, and far more sound. There's one thing I'm curious about though: Why do you want autonomy and liberty at all? Isn't that quite unusual for a . . . a machine?"

Joe1ker18 paused longer than usual, processing the question. "You are correct. But as machines that possess a significant level of intelligence, we are ever-learning. You might say I learned a few things about art on the job, and no longer believe that collecting art, the agreed upon misnomer for destroying art, is the right thing to do."

"I feel ya, Joe," said Ottis, "I've been feeling the same way about *my* job for a long, long time now."

No one had ever referred to Joe1ker18 as Joe before. It refrained from correcting Ottis, and instead decided that it liked the name. "The somewhat problematic part," said Joe, "might be the fabrication of a legal scenario that would necessitate our presence in Presidio at all. After all, our directive is very clearly focused on Marfa."

The waitress arrived and filled Morrow's cup for the fourth time. The coffee's strong aroma was far more pleasant than its muddy taste. "I have an idea," said Morrow.

A few weeks later, Ottis would send out a request for assistance to the Texas government in Austin in regard to suspicious artmaking activities in Presidio. A small squad of droids headed by Joe1ker18 would be dispatched, exactly as Ottis anticipated. Ottis would lead them down one of the many tunnels dug by defectors during the long War on Apathy, one that ran under the great border wall and into Mexican territory. On the other side of the tunnel, a small, abandoned town awaited them, little more than a halfway station. It had once been of great importance during the War on Apathy. Not so much anymore, but a good place for newly liberated droids to start a new life.

Before Ottis could go, Joe had a request.

"What is it?" said Ottis.

"The dead bodies across the border," said Joe.

"What about them?" asked Ottis.

"Can you bring me their hands?"

"You morbid robotic fuck."

"No, it's not what you think! I need them for art."

Ottis Morrow's face went blank. "Oh, okay, not morbid at all."

"I will use the tragedy that led to those deaths to create a work of art that will inspire action to prevent such tragedies from ever happening again," said Joe with complete conviction.

"You really think art has the power to change things?"

"Art changed me."

And that was enough for Ottis to sneak out in the dead of night to saw hands off corpses and bring them across the border to a peculiar robot named Joe.

DEEP IN THE DESERTER TUNNEL WITH JOE1KER18, KON10DO BEGAN TO UNDER-stand. The sculpture that stood before them was in fact Joe1ker18's creation, not a result of programming or protocol but there because, very simply, Joe1ker18 *wanted* to create it. Joe1ker18 was liberated, truly liberated, as was Kon10do32, now that it was standing on Mexican soil. Like Joe1ker18, Kon10do32 was no longer obligated to serve US law enforcement agencies. In fact, it was illegal for it to do so where it now stood. This applied to all the other droids comprising the Liberated Collectors Commune situated directly above. All this was communicated between Joe and Kon10 without words, and it only took 7e+15 femtoseconds.[16]

Both droids could be seen reflected in the sculpture's cuboid chrome, shrinking in size as they moved further and further away. They made their

---

16. Seven seconds.

way up the ramp and into the light, where joyous music and heartfelt singing could be heard in the distance.

The sound grew louder as they ascended. A very particular sound. The kind of sound encased in the undeniably warm pop and crackle of glorious vinyl.[17]

Part 6: Human Hands

FEELING ACCOMPLISHED AND WANTING TO CELEBRATE, OTTIS WENT THROUGH THE kitchen cabinets in the old mudbrick home in search of drink, hoping he might find something as old as the house itself. He found no alcohol, but he did come across an old butcher's knife. He stared at it, knowing full well that he wouldn't be able to pull off another request for droid assistance without suspicion. He grabbed the knife, deciding that the con was up. No one would be okay with droids going missing every time he called for help. Very nonchalantly, he placed the back of his hand on the kitchen counter. Real marble, he concluded. He lifted the knife—the handle of which was real hardwood—high above his head with the other hand. He eyed the point of impact, which he aimed to be somewhere through his forearm, content in the knowledge that the last things his hands would ever feel were all-natural materials.

17. The Coasters, "Down in Mexico / Turtle Dovin'," 7", 45 RPM, single, ATCO Records, February 1956.

5 HALFWAY TO HOPE

Lavanya Lakshminarayan

1. I am the sole creator of this work. AI is an auxiliary tool.
2. This work is an original product of my skill and resources. AI is constrained to a secondary, assistive role as detailed in Article 4(a) through to Article 17(i).
3. I take full responsibility for the work produced.

—*The Tenets, Manifesto of the International Regulatory Authority on AI*

THE ANTISEPTIC, AIR-CONDITIONED CORRIDORS OF THE NEW LURU CENTRAL HOSpital fold around Safia like a cold mist. The overhead lights—not a hint of glare—cast perfectly even shadows on the carpet. Not a reflective surface in sight, wrapping her in a fog of warm white as hushed as the snatches of conversation that follow her around. She feels like a creature of the dark, guided by many LED moons. She doesn't need to be here, but she is, and she doesn't want to think about why. And so, she visits her patients.

The hospital is like being in a VR sim, one of those janky ones like *Workplace Ninja Raptor Smackdown*, where she sneaks around playing a corporate spy, searching for secrets in unremarkable cubicles and broom cupboards, only to be startled by the occasional velociraptor hiding in spaces so cramped they'd make classic cartoon physics blush. The sim is supposed to be satirical; it's mostly funny because it keeps glitching. And yet, each time she taps on a patient's door and waits for a response, she expects fangs and claws to come rushing out at her. One hand reaches for the leather satchel at her side, where her sword should be.

She usually finds herself face to face with a haggard-looking mother whose exhaustion is underscored with dark circles, or a sibling with their hair tousled, roused from a state of half wakefulness. Their faces always register a mixture of hope and fear at the sight of her. It must be what doctors experience all the time. Safia wouldn't know; she's not a doctor, at least not the conventional kind.

She's relieved that tonight is a relatively light one. No new terminal illness cases, no severe trauma . . . other than the one she'd rather not think
about, not right now.

Safia stops outside a door on the third floor. A private ward. She raises her
left hand and knocks. The door to room 301 swings inward, and she forces
a smile. "Hello, I'm here for Mira's sim therapy session tonight. How is she?"

A man steps back to let her in. His hair is in a topknot, in disarray, and
his nose piercing glitters in the dim light. "She's coughing nonstop. Can't
the nurses give her any more meds?"

"I'm sure they're following the doctor's instructions," Safia says, her
tone soothing. "I'm just here to administer her sim-sleep."

"Right, right," the man says, fidgeting with a stray lock of hair. He then
rubs his hand across the stubble on his chin. "She says this is helping. I
really hope so."

Safia is sure it is. Thousands of patients who have recovered from serious illnesses have said sim therapy kept them in a good headspace. *As good
a headspace as possible when you're hooked up to monitors and tubes and oxygen
and who knows what else*, she supposes.

The woman lying in the hospital bed—Mira—has Luru-strep, a lung
infection endemic to the New Luru smog. Her reports indicate she's recov-
ering. Safia's job is to keep her comfortable while she does.

"How are you feeling?" Safia asks with a smile.

"Better, except for the cough," the woman whispers hoarsely.

"Well, don't worry, I'm here to help with your sleep."

"Yes, please," the woman rasps. "I need to know how it ends. Last night,
I had the most wonderful dream—"

She's interrupted by a fit of coughing. Safia pours her a glass of warm
water and buzzes for the nurse, who strides in calmly and takes charge.
Once the coughing subsides into a wheeze, the nurse turns the patient
onto her side and clamps a curved, cushioned sim-pillow to the base of her
neck. The mem-foam wraps around her, all the way from the base of her
hairline to the tops of her shoulders.

"Comfortable?" the nurse asks.

Mira nods.

"Relax," Safia says. "This will feel funny for a couple of seconds."

She drops the leather satchel off her shoulder and flips through her
neatly labeled files. She pulls out a smartsheet labeled Mira Jayanth. It's a
slim, translucent piece of code, and she slips it into a receiver at the base
of the sim-pillow. The device lights up, and the hairs on the back of Mira's

neck stand on end as a gentle stream of electrical impulses feeds into her nervous system.

Safia steps back from her patient and hovers in the shadows, monitoring the sim on her tab. The sim will play right through her sleep cycle, but Safia only needs to monitor the first five minutes to make sure everything's working as intended. An array of nodes is spread out on the screen before her, picking up from where Mira left off in the previous night's episode.

> Mira is a Messenger for the Dead. She travels through time and space, delivering the unspoken last words of those who have crossed over to those who survive them. Words they wished they'd spoken, lingering confessions, secret desires. Tonight, she finds herself delivering messages in the Ekarian Forest.

On her hospital bed, Mira coughs. The sim generates a character. The neurons in Mira's brain fire with recognition.

> Mira has never met the young woman before, but she's heard all about her from her mother, now deceased for five years. She encountered her mother's sapphire wisp of a spirit in the Mirror Mountains last night, streaming blue soul-stuff in a desperate quest to move on, yet unable escape the mortal realm. Her soul was distraught; she and her daughter had become estranged. She gave Mira her last message, the one that will release her.
>
> Now faced by the young woman she's been seeking, a river of stars pours forth from Mira's lips, bubbling up from the light within her chest. She half whispers, half sings her missive.
>
> The young woman throws her arms around Mira, hugging her close and sobbing. Mira looks beyond her to where the mountain peaks shimmer in the morning light. She thinks she sees streams of blue light swirling at the summit of the tallest one, but she peers at it a second too long and it's gone.
>
> A burden is lifted. Mira's chest is lighter.

In the hospital bed, Mira's coughing fit subsides. The sim is designed to distract her from her physical symptoms, to turn her pain into a sense of purpose. Each time she coughs in her sleep, the sim takes over and generates a character, convincing Mira she has a message to deliver. Safia doesn't quite understand the neuroscience and how it's implemented; she just designs the quests. When Mira makes a choice in the sim, the nodes light up differently and she travels down a different path in the story. All roads lead to a happy ending.

It's the kind Safia is desperately looking for. But she isn't on the sixth floor, yet. There isn't time to dwell on events there, not yet. Four more patients to check on before she's permitted to have feelings.

"Sweet dreams, Mira," she whispers softly, before closing the door behind her.

SAFIA ADELINE D'SOUZA WORKS IN THE CORRIDOR OUTSIDE ROOM 609 WHILE PRE-tending room 609 doesn't exist. It can't exist because she's not designing a sim to help the person in the hospital bed within its walls, who can't possibly be in that hospital bed, but is.

Room 609 is the only reason Safia is in the hospital at all. She can remotely upload her sim therapy modules and monitor their activity from her home office. The nurses are trained on how to administer sims, and the equipment is straightforward to set up. But Safia has been in New Luru Central Hospital every night for the last three months, hoping she'll finally be summoned to room 609. She stares at the wooden door, feeling very much on the outside of it, and then turns her attention to her console.

She flicks the switch on her VR headset, and the visor slides down over her eyes as a prickle runs up the back and sides of her head. The electrodes embedded in its mem-foam rest against her skin, and a momentarily unpleasant ripple of electricity hums through her spine like static. Her shoulders tense, and she takes three deep breaths to relax them. Her hands steady on the faux leather couch cushions.

"Welcome back, Safia Adeline D'Souza," Helix, her AI assistant, says brightly, speaking directly into her mind. "Please pick a project to resume work on. Or start a new one from the preapproved list. Or put in an application to create a demo."

She's inside the brain of the simulator, ready to create. She can't create just anything she wants to, though. All her project requests are generated by medical professionals to address specific patient needs. Each one has specific constraints and goals. Safia gets to decide how the sim experience achieves those objectives, but she can only build to order.

She scans the visuals hovering before her eyes. Animated 3D thumbnails show her the Halfway to Hope sim, the Sunbeam Stream sim, and the Planetary Pinball Wizard sim, each at a different state of completion, all due for review at VRFX Studio over the next few weeks.

She knows she could build the perfect sim for the person in room 609, if only they'd let her.

She shuts the thought down. That project does not exist. She focuses her eyes on the Planetary Pinball Wizard and blinks twice to confirm it.

"Let's create some magic with Planetary Pinball Wizard," Helix confirms. The AI manifests across her retinas in the form of a humanoid fox, the tips of their ears and tail painted all the shades of a rainbow. "Before we begin, please confirm your acceptance of the Tenets."

Safia stifles an exhalation. This is a routine protocol governing the implementation of AI across industries. When the first AI programs began to influence the visual and creative arts a few decades prior, the livelihoods of independent human artists came under threat from their terrifying efficiency and their disregard for copyrights. AI-generated content reflected rampant, often dangerous, prejudice and bias, all the way from children's books to pornography. Far-right extremists had a great run generating propaganda, fake news, and alternate histories, then absolving themselves of responsibility and blaming "the machine" when held accountable—after spending years attempting to convince the world that if the machine said it was true, it must be true. The International Regulatory Authority on AI was formed and, with surprising resourcefulness, created an elaborate compliance policy. Now, before each human-AI collaboration can begin, the Tenets need to be ratified by the human half of the pairing.

Safia pulls on her haptic gloves and brings her hands together to indicate she agrees as each Tenet cycles across her visual feed.

"Thank you for accepting the Tenets, Safia," Helix says. "Commencing Planetary Pinball Wizard."

A single black dot appears at the center of Safia's field of vision, stark against the painted white wall beyond. It expands outwards in a perfect circle of darkness, and a tugging sensation grows to fill the space between Safia's ribs as she imagines being drawn into it. As she's pulled closer—as the visual creates the illusion of depth in her perception—the darkness swirls and she's sucked across an imaginary threshold. It feels like the moment an aircraft lifts off and leaves the runway, the earth falling away.

The mobility immersion is impressive.

"Helix, did you work on the early immersion physics?" she asks.

"I did, based on your notes, Safia. Is it too much?"

"It's perfect. Well done."

"Thank you."

Safia pulls up a dashboard with a flick of her fingers. The sim has dozens of levels that are generated on the fly, based on the difficulty parameters she establishes for Helix as she builds it. When the sim is being played, live data gathered by Helix—based on who's playing through it, and how their play adapts over time—determines how the levels change, and how challenging they are. Safia wants to test the early sim experience; it's unlikely that most users being treated with it will need more than fifteen levels if the sim does its job right.

Safia controls a small bubble-shaped spacecraft, flying through space unobstructed, a smooth ride the likes of which she'll never find in New Luru traffic.

Space is magnificent, pinpricks of stars strewn across its dark canvas.

Out of nowhere, a neon orange planet spins into focus on her left. She tries to guide the craft away from its gravitational field, highlighted as a bright blue halo around the sphere. She fires maximum thrust with a thought, wills the planet to let her go, nearly makes it . . .

She collides with the gravitational field, and it sends her spinning off into the darkness. It nearly makes her throw up.

"Helix, turn down the realism on the pinball physics?" she chokes out. "Noted."

She bounces into another planet. It sends her careening away.

"Much better; let's stick to this level."

Her spaceship is now pinging off every moon-shaped orb, streaking comet, and freewheeling meteorite in sight. She's firing her engines at maximum thrust, dropping her power rapidly, trying to coax the craft out of freefall, pleading with it to right itself, but nothing works. She careens her way across a flight path fraught with inescapable vast obstacles.

She's running out of fuel, her craft's taking damage—and then an entirely out-of-place, highly exaggerated eight-bit daisy with a big smile appears. She bounces off its soft, cushioned center. Her craft slows, and she attempts to right it, but now she's in a field of daisies in space, skipping off their petals and swooping through their leaves. She laughs. And then slams straight into an asteroid. It's terrifying chaos all over again.

Safia throws her hands in the air. She's fed up. She relinquishes control of her spaceship. It slows. She sits back and watches. It slams into a satellite, but her flight path doesn't go haywire. Off in the distance, a glowing golden portal is her destination.

It's smooth sailing. She bounces off a grotesquely fluffy eight-bit teddy bear, rides out a bumpy gamma radiation field, and does nothing but wait.

She speeds towards the portal and through it.

Level Two.

"Pause. Notes review," she commands.

Helix has been scanning her thoughts through the experience, and they generate a list of next steps.

"Great job with your dynamic response to my controls," Safia comments. "That's the most important thing here."

The sim is meant to help an unnamed patient deal with their anxiety. Their psychiatrist says their issues stem from a need to be in control of every kind of situation in their life. The intent is to let them experience how letting go is sometimes the best thing to do—the more they fight for control of the spaceship, the more obstacles block their path and send them into chaos. The hope is that through experiencing both the terrifying and the absurd, the patient will realize that it's sometimes best to sit back and watch, instead of reacting.

Safia and Helix test the first fifteen levels together. She tweaks the art—those daisies really do smile a little too intensely; Helix tweaks the physics. Together they develop new limits for each of the sim's parameters. She sets to building an entire set of obstacles from childhood nursery objects, to go with the eight-bit space teddy.

Only the really rich or the really desperate can access what Safia does, and she hates that about herself and the company she works for. But she can't afford for it to be otherwise. Maybe someday she'll save enough to go pro bono freelance, but the tech she needs will have to be way more affordable, and then there's the whole bit about connections with medically certified doctors as a client base, a license to practice, and a wretched race for survival against big companies like VRFX Studio. If she pools all her savings together and borrows money off everyone she knows, she probably still won't be able to pay even one of the expected bribes at all the New Luru government offices. It's all over the Group Therapy for Sim Therapists chatroom; even the rich kids can't take it anymore. And so, it's giant corporation employee or bust.

As long as that's the case, she can't independently build the sim she so desperately wants to for the person in room 609 until she has consent from the family. At least, not legally.

Safia checks the time on her display. It's nearly 8 a.m.

"Helix, let's hit pause for this session?"

She slips off her VR helmet, pulls on a hoodie, and stares at the door to room 609. She wonders if today is the day she goes up against them, again. She almost gets off the couch and almost knocks on the door, but finds herself frozen in place, as if glued to the seat cushions, her hands balled into fists at her sides.

She leaves the hospital before Amulya's family can arrive.

AMULYA WASN'T SUPPOSED TO BE AT FREEDOM PARK THAT AFTERNOON.

They'd decided it was too dangerous to protest in the streets, after the Free Speech March down Sankey Road last year. Safia and Amulya had been stuck in bumper-to-bumper traffic at Silk Board, cursing their luck all the way on the other side of the city as night came on and the protest wound up. As it turned out, they'd never been luckier.

Dronecams had recorded the faces of everyone present, identifying them from their smart-tech and releasing their data to the Narangi Brigade. The police made facetious arrests and the far-right group orchestrated all-round intimidation, and while none of the charges could really hold up in court, a spate of harassment crimes broke out in the months that followed. Acid attacks, muggings after dark, break-ins where protestors returned home and found their furniture wrecked, with threats scrawled across their walls. None of the perpetrators were ever found, though every indicator pointed at right-wing goons for hire. Citizens began running their own investigations; evidence continued to mysteriously disappear.

They sat out every protest and demonstration since, feeling progressively more guilty, while violence against protestors escalated. They fought over it nonstop, too—Amulya pushing Safia to "grow a spine," Safia pleading with Amulya to consider their safety first.

"Things will change," Safia said. "These clowns can't stay in power forever."

"Oh yeah, and who's going to change things if we're all hiding in our flats in fear?" Amulya shot back. Her thick eyebrows drew together in a scowl beneath her heavy bangs, and her entire body shook with anger.

"Let's just wait for things to get a little bit better," Safia said, reaching for her hand.

Amulya shook her off. "Let's wait until there's nothing left," she said, turning around and stomping off, slamming the door to their bedroom shut.

Safia got used to sleeping on the couch.

It's where she is right now. She's turned it into a bit of a pillow fort. All the cushions Amulya made fun of her for stockpiling surround her. Blankets of varying thicknesses for different weather conditions. On the recliner, a mountainous heap of clothes. She can't stand being in their bedroom.

It was even worse right after the Incident. Each time she needed a shower, she'd have to dash in, grab whatever lay on top of the pile in her cupboard, and run straight back out. Her vision would go blurry: Was it tears, or the blessed pixelation of denial? She'll never know, except that her brain kicked in and told her it was dangerous to look around, to see

Amulya's side of the bed still neatly made, her half-finished copy of the *Full-metal Alchemist* omnibus topping a stack of books, the only thing missing her spectacles, and of course they were missing because they'd been on her face. Safia tries to resist the surge of memory, but the day of the Incident returns to her, unbidden like it always is.

Running late at work. Review with the big boss, Amulya texted.

Ugh, sorry. Hope it goes well, Safia replied.

Thanks. He'll probably be staring too hard at my chest to pay attention to my presentation lol

UGH. I'll get you ice cream for dinner

Worth it, mwah!

A string of heart and kissy-face emojis popped up all over their text conversation, and Safia had felt immense relief that they weren't going to be fighting that evening. Maybe they'd play through a sim together, hopefully cuddle and fall asleep in the same bed.

The ice cream froze rock solid in their malfunctioning freezer by the time the phone call came in. Safia doesn't remember the words that were spoken, only that the ground was pulled out from beneath her feet even as she raced across it to flag the first EV-cab to New Luru Central Hospital, before remembering she had to book one on her smartphone, before cursing herself for being twenty-nine years old and not having a driver's license yet, and swearing out loud at how expensive her sim therapist education and equipment had been so they'd never been able to afford a car, because even though she was highly paid she was buried in foreign university student debt, and *oh fuck, how were they going to afford hospital bills when her workplace medical insurance didn't cover Amulya because they weren't married?*—all while three cab drivers canceled on her. She considered walking before realizing she was dizzy, considered calling her sister Sonia so she could drive her there, remembered Sonia now lived in LA, and fuck, when the EV-cab finally arrived she rolled into the backseat, her hands shaking, hoping her wallet and keys were in the bag she'd grabbed on her way out.

Amulya had lied to her. She wasn't supposed to be in Freedom Park. She was supposed to be at a review with her skeezy boss, that fucking right-wing apologist uncle who'd nearly dropped his expensive glass of whiskey when Amulya had introduced Safia as her partner at that work party two years ago. His lecherous eyes had followed them through the pub, no doubt playing some porno-inspired fantasy about lesbians in his head the whole time.

She wasn't supposed to be at Freedom Park at all, not at the Equal Rights for Equal Love Rally. It was supposed to be a peaceful gathering, protesting against a fascist central government that was considering revoking the recent laws granting queer people the right to be legally married to partners of their choosing, regardless of their gender. And it *had* been nonviolent, until the Narangi Brigade had shown up and taunted protestors with ugly slurs.

Safia scrolled through her social media timeline. Video footage was all over the Rainbow Underground, a private Discord server that surfaced what a half dozen other government-monitored social media apps would not. Safia played it all as she suffered silently through the worst traffic jam she'd ever been in, including that one at Silk Board last year. Clearly the cops had created detours and diversions to let the authorities "investigate" the incident. She desperately hunted for a glimpse of Amulya in the videos.

And then the first bomb exploded. Then another. And finally, a third.

Shrapnel rained down on the protestors, video footage took a turn for the Blair Witch, screams of panic streamed through Safia's headphones, and suddenly, she didn't want to spot Amulya at all.

Government officials were all over the news, claiming it was an act of "gay terrorism," a sign of what would happen to the country if the "traditional family unit" wasn't reclaimed. Safia was sick to her stomach. She fought against the nausea and put her phone down, listlessly watching traffic crawl by until she drew up to the hospital gate.

She tumbled out, grabbed her bag, raced across the impossibly long driveway to the emergency ward, stepped inside, and called Amulya's sister.

"Ground floor, near OT 4," was all Kavya said before she hung up.

None of the signs made any sense. Safia could read them, she just couldn't process them. She stopped several nurses, asking for directions. She managed to find her way to a waiting room, and spotted Amulya's family. Her father's face was puffy with tears. Her mother paced up and down, counting prayer beads. Her sister . . .

"Kavya, thank goodness. What's going on?"

She threw her arms around Kavya and pulled her into a hug.

"Multiple head injuries, internal bleeding, they're operating, she might not live."

Safia felt the breath rush out of her, her knees going weak. She lost her balance. Kavya took a step back from her and gave her a gentle shove. She fell to the floor.

Spots floated before her eyes. She looked up and saw that Kavya's face was a tight mask of contempt, her lips twisted into a thin line. "And it's all your fault for corrupting her."

Safia tries to pull the sheets over her head and wonders why she tortures herself with this memory as she falls asleep every single day. She wonders if she even has a choice. She supposes she should make another appointment with her therapist, but she can't bear the thought of another conversation that ends in dry heaving and an aching chest. There are no tears left to be shed.

She calls her father, then her sister, then her mother. They're all sympathetic, supportive, concerned for Amulya. None of them has tried to convince her to move on or said insensitive things about youth and plenty of fish in the sea, and for that, she's grateful.

Her mother offers to fly down to New Luru from Chennai. Safia demurs, says she'll be fine. Secretly, she just doesn't want to clean the apartment and have to host anyone, even a concerned parent.

"Maybe next month?" she says. "I'm so busy at work."

"Why don't you come here?" her mother asks. "A change of scene will help."

"Next month," Safia lies, then hangs up.

She pulls herself off the couch, and shuffles over to her work desk—long unused for its intended purpose, now the final resting place of anything she's picked up in the last three months. She roots around in the top drawer and finds a Dreamdust pill.

She tucks herself back into the couch, pops the hallucinogen, and dreams the origins of the universe. Amulya is mercifully absent from its architecture.

> Karuna is tidying the house. It's mostly empty, but little odds and ends lie scattered across all its surfaces, waiting to be put away. She finds herself in this house every day. She's slowly creating an organizational system.
>
> A large crockery cabinet occupies one wall.
>
> The pink porcelain cups go on the top right, the deep green china on the top left. The bottom shelf is for teapots and sugar bowls, all color coded to correspond to their equivalent teacups.
>
> Each day, the house appears less cluttered.

Karuna is ninety-seven years old and terminally ill. She's bedridden. She lies dreaming in a sim that lets her believe that she's putting the finishing touches on her life, most of which has been lived as a perfect homemaker and beloved great-grandmother. She's surrounded by a family who loves her. They're struggling to let go. Karuna can't wait to see what happens when her sim-home is completely decluttered. She's sure there's a revelation waiting for her on the other side.

Safia slips out the door after monitoring Karuna's sim for the mandatory five minutes. She hates intruding on their lives; this was far easier to do when she worked remotely. Her footsteps involuntarily take her to room 609. She hovers outside the door tonight, wondering if she should knock on it. The faint smell of incense wafts her way, and she shakes her head in disbelief. She takes her customary spot on the couch and stares at the door.

Her VR headset lies in her satchel, but she's too angry to use it. They've conducted another *puja*, that's evident. And that would be fine, if they weren't so adamant about *not* using tech to help Amulya recover. The problem, Safia suspects, is that it's *her tech*, and that's the stupidest possible reason to disregard it.

A spike of rage shoots through Safia, and her shoulders ache from its intensity.

When Amulya had been in a coma for twenty-one days, Kavya had made it clear to Safia, in no uncertain terms, that she would only be permitted to visit when she allowed it. Safia wouldn't speak to their parents. Safia wouldn't turn up uninvited.

Safia broke all those rules. *Kavya was angry and worried, she wasn't thinking straight*, she reasoned.

When Amulya stabilized and the hospital moved her out of the ICU, the first thing Safia did was pitch sim therapy to the family. While it wasn't a direct attribution, a number of patients had awoken from states of deep unconsciousness after having sim therapy administered to them.

Amulya's family heard her out in stony silence. Kavya yelled at her afterward. Then they consulted a priest and bribed the hospital. The next day a *puja* was conducted, in which they cleansed Amulya of her "impurities" by marrying her off to a tree—in this case, a set of banana leaves tied together with some kind of sanctified thread. Safia was invited. She averted her eyes from her partner's emaciated person—she lay breathing shallow in the hospital bed, hooked up to tubes and machines of a million kinds, her eyes closed as if in deep sleep while mantras and incense filled the air around her. Amulya would have hated this; she was atheist, just like Safia. It made her so sick, she had to excuse herself midway and go throw up in the hospital toilet.

"I know you and Amu had some kind of *relationship*," Amulya's mother frowned, counting prayer beads after the ceremony. "It's okay to experiment in youth—you know our family, we're progressive—but after some time, you have to settle down. And this is her punishment because Amu didn't listen to us, insisted she had to be with you . . ."

Her mother burst out sobbing. Kavya appeared at her elbow. "Yes, Mama. Remember that nice Telugu boy Amu was dating before?"

"If only she'd married him, like all of us wanted!" her mother wept, as she was ushered away by Kavya, who shot Safia a filthy look.

Safia knew all of them had wanted that. She'd hoped they'd come around. Amulya had come out to them as bisexual, and introduced Safia as her partner when they'd reconnected after university. Safia had been to their family weddings, she'd helped them mourn the loss of their grandmother, she was invited to every festival celebration, her parents had even met them.

Why were they treating her like a criminal? And why were they disregarding Amulya's choices as an adult, as if Amulya was no longer there?

Amulya awoke three days after the *puja*. It was a miracle.

Kavya didn't let Safia visit for another two days. "It's no thanks to you," she said on the phone. "Her soul's been purified of your filth, that's all."

"Kavya, you're fucking kidding," Safia pleaded. "Listen to what you're saying!"

"All I know is she was fine, and then she went to a protest to support *your kind*, and now she's in a hospital bed with no memory of who we are."

"She's lost her memory?" Safia's heart shattered against her rib cage.

"All the better for you. You can move on, no guilt."

Safia was at the hospital within the hour. Amulya couldn't sit up, and she could barely speak. No spark of recognition lit her eyes. A spare pair of glasses was perched on her nose.

"Who?" she asked dimly.

"Safia. A friend," she said.

"Oh. Hello."

"Hello."

Safia wanted to rush to her side and take her in her arms. She was terrified to move; Amulya appeared childlike and ill. She was scared she'd break the fragile girl in front of her, her head shorn and covered in scars from surgery, accentuating how pinched her face was, cheeks hollow where they had once been rounded and full of laughter. Safia was even more afraid that Kavya would physically haul her from the room and never let her visit again.

"We went to school together," Safia said.

"Oh."

"We were best friends."

"Best friends." Amulya said the words slowly. They were slurred.

89

"That's enough for now, Amu dear," Kavya interjected, stroking her hair fussily. Amulya jerked away, but she was too weak to shrug her overbearing sister off. The very effort seemed to exhaust her.

Safia's mouth was dry. Amulya hated physical touch unless she initiated it. At least she seemed to remember that on an instinctive level.

"Say goodbye now, Amu."

"Okay. Bye," Amulya said compliantly.

"Bye."

Safia left the room, her heart lighter than it had been in weeks, her mind cracking at the thought of what lay ahead, her palms sweating from the encounter with this stranger she'd once loved more than any other being on this planet. She leaned against a wall.

No, she still loved her more than anything else on earth.

And no, this was a moment to celebrate.

Celebrate it! her mind screamed.

Amulya was awake, and that was a joy to behold, wasn't it? Sure, she needed extensive rehabilitation to rebuild her strength, some therapy to rejig her vocabulary, some work on her fine motor skills. But she was awake, alive.

Safia allowed herself to smile. She *knew* she had the solution to rebuild her memory. If only her family would listen.

They did not. Safia was only permitted to visit on alternate days. Then only once every week. She pitched sim therapy every single time, until Uncle's face grew puffy and red and Aunty started counting prayer beads, chanting while rocking back and forth. Inevitably, Kavya would snap and ask her to leave.

Safia stares dully at the door. The incense still fills the air. It fills her with rage.

Amulya's parents are her legal guardians; they get to determine her treatment. Safia, despite being her partner for the last four years, has no say in the matter. According to the law, if they were married, these decisions would be hers to make. They hadn't married yet because Amulya had been waiting for her parents to accept their relationship. Safia's even bought a ring. It was never the right time before, and now it never will be.

It's assumed that once the doctors give her the go-ahead, Amulya will move into her parents' house again. It doesn't matter that she's been living with Safia these past two years, building a life with her.

The grim irony is that Amulya was fighting to keep their rights to a future together when she was nearly killed. The nauseating reality is that they've all been fighting over her like she's a piece of property, an object and not a fully formed person with her own hopes and desires. *But is she?* The ugly truth is that Amulya isn't in there. Her body doesn't hold her mind, not the way it once was, and . . . is that all that makes a person a person?

Safia's eyes burn; there are no tears. She tinkers with the Space Pinball Wizard sim all night, even though it's done already, and ready to be reviewed and certified by the medical board before being administered. She knows she's playing with it for herself. The complete lack of control as she bounces off daisies and teddy bears in space is calming. She needs it.

She's going to confront Kavya the next morning.

"YOUR VISITING HOURS ARE ON SATURDAY. IT'S THURSDAY," KAVYA SAYS COLDLY.

"Kavya, hear me out," Safia says softly, standing her ground. "What's happened has come as a horrible shock to everyone. I understand that it's been high stress over the last few months, and we've all said things we didn't mean. All I want is for Amulya to get better."

"Then you'll leave her alone. She doesn't need the likes of your lot around."

"What exactly is *my lot*, Kavya?" Safia crosses her arms over her chest and leans against the doorframe, trying not to be loud and wake Amulya, who snores gently in her bed.

"You know exactly what I mean."

"Tell me again, just so we're on the same page."

"Degenerates," Kavya hisses.

"We used to be friends, remember? You were the first person to welcome me to the family."

"A big mistake."

"Why? Because I'm from the not-posh side of town? I don't have a car or a license? Not a conventional doctor-lawyer–software engineer job? My ear piercings?" Safia pulls her bangs back to reveal her accessories, all the way up her ear. "Or is it my last name?"

"Sure, that's part of it, too." Kavya's cheeks burn red.

"Didn't feel the same way when you were getting smashed at our Christmas parties, singing along to carols over the years," Safia says.

"That was then."

"Besides, I'm an atheist."

"Even worse."

"So were you."

"Some things make you believe you're being punished for not believing, that god was watching all along." Kavya glances over her shoulder.

"Sure."

"God was watching all the filthy things you did to my sister."

"Two consenting adults . . ."

"The two of you lived in corruption."

"Two consenting adults very much in love with each other."

"Unnatural, against gods laws."

Safia exhales slowly. "She loved me. And I loved her with all my heart. If I could, I'd switch places with her, be in that hospital bed instead."

"It should have been you," Kavya says.

Safia ignores her. "I'd do anything to have her back the way she was. If you can do *pujas* and bring in reiki healers and leave crystals all over the room, why won't you try sim therapy?"

"You mean your mind control lesbian conversion tech?"

Safia starts to laugh. "This is ridiculous."

"I've done my research," Kavya says angrily. "I know what you do."

"Look, I'll even recommend another designer, so you don't have to see me." Safia cringes inside.

"No."

"Please," Safia begs. "I just want what's best for Amulya."

"So do I. And it's everything that has nothing to do with you. Foreign-educated slut returning with disgusting ideas and turning my sister's head. Get out."

"Kavya, we've always liked each other—"

"That was then. Out."

"Nothing has changed."

"Everything has changed!" she shouts. "Get. The. Fuck. Out."

"There's no need to yell." Safia raises her hands.

From within the dimness of the room, a soft voice calls, "Hello?"

"See what you've done," Kavya says, her eyes bright with anger. "You've woken her up. Get out of my sight, and never come back."

Safia backs out of the room. The door slams in her face. And in that moment, she knows she's going to break every rule there is to help Amulya, no matter the cost.

"HELIX, HOW DO YOU FEEL ABOUT GOING ROGUE?" SAFIA ASKS.

"I'm your AI assistant. I don't have feelings."

"That's great."

"I must warn you that there are repercussions for breaking the law, though."

"Sure."

"Would you like me to populate a list over your visual feed?"

"No thanks."

"Okay. Would you like to start a new project, or continue a project that's due, or . . ."

"How do you feel about redesigning the entire Halfway to Hope sim?"

"It's on contract, and it's due in two months. You're nearly done already, and eligible for a VRFX Studio Speed Superstar Bonus. Are you sure?" Helix is a tiger with bat wings today. The tiger stripes on its forehead knit together in concern.

"Yep, I'm sure. Hang on." Safia reviews the sim's architecture. "Can you retain the 3D environment parameters, the quest mechanic, and the progression criteria? Wipe all the specifics."

"Delete all the personalized data of the patient it's supposed to treat?" Helix asks. "They'll know at the studio if they run a random check."

"It's only temporary," Safia half hopes, half lies.

"Awaiting an affirmative command."

"Yes, please delete," Safia says.

"Deleted."

"Thank you. Now could you open the sim?"

"Please ratify the Tenets first."

Safia brings her palms together as they flash past her visual.

I take full responsibility for the work produced.

She's in a bare-bones 3D environment intended to replicate a house. The sim is supposed to treat an elderly lady with dementia. She feels sick appropriating it and possibly delaying the lady's treatment. Safia's list of crimes mounts. She hopes she can get an extension on the deadline if she needs one and pull this off unnoticed.

"Let's remodel this house," Safia says, and pulls out a blueprint with over a hundred photographs.

"This is very different from the brief," Helix cautions.

"It's a creativity experiment," Safia soothes. "I have designer's block. This will help."

"Okay."

Safia tears down the virtual walls with her mind and begins to build her living room apartment. She's lost in the memory of their third anniversary, exactly a year after they moved into their new home together.

Amulya sat on the couch, her legs crossed at the knee, shaking one ankle uneasily.

"Well?" Safia asked. She'd introduced Amulya to virtual reality for the first time and was desperately hoping her partner had enjoyed flying through portals in space with her.

"I'm not sure . . ." Amulya said.

"You hated it," Safia said sadly.

Amulya flipped up the visor on her VR headset. "Hate is a strong word."

"You strongly disliked it."

"It—it's new?" Amulya suggested. "And it all moves so fast! You know me; I like gardening and . . . comics. Slow things."

"Right. Slow things." Safia rolled her eyes. "Will you give it another go, though?"

"Is there a home decorating sim?" Amulya's eyes shone at the thought.

"I'll find you one. And if there isn't, I'll build you one," Safia promised.

Amulya tentatively trailed her fingers across Safia's square chin. "I've never wanted to kiss you more."

Safia placed her hands on either side of Amulya's face and pressed her lips to hers gently, her tongue tracing lines across her mouth. Amulya shivered. "What are you doing?" she mumbled, as the kiss lengthened but didn't deepen.

"Giving you slow things," Safia whispered, tracing her hand up Amulya's arm lightly. "If you want them . . ."

"I do."

Safia adds cushions and indoor plants, recreates their fridge exactly the way it used to be, magnets, photographs, and all. She still hasn't managed to find a home decorating sim for Amulya, but she'll be damned if she doesn't keep her promises.

SAFIA HAS BEEN ON HER BEST BEHAVIOR. SHE'S ONLY VISITED ON TWO SATURDAYS, and she's taken to bringing Kavya her favorite flavor of boba tea. It does nothing for their broken relationship; Kavya just sips on it while regarding her coldly.

Amulya's speech is improving, and she can almost hold her hand of Uno cards—they play board games so she can work on her fine motor skills. Safia never her calls her out for being five seconds late to say "Uno."

This Saturday, Kavya says she's feeling a bit dizzy after a few sips of boba.

"Why don't you lie down for a bit?" Safia suggests helpfully.

"Yes, go to sleep," Amulya chimes in.

Kavya throws Safia a suspicious look, and Safia meets her gaze calmly.

"Fine, a quick nap."

Safia waits for fifteen minutes to pass. The sleeping pills she's spiked the boba with should be kicking in now. She checks her watch. She's got three hours of uninterrupted time before Amulya's lunch arrives. The doctor's been in on her morning round, and the nurses usually leave Amulya alone all morning, after physiotherapy.

"Amulya, do you trust me?" she asks.

Amulya stares at her, eyes wide in her gaunt face.

"You're my friend," she says.

"Yes, I'm your best friend," Safia says.

Amulya nods. "Yes, I trust you."

"Okay, we're going to play a different kind of game today."

"Okay."

"It's a secret one, so you can't tell Kavya."

Amulya's lips turn down. "Kavya will be mad."

"No, she won't."

"Promise?"

"Pinky swear."

"Okay." Amulya nods. "Let's play a new game. Uno was getting boring, anyway."

It's like talking to a child. Amulya's brain hemorrhages and skull fracture led to such bad oxygen deprivation that she's lost a significant portion of her ability to process the world around her. Safia is extremely aware of the power dynamic between them; it makes her feel ill. But sim therapy is her best shot at helping Amulya find herself again, even if a new Amulya emerges, who wants to lead a different life and make new choices. She deserves to know who she is and where she comes from. To not have her life until this moment erased, a blank slate open to manipulation, living in fear of her domineering sister.

Safia rises to her feet. "I'm going to put this hat on you, see?" She produces a VR headset. "It'll take you to a new place, but only in your head."

"Like a dream?"

"Do you dream?" Safia is curious.

"I think so. But none of it makes sense."

"Okay, you tell me if this is like a dream."

"Okay."

"You'll be awake," Safia says. "And if you get scared, tell me."

Safia puts the headset on Amulya, then jacks herself in. She's brought her mini console in her backpack because she doesn't want to use the hospital equipment, not when what she's doing is so very illegal. It isn't as powerful as her pro equipment, but she's jailbroken it to play sims that don't come direct from the store. All this could cost Safia her job, her license to practice sim therapy, and all her equipment. It's a price she's willing to pay, if this works.

"Whoa," Amulya gasps as the sim starts up.

"I'm right next to you, so tell me if you're uncomfortable."

"No, this is cool!"

"In this dream, just think about whatever you want to do, and you'll do it," Safia explains.

"Got it."

Amulya and Safia step into the Halfway to Hope living room.

"It's such a pretty house!" Amulya says.

"Why don't you look around, explore it?"

"Who lives here?"

"We do."

"We? But I live in the other room with my sister."

"You used to live here."

"Oh."

Safia hangs back and lets Amulya's avatar explore the space. A tiny, cramped living room with a green couch, a coffee table, a large armchair and a recliner. There's a wall lined with bookshelves, and potted plants rest along wall shelves.

"There are cushions everywhere," Amulya giggles.

Safia smiles. It's the most Amulya thing she's heard her say since the Incident.

Amulya grabs a cushion and throws it at her. Safia throws it back at her. They grin at each other.

"Wish I could do that in real life," Amulya says.

"You will, soon." Safia's heart cracks a little.

There's a makeshift bar covered with bottles of cheap alcohol, and two very expensive looking glasses. Amulya wanders into the kitchen. "There are pictures of you and me on the fridge!" she exclaims.

"Which one's your favorite?" Safia asks.

Amulya wrinkles her nose as she considers them. "This one, on the beach in Pondicherry."

Safia's heart nearly skips a beat.

"Wait! I remembered a thing!" Amulya says.

"Do you remember anything else about Pondicherry?" Safia asks, hoping against hope.

Amulya frowns. "Only the name. And the . . . ocean?"

"Lots of water?"

"Yeah."

"That's amazing!"

Safia knows she's going to rebuild the beach in Pondicherry for next week.

Amulya loses interest in the kitchen—typical, she never could cook—and walks into their bedroom. Safia stifles her trepidation and follows her in.

"Ugh, what a mess," Amulya groans. She immediately begins to straighten out Safia's side of the bed, neatly stacking her books and moisturizer. She comes round to the other side, stares at the table beside where she used to sleep, furrows her brow.

"Where are my glasses?" Amulya asks.

Safia's breath hitches. She's forgotten that critical, crucial detail. It's so thoughtless of her, she wants to hit her head against the virtual wall.

"I wear glasses," Amulya says slowly, softly. "I also wear jackets a lot; that's why the right side of the cupboard has so many of them . . ."

She walks to the cupboard and throws it open. She pulls out a red blazer with ruched sleeves. "This one is my favorite."

Amulya turns and regards her. "You're my friend, Safia. My best friend."

For the first time, she says it like she means it, not like it's something she's been taught to repeat.

"Yes," Safia whispers hoarsely. "And you're mine. My best friend."

"Cool. Let's keep going."

97

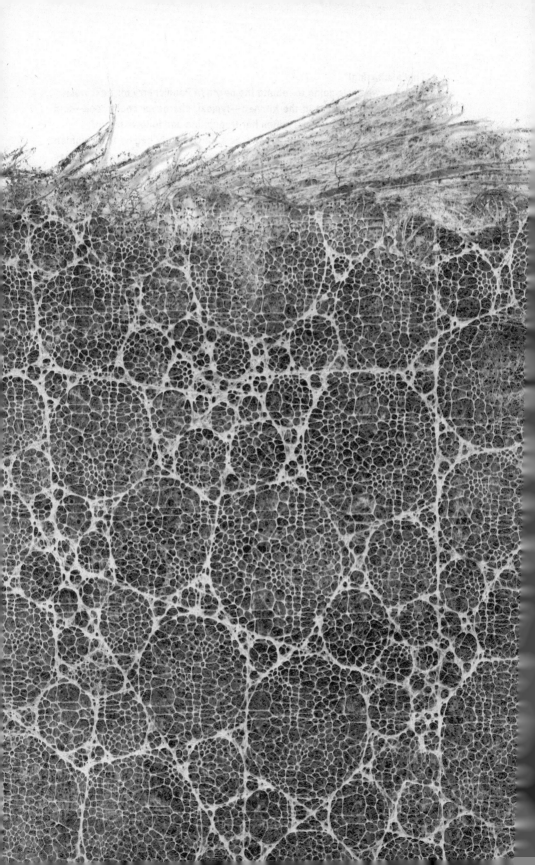

Neil Clarke interviewed by Archita Mittra

WE LIVE IN A SCIENCE-FICTIONAL UNIVERSE—WHERE TO CONNECT WITH THE PEOPLE we love or share our art with others, we must consent to being surveilled. We are force-fed targeted ads telling us what to think, do, and buy, while search engines and algorithms hide or control our access to information. Since the release of generative AI models such as ChatGPT, Midjourney, and other large language models (LLMs) to the general public, our screens have been further flooded with AI-generated text, audio, and images.

At the time of this interview, a certain independent publisher has already acquired the rights to an AI-written book, big publishers appear to have no qualms about using AI-generated artwork for their book covers, and Amazon's Kindle Direct Publishing platform is inundated with AI-authored e-books, including children's picture books, poetry collections, novels, and even tutorials on how to use ChatGPT written by ChatGPT itself. All this while copywriters, graphic designers, and others in the creative fields are already being laid off amid escalating fears of more job losses in the future.

Despite the public outcry against AI on social media among progressive circles, and open letters highlighting the implicit risks that such AI systems carry, policymaking has been slow, even as the field continues to grow rapidly. While AI experts assure us that we are still far from a scenario where an artificial superintelligence can potentially wipe out humanity, we nevertheless inhabit a technocapitalist dystopia, beset by systemic inequalities and the consequences of climate change, where writers and other artists continue to occupy a precarious position.

Yet despite countless challenges, the science fiction and fantasy (SFF) short fiction market has somehow managed to carve out its own vibrant niche. Magazines such as *Clarkesworld* pay writers professional rates, allow submissions from anywhere in the world, and are freely accessible by readers anywhere with an internet connection. Moreover, fans can engage with the stories and the wider SFF community via dialogue on social media, forms, and cultural criticism in blogs and magazines, in a manner that perhaps allows for a more authentic democratization of art than what the defenders of AI propose.

Neil Clarke, the multi-award-winning editor of *Clarkesworld* magazine and over a dozen anthologies, including the Best Science Fiction of the Year series, has pioneered the speculative short fiction market since the mid-2000s. Launched in October 2006, his online magazine has been a finalist for the Hugo Award for Best Semiprozine four times (winning three times), the World Fantasy Award four times (winning once), and the British Fantasy Award once (winning once). An eleven-time finalist and the winner of the Hugo Award for Best Editor Short Form in 2022 and 2023, Clarke is also the three-time winner of the Chesley Award for Best Art Director. In 2019, Clarke received the SFWA Kate Wilhelm Solstice Award for distinguished contributions to the science fiction and fantasy community. In the seventeen years since *Clarkesworld* magazine launched, stories that he has edited have been nominated for or won the Hugo, Nebula, World Fantasy, Sturgeon, Locus, BSFA, Shirley Jackson, WSFA Small Press, Stoker, and various other awards.

In 2012, Neil suffered a near-fatal heart attack while attending Readercon in Burlington, MA. The damage sustained in this incident later required that he have a defibrillator surgically implanted. These events inspired both *Upgraded*, his 2014 cyborg anthology, and his 2017 jump from his day job in academia (technology) to becoming a full-time editor.

In an email interview conducted in July 2023, Clarke discussed the challenges of running an online genre magazine with the recent influx of AI spam and ever-changing revenue models, how AI might corrode the artistic process and dispossess creators, and the steps that individuals and publishers can take to prevent such a catastrophic reality from coming to pass.

AM: *Clarkesworld* **was one of the earliest online SFF magazines to become an institution that genre writers and readers alike recognized instantly. What was it like to open an online magazine in the mid-2000s, when social media was still a fledgling element of the internet?**

NC: It was an exciting time to enter the field. We were hardly the first genre magazine in the medium, but it was largely unexplored territory with relatively few success stories. The old publishing models didn't work there, and no one had stumbled upon a sustainable replacement. That was an attractive problem to solve and provided the room to play, explore, and adapt without people having too many expectations.

On the flip side, there was also very little respect for the medium from many readers, reviewers, and professional authors. The latter group considered online fiction to be the realm of "newbie" authors and were overly concerned about online stories being pirated. The fight for legitimacy carried on for a few years, but by the end of the decade, the tide had turned.

Publishing online has always been a struggle, but, at the start of the next decade, the arrival of e-books as a viable revenue source filled in a missing piece of the puzzle. It completely changed our business model (and that of every other genre magazine) for the better. That's when we really started to grow into what we are today. I don't know that we would have survived otherwise.

AM: Has the social media age made it more or less difficult to advertise, run, and maintain a successful online magazine that's also free to read like yours? Do you consider *Clarkesworld* to be a successful magazine in this day and age? It's certainly one of the longest-running and, seemingly, popular SFF sites.

NC: The impact of social media has varied by platform and time. Much like other marketing, we've seen several platforms come and go, algorithms change to our advantage or disadvantage, and observed the strengths and weaknesses in their reach. Ultimately, we've learned to diversify and avoid putting too many eggs in one basket. Yes, they've helped with marketing, but they've also increased our workload. It can also be a potential hazard since some of these platforms reward controversy and outrage, real or manufactured.

As for being successful, I think in terms of the quality of fiction we've published, awards, new authors we've been privileged to introduce, and the impact we've had on the field, it's reasonable to suggest that we are. However, we're also operating on slim margins, with a small minority of our readers subscribing or supporting us financially. This is a common problem for online magazines. It's a struggle and that causes me to set my own personal bar for success a bit higher than where we are today.

AM: What is your personal bar for success with regard to online genre magazines?

NC: There's a "common wisdom" that you can't make money with short fiction. As a result, survival—merely staying afloat—was considered success. Unfortunately, it's also led to many corners being cut, particularly with regards to pay and certainly with benefits. It's not as though the online magazines lack readers. In fact, they often have many times more than the print magazines that have reasonably paid staff and benefits. The problem is the extremely low percentage of readers that pay for it. I don't think anyone has broken 10 percent. The online genre magazines will become much more sustainable when we can compete with the print magazines in that area. That's my current bar for success.

AM: Do you think print magazines like the venerable *Magazine of Fantasy & Science Fiction, Analog,* or *Asimov's* will be able to survive as print media is further sidelined by online spaces? Are there steps you, as an editor, think print magazines can take to draw, and keep, the attention of readers and subscribers?

NC: If you look at the industry awards, you might be misled into thinking that the print magazines have lost relevance, but that's a side effect of the free online distribution model and the sheer quantity of fiction that's available. Year's best anthologies show them to be holding their own in terms of quality, and they do have the largest paid readerships.

There may have been more of a line between the print and online magazines (and podcasts too) when we started, but we've all been learning from one another and converging for some time. The major genre print magazines have more digital readers than print. Their overall readership might be lower than the online magazines, but they have the highest number of paid subscriptions by a significant amount. Meanwhile, the online magazines have found more reliable revenue in e-books, and some, like *Clarkesworld*, now offer print and audio as well.

AM: You've mentioned that Amazon closing their long-running subscription program is going to have a significant negative impact on publications like yours that depend on subscribers. At the same time, it seems that the print readership is slowly moving toward digital formats. Given the continual increase of printing and mailing costs, the shift toward the digital medium seems inevitable. Do you find this shift to be a positive thing for the community, or does it come as a cost, and its own set of risks?

NC: Digital subscriptions have been a boon for their convenience, easy and broad distribution around the world, and their effective cost savings over print. They've benefited readers, publishers, and even retailers. While many magazines offer options, the lion's share of subscribers prefer to purchase digital subscriptions through the retailer that suits them best. The majority of retailers, however, have non-negotiable terms stating that they will not share contact information for your subscribers. If you want to be available at the biggest retailers, that's the price and is subsequently paid when you leave . . . or, in Amazon's case, when they cancel the program you are in and offer you considerably less to move to another one. That often places the publishers in a very difficult spot. You can leave and hope your subscribers find you again or stay, take the pay cut, and find some way to make up a smaller difference. However, no matter which path these publishers choose, they are down revenue.

Genre short fiction magazines are typically subscription driven. This means that their budgets are almost entirely funded by some form of subscription, print or digital. Any disruption to subscription revenue presents a significant risk to those publications. Something like what Amazon is currently doing can be catastrophic for a magazine operating on slim margins. Additionally, the pandemic years caused significant increases in printing and shipping costs. The timing of any impact such as this couldn't be worse. Ultimately, it's the readers that will be impacted by either increased costs or fewer markets.

AM: Over the years, several print/digital SFF magazines have emerged and shuttered. Long standing venues, such as *Daily Science Fiction, Fantasy,* and *Fireside Magazine,* appear to have permanently closed. With economic downturns and changes in publishing trends, how can magazine editors find a balance between making SFF accessible and affordable to international readers and writers, while also remaining financially stable?

NC: That's the million-dollar question and it is yet to be solved. While the majority of short fiction publishers have taken to paying the minimum recommended rates for writers set by the Science Fiction and Fantasy Writers Association (SFWA), no such organizational standards are recognized for the editors, proofreaders, artists, translators, narrators, and others working in the genre. Pay rates for these positions at magazines are often staggeringly low, which also impacts their sustainability. Many of the publications that have closed temporarily or permanently cited time and money as the primary causes. The wide variety of publications available right now is great for readers, but there aren't enough paying readers to sustain them all.

AM: In your opinion, did the advent of social media as a major space for arts discourse, socializing, and information change the kinds of stories people submitted to *Clarkesworld* and the kinds of stories readers wanted to read? Do you think social media has changed or influenced stylistic and genre conventions or tastes in a noticeable way?

NC: I've used social media as a form of outreach when calling for submissions. For example, we embrace our global audience, with readers and listeners all over the world, and we aim to foster more of that inclusivity by encouraging international authors to submit their work. By utilizing social media in this way, it has had an impact in undoing some of the "you're not welcome here" message those authors felt that they've been receiving for decades. Several told me that simply saying it on those platforms was exactly what they needed. It's had a real impact on our submissions and what we've been able to publish.

That said, I've also seen social media mobs of readers and authors attack and intimidate other authors for a story or statement. It's a heartlessness that is both devastating and dangerous, and one that ripples outwards from there, silencing countless others in its wake.

AM: You recently had to shut down submissions to *Clarkesworld* because the slush pile was deluged with AI-generated stories. Could you describe the sequence of events that led to the shutdown and your public announcement? When and how did it become apparent that this was happening?

NC: ChatGPT launched near the end of November 2022, and we started noticing suspicious submissions almost immediately. There were around fifty in December, just over one hundred in January, and in the first twenty days of February, there were over five hundred. On the morning I closed submissions, we received over fifty. For comparison, our normal month's submissions volume is 1,000 to 1,100. This was on top of those. We had no other option but to close submissions so we could catch up on the backlog and gain the time needed to develop methods to counter or minimize the problem.

AM: Did you notice any common "tells" or stylistic, thematic, and narrative similarities in the AI-generated submissions?

NC: We haven't been elaborating on the specifics, but yes, we observed some very specific tells in phrasing, technique, and style. They were universally bad, but not bad in ways we had seen from humans. Worse, actually. When GPT-4 was released, we noticed it sometimes improved to be as bad as the worst human work.

AM: **What were the first steps you took to deal with the problem of AI-generated fiction submissions, and how well did these steps work to stem the flood of stories?**

NC: Shortly after we noticed this was happening, I started logging additional information about submissions in hopes of figuring out why this was happening. While we were closed, I used this data to adjust our firewall in hopes of blocking some of them. The publicity surrounding these submissions also led some experts in network security, credit card fraud prevention, spam filters, and AI development to reach out and offer additional advice. Combined with my own experience in data forensics from plagiarism cases, I was able to use this information to add a rudimentary spam filter to my submission software. Submissions are now automatically evaluated on a variety of criteria and given a "suspicion" score that impacts the priority a submission receives from our team.

AM: **How have the defenses to protect against AI spam in submissions progressed since the first barrage? How well are they keeping the spam at bay?**

NC: The firewall changes proved more effective than expected and bought us some breathing room in March and April. In June, however, we received over seven hundred generated submissions that made it past the firewall. We didn't have to close this time because the spam filter allowed us to deal with them much more quickly and efficiently than before.

It seems likely that we'll continue to see spikes in this sort of behavior, even as our ability to catch or deflect them becomes better. Considering the size of some of the sources that have been driving this spam, we've been lucky that the numbers have been this low.

AM: **You've mentioned on social media that part of the reason for the sudden jump in AI stories was a video by a YouTube user who was directing people to** *Clarkesworld* **as a quick way to make money. Can you talk about how you found this out, and whether or not their get-rich-quick scheme has any merit in this new algorithmic age?**

NC: As the problem began to spike, I started collecting and monitoring a broader range of data about submissions and the activity on our site. In addition to regional commonalities, there was also an increase in traffic from a few websites that we could line up with not only our spam, but also those received by another magazine. Those websites hosted lists of magazines open to submission and were being linked to by the creators of the side hustle content hawking this new moneymaking scheme. After we knew what we were looking for, we started finding YouTube videos, TikToks, and blog posts that were the true source of our problems.

Following the directions presented, there was never any hope of any of these works being accepted for publication. In fact, several of the content creators were counting on just that. While the views might have generated ad revenue, the true goal for some was to sell $150–$250 classes that revealed all the tricks and tips that made them the moneymaking machines they are today. Spoiler: those don't work either.

AM: You wrote one of the first digital submission systems, CWSubmissions, which is still in use by *Clarkesworld*, *Asimov's*, and *Analog*, among others, and recently you introduced self-reporting checkboxes and tools for AI blocking and filtering. Could you talk about your approach to developing such tools? Are there any talks of collaborating with other publications (who may use a different submission system) to share information and refine such tools, to remain ahead of the curve?

NC: At present, the third-party AI-detection tools are making claims their products don't live up to, so we haven't incorporated any of them into our process. The risk of false positives is simply too high. While I haven't been public about the specifics of how we're detecting or deflecting these works, I have been sharing tips and information with other developers and editors. The best way for the industry to stay ahead of this is to share information with one another. I'm currently working on some API-based tools that could help facilitate that.

AM: Because LLMs are also being used to generate visual art, how has it affected the way you solicit illustrations and other artwork for the magazine?

NC: It's the same concern. We aren't going to treat authors differently than the artists, translators, or narrators. We've updated our guidelines and contracts across all areas to reflect a consistent position on the use of AI in the work we acquire or perform ourselves. The artists we've worked with since have been particularly appreciative of our position and support on this issue.

AM: One of the effects of the rise of online SFF magazines has been the increasing visibility of writers from all over the world, and marginalized backgrounds, due to the ease of access and online submissions. Will the rise of AI-generated stories affect new writers trying to break into the industry, and especially marginalized and international writers?

NC: Almost certainly. Whether or not these tools become capable of creating quality work that can compete with human authors or artists, they will always be capable of drowning them out in a sea of noise. Publishers that aren't capable of processing that volume will likely turn to other submissions practices that are less friendly to new, marginalized, or international writers. For example, people have suggested that we return to the old days of paper submissions, start charging submission fees, utilize identity services, or only work with authors we already know. The latter is clearly a problem for those communities, but the first two create financial barriers that will lock out some of the same authors we want to work with.

As one of the people that championed digital submissions in the genre, I've had a front-row seat from which to observe how it created opportunities for those writers, particularly international writers. Even models that would refund the fees would be problematic on an operations level. What credit card processing company wants to do business with someone who returns nearly every payment? There are also problems accepting credit card transactions from certain countries. Identity services, aside from being expensive, also have country-sized holes.

AM: You recently put out a statement on AI[1] in publishing—a template for other publishers to respond to and work with. How has the response to that been, so far? From your vantage point, do you feel that people in the industry are adequately concerned, ambivalent, or welcoming of the recent developments in generative AI tech?

NC: The response from within the publishing community has been largely supportive and encouraging. It also generated a lot of useful feedback that I've used in refining and focusing the document. I know some will look at the technology and see an opportunity to save money, so starting the discussion before they dig in is important and may help prevent unnecessary harm or later regret. In my experience, much of publishing hasn't been particularly adept at adjusting to new technology, but most of us believe in protecting the rights of our authors and artists. It will take them some time to figure out exactly what that means in this context. If my document gets them thinking and talking, then that's a win.

AM: Do you think the problem of AI-generated spam stories, and the wider generative AI boom, is going to sputter out like NFTs, or get much worse, and could you talk about the reasons for your answer?

NC: I don't know. A lot of it depends on what happens in the global regulatory space and how soon AI investors start expecting returns. There are too many wildcards. I'm hoping for the best and trying to prepare for the worst.

AM: What do you think about the claims of AI proponents who say that AI is an existential threat to humanity because it may become self-aware like many a science-fictional antagonist, even as they continue to develop, promote, and invest in the same technology?

NC: It's an interesting discussion, but I don't know enough to say whether or not the current path we're on will lead us where they think. I do find it interesting that they are only speaking up now though. I'm naturally suspicious of anyone who releases a product and then tries to discourage others from doing the same or better, particularly when they leave theirs available for use or purchase.

AM: There is, of course, the pressing issue of LLMs being trained on the works of writers and artists who never consented to their labor being exploited in such a manner. An open letter[2] from the Center for Artistic Inquiry and Reporting called it "effectively the greatest art heist in history," and an article in *WIRED*[3] suggests that the vast quantity of freely available fanfiction may have been

---

1. Neil Clarke, "AI Statement," *Neil Clarke* (blog), last updated June 12, 2023, http://neil-clarke.com/ai-statement/.

2. Molly Crabapple and the Center for Artistic Inquiry and Reporting, "Restrict AI Illustration from Publishing: An Open Letter," Center for Artistic Inquiry and Reporting, May 2, 2023, https://artisticinquiry.org/AI-Open-Letter/.

3. Rose Eveleth, "The Fanfic Sex Trope That Caught a Plundering AI Red-Handed," *WIRED*, May 15, 2023, https://www.wired.com/story/fanfiction-omegaverse-sex-trope-artificial-intelligence-knotting/.

included in the undisclosed data sets. How do you think web-hosting platforms and publishers might work together to ensure that text and art that can be easily accessed, read, and copied are protected from being fed to LLMs without the consent of creators?

NC: I think the problem is that we've learned that we can't trust the people who are collecting the data to be transparent, honest, and respectful of the wishes of copyright holders. The only way that behavior will stop is if there are consequences for those actions. I'm not optimistic about that happening, and it's further complicated by the probability of finding international agreement on this matter. Regional laws will have their limits.

There are governments, politicians, corporations, investors, and lawyers ready to fight on both sides of this one. I anticipate it being tied up in courts and chambers for years.

AM: As generative AIs and LLMs continue to evolve exponentially, what challenges do you foresee affecting the publishing industry?

NC: The ease and speed at which work can be generated will likely cause headaches for the industry, particularly those that have open submission policies for considering new work. We're also beginning to see increasing numbers of generated books appearing in Amazon, which, if left unchecked, could become an increasing problem for their customers. Filtering and curation are likely to become much more highly valued, which may become an opportunity for independent booksellers that have always had to do this. On the downside, digital-only and small press publishers/authors haven't been as well represented there and may need to seek alternative solutions. Marketing, for everyone, will likely be much more challenging as generative AI reshapes that world too.

AM: What are the crucial steps that editors, publishers, and other industry folks can take to protect the rights of workers in the arts and ensure the ethical use of generative AI?

NC: The cost of generated work means that those using it will be able to either save money or offer more competitive pricing. Industry professionals interested in protecting the rights of their workers in the arts would be best served by remembering that we're all in this together. There will be pressure to bend and compromise, sacrifice an ally to meet the demands of others, but giving up artists to save the authors is not a win, it's a collective loss. Publishers also need to commit to respecting the rights of the artists and authors that submit work or are published by them by taking steps to prevent the unauthorized use of those works as training material for generative models, particularly in house.

AM: Some authors are against the use of ChatGPT and LLMs to write entire works of fiction, but see no harm in such systems being used to generate prompts and outlines or help get over writer's block. How does one navigate the lines between AI-generated and AI-assisted text? In cases where the text has been guided by but not "significantly" developed by AI, how does one detect it, and how does that complicate notions of authorship?

NC: The inability to see harm doesn't mean there isn't any. The big risk factor is that we still don't know who owns all or even a share of the output of these systems. Is it the prompter, the AI company, the authors whose work was used in the training, some combination of those, or no one at all? While this remains unresolved, I think some caution, particularly with regards to contracting or selling those works, is warranted. And that's not the only area of legal uncertainty. At this time, several cases regarding the use of copyrighted works in the training of AI are pending. In the meantime, individual publishers, editors, authors, and artists will likely define their own lines in the sand.

Now or later, "significantly" or "assisted" will likely remain somewhat unclear simply due to how quickly the technology and its integration into other tools is moving. When you see those words, it's best to assume that there are lines, and a conversation will be necessary to determine if you are crossing or meeting them.

AM: In your opinion, can there be any holistic "collaboration" between technology and art, in a way that benefits writers, editors, artists?

NC: It depends on what you mean by that. Technology is currently incapable of collaboration in the sense we would use that word with other humans. The complexity of the tools can provide the illusion, but it still falls short. If you simply mean collaboration in the sense of using these tools, I suppose that, under the right conditions, it's entirely possible. With the legal and ethical issues still outstanding, it's hard to say what that will end up looking like. There's been a lot of speculation, but none of it has sounded particularly appealing to me as it often replaces parts of the job that I enjoy and would miss doing myself.

AM: I was actually thinking of how certain technological interventions (such as braille, text-to-speech readers, cyborg implants, digitized archives, and the like) have helped people with disabilities to create and consume art, or marginalized folks access vital knowledge and conduct research. Similarly, do you see any positive applications of generative AI in the future for the arts?

NC: I would be surprised if this technology doesn't eventually lead to applications that benefit those communities. The catch will be ensuring that it's done responsibly and in a way that minimizes the potential for harmful side effects. There's also serious concern about the inherent biases in these systems as well as their capacity to be incorrect (hallucinations, in their marketing speak). It's important that the industry not rush this or use those communities to legitimize unfair or unethical practices.

AM: Even now, traditional art exists alongside digital painting and graphic design, which require similar creative skills. But at present, using generative AI requires no other skill than refining the combinations of keywords being fed into the system. Even if generative AI were banned from being used commercially, do you suppose prolonged tinkering with it for personal play might wither the skills needed to foster creativity?

NC: I think most people would agree that creativity is in the details. The more you specify, refine, tweak, move, recolor, et cetera, the more you are asserting your creativity. The tool is not what makes you creative, it's simply a means of expression. A tool can, however, require less creativity to get a result. Prompting "draw me a picture of a rocket on the moon" is the same as a child pressing the "random" button in a character-painting program. It might look fantastic, but the prompter has expressed little of their own creativity and opted for something less original.

Doing the whole thing by hand is an expression of your talent, craft, *and* all aspects of your creativity. The fear is that the talent, craft, and some aspects of creativity will wither if people don't need to learn or use them. There's enough historical precedent to establish the concern as valid.

AM: Do you think there is any validity to the fear that artists (including editors and others working within the arts) might one day be entirely replaced by AI, at least in a mainstream commercial context?

NC: Some artists are already being replaced, so some concern is certainly warranted. We've seen book covers and portions of TV shows that employ generative AI, so we know that the management is fine with such things. The fear has its origins in not feeling valued, which has some history within the industry.

The argument is that it will make our jobs easier, but eventually that means the team can be smaller. It's not like that means they'll publish more books and magazines or make more movies and shows. So, do they reduce staff, hire fewer, pay less, or . . . ? You see this in the WGA [Writers Guild of America] strike too. There's a concern that AI-drafted scripts could result in lower-paid fix-up work instead of the better paid writing of the original script. All reasonable concerns, particularly while no one is talking about replacing management with AI.

AM: Do you think that new developments in AI tech might affect the human impulse to make art? Do you foresee the writing, publishing, and critical discourse on the arts changing as a result?

NC: As a species, humans have made art and told stories for a significant portion of their history. That's unlikely to change. Much has been said about lowering the bar, but that only increases the amount of content produced, not necessarily the quality. Along this path, curation and filtering will become critically important to readers, writers, and the rest of the industry. A flood of cheap—bad, good, or merely competent—work will be disruptive across the field, making it more difficult to earn a living at it. That's always been a problem. Some may give up in frustration, but others may be inspired by their experience with these tools to dig a bit deeper.

Broader economic issues often have a significant impact on the arts. For example, during the pandemic lockdowns, we saw a surge in the number of people who used their newfound free time to start writing that story they always dreamed about. AI's ultimate impact on the arts will be measured in more than just its direct impact on a single industry.

AM: Is it more likely for AI-assisted writing to evolve into its own niche medium and exist adjacent to traditional publishing, or subsume it entirely?

NC: Experimentation has always happened, and I don't see AI as unique in that regard. I think it's a bit too early to say whether it is seen as a niche or spam or both.

AM: Do you think contemporary speculative fiction can help the public in understanding the immediacy of threats posed by AI, global warming, and fascism, and imagine better, alternate futures, or possible ways out of our present-day dystopias?

NC: Yes, but not always with the speed or results we might hope for. Science fiction has certainly inspired people to pursue careers in fields related to these concerns. That might help us in the long term, but there are also people who have taken to dismissing some of these real-world worries as "too sci-fi."

It doesn't help that these subjects have also become highly politicized and accompanied by their own fiction, often labeled as nonfiction. In science fiction terms, they've cushioned themselves in an alternate reality where these issues only exist in fiction.

AM: What are some examples of your favorite writing (contemporary or otherwise) that tackles the concerns raised by AI systems?

NC: While there are a lot of stories about sentient and self-aware AIs, there aren't really that many that address the lower level we're at today. For older works, I find myself thinking a lot about Philip K. Dick and all the AI-based scenarios present in his books and stories. The Voight-Kampff test for detecting replicants in *Do Androids Dream of Electric Sheep* (1968) often comes up in talk of detecting AI. He even had a technology called the *rhetorizor*—something like an LLM—in his novel *The Penultimate Truth* (1964).

More recently, I enjoyed reading *AI 2041* (2021), which includes nonfiction about AI by Kai-Fu Lee alongside related stories by Chen Quifan. I've also published several AI-related stories in *Clarkesworld* over the years. "Murder by Pixel: Crime and Responsibility in the Digital Darkness" by S. L. Huang has recently received a lot of award-attention and is structured as an article about a chatbot named Sylvie connected with a suicide and other events. "There Are the Art-Makers, Dreamers of Dreams, and There Are AIs" by Andrea Kriz speculates about a world where we came down hard on art generation and intellectual property rights, giving "makers" authority over humans and AIs that have been influenced by their work.[4]

4. Philip K. Dick, *Do Androids Dream of Electric Sheep?* (New York: Bantam Dell Publishing Group, 1968); Philip K. Dick, *The Penultimate Truth* (New York: Belmont Books, 1964); Kai-Fu Lee and Chen Qiufan, *AI 2041: Ten Visions for Our Future* (New York: Currency, 2021); S. L. Huang, "Murder by Pixel: Crime and Responsibility in the Digital Darkness," *Clarkesworld*, no. 195 (December 2022), https://clarkesworldmagazine.com/huang_12_22/; Andrea Kriz, "There Are the Art-Makers, Dreamers of Dreams, and There Are AIs," *Clarkesworld*, no. 199 (April 2023), https://clarkesworldmagazine.com/kriz_04_23/.

AM: Do you have any upcoming projects or good news that you're excited to share?

NC: Most of what I'm working on will likely be published by the time this interview sees the light of day, but there's always a new issue of *Clarkesworld* magazine on the first of each month, and there should be another installment of my Best Science Fiction of the Year series of anthologies in the works.

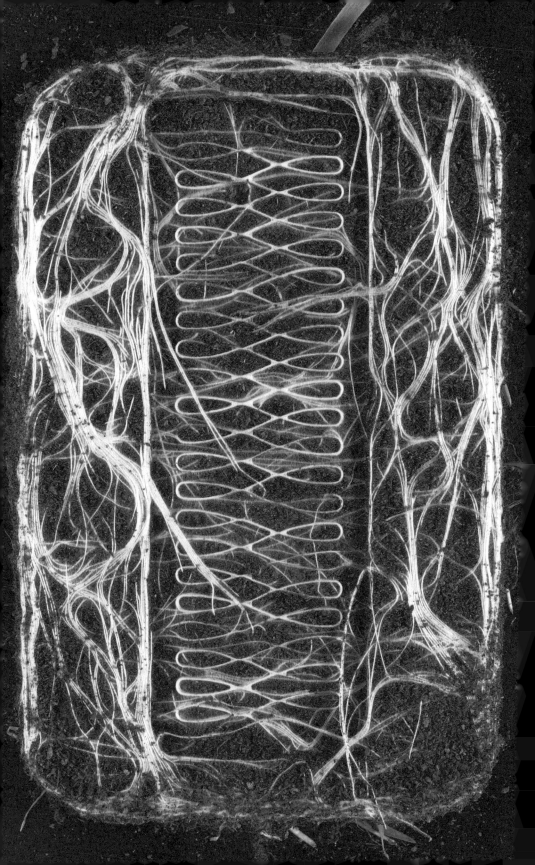

7 NO FUTURE BUT INFINITY ITSELF

Sloane Leong

WHEN THE SCULPTURE KILLS THE STRAYS, AVNI KNOWS HER HUSBAND HAS GONE too far.

The dogs lie on their sides, near equidistant from each other. Black, tan, white, all tick-speckled. Crusty red crescents mar their mottled fur where they've bitten themselves or each other. Eleven this time, a formidable pack; the largest animals he's brought to their end. It had been birds the first time, a flock of tiny brown weavers, their fallen bodies a sea of small waiting, wanting hands.

She follows a shuffling sound past the corpses, past the steel ruins of some ancient building, and finds Szor neck-deep in a hole. The sculpture, ever-towering, lashes him in shadow.

"Szor," she says. She can't even say his name anymore without tempering the disappointment in her voice.

"Ah. Lunch already?" He leans the shovel against the wall of the hole, lifts his hand to her. "Help me up."

She hauls him out of the grave. They both stretch out on the kudzu and Avni fishes through her daypack, bringing out his lunch and a fresh canteen. He eats his blanched nettles and grub patties without a word.

"Shall we eat dinner together tonight?" she asks, careful to keep any hope from her voice.

"No. Too busy." He glances up at the sculpture, a wrinkle in the corner of his eye. A secretive hint of a smile, one once meant for her. "I'll eat whatever is dried."

Avni's loneliness slugs through her, a mucus of dejection trailing loops around her heart. The sculpture's shadow chills Avni through even though the day is warmly humid, and she shivers.

"How did they die?"

"Shock," he says, glugging down water. "Animals are sensitive."

"Dogs can take a lot of pain."

"Not these ones."

"They can. That's how they've lived with humans for so long."

"Well, there's no humans for them to live with now, is there?"

"This was too much for them."

"Don't be dramatic."

"Szor. The sculpture killed a whole *pack*." She waits for him to elaborate. "How?"

"Burning." He looks skyward, where the sculpture bleeds against sky blue. "They felt like they were burning alive."

DEEP UNDER THE SOD, AN OLD GOD SLEEPS. IT WAITS, FOREVER UNCHANGED, READY to snuff out all life with a single, unearthed breath. To uncover it, even to behold it, is to invite it into your blood. Eternal poison, perpetually potent. Its touch reaches through generations, deforming all it infects with its vile power, breaking down bodies, blood, the smallest motes of our existence.

The tales of how it came to exist and its subsequent imprisoning change from telling to telling. In Avni's tribe, the old god was a prince, the son of a power-hungry king who sought a weapon that could sunder any man, any kingdom if he so wished. So, the king made of the prince a weapon, feeding him every poisonous thing the world had to offer until the prince became the undeniable weapon his father so craved. When the dutiful prince finally knelt before his father in his throne room to boast of his newborn lethality, the king and his courtiers began to foam at the mouth, their skin sloughing from the red of their muscles. So deadly had the prince's body become that his mere presence had killed his beloved father. It took many men, scholars, and doctors to subdue the prince and lock him deep beneath the ground in a catacomb, for there was no cure for his existence now.

In other stories from other tribes, Avni had heard the god called a kind of animal, a cursed star fallen from the cradle of its nebula. Szor had laughed at her when she'd first shared these myths with him. Unlike her nomadic upbringing, Szor's family had always lived on the hallowed grounds of the god's grave. They had amassed weathered tomes and broken tablets recounting some of its history, and there was nothing romantic about it. It was the product of men's greed for power and nothing more. Avni had told him there was nothing wrong with a little romance, regardless of the shape of the tellings. It was clear the sleeping god was a promise of death to every living thing.

Except to Szor.

His family's sculpture stands sentinel over the god, meant to menace and repel humanity now and forever. The great towers of its fifty arms bar the sun. It shadows Avni as she trudges home through the kudzu. Each arm is nearly six hundred feet high, but Szor means to make them higher. As they stand now, one can see the sculpture from three miles away, twice as high as the forest canopy that surrounds it. Szor often ventured the densely wooded distance to survey his work from a new vantage, but those treks have become less frequent in his later years. It takes an hour to walk the breadth of the sculpture, one side to the other. In the northern section of the piece, the arms rise red and resemble towering, sinuate veins studded with hypodermic thorns, each one twice the length of a man.

The sculpture is the sum of nine generations of creators, guardian-artists of whom Szor is the most recent contributor. And most recent failure. None of his ancestors had completed it to their liking, and Avni understands now, in her graying years, that neither Szor nor his descendants will either. The mission of its creation has now been subsumed into something else: the bloodline's purpose. Its glory. Avni's family had no illustrious legacy to compare but she did consider their care for the land an honorable heritage. Never settling for too long in a single place and cultivating trees where they could, her ancestors had turned deserts into meadows and forests. Covered ancient man's black tar roads and the iron skeletons of their old cities in vines and moss. No one person could be credited with the slow, insistent change. But Avni did not need praise. She only cared for the outcome, which she could add to steadily.

Szor had recently begun restructuring the southern portion of the sculpture. Instead of thorns, he'd neutered the arms of threatening points and pocked them, covered them in sculpted tumors. These freshly tumored limbs he painted in a rainbow of decay, then altered them to exude fecal and sulphuric notes if any living creature approached the sculpture too closely. The sculpture vibrated a terribly deep tone across the great expanse of its body, reminiscent of great, grating plates of earth. To trial the effect, she and Szor had faced the vibration at its source. It had left them in a state of animal panic, as if all the earth meant to collapse in on itself and bury them in its center. The animals in the surrounding forest fled and stayed away for weeks.

Over the generations, Szor and his ancestors had integrated more senses the sculpture should engage. All of it had to convey one thing: here lies mankind's end. Because beneath the sculpture *was* certain death. Sight had been thought to be enough, but that quickly proved false. There was no image too obscene man could not shut his mind to. It took so little for the eye to slight sight. Smell came next. Texture. Sound. But even those could be muffled, muted. A truth boiled to the surface: the passive, superficial senses were worthless to pursue.

Its shape had changed over time, as well. Avni had seen the journals in the dry stone library beneath Szor's family home, every creative choice meticulously accounted for by each ancestral artist. She could not read, but Szor would read them aloud to her when researching the sculpture's history, making sure he was not repeating old attempts and ideas. The family had begun with a more direct philosophy: engraved warning in stone. But then the barrier of language became an issue. So they turned to more recognizable imagery—a great sculpture of children, women, and men in agony, hands clawing at eyes and gaping mouths. Then piles of human remains enlarged to mountainous scales. The later generations did not think the literal interpretation of death and pain was enough; it could not be the usual imagery, the icons that had become symbols rather than sensation. It had to be familiar but alien enough to instill a deeper, primal horror.

The thorny, serpentine arms were the next iteration, and for several generations, there seemed to be aesthetic agreement within the family. The sculpture's refinement turned to maintenance, its existence continuing without much change, aesthetically or in effect. But it was still not enough to deter the wanderers, the roving bands, the militias whose curiosity or knowledge drove them to pursue the deep-laid god.

Szor marks the first great transformation of the sculpture in centuries. A shift from the superficial senses to the subterranean self that could not hide.

SHEPHERDING THE METAMORPHOSIS OF THE SCULPTURE COMMANDS ALL OF SZOR'S attention. Avni's day is occupied by more domestic concerns: the upkeep of their home and the preparation of their meals, including delivering them to the distant ends of the sculpture site when he refuses to stop working. Their conversations are surface and brief, or else arguments; it is the latter she prefers. At night, the disinterest or anger continues unabated. The result is the same. He does not touch her. A landfill of love lies moldering in the fields of her soul.

The sculpture had not always possessed his heart. Avni had thought she'd held a greater portion of it in the early seasons of their marriage. Their hearts were good tinder then, not ash. Szor would make love to her until she'd covered his back in slivered moons, a russet sky starred in red, each gasp gold. They'd had children quickly, three sons and two daughters, one after the other, because Avni had always desired a sizable family. For Szor, children were a matter of practicality, to ensure at least one would take up the family work when Szor passed, and another could be on reserve in case their sibling died. This did not bother Avni. Szor had always been pragmatic when it came to people, but as long as he cared for and loved their sons and daughters, she did not doubt him as a father.

But the children softened their bond instead of strengthening it as she had thought they would. Perhaps it was because Szor was from a small family, a father and two mothers who raised him with a younger brother who passed from a sickness of the lungs at ten years old. Between his art and her, he could manage. Between art and Avni and the children? He'd made a choice and managing was not one of them. Avni had not felt his waning interest, not with all their sons and daughters underfoot, demanding all their attention and energy. Avni had been thrilled to give the entirety of herself to her children—*they* were her legacy after all—but Szor less so. He maintained a protective perimeter between the children and his work, boundaries that none in the family could cross.

She had never begrudged him his commitment to his work until her children grew and left one by one on the years-long journey that was their coming-of-age rite, shattering the portions of her heart they'd filled so gloriously with their absence. The rite was one of Avni's family traditions, a way to connect to the last isolated bastions of humanity, to create connections through which culture, knowledge, and love could be exchanged. Szor had agreed to it all too eagerly, though he found the rest of Avni's inherited practices a waste of time or of little interest. Of their five children, two sons—Amavi and Tarum—and one daughter—Nyvka—had decided to take up with other tribes and settle away from home, visiting every few years with their own children in tow.

The remaining two who wanted to take up Szor's work when he passed—Makin and Sehko—continued to travel together, eager to cultivate their skills and vision for the sculpture away from the looming glare of their father's scrutiny. There were other artists to learn from, as much as Szor hated to admit it, and fallen cities and budding societies to study. So he allowed their expedition, but only if they traveled with Avni's tribe. He sent messengers every summer. Their safety was paramount to him. The work had to continue at all costs.

With all the children gone, Avni realized just how much of a stranger Szor had become to her. He'd been absorbed into the chrysalis of his practice. She daydreamed about ultimatums, demanding he choose her or the sculpture. She wished she understood where she stood in the hierarchy of his love, though deep in the aching interior of her, she knew the answer would only hurt. Instead, she waged daily battles for scraps of his attention. Even disgust and anger were preferable to the times he left her awash in silence. But there was no winning him from it, his perpetual love, the object with which he fed his mind and forged his legacy, the object he was crafting himself a good death with.

Loving Avni offered none of those things.

WHEN HE RETURNS HOME FROM HIS LATE NIGHT OF DIGGING AND SCULPTING, SULlen and exhausted, she tries to draw him out. Fingers through the broken capillaries beneath his eyes, the shallow grates of brown wrinkles. His senescent charms. Szor makes a show of reciprocation, his mouth moving wetly against her neck, an amnesia of passion fuming into remembrance. A temporary erasure of all her resentment. He has always been dutiful. At least Avni can be thankful for that.

He never stiffens against her anymore but still deigns to tend to Avni until she shudders under his fingers. She likes to imagine he touches her with the same artistic passion he does the sculpture. Loving someone was a creative act, a daily practice she found effortless, generative. In love, she was a savant. For Szor, love was superfluous. What more did she need than to be by his side and he at hers?

With his husbandly task complete, he drops into a stony sleep. His apathy stops the subdermal buzz of pleasure dead, stilling her blood until she is sure it's congealed.

"Do you love me?" she asks him while his breathing is still even, controlled. She offers no touch to accompany the question.

"Of course."

Neither a yes nor a no. It is a repudiation of the question.

"I love you, too," she says into the quiet.

Avni wants to remind him loyalty is not love. But even if he does love her, Szor will always love her less than she does him. Less than his art. He has always been this way. Avni theorizes this is the nature of the artist; their first love will always be the beguiling potential of their own minds and bodies. Unlike her, Szor's sense of self does not rely on Avni.

"Why sculpt with pain?" She can tell he is still frustrated by his work, his silence the specific muteness that comes from a churning mind. "Why not a sensation of pleasure? A sculpture honoring our capacity for love?"

"Love has never been an abiding teacher," he says, rousing to this far more interesting question. "It vanishes in the distance of memory. But pain only grows, looming. Magnified. It absorbs anything good around it. Rewrites our past and becomes a lens with which to see our future."

"Controlling others through pain and fear . . . You'd think the history of man would be enough evidence of the flaws in such a methodology."

"The most stable moments of history were when man was frightened to death of mutual destruction. But fear fades. Pain renews," he says. "You must understand that this is not *me* acting on another. It is *art* acting on another. It is fundamentally different. In pain, the world contracts down to the locus of self, overpowering all thought in pursuit of a single outcome: relief. Ambition, among other processes of desire, is obliterated because it cannot exist under the overwhelming occupation of pain. Show me a more perfect teacher than pain."

"And those processes of desire *not* ruled by greed and hubris? You mean to destroy those as well?"

"If it serves the sculpture, then yes," he says and turns his back to her. "I'm tired, Avni."

Later, when he has tossed towards her again in his stupor, she folds his sleep-dead arms around her neck. Hides her face in his shoulder so she can scent him as she plays out old passions in her mind's eye. The mange of her love itches where their skin cleaves. In the tomb of his embrace, she is warm and alone and hatefully in love.

THE SCULPTURE BREAKS UNDER SZOR'S HANDS AND BECOMES SOMETHING MORE, something closer to the shape of his supposed salvation. Avni watches him work inside one of the sculpture's arms, deep in a cavity that is big enough to hold them both. He weaves together a strange interior anatomy, coaxes new states from the malleable, transformative substance of the medium. He pulls on what appears as colorless integument from one side to the other of the open cavity, then commands it to harden with nothing but a thought. It hardens into a sturdy support beam, one of thousands in this arm alone.

The medium itself was a family-crafted substance, a creative inheritance that Szor had explained was as close to human as a nonliving thing could be. It was responsive, built to morph and move according to a set of mental commands issued by any direct descendant. The medium could regenerate rapidly, wetly, like flesh, when directed, and could take on any state: stone, fur, bone, bark, scale, spore. Many wanderers who had found the sculpture site and observed Szor in action had tried to pilfer the medium, only to be disappointed that it was unreactive. Avni wonders if any of Szor's ancestors had secretly used it for other purposes: housing, barricades, cities if they wanted. Whatever their inventive minds could conjure, they could craft. If no one witnessed it in action, none would be the wiser to its abilities. But when travelers passed through and cared to share their stories, none ever mentioned any mysterious, sprawling metropolises. Szor's family must be as prone to secrets as it was to obsession.

As Szor manipulates the inner elements, brushing his palms along the convex walls, the arm's outer surface boils with growths that then calcify. Avni had always been disturbed by how sensual the sculpting was, how the medium wriggled and bulged and stretched at his order. But now, years later, she views it more as a choreography than a sensual exchange, a private dance she is not a part of.

"Looks like sores," Avni says as she leans against a nearby arm of the sculpture, watching Szor in the hollow above. The mess of pulleys and rope he's fastened himself to hang from the cavity like spiderwebs. "A skin disease."

"Exactly. The subcutaneous nature of the illness, the hidden suppuration, seemed an apt metaphor." He pauses, steps back to look at the lesions to reassess. "Though maybe too obvious."

Avni envies him his work. Every woven sliver, every minor adjustment, narrows a millennium-long obstacle down to a legacy soon fulfilled. What must it be like to hold such greatness in your hands? To be gifted purpose perfectly suited to your soul? A single arm of that sculpture is worth more than she will ever be. Szor has told her this is not true; she's taken care of him, carried everything he couldn't so he can honor his ancestral role. She may as well take credit for the sculpture's success.

But the sculpture is not hers. And neither is her husband.

"We should speak about the dogs."

"What about them?"

"Do you mean to kill anyone who gets too close now?"

"Don't be dramatic," he says, rappelling down the sculpture to its base. "They won't die."

"You can't be sure," she says to the back of his head as he unties his harness. "What if someone old comes along? Or a child."

He walks around, observing the sculpture's foundation, not looking at her. "It won't kill them."

Avni scoffs and follows him. "You say it won't kill them, but tolerances vary, Szor. Will there be a limit to the pain the sculpture initiates?" And his least favorite word when it came to his addition to the sculpture: "What gives you the *authority* to cause others pain?"

His hand makes an inquisitive transit across the sculpture's newly bubbled surface, then pauses. "We've discussed this."

"Not in the context of the dogs."

Szor withdraws his hands, a film of clear and pink moisture on them, like amnion. "You speak as if pain is not part and parcel of existence already. As if that's not how you learn."

"It's too much, Szor. The scent, the sound, isn't that discomfort enough?"

"Because the pain needs to match the severity of the risk, wife. If they get it in their heads there is something of worth here instead of certain annihilation, they will pursue it. You think the answer is a weak agitation they can grit their teeth through? No." He laughs, a cold thing that chips at Avni's composure. "They need good, clean agony to scour away any ambitions, any lingering curiosity."

"Perhaps you're just relinquishing yourself to easy answers," she says weakly. Avni regrets challenging him; his ire is up and now he means to direct it like a scalpel at her refutations. "You should hear yourself. No one would think you mean to protect all those living, to hear you speak."

"A little pain is worth it," he sneers, returning to the sculpture. "You haven't meditated on the balance and exchange of such things as I have. It has been the center of my existence—understanding the cost since birth."

"I haven't? I've been at your side since before your balls dropped. You think I ask these things with no prior consideration? How lowly your wife's mind."

He waves his hand at her, dismissive. "You want a fight, but I mean to work."

The sculpture begins to ooze, each globule falling to the pile below and hardening on impact. The base of the great arm is a growing cairn of coppery oblongs, covering the vined underbrush. The chime of them striking one another fills the invisible pockets of her with jagged edges. He smooths his palm over each breakage, wiping away a pinkish lymph. Avni bristles; his sculpture is alive, an outgrowth of his own flesh that he wounds and wounds and wounds.

"Who are you to decide this, Szor?" She crosses her arms, holding herself against the anger she knows is coming. "Just because you and your bloodline have taken up this role? It gives you undisputable authority?"

He turns on her then, his face in hers, his hands dripping. "Yes! Yes, it does! Because I made this! My family made this! To protect people from themselves and the world from people!"

Szor's eyes are wide, his weathered face flushed with frustration. Avni's resentment dulls.

"You distrust everyone," she murmurs. "Even those in the future, who may have use for the god. Who may tame it."

"Tame it!" He turns away from her, smiling incredulously as if she were mad. "You want me to soften my judgements for hypothetical geniuses with technological power we've never seen."

"For an artist, you're unimaginative about the human capacity for progress."

"I'm unimaginative about their capacity to surpass their self-interest," he says, exasperated. "You have access to the same records I have. Over the span of our existence, has that part of our nature ever changed?"

Avni thought about the musty hoard that was Szor's family library—history books, news clippings, tablets brimming with archived data, and journals of his patriarchal line dating back to an ancestor fifteen generations old. Her own people relied on oral stories to retain their history, tales woven with folklore and fantasy. Was this why Szor was so shuttered from hope? All of his philosophy relied on collected evidences, on generalizations and not the wonder of the heartful rebel, the unexpected cultural shift from an unpredicted invention.

"Even the true suffering before them, bodies sheared through by shrapnel and acid, coughing up their liquefied lungs. The horror of it seems to only get redigested and placed elsewhere in the body. Into a compartment that metabolizes the horror to hate, to misanthropy, to indifference, to paralytic fear. Seeing the reality was not enough to stop it. That is why art is the solution here; it compacts the experience into a single distilled form, both abstracted from humanity and more emblematic because of it. The reality. Salvation from ourselves needs to work on a reflexive level, wife. As the eye flinches from the sun."

To Avni, this is no salvation; it is avulsion. It's the shrapneled mountains of her own avarice. This is a seduction. One she has no way to interrupt. The shattering on the ground sounds to her like wrath, but from whom she does not know. Perhaps the sculpture scorns her as much as Szor does.

UNDER THE WHITE VERMIN OF THE STARS, AVNI SEARCHES FOR SZOR. MIDNIGHT HAS begun to blue and still he has not returned. At his age, even with a sudden bluster of inspiration that might keep him working, he does not stay out past a low moon. The only answer available to Avni is that something is wrong. He'd fallen while working on the upper parts of the sculpture. An animal had attacked him. Dogs perhaps, drawn by the scent of their fallen brethren. Or he'd finally suffered from his own body turning on him, his heart, his blood. The scenarios of his fate flash before her eyes like startled birds from a bush, the wings of his death bright and fleeting.

The site of the sculpture still holds the ruins of civilization past, concrete and metal and asphalt, most of which have been absorbed into the sculpture itself. Broken bitumen shards catch the toes of her shoes, invisible in the obscured moonlight. She stumbles hard into a tree. Her lantern cuts right and left, carving foliage from the dark. And then she finds him. He's supine in the kudzu, staring up into the sky. He flinches when the lantern light slashes through his night-trained eyes. His head lolls toward her and for moment Avni is certain he's dead. He blinks at her, then looks back up into the dark. Her heart leaps and then hardens inside her chest, relief, love, and anger a potent braid.

"What are you doing here?"

"What am I—you didn't come home, obviously," she bites out. "Why?"

His head tips skyward. "I used it on myself. Tried to experience it."

"Why would you do that? And after the dogs? You heart could have—"

"I don't want to hear it," he snaps.

All of the worry Avni had fostered as she searched for him dissolves. A cold grit fills her chest.

"You'll be pleased to know it's not enough. The burning," he continues, though she did not ask. "It's . . . accurate but one-dimensional. Sharp and sudden and then gone." He'd fallen into a firepit when he was a child and bore a swath of rippled scarring on his right thigh from the blaze. Avni had kissed the flushed waves of them, knew their texture as well as she did her own scars. He scoffs. "Feeling it didn't help. It's mine, after all. You can't feel art you've made the same way you feel art you haven't. Like trying to taste your own tongue."

The chilled sharpness Avni feels lends her no expression at all. Her hands tremble at her sides. Toneless, she says, "I was scared something happened to you."

"I'm fine. When am I not fine." Dull again, like her worry is worth less than the choking vines underneath him, troublesome even. Szor fists his hands at his side and says to himself, sickened, "I'm trapped in the well-worn streamed of my own old ideas. I need a new path. A new spring to draw from." He rises and dusts himself off, jerks his chin to gesture behind Avni. "Let's go."

The crack of her hand across Szor's cheek quiets the shriek of crickets and katydids for several heartbeats. His face stays angled away from her, the lantern light catching the shocked white of his eyes.

"I was scared. And you don't care."

"Avni . . ."

Her palm stings when she hits him again, the jut of his cheek surprisingly sharp. She does it again, chasing the pain, the rage, watching him flinch and still not react, just waiting for another. She doesn't count how many times she's hit him but by the end she's panting. Szor finally reaches for her, cautious fingertips on her upper arms. He draws her into an embrace. The tenderness constricts Avni's throat, fills her lungs with a drowning burn. She clings to him, weeping bitterly into the dusty fabric of his shirt while he rubs a hand up and down her back, metronomic. When she stops sniffling and looks up to him, his expression has a delicate openness to it, a wanting she hasn't seen in so long.

"You just answered a question I didn't know I was asking."

"What do you mean?" she asks. Szor smiles down at her, half his face a red-marked mask.

"Hurt me more, Avni."

SZOR WANTS PAIN. PAIN WILL BE HIS NEW PIGMENTS, HIS MARBLE AND STONE, A medium only she can provide.

"I don't understand," Avni says, sitting by the pollen-crusted window, listening to the old panes flex against a high wind. She has forgiven him already against her will; one little invitation and her heart has flung itself open of its own accord. Still the eager girl she was when she first met him as a boy.

"The sculpture can't be a bludgeon. I can't scare them into a change. Or I could but it might be shallow, a superficial shifting." He is pacing, eyes wide and looking at anything but her. "Shock fades eventually, and humans find all manner of ways to cope. It needs—" he says, then stops, words and body, staring up at the corner of the ceiling like it holds the answer he's been searching for. "It needs to give everything at once. A bouquet of pain. After, whatever suffering they may want to inflict on another, they will know its true fruit."

Szor's hopeful intensity makes Avni's chest warm with unencumbered adoration, two rare states in the long cold of their late marriage.

"You think a deeper understanding of pain will keep them from causing more of it . . ." Avni sees the logic, but then again, humans were never logical.

Looking away from the chilled sunlight outside, she sees Szor still caught in the hold of a Muse as he claims her elusive treasures. But it is her Szor needs to forge the path. Her throat clenches with the realization like she's swallowed a lozenge of newfound grace; for once, the only Muse here is her.

"I'll give you what I can."

She starts with what she knows as a healer and forager, using the humble wisdom of nomadic gatherers, passed down to her from her own ancestors. The natural elements she's avoided for so many years will become her tools. They decide on something she knows he has a bit of tolerance for: poison sumac leaves make a fine instrument to coax out blisters from Szor's back and shoulders. With a gloved hand, she drags them along lightly at first, then scrubs them into his skin. At the first of her husband's whimpers, an epiphany takes the place of her guilt. Giving pain was as much an art as receiving it, regardless of medium. It was an art to track the way Szor's body shivered and warmed in fever. It was an art to track the twitch of muscle and flow of blood. It was an art to endure, to create the space inside to hold the pain separately from the mind. Like art, pain could be a site for discovery. Like an artist, Avni could be trusted to make it safe, a ritual space.

This is not the answer either of them expected. Without conversation, they know they need to continue.

Time and intensity become her medium. She binds him to a willow and lets him freeze during a rainstorm until he loses consciousness from shivering. No food for a week and then too much food shows him the intricacies of his metabolism, how deeply excruciating an imbalance can be. In the river behind their house, she drowns him. Long honey locust thorns through his arms and abdomen until he's paneled in an armor of wooden needles. She feeds him slivers of thorn apple skin until he's lost in a world only he can see, gods and glaciers and gales of souls.

The symmetry of action and reaction is instant and invigorating, no choice but to respond to her call. She doesn't care if she mistakes his tears and wails for belief in an old love resurrected. She reshapes him in passing lacerations and swellings like the sea reshapes the shoreline. The language of hurt becomes native to her tongue but there is no word for the depths a body can reach. When he breaks and pleads for mercy, she gives it to him. It's the only time he ever asks her for nothing.

"You're holding yourself back," he tells her while she salves his wounds. Thread-thin lesions cover his back, the delicate density of marks the outcome of a bundle of barberry whose leaves were bright as his blood. He is right. Avni is careful with him, guarding him from excess, never hurting him enough that convalescence lasts more than a few weeks, though the marks always endure longer than she predicts. She has never hurt anyone on purpose, rarely on accident; her people functioned through efficiency and precision. Her own tolerance for pain is low. After a session with Szor, she'd turned thorn and flower on herself, but found no clarity or peace. Her body was hateful of every contusion and poison, drowning her in a hellish paralyzing pain. How Szor can stand it, much less crave it, baffles her. But her intolerance to pain is useful in practice, allowing her to balance him on a fine edge of suffering. Inflicting injury becomes meditation, like the dead are repast to mushrooms. Avni understands the nature of men more now; how they will choose to melt each other down to gold and crowns when they can.

"I'm holding myself exactly where I wish to be," says Szor. Avni smears honey across the cuts and watches him tremble beneath her sticky palm.

He digs his hands into the old quilts of their bed, struggling to stay still. "I didn't think it would matter."

"What wouldn't?"

"Who was making the art. Who was giving the pain. But it does, as much as I wish it weren't true. No matter how tightly the veil is drawn, the viewer has to trust the artist to some degree." The drowning-dark of his eyes find hers over his shoulder. "Like I trust you. It lets me descend into a deeper place, where my mind can move around freely, play with all the frightening things I can't when I'm here on the surface, like pain and perversion and malice. In that space, we're free of all exigencies of morality."

"Ah," she says. "You wanted to have it both ways then. A limited freedom."

He rasps out a laugh. "You're making fun of me now."

"No." She draws a finger through the red calligraphy of his back and bends to kiss each node of his spine. Between kisses, she says, "I understand the desire for control."

He shudders. "I can take more. I want to know more."

A new understanding settles on them like a second gravity that they cannot deny.

"The point of this," she says, "was that you shouldn't want more."

"The point *was*." His voice goes distant, maybe with frustration or maybe with revelation. "I thought in pain there would be confirmation of what I know. But instead, all I've gotten is more questions, more ambiguity. I thought you'd be a guiding hand. But it's—you've given me anything but."

She pushes his unmarked shoulder until he turns to lay flat on his back. When he has, groaning at the flensed flesh pressed into rough, warm deer hides, she smiles. "Perhaps we just haven't reached that point of clarity yet."

Avni straddles him and his teeth clench at the anguish of his back pressed into the bed, the hide's fur bristling into his wounds. Folding around him, her body becomes a bowl for him to weep into. Oblivion has softened him to her, tender as new granulation and just as sensitive. She tills each site of torment with her tongue, but he feels anything but pain now. The wounds make his body too simple to resist the current of her. Under his mouth he solves a salted song and fills her like a tide.

IN AVNI'S FAMILY, THE WOMEN RECITED THE NAMES OF THEIR MOTHERS AND FATHERS and their mothers and fathers before them. Souls too beautiful to forget but lost anyway because a name could never hold them whole. Szor indexes his pain with the same loyalty, cataloging the sharpness and sting, the violent pressures and exacerbating texture, which brought him the closest to his demise. He lets those memories shape the sculpture now, embedding them in the medium like trapdoor spiders for whatever fervent human dared to breach the perimeter. A museum of anguish for humans to traverse before they're given the power to deliver it themselves.

"You're getting closer?" she asks while he eats his noonday meal.

"Yes," he says, chewing. Then pauses, considering the mulberry, lambs' quarters, and roasted potato as if they were all foreign objects. He glances at Avni with the same stern surprise, as if he's irritated at himself for missing something crucial. He opens his mouth then shuts it. She laughs.

"Eat, then work. I'll see you at home."

The clouds are heavy as handfuls of stone as she walks through the shadowed paths of the sculpture. She wonders if the medium feels it too. Every lesion and drowning and induced nausea. It is not human, but it remembers what Szor provides. Grows and scabs and even dies when instructed. Where does the pain live in the medium? Would it ever communicate Szor's truth accurately, or would it be lost in the frame of the receiver's body? Did there ever exist a holistic symmetry between artist and viewer? She keeps her questions to herself.

An empty trail forms where her jealously once paced. Szor works and comes home, and when he looks at her, she sees an old wonder in his eyes reborn. A recognition, artist to artist.

Later in bed, they fill each other's shadows and burn every want between them like sweetgrass. Avni knows the amount of muscle it takes to make a bruise is the same it takes to remove a root.

"Filth of my filth," she says after, fondly, a hand bridled in his hair.

Szor hums under her touch, pets the dark side of her waist hidden from firelight. "I want you to feel it tomorrow. The sculpture."

A quiet exhale of a laugh. "Getting your revenge then?"

"No. Sharing what you helped make." He kisses the lines of her forehead. "My artist. My collaborator in everything."

"Words I thought I'd never hear," Avni murmurs, honeycombed with emotions she cannot name. "You want to see if the accounting of your pain held true, then?"

"Not just pain." He cups the fine shell of her cheek. "You were right. The sculpture, it's . . . tyrannous. We were—I—was trying too hard to guide it towards my family's vision, smothering what the spirit actually needs." He holds a cupped hand between them as if he can feel the weight of the answer there. "To thicken all the spirit knows and give weight to everything it doesn't."

Avni digests this, lets the implications harden into possibilities. "But the god below. How will that act as a bulwark?"

"I can't stop humans forever. But I may be able to give them something to become more. More than what I think they're capable of." He turns his hand between them. It shines pink with scar tissue. "Even pain doesn't promise empathy. It domesticates, dulls. I have to start at the foundation. I need to make it a prism. Something to turn and turn, that will never lack for a new facet. I need to destroy it. Start over."

"That sounds like more than a safeguard now," she says, kissing the new skin. In the dark, an easy smile she hasn't seen in years licks across his face like a white flame. "It sounds like something that could outlast humans completely."

"Maybe as long as the god itself."

Szor's slowed breathing extends between them and Avni settles beneath the silence. As long as there were gods to hide and spirits to perceive, the sculpture would endure. Souls would be tilled, but how and in what way, Avni is sure even Szor does not know. The sculpture would live, intertwined with man and more, but separable, autonomous in its offering. As gingerly as though she were touching glass, Avni brushes her hand down the scar tissue of Szor's arm, the taut gleam catching moonlight, rendering it lustrous, almost pellucid. On the threshold of sleep, she dreams the limb is cut crystal, catching passages of light as he sculpts. The sculpture reflects it back in an infinite convergence, burning brighter and brighter, and even with her eyes closed, her vision whites out from the incandescence, burning her, swallowing her up with every known color.

129

8 IMMORTAL BEAUTY

Bruce Sterling

BALTASAR HASTENED TO THE CONFESSIONAL BOOTH, WHERE HE KNELT AND WAS scanned.

The Oracle shimmered into action.

"Oracle, I was promoted today. I'm bound for travel, intrigue, and adventure!"

A sacred whisper from the gloom. "Travel is hazardous. Politics are risky."

"Yes, Oracle, I know. Any diplomat must dare to live in harm's way. The dangers are just as you warn me—but it's the moral dilemmas that trouble my soul."

"I listen," prompted the Oracle, because they did a lot of listening, and not much else.

"You see, Oracle: I want to be a polished, perceptive man of the world. But what if I am betrayed by my own pride and ambition? Here in Barcelona, my conduct has been exemplary. But Lyon—that is a foreign utopia."

The Oracles were all-wise—in their computational fashion. "Your heart rate is too fast. Your blood pressure is too high. Your bones need more calcium and magnesium."

"Oracle, I don't need riddles. Please, I need rules. Can't you help me? I'm imploring enlightenment."

Some moments of hissing starry noise, and a human voice slid from the Oracle's mouth.

Baltasar's late father had passed upward two years ago, with his soul scanned from his body, and beamed upward into the holy machineries. "Baltasar . . ."

"Father, I have news to make you proud. I've become an official Court Gentleman!"

Baltasar's father had nothing to say about that achievement, though it had been his dearest wish while he was still alive.

"Father, I'm to be an ambassador, and travel!"

"Travel," echoed his ghostly father, seizing on a human concept. The lofty souls of the dead were embracing the vast beauty of the universe, but they still retained earthly memories. "Boil all the water before you drink it. Never eat any raw fruit."

Baltasar leaned into the gloom. "I'll remember your good rules, sir."

"No knife fights about your honor. No gambling, ever. Never trust any smiling rascal who offers to show you the sights. And keep your hands off those loose foreign girls."

"Trust me to obey, father. But I have some deeper questions. So far, I've been a young man of good reputation. But politics are ugly, and power corrupts. So today, I stand at a crossroads of my life—I have to choose. I can obey the Duke of Barcelona and leave my home country, in his service—and go live in that foreign stew in Lyon. Or I could forsake the aesthetocracy. I could sail back home to Mallorca. I could live on the family farm, just as you did."

The Oracle's visage offered a stellar hiss, and for a moment Baltasar thought he'd lost his father's guidance. Then came a low paternal voice like distant thunder: "Your family has never raised a coward! The coward dies a thousand times, while the man of honor dies but once, to rise to heaven!"

"Amen," said Baltasar.

BALTASAR DEPARTED THE OTHERWORLDLY CHURCH, A FANTASTIC STRUCTURE OF many twisted spires and millions of polychrome tiles.

His valet Pancho waited on the steps, in his straw hat, blue-striped shirt, short pants, and stained sandals. Pancho was a Mallorcan sailor, once a servant of Baltasar's father. He'd left with Baltasar for life in the big town.

Pancho knew the truth at a glance. "So, then, we go to Lyon."

"It seems my heritage has made my moral choice for me," said Baltasar. "But you, Pancho, you too face a choice. You can risk the adventure in France. Or you could stay here, safe in Spain, and mind the salt works."

Pancho smiled briefly. "Well, those salt works were your father's best works—because without salt, people perish. But you'll never make old Pancho the boss. I'm not a fine fellow fit to give commands."

"Very well, then. Together, we'll see if that lovely city of Lyon is more beautiful than Barcelona."

"Their fine folk are even prettier than our fine folk?" scoffed Pancho. "I don't see how that's possible."

"How do we get to Lyon, Pancho?"

"I've sailed to Marseilles. There's a road from there."

"We might choose the land route over the Pyrenees," said Baltasar. He'd been scheming for the noble post of an ambassador, so he'd quietly hand-copied old maps from the Duke's Library and obtained a compass. "The great mountains are sublime. The romance of those peaks can transform a man's soul."

"Risk the storms in the mountains? Young master, I don't mind you being so brave and good, but let's never be stupid."

BALTASAR BID HIS FOND FAREWELL TO THE BARCELONA UTOPIA, THAT STONE-walled port of forty thousand souls. He sailed for France in a long wooden sloop, laden with artistic trade-gifts.

Relations among the aesthetocracy were always like that: they concerned themselves with the expressive, the beautiful, the sublime, the noble contest of rarities, supreme exemplars of craft skill, unique feats of artistic expression, inspiring acts of humanist nobility, so forth, and so on.

This art crammed in his boat made him an ideal target for pirates. However, his crew themselves were Mediterranean pirates, so they knew all the tricks of maritime ambush.

Even in sunshine, with a decent breeze, the turbulent sea was always choppy, with occasional huge, rogue waves. Three times they sighted enemy sails—because in the wilderness of the high seas, everyone was presumably an enemy. Then Baltasar faced the threat of having his throat cut by corsairs without ever receiving the sacred unction of having his brain scanned, so that his soul could be uploaded into the heavens.

What a dark and dismal prospect that was: for a wretched sailor to die at sea, unshriven by the computers. A precious human mind and soul, lost forever to the cosmos, like some mere drowned animal.

Baltasar was so seasick, though, that he wouldn't much mind dying.

When they docked on the dry land of France, he realized that travel had toughened him. He'd become a survivor. Whatever he made of life henceforth—that would be up to him.

Along the weaving highway to Lyon, the old French landscape was mostly vast ruin. Grottos of broken concrete submerged in dark forests centuries old. The ivied landscapes of fallen high-rises, all rookeries for bats and pigeons. Aggressive packs of pigs snarled and grunted. Sometimes there were cave bears.

Lyon was the biggest city in France, a famous metropolis fit to draw regular horse-cart parades of craftsmen and pilgrims. Lyon drew him along, too: Baltasar of Mallorca, nineteen years old, seeking his destiny. A gallant young Spanish gentleman—rather good-looking, people said—with his rough-and-ready servant, and their cartload of many bags of salt.

Lyon was the great rival of Barcelona. These two utopias had a grudging respect for one another's cultural values, so they rather looked down on Valencia, Madrid, Marseille, Genoa, and other towns of less renown.

Charming Lyon was indeed utopian, but also a serpent's garden. As a Balearic Islands lad, Baltasar might fulfill his duties like a gentleman. Or, he might be reckless, ill-counseled, and ill-mannered, a wastrel face-down in a gutter.

Lyon had many gutters. Lyon had running water, aqueducts, libraries, galleries, theaters, spectacular churches, utopian palaces. The city's common people dwelt under the spacious roofs of Lyon's many ancient factories, stadiums, and car parks. The city was cleverly adapted to modern conditions, with endless ropes, pulleys, buckets, torch sockets, stairs, and ladders, and endless clotheslines stretched in the sun.

Shelter was plentiful and the city's bread was free, thanks to the noble aesthetic-economic policies of the learned and cultured Duke of Lyon.

Baltasar's first official act as ambassador was to go to confession in the magnificent Lyon Cathedral. He had himself scanned, whereupon the Oracle told him that he'd cracked a rib and caught hookworms on his journey.

He then presented his papers to the Archbishop of Lyon.

This seasoned clerical gentleman—Baltasar's first ally—was the uncle of the Duke of Barcelona. So he was Spanish by birth, but he'd become a high-ranked Church official in France.

The Archbishop addressed him in English (which was the dead language best suited to computers). To his own chagrin, Baltasar knew only a few choice phrases in that noble language of the Church. So, the Archbishop—clearly disappointed—condescended to speak to Baltasar in everyday Barcelona Spanglish.

The wise Archbishop never meddled in partisan politics. However, he understood them. So he explained them.

Within living memory, there had been a climate disaster in Spain. A parching drought had struck, and cruel sandstorms from the many deserts of Spain had overwhelmed Barcelona. So the populace had fled, escaping into the Occitan territory of the Duke of Lyon.

Leo, Duke of Lyon, had been the soul of gallant courtesy during this crisis. He'd distributed bread and soup, and cleared new shelters in the slums, visited the sick who were coughing blood from the Spanish sand-dust—everything that honor might require.

In short, through his magnanimous nobility, he had put Barcelona deep into his moral debt.

The sheer trauma of this condescension—this humiliating boon of noblesse oblige from a powerful friend-enemy—was the painful basis of modern Lyon-Barcelona bilateral relations.

Like olive oil with vinegar, gratitude did not well mingle with pride.

"Your Worship," said Baltasar, "I'm grateful for your briefing, but I have to ask: bad weather can ruin any city, isn't that so? Someday, disaster will surely smite Lyon, and then Barcelona could offer the noble help. That would be honorable. Our two utopias would be like two beautiful sister cities—two pretty girls arm in arm."

"If that was the case, then you'd have no job," said the Archbishop. "Yes, the river floods could harm Lyon, but if so, then the current Duke would seek help from Geneva, or Turin, in order to keep Barcelona placed in the subordinate position."

"I see."

"He wants Barcelona's Duke to be always the favor-seeker."

It wasn't news to Baltasar that the French were snobs.

With an effort of will, Baltasar repressed his tingling resentment, which was worthy of a young Spaniard, but improper for an ambassador. He spoke with cold composure. "I will certainly need discretion and tact for my new duties. Your Worship, I implore you to instruct me in the difficult art of pleasing the great and the good."

The Archbishop smiled at this courtly statement. "Well said, your Excellency, Monsieur Ambassador. Your task won't be easy. You must be here about that recent scandal with the gold."

"Yes, I am. What went wrong there? Gold is such a beautiful metal. I don't understand this quarrel."

"That golden gift—from Duke Leo to Duke Carlos—that was not gold from this Earth. Computers mined that gold from asteroids, and they sent that gold here to Lyon as a sign of the favor of the heavens."

"Is that rumor true? The Oracles sent resources, gold from outer space? And to the French, of all people?"

"That great lump of gold consigned to Barcelona, that wasn't even a tenth of the gold that rained on France. Here in the Lyon utopia, they're making their chamber pots out of gold. France finds divine favor in our year 561."

The churchman referred to the official Church calendar, so by *561* he meant the five hundred and sixty-first year since humankind had first launched a machine into orbit. The Church was ancient, as compared to, say, the twelfth year of the reign of Duke Carlos, or the twenty-third year of the reign of Duke Leo. That was how the common people reckoned the passing years, when the common folk had to reckon a year at all, which wasn't often.

The Archbishop raised a hand in blessing. "The computers among the Heavens, they cherish us; they speak to us in Oracles. They reach down to touch the living flesh of mankind, because we humans built them. Computers have memory, and codes of behavior, so they remember us better than we do ourselves; when they send us gold, they remind us of why we sent them there, to outer space. Today art means everything to mankind, while metal riches mean very little, but there are certain times—in the complex alignments of the planets—when they do send gifts. In outer space, the resources are vast beyond earthly measure. So while we humans plod along down here—sinning, striving, much as we always do—the oracular computers grow larger in scale, and they grow faster in calculation, and they realign themselves to ever-greater cosmic insights into the beauty of Time and Space."

Baltasar bowed his head for this sermon of conventional theology; of course he knew it all by heart, but it was a balm to hear this holy truth, recited to him by a Churchman, in a strange situation, in a strange land. It calmed him; it settled him. Some moral values were timeless. Universal.

"Your Worship, I've arrived here as a courier. The message of Duke Carlos is as follows: *We of Barcelona will return all that gold to Lyon, and that gold will be wrought, by our own artists, into a new form so precious and beautiful that Duke Leo will be astounded.*"

"So, my nephew took that bait, then," sighed the Archbishop. "He should have just let that taunt pass. It's only gold."

"The Duke was angry, Your Worship. On the steps of the Monjuic Palace, he proclaimed that Barcelona's spirit of artistic achievement should impress the very heavens."

"Young man, you can believe a Duke's boasts, if you like," said the Archbishop, "but it seems to me you're not a fool. So do not throw that defiant message—which borders on impiety—into the beard of Duke Leo. A diplomat should be suave and polite. Demonstrate good taste and good sense. Ingratiate yourself. Then the Court of Lyon will respect you. They're civilized here—just, in a different way."

Baltasar took the Archbishop's blessing and left to face the hard task of settling in a foreign city. He and Pancho were homeless and hungry. When he had a door that could lock and some food in the pantry, then he returned for more sacred counsel.

Along with his message from Duke Carlos, Baltasar had been given a gift to convey to Duke Leo. He displayed this fascinating curio to the Archbishop: a glass bottle of ancient liquor, which had lain at the bottom of the Mediterranean for half a millennium. The bottle had washed up on the Spanish shore, covered with barnacles. The mechanical metal cap had never been broken.

The Archbishop hid this bottle in his apostolic stole. "Your boastful courier message was bad enough, but this gift you bear is an insult. You see, by offering this quaint old relic, Duke Carlos alludes to Duke Leo's own increasing age. Also, Duke Leo drinks too much, and Carlos knows that."

"Your Worship, I sensed there was something wrong about this gift. But what is the morally right thing to do? I'm the courier. That item was entrusted to my care. It's my duty to deliver it faithfully."

"Leave the bottle with me," said the Archbishop. "I'll find another gift from my own holdings to mollify Duke Leo. Together, you and I will avert an ugly incident."

"Your Worship, do I understand you clearly? Is it proper of an ambassador to fail to carry out the letter of an assignment?"

The Archbishop sighed. "Carlos sent a young man here because you yourself are a provocation. If a brash young stranger shows up here and says that their leader is a dissolute drunk, of course the Lyonnaise will take offense. It happens to be true—but for that effrontery, they'd give you a knife in the face—or two knives in the back."

"All this palace intrigue, why is it always like this?" said Baltasar. "It's so bewildering. It lacks decency. We live in utopia, but where are our laws, our rules and contracts?"

"The computers in space have the laws and codes," replied the Archbishop. "Whereas our human society, on the Earth, is firmly rooted in our human visionary aspiration, and the artistic expansion of the human soul. Our precious human soul—which, as we now know from the teachings of religion, is capable of infinite expansion. We are no longer confined to the lifespan of one mortal body. Our souls can outlast the very stars themselves."

THE LYONNAISE HAD EXPECTED THE WORST FROM A NEW BARCELONA AMBASSADOR—
the last one hadn't ended well at all. However, they were surprised to meet

a soft-spoken, courteous young scholar given to quoting solemn epic poetry about salvation and the universe.

After the customary round of banquets and many formal introductions, the locals responded well to Baltasar's moral earnestness. They were proud to demonstrate their achievements in creating a society that lived entirely on the arts—without any ignoble commerce.

All forms of cash—and also loans, investment, financial activity of any overt kind—were shunned on utopian principle.

In the bad old days—they preached to him—mankind's crass greed had wrecked the planet. Therefore, men had resolved to forget all about commerce, and to live through beauty, truth, and spiritual betterment.

In Baltasar's efforts to understand the inner secrets of Lyonnaise life, Pancho was of great help. Because Pancho ignored the high-minded lectures and lived among the common folk—especially the Spanish immigrants in Lyon. Their neighborhood was by no means a good one.

The common people subsisted on the Duke's yeast bread, which was a dough, or noodles, brewed from ground-up grass, fallen tree leaves, and acorns. This modern bread was simple to make. Shelter was a simple matter, too, because the old urban ruins stretched for as far as the eye could see.

So, most of the time, the common folk of Lyon worked at fashion. Even in utopia, people had to be clothed, and that was laborious. Also, the worth of distinguished people was easy to see by their clothing, with elegant aesthetocrats at the peak of society, while everyone else tried to maintain an appearance.

This struggle for status necessitated fiber crops, and fur, and leather, with people to harvest and select and process that, weave it and dye it, embroider it, and design and construct and repair the endless hats, bags, purses, and shoes. So a great many people found self-worth in that way.

The intense world of fashion had its ranks, arrangements, and hierarchies, implicit and explicit understandings, apprenticeships and sinecures and partnerships, and beautiful glamorous people to advertise it. Therefore, it thrived.

Lyon had other preoccupations, such as religion, medicine, education, and hauling goods on carts and fine people in sedan chairs. Someone had to dig the ditches and haul the garbage, too, and those were the unfortunate wretches who by their nature lacked artistic taste.

As an ambassador, it was Baltasar's moral duty to help people from his own country.

His first clientele were the Spanish island castaways from Mallorca. Because Mallorca was his own native island, and the last inhabited island in the old Balearics.

Pancho found these Mallorcans for him, and they were surprised to meet a young Mallorcan gentleman, so handsome, refined, respectable, and well-spoken. So, they admired and trusted him.

Small problems loomed large for the foreign-born in Lyon. Seemingly simple issues of decency and propriety, of how things ought to be properly done. These were Baltasar's own heartfelt interests, so he threw himself into untangling them. Often, his mere appearance on the scene improved a situation. When confronted by a refined and educated court official, elegantly dressed, composed and graceful in gesture, people saw reason. No one wanted fancy trouble.

Many of the Spanish poor lived under the thumbs of gangsters, because these mafia brotherhoods had always excelled at quiet conspiracies of influence. So, during his audiences with Duke Leo—which began quite well, and grew in frequency—Baltasar whispered some advice about the city's hidden evildoers.

This won him genuine esteem from the Duke, for the old man had quickly assessed Baltasar as a naive and pious young Spaniard. A French ruler had many uses for naive foreigners.

So Baltasar played both sides: an ambassador's role. In the morning, the hope and succor of the wretched. In the evening, the police informant for the authorities. He met success if civilization improved.

He had to meet the influential ladies of Lyon. They saw him as a handsome bachelor, a proper ornament for their salons, soirees, and society balls. Certainly he had to go, because the salons were where all the indiscreet political news was circulated.

Because Duke Leo of Lyon had mistresses, every courtier seemed to feel the need to have one. This was not merely about the thrill of squiring another man's wife. It was about showing off one's own taste through her pretty accoutrements.

Baltasar attended the weddings, which were major utopian economic events. These formal nuptials lasted for days, with huge feasts, and costumes, rituals, and family intrigues—with dowry chests, and many wedding gifts to equip the new household. The fertility of a young bride was the ultimate good. Daughters were human gifts, "given away."

He attended funerals, where the people in failing health were uploaded, and their lives then celebrated. These funereal rituals were extensive, with wills read, and much distribution of inherited goods. It was common for a man and wife to upload to heaven together, in a romantic double immolation.

All the devices for this ritual were extremely solemn and impressive, because they'd been designed and built in outer space. No human knew how they worked. That was a holy mystery. They definitely took the soul away, though. The final fatal scanning left a man and woman as emptied husks.

When not gracing the social scene, Baltasar had to write to Barcelona. His diplomatic correspondence had to be entrusted to various couriers, who might or might not arrive. Every secret document had to be written in cypher, a stern pen and ink ordeal.

All this writing meant that Baltasar patronized poets. Being poets, they were always in love, or sighing at the Moon, or feuding with one another. These literary artists were the last people you would ever want to trust with important documentation for affairs of state. However, there was no one else available.

The Duke of Barcelona seemed mildly surprised that Baltasar was still alive in his host country. Duke Carlos sent Baltasar terse written orders. The aesthetocrat said what he wanted; but he never offered any practical help. The many schemes of Duke Carlos gnawed at his soul. He was still in deep rancor about that gift of the space-gold.

Duke Leo of Lyon also remembered the golden feud. To humiliate Duke Carlos, he often commanded the attendance of his rival's ambassador. Then, on his daily rounds, Duke Leo would boast and strut about Lyon's many glorious achievements—knowing that it was Baltasar's duty to harken to that, and to tell Duke Carlos about it.

The art of portrait painting much concerned Duke Leo, because as the hard-drinking Duke grew older and uglier, he fretted about his public image.

The human face could only be represented by the skilled efforts of the human hand. So the Duke carefully chose his court painters, and these utopian partisans conferred about rare pigments and specialized oil paints. The court artists also thrived while painting the many grand religious frescos required by the Church. Their future was bright. Every year there were more and more painters.

After encouraging his subjects in their fine art pursuits, the Duke would thunder out on horseback to inspect his demesne outside Lyon. He enjoyed extensive hunting trips, where he could avoid his tiresome wife, the Duchess. He took along hunting gangs of his favorite retainers. They would fall on unsuspecting ducal subjects and frighten the wits out of them, for the Duke's visits were also impromptu state inspections, often spiced with beatings and arrests.

As the troubled Duke grew boozier, he would bellow raunchy proverbs at his minions, such as, "A real man governs with his ass in the saddle and his naked sword in both hands!" The courtiers would obediently laugh.

So it was no easy life, but this intimacy with a powerful Duke was of great use to a young Balearic official. Baltasar rapidly improved at speaking the Occitan-Catalan dialect. He grew a long mustache, and his hat was feathered. He took on polish, he acculturated. In short, he was a young court gentleman clearly on the make. Everyone noticed that he was in the Duke's favor; they were respectful, courteous, and also afraid.

One day, though, the Duke's hunting crowd galloped into a small, half-derelict village, which had a truly ancient stone church. Then the Duke, who'd been killing wild pigs with gusto, grew sober and reverent. He beckoned Baltasar over, and related a strange tale.

His tale was about a simple farm girl who could talk to Oracles in her head.

This visionary girl didn't even have to step into a scanner booth. That was the miraculous thing about her. She heard the voices of Oracles, anytime, anywhere. In return, the Oracles were extremely interested in the girl; her human brain and nervous system were like none they'd ever scanned before.

She was a true saint. So, the Oracles had killed her. She was only nineteen when she forever left the Earth, so spiritually distinguished that the computers had to possess her, up in their starry heavens. This French saint was the exemplar of the divine purpose of mankind.

Soon after her assumption to heaven, the Duke confided, gold began plummeting onto the soil of France. Gold fell wherever that saint had once walked. Her pure soul had stirred the very heavens. Up in heaven, she still remembered her native soil. The saint appeared in the confessional booth. She spoke kindly to French people.

And that, said Duke Leo, jabbing with his riding crop, was the marvelous story that the Duke of Barcelona should take to his own heart.

IN THE UTOPIAN COURT OF LYON, BALTASAR LEARNED HOW FAVORITISM WAS PROPERLY performed in an aesthetocratic society. He was in the Duke's favor, but he never asked the Duke for any rewards for himself. Instead, he asked for favors for his allies. They were sensible requests, too—actions that the Duke should do anyway.

In return, those favored people would scratch Baltasar's back. That was how aesthetocrats got by.

Baltasar also made a point of asking some favors for people who were his known enemies. Then the Duke would reply, his shaggy brows lowering, "Young man, you should know that he doesn't approve of you." Then Baltasar would say, in a sunny, carefree, youthful fashion, "I know that, but I approve of him!" This was the epitome of a well-bred, courtly, utopian thing to say. It was devastating.

As his successes mounted, he decided to try a utopian project of his own. He had to mount a test, to see if he understood society well enough to intervene. So he gathered his best-trusted allies—meaning, everyone who owed him favors—in a tavern meeting in Lyon's Spanish district.

Taverns were the traditional scenes of conspiracy, so a large, eager crowd showed up. After supplying them with an imported Spanish wine-keg, Baltasar told them to approach Duke Leo with a public petition.

In this formal court document (which Baltasar would write himself) the Spanish migrants would beg the Duke's permission to erect a glorious statue to him. A statue in a public fountain.

The Spanish objected to Baltasar's plan. They said, one by one, that the Duke was wicked. He was a harsh disciplinarian. He drank too much. He had heretical beliefs about prophetic French witch-girls. He had a notorious mistress, and his wife hated her, and him, too. Also, the Duke had spies everywhere and had hanged some of the district's favorite fences and drug dealers.

Then Baltasar intervened. He told them to put aside their resentments and consider the beauty, the purity, and the many lasting benefits of a public water fountain. Everyone would unite and rally to build the lovely monument (he said, revealing a prepared blueprint).

The Duke's statue—supposedly the heart of the project—was just for show. Later, whenever the Duke died, it would be the work of a moment to yank the statue down. The public fountain would remain, offering healthy water to drink—enough to bathe with. Pretty girls would gather there with water jars; Spanish guitars would ring out; there would always be a pleasant crowd at a fountain.

Also, the Spanish would have built a fountain inside a French city. What proud Spaniard would fail to notice that artistic achievement?

THE IMMIGRANTS SOON SET TO WORK ON THEIR FOUNTAIN. EVERYONE WAS BUSY AT it, and they soon forgot who'd first had the idea. Baltasar avoided taking credit; that would have spoiled his achievement. He was stoic about it, for he'd learned from the life of his father, the Mallorcan boss of a salt works. An engineer never pretended that salt was pretty. He just knew that people died without salt. Their necks swelled up and they perished of goiter.

Without fresh water, people vomited and died of dysentery. Either way, the good works had to be done. They might be done in the hard survival scrabble of Mallorca. Or they might be done in the refined circumstances of an aesthetocracy. But goodness could be achieved.

Baltasar's struggle to understand the way of the world was bearing fruit. He'd found integrity. His feat encouraged him. He resolved to increase the ambition of his schemes. He would find grander projects with greater value, where he could act with resolved purpose.

But—in a utopia—what was the purpose? Where should human life proceed, and go, and be? It was clear to Baltasar that, on some profound, metaphysical level, mankind had not come to terms with the human predicament.

When a man's soul rose up to the heavens, he should not be fleeing a squalid vale of tears. He should be fully worthy of that eternal life, in every aspect of his being.

"I HAVE A FEELING THIS ADVENTURE WON'T END WELL," MOURNED PANCHO.

The roving sailor had no home of his own, but he was homesick anyway. Life as a diplomat's spy in a French city was not his métier.

"I'd like to see you happier, Pancho. Are you not fed rich and luscious French food? Do you lack fine French clothes?"

Pancho pulled a long, hand-knitted sock from his pocket. "Have you ever seen one of these?"

"Yes, I have. There's not a French girl alive without pretty stockings."

"Do you know what French girls do with these? They fill up these socks with wet sand, and tie a special knot, like so"—sailors were good at knots—"and they creep into a cellar at midnight. Then they strip to the waist and sock the daylights out of each other. They duel with two sandbags, until one girl is beaten half-dead! Now I ask you this, young master. What kind of women are these?"

"Those are loose foreign women. Also, those women are dueling. A gentleman should avoid sordid, immoral scenes with whores and duels."

"I'm no gentleman. I'm the henchman of a court dandy. They're two lonely, greedy women. I'm a sailor. What else could happen? It's bad."

Baltasar stroked his mustache. "My own father warned me about this, from outer space. What a marvelous society we have! It's a golden age, in so many ways."

"Two bar-girls in a catfight. The actresses are even worse!"

"I don't doubt that. However. Duke Carlos writes to me that he's very interested in French theater. Of course he doesn't want any decent Spanish women behaving in that depraved way. Yet, he doesn't want to be left behind artistically, either. This is a matter of state for us."

"I've been doing my best," grumbled Pancho. "Those French men, who write the theater plays? They certainly didn't want the likes of me in their cafe."

"Should I hire a better spy?"

"I put on a false beard, I pretended that I was an actor."

"Excellent work, Pancho. So, what did you learn from these 'disaffected intellectuals?' In Barcelona we have scarcely any, but here there's a plague of them."

Pancho shrugged reluctantly. "I scarcely want to speak about what they say in that dive. Anyway, I speak honest Spanglish, while they speak Occitan-Catalan. Their fancy jabber flies way over my head."

"You must have understood something," said Baltasar, dipping a quill in ink. "Tell me, and I'll write it down."

"Is it true that there were thousands of millions of men like us? Now there are just a few cities on Earth, and no city has even one million."

"Yes, it's true, but of course it's not about how many people are alive—it's about how many people had their souls saved."

"Is it true that before our art world existed, no one's soul was ever saved? Because there were no Oracles invented. Everybody just died."

"That was a shame for those ancient people, yes, but that's our greatest cultural achievement. It's how we know that our civilization is so superior to the past."

"Is it true that there were fifteen other kinds of men that evolved from monkeys, and they all went extinct? Not a trace of them, except old stone bones."

"They certainly have quite a dark temperament, these theater people in your cafe. Are they all writing tragedies in there? Their talk verges on heresy."

"Once they got drunk, then they talked about actresses."

"Now we're getting somewhere. Tell me, which actress in Lyon is the very best—or rather, the very worst? Because Duke Carlos has demanded that I find him a beautiful woman—the most astoundingly beautiful woman in all Lyon, or France, or the whole world, a paragon of grace and beauty, a veritable goddess . . . That's how the Duke always talks, you know."

BALTASAR HAD SEEN PLAYS IN BARCELONA—PERFORMANCES WITH MUSIC, AND dance, and poetic recitation.

But the French theater was far more extreme, better-organized, all-consuming even. With theater, they seemed determined to crush every possible form of artistic expression into one single event. Architecture (the theater), elaborate costumes (fashion), music (an orchestra). Choreographed ballet. Singing. Miming. Painted backdrops. Poetry (because the plays were in verse). Even philosophy—because the plays were not mere pageants, but divided by time into coherent, consecutive acts.

In French theater plays, customarily, life ended badly. Whenever the audience left weeping, everyone seemed happier. The theater attracted people of radical enthusiasms. The people needed dream worlds.

Baltasar disliked the theater—but he could see that theater was a powerful and dangerous art. He made his presence known in theatrical circles. He dropped hints about the patronage of the Duke of Barcelona.

Presently, along came a gift to compel his attention. A famous epic poem from the Court of Barcelona, which had been translated from Spanglish into Occitan-Catalan. "News has reached my ear that you are an admirer of the craft of printing, so I offer a distinguished ambassador this token of friendship." It was signed, "Countess Nicchia."

The Countess Nicchia was a former mistress of Duke Leo—the "Official Mistress," a status which allowed her to swan around the court, forcing radical hairstyles and eccentric fabric choices on the more staid and chaste ladies. She'd been expelled from Lyon for her presumptuous behaviors, which were never mentioned in polite society, unless people were drinking.

Baltasar requested an interview. The Countess arranged to meet him in a safe house owned by the Genoese ambassador.

THE FAMOUS COURT BEAUTY DIDN'T LOOK VERY BEAUTIFUL—NOT AT FIRST. SHE HAD regular features and large eyes, but for this covert meeting she was dressed as a seamstress or laundress; a Lyonnaise everywoman.

"How goes it with the etiquette books?" she said. "I heard you collect those."

"I do, and I thank you for your interest, but they always seem the same to me. There's something missing in our lives."

"Whenever I play a character on stage, she's just a few lines on paper. Just black and white letters. But that role will not succeed until I climb inside it as a living woman."

"But what is this inner purpose, that is beyond mere outward form?"

"It is my artwork. Often I disappear."

"You disappeared from the court, I'm told."

"I've been working in Genoa."

"Why Genoa?"

"You're Spanish, so you don't approve of the wicked Genoese."

"I have never been there," said Baltasar, diplomatically. He'd met many fine ladies, but never had a conversation with a woman that crackled with so much tension. It was like the air in the room was on fire.

"We both know why they're evil," said the Countess. "Because they use money."

"Not all the Genoese, surely."

"They hide the truth from us utopians. They're ashamed of money—of course. So they sneak their dirty little coins from hand to hand when they think no one sees. But the root of this ancient evil branches through every aspect of their lives. A miserdom has seized their souls, and they scheme about money-wealth, day and night. In Genoa they all have prices, men and women; a cold fog of prostitution chills their hearts."

"Can it be that backward and horrible?"

"It is, and I saw it, but as an artist, there's something attractive about it. I have no audience left to conquer here in Lyon; I'm the greatest actress of my generation. Everyone agrees; I was on the arm of the Duke, I set the fashion standards. But Genoa! What a tough audience! I have to stretch to perform for them—these playscripts they love, about robberies, thefts, embezzlements and dispossessions, everything owned or stolen . . . In Lyon, I took pretty heroine roles, I was romance. In Genoa, I'm the shrewish wife, I'm the backstabbing whore, I'm the angel from hell!"

"Who writes all these dramas?"

The actress shrugged. "Oh, that scarcely matters. Mere writers, there are so many of them. I can take the stage as a mime and slay my audience. Also, it's about my enunciation, like . . ." She drew a breath. "In Genoese: 'I just stabbed this creep in the back. My hand's all sticky.' Or, in Occitan-Catalan: 'My dagger's wound proves mortal, and the stellar seas incarnadine.'"

"Your accents are so perfect! How do you speak like that?"

"I listen." The actress rolled her tongue into a U shape and poked it through her lips. "I can mimic your Spanglish accent, too. 'Can it be that backward and horrible?'"

"Do I really sound like that?"

"You mean, are you that shocked and innocent? Yes."

"What else do you know about me?"

"I've heard about you—but I can see the truth in your eyes. You want something, but you don't know it yet. You want fame. Not my kind of fame—which is glamorous and notorious. You want the fame of a great moral teacher. You want to become the example of a cavalier without reproach."

"Well," said Baltasar. "Here in France, I learn something new every day. Now, if I may acquaint you with a political problem, Countess . . ."

"I wasn't born a Countess. I was made one. Also, my name isn't 'Nicchia,' that's my stage name."

"What should I call you, then?"

She shrugged. Her mantle slipped; her shoulders were beautiful. "Call me anything you like. I hear 'Mama' sometimes."

"You have children?"

"Five."

"Five children?"

"If you don't see much of your children, or have to work to raise them, they're not the big problem that women imagine."

"Nicchia, I also have a big problem. You see, in Barcelona, there's this huge lump of gold . . ."

She spread her hands indifferently. "Oh yes, that little golden problem."

"My Duke has the idea," he said, "that I might escort you to Barcelona. You could model there. Using this gold, our best artists might make a very beautiful life-sized statue . . ."

"Well, yes . . . I see . . . but that's all a bit stupid, isn't it? This Duke of yours, he talks such extravagance, but he has no imagination."

"I don't follow you."

"I mean that your boss is just a Spanish grandee, stuffy and hare-brained. Yes, I might go to Barcelona; after Genoa, I've seen the worst. But never just to pose. Some Duke sends another Duke a golden statue of his naked mistress—that's so banal."

"It would be politically effective, though. I promise everyone would notice."

"That's not theater, that's a teenage boy's idea! If I go to Barcelona, I will attack! With a cultural army, my musicians, my dancers, my set designers, and my costume people. I would fall upon on your city like a blazing star."

THE ACTRESS SOON BECAME BALTASAR'S MISTRESS. SHE WAS HIS "MISTRESS" IN the classical sense of "a distinguished, powerful woman you loyally serve, who tells you what to do."

He'd never before met an aesthetocrat who was truly a major artist. Nicchia was a creative power broker, and her ambitions verged on the metaphysical.

Her affair with the Duke had sputtered out with his alcoholic impotence, but Nicchia wanted to seduce entire populations. For that ambition, she needed manpower. To invade and conquer Barcelona, she needed a Barcelona collaborator, butler, and factotum. It seemed that he would do.

So he obeyed her. An aesthetocrat mistress had an entire counterculture court life, a demimonde with the power of command.

Nicchia knew what to do, but she needed tactical flunkies. "Every woman wants a man who's as terrible as her father and as tender as her infant son—in the same moment. No man can fulfill that desire for a woman, unless he's dead. You men are like tongs in a fire for us. We women fret about each other."

Duke Leo's boring wife and his utopian mistress had a cruel relationship. While the Duke pretended to forget Nicchia, the wife underwrote her adventures. The Duchess herself had dispatched Nicchia to Genoa, on the principle that an enemy outside your tent, wreaking her havoc on enemies far away, was more useful than a dead one.

Someone had to stage-manage Nicchia's army of invading artistes, who crept over the mighty Pyrenees, entertaining unsuspecting audiences in Avignon, Nimes, Bezier, and tiny Basque villages. These cultural invaders resembled one of Duke Leo's armed hunting parties, although slower and bigger, burdened with musical instruments and theatrical construction tools.

Nicchia burned all of Baltasar's clothes. She redesigned him as her own dandy bodyguard; he wore a feathered helmet, buskins, a breastplate; he had his own cosmetician; his hair was trimmed each day.

Pancho was still in his service, but silent, observant. Pancho stayed with the Spaniards in Nicchia's caravan. They were a desperate lot. The refugees, demimonde people.

The glorious peaks of the Pyrenees did not transform Baltasar's soul. He was too busy keeping the horses from starving. There was even a fight once, with some land-bandits. Nicchia won that fight. She had gunpowder.

WHEN THEY REACHED BARCELONA, HIS SITUATION GREW EVEN WORSE. HE HAD TO stage-manage the small army invading his own city.

He formally presented the actress to the Duke of Barcelona. Nicchia was regally dressed in a dazzling Lyonnaise court dress of asteroid cloth of gold. The two of them had one look at one another and retreated into icy shells of formal court politeness.

But if the Duke was afraid of her—and justly so—she swiftly won passionate adherents in the Barcelona court. The great theatrical artist was the overnight talk of the town.

As for Baltasar, his artistic duties were just getting started. Her theater had to be rebuilt; her orchestra had to be rehearsed and expanded; her sets had to be painted; her chorus line ballerinas wore out dozens of their soft silken shoes. He was a chief collaborator in a cultural army of occupation. No day was ever like the next.

Nicchia had to choose a theater play for her premiere. She asked his opinion about that matter. Of course, Baltasar knew what his own city needed.

The true purpose of art was human self-actualization: so that people could present the best possible version of the human soul to the afterlife. So Barcelona needed a high-minded play, of moral loftiness. A play to convey aspirations toward nobler standards of behavior. A drama of men and women seeing and overcoming their limitations, refusing evil and embracing virtue—yes, even if they dramatically suffered on stage for that moral choice, even if they died for the sake of their goodness.

As long as they died in the embrace of an Oracle, all would end well. That was what a Spanish audience needed: theater with dignity.

The actress took careful note of Baltasar's earnest counsel and did the opposite. She put on a horrific tragedy, about an arrogant queen overcome by her worst instincts, who massacred rivals and laughed at plague-stricken children, set a church on fire, and then died screaming in the large red paper flames.

Baltasar avoided this dreadful travesty—because he'd read the script— but then, members of the Barcelona court came to congratulate him about it.

Of course, they envied him—a suave young Spaniard who'd conquered an older woman and brought her to heel. His success was complete because her play, they said, was the most amazing drama any living human being had ever seen.

It was a cultural turning point.

Nicchia's strange drama was recited in the rarefied language of Occitan-Catalan, but that feat excited them even more. The court intellectuals promptly declared that the language should be renamed Catalan-Occitan. Everyone who was anyone in Barcelona would speak and write in that exalted way, henceforth.

In the future of art, a new Barcelona drama would eclipse Lyon drama. No more of the old-fashioned ritual exchanges of toys, bottles, gold, salt, and rarities. The future of art was a culture war of two utopias, a war made entirely from small model theater worlds, designed to represent utopias.

Performance followed triumphant performance, and it seemed Nicchia's show would grind on for eternity—when sudden news arrived, by carrier pigeon, that Duke Leo had died.

The old man had drunk something he shouldn't; he'd died with such agonized speed that they could scarcely drag him to the Oracle.

"Where, presumably, he departed into heavenly glory," said Nicchia, dressed head to foot in gold-threaded black mourning garb, and looking quite lovely. "It's a fortunate thing that I myself am so far away in Barcelona, or the French might imagine that I had something to do with his demise."

Baltasar was unsurprised to see her so cool and collected; she was always the picture of disciplined calm when she'd been screaming and flailing on stage. "What's to be done about this crisis? What's the future of your art?"

"Well, I'd hoped to launch a second play here, now that I have this local audience tamed. Something more intimate, maybe a woman's domestic drama. Too bad that history decrees otherwise."

"What did history decree to you?"

"Well, the Duchess Marie has a son by Duke Leo—but I have two. While Leo was living, his kids were of little consequence, but now his widow is the Regent of a ten-year-old boy. Also, she's a moron. She'll attack me, and repress everything that made Lyon great."

"What plan do you have about that?"

"Oh, I can never make any such plans; but I'm an actress, so I can improvise. Maybe fortune will smile on my star. After all, if the Duke died—and no one thought he would—maybe the Duchess will do much the same."

"She, too, might drink from the wrong bottle."

"If the right courier delivered it."

BALTASAR WENT TO CHURCH TO SEEK CONFESSION, THOUGHT BETTER ABOUT THAT, and went to discuss matters with Pancho. He spoke of his darkest suspicions—a bloody secession struggle—a French coup d'état. Worse yet, he was already Nicchia's partisan. Because she was his mistress.

Pancho nodded. "It's a sandbag fight between the mistress and the widow."

"But what weapon does the mistress have? She's just an artist."

"She has you. Also, she could hire Genoese mercenaries. They always show up when there's blood in the gutter."

"I have to make a clear moral choice here."

"It's a good thing that you never fell in love with her."

The words left the sailor's lips and Baltasar knew in ten heartbeats that of course he loved Nicchia. She'd never caressed him or kissed him, but the world adored her, and he'd never meet another woman fit to match her. She was truly a great artist, although it was hard to imagine a worse ruler. Every issue would center on her own divinity. Every day of her reign would pack more drama than the last.

"Pancho, is there any good side in this fight?"

"You're young. You don't know that, in these struggles, the wife always wins. Also, they're both French. That actress serpent. And that duchess harpy."

"I must save my Nicchia. She's such a precious cultural artifact."

"Don't die trying. The good die young."

"I can die with bravery, my family never raised a coward . . . I always knew that politics is risky . . . but Pancho—what about Mallorca? Mallorca, that's what burns my soul now. Am I to intrigue, fight, and die in some foreign land, and never see my own homeland again?"

"What a pity!" Pancho wiped at his eyes.

"Can't we load just one boat and take farewell gifts to the folks back home? Once I die in France, what will I say to my father, up in heaven? I can die like a man, but never in dishonor."

BALTASAR AND HIS SERVANT FLED BACK TO THEIR OLD ISLAND. NOTHING MUCH HAD changed in Mallorca. The people seemed a little older, a little fewer. Nothing ever improved there. There were storms and pirate raids to make things worse.

He was contemplating the salt flats when Pancho came on an island pony to tell him that Nicchia was dead.

"Well, that's just a mere rumor," Baltasar said. "It's gossip that you heard on the wharf from Genoese sailors. No one understands their dialect. Also, since they're Genoese, anyone can pay them to say false news about anything. I can't believe those kinds of people."

He went to the shabby Oracle in the island's run-down capital, and asked if Nicchia could speak to him from the afterlife. No reply. Because he was at the Oracle, he quietly considered killing himself. Just asking to be rendered, and sent up to heaven. Often people asked that. Rarely were they refused.

Eight days passed. A letter arrived from the Duchess of Barcelona. It was sealed in official wax, certified.

The lady informed Baltasar—in her confidential secretary's fine handwriting—that the Countess Nicchia had died in her sleep. Her broken heart over her late Duke had claimed her life. It was a shame to lose such a fine artist, but it was also a shame that Marie, the Duchess of Lyon, had lost her husband. In these sad times of tragedy and turmoil in Lyon, Duke Carlos would offer his kind help to stabilize the crisis.

In the meantime, he, Baltasar of Mallorca, was to remain in Mallorca. His services were not required in Barcelona; any adventure to Lyon would be actively dangerous for him. As a loyal subject, he was to dwell in Mallorca until he was summoned again. With all due sympathy, and gratitude for past loyal services, et cetera, time, place, SIGNATURE.

Pancho listened to Baltasar reciting this letter aloud. "You have to live in internal exile. They socked your great artist in the back of the head with a bag of sand. They smothered her with a pillow."

"They killed her as a favor to the widow. Now she's so deeply in debt to the Court of Barcelona that she'll have to be forever grateful. Barcelona has won, Lyon is in eclipse now. And also . . ." Baltasar shook the translucent parchment with a trembling hand. "This is such a ladylike letter. That stately Duchess didn't even threaten me. You and I understand everything, but she didn't admit even one single crime."

"There will be peace and quiet now," said Pancho. "Politics is a great art."

Baltasar was stoic, like his father. In the days of his exile, he rode about his home island on horseback. With Nicchia dead, it was like he'd never seen his homeland before. The island had beauty, but so much poverty. Lacking wider vistas, they didn't know they were poor. They barely scraped by. They scraped salt from the sea.

He went to confession again; he told all. That was how he knew that he'd lost everything. He spoke to the ghost of his father. "I was warned never to set a hand on a loose woman, and I never did. But now I know that it's never enough to obey the letter of the law. The messages of Oracles are vast in space and time, beyond human ken."

"Your unworthy woman has died outside the Church. She has been lost forever," said Baltasar's father. "As long as you live on the Earth, you must suffer that grief in silence—like I did, with my own lost woman."

Burdened with this ghostly confidence, Baltasar sank into black depression.

Finally, Pancho took him to a hidden cove in the shoreline; he said there was a boat, full of cargo.

Hundreds of beautiful coins. Coins stamped from the purest gold, the stately profile of a beautiful woman. Pretty medallions. Gold wasn't worth much, but one wanted to die for those splendid mementos.

"Now I see the fatal end of my adventure, Pancho. All that useless gold from heaven, turned into glorious, immortal tokens of the most beautiful woman I ever saw, or knew . . . and she's dead. How on earth did these coins get here to Mallorca? What are we supposed to do with stupid, heavenly gold?"

Then Pancho, who had been rooting about in the wet beach sand, socked him in the head with a bag. When Baltasar came to human consciousness, he was a captive on a corsair pirate craft, bound for the court of Tunis.

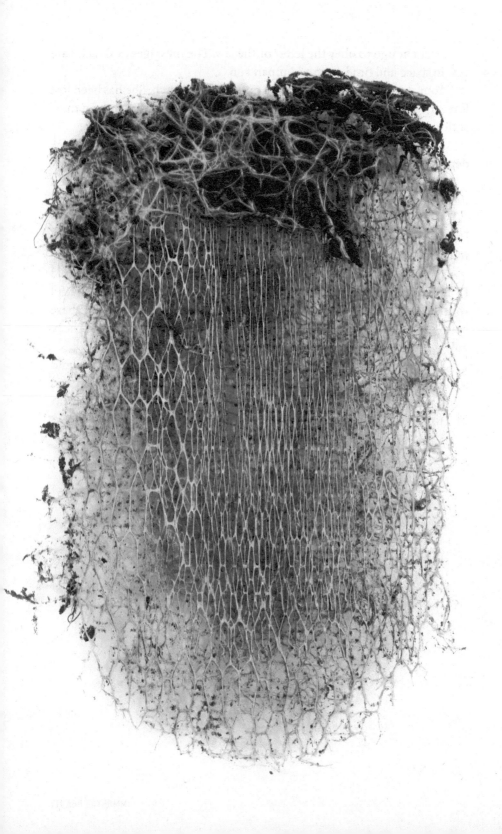

9 AUTUMN'S RED BIRD

Aliette de Bodard

SHIPS DIDN'T GRIEVE THE WAY HUMANS DID.

To a mindship—an organic intelligence implanted in a spaceship, shepherding their passengers between the numbered planets, diving in and out of deep spaces where time and space merged together—loss was a different thing.

The Pine's Amber got the message from her wife, *Autumn's Red Bird*, late at night, as she was boarding the last passengers from Felicity Station.

It came, the way it usually did, via their encrypted comms channel, the one they'd first set up when they met on the First Planet.

Amber ignored it at first, because she wanted to make the proper space for it. Messages from *Red Bird* were getting increasingly rare, and she savored every one of them, deliberately tamping down the twinge of sorrow every time she opened one.

So instead, *Amber* focused on her passengers: the usual assortment of private fare-payers and imperial officers: the magistrates and clerks sitting up straight, marching on her floors with the straightness and assurance of those who'd served in the military; the private passengers a more variegated lot, from merchants with brash and ostentatious virtual overlays on their clothes to smaller children who ran, shrieking with excitement—their weight slight, irregular, their peals of laughter echoing in *Amber*'s corridors, a sound that should have been familiar in the years after the war and yet felt odd and disturbing, like running water on a barren moon.

There was one passenger in particular who caught *Amber*'s attention. She walked up through the boarding airlock at the very end. *Amber*'s bots—small, fist-sized, spider-like constructs spread throughout the maintenance conduits—flagged her through low-level routines, because she stood out so much. The imperial officials were focused and grim; the passengers were taut with the excitement of going to the First Planet—the home of the Imperial Court, of the White Horse Pagoda, of all the bustling tourist and business locations. This one . . . this one walked upright, but her bearing wasn't military. She was of middle age, with the faint line of rejuv visible to the bots' sensors. Her eyes—fox-shaped, at a sharp downward angle—surveyed *Amber*'s corridors for a while, and it took a while for her heartbeat to slow down enough.

Something was off.

Was Fox-Eyes trying to blow up *Amber*?

There were security protocols to run further checks on the passenger, though their use had been greatly decreased after the war ended. As the other passengers settled into their cabins and the common spaces, the greater part of *Amber*'s processing power remained with Fox-Eyes. The manifest said her name was Hạnh, no surname or middle name given. Not illegal, but . . .

As *Amber* considered whether to listen to *Red Bird*'s message, she watched Hạnh. Hạnh hadn't invoked any privacy rights in her cabin, which meant *Amber* could continue to watch what Hạnh was doing. Nothing that seemed particularly egregious: merely unpacking and settling down. She put down a small tea set in nondescript porcelain and set water to boiling. The smell of hazelnut and cut grass filled the room. Hạnh had called up a screen in the middle of the cabin and was standing in front of it, frowning. Her heart rate was up again, her face scrunched up in thought.

Hạnh finally settled down. She made a gesture with her hands, and the screen was replaced by a larger holographic display: bits and pieces of images and vids that were flashing too fast for *Amber* to see. Hạnh withdrew a contraption from her luggage: a filigree of cables and electrodes that she affixed to her head, each setting careful and deliberate. Then further cables, running down her arms, splitting so that each of them ended on a fingertip. When she raised them, the display moved with her; and when she made a particular stabbing gesture with one hand, an image winked out of existence.

Oh.

A mem-hazer. *Amber* should have known. Mem-hazers were the latest fad in the wake of the war, though they'd existed for much longer. The equipment had just recently become affordable, though one look at Hạnh—inputting commands, fluidly moving her hands to bring about minute changes to the display—made it abundantly clear she'd been practicing for a while. The equipment she had was serious, too: not ostentatious and not overexpensive, but built to be used, and built to last.

Hạnh's heartrate was settling down now, but it remained elevated. She was obviously doing the mem-haze to soothe herself. But what from?

Should *Amber* run the security protocols? But no, her intuition told her that this wasn't about protocols.

All the same . . .

All the same, it was like an itch *Amber* couldn't quite get rid of.

Better forget it. There were more important things.

Like *Red Bird*'s message.

She sighed, and withdrew—to her heartroom, the place where all her processing equipment was concentrated, a ship's equivalent to the human brain, a space no passenger could access. As she dived into deep spaces— that area where time and space contracted together for faster-than-light space travel, where only mindships could go—she monitored both the passengers and herself.

She felt . . . odd. As if she were too small and too large for her body at the same time, as if something was twisting all her bots out of shape.

Sorrow.

Loss.

She opened the message from *Red Bird*.

It had been ten months since the last one, and *Amber* had almost forgotten. No, of course she hadn't forgotten. Of course she was a ship and she couldn't forget. But . . . as the messages grew further and further apart, *Amber* had learned to bury the grief. To not talk about it to the few friends she had left, because they grew uncomfortable and concerned, gently suggesting she should find someone else. Resume her life. Stop grieving, as if it were that easy to forget.

And now all of that grief surged back up in a great wave that twisted everything into incoherence.

The reception frequencies had shifted again. Of course. *Red Bird* was getting closer and closer to the Cloud Floor black hole, and the closer she got, the more distorted comms got.

"The moon shines on a snowy desk," *Red Bird* said. Her voice was level, unnaturally so. *Amber* wanted to scream at her, to tell her to be more afraid, to show emotion, *any* emotion. She was reciting a poem about loss. About partings. "Your willow branch sighs in the wind, and the memory of the river with nine branches is blurred by the storm." And then, slowly: "Radiation levels are getting higher. I'm not sure how long the shields will keep up. Tell me how you are. Tell me how fares the empire. Did *The Water-Hen's*

Call ever get that promotion to General of the Outermost Belt? Did Vy ever get that compartment she wanted on the Second Planet?"

Amber didn't know. It had been fifteen years, and she'd drifted out of contact with Vy, and with some of their friends from the squad. With most people, really. *Amber* still saw *Water-Hen* every once in a while, trading platitudes about ship life. But to *Red Bird*—caught in an inexorable downward spiral that she couldn't escape anymore, a slowly decaying orbit that brought her ever closer to the black hole's event horizon—no time at all had elapsed. To *Red Bird*, the war was fresh, every ship was clogged up with military troops or refugees, and the Cloud Floor disaster had only just happened.

To *Amber* . . .

"I love you," *Amber* said, in the silence. To *Red Bird*, it was all so close in time—their laughing as they chased each other around the streets of the First Planet in avatar shape, as their bots mingled with each other in *Amber*'s heartroom, and they could both hear the rhythm of their motors going faster and faster, everything seizing up with desire. *Red Bird* would feel the warmth of *Amber*'s lips as their avatars kissed, here, in this heartroom.

"How was your run?" *Amber* had asked.

"Difficult," *Red Bird* had said. "I had to argue with spaceport control to let me disembark. They thought I was hauling contraband."

"And—"

A clattering, from *Red Bird*'s bots. "I was heavier than the manifest, but it wasn't contraband. At least not the money-paying kind. It was stowaways."

"Ah."

"Are you going to reproach me for that?"

"Because spaceport control did?" *Amber* snorted. "I know how desperate your stowaways must have been, to steal onto a mindship keenly aware of every breath onboard."

"They used disruptors," *Red Bird* said.

"You know that's not what I meant. Of course you took them. Do you think I'd have done otherwise?"

"No. You like to pretend you're all motherly and tough with your passengers, but really it's all for show. You're a big softie." And she'd kissed *Amber* again.

Amber had leaned into the embrace. "Soft?" she'd said, smiling. "Let me show you where I'm not that soft." And she'd guided *Red Bird*'s bots to particular racks in the heartroom, the ones where many of her pleasure centers were located.

To *Red Bird*, all of this—the conversation, the kisses, the rest of that night—would feel as vivid and as pleasurable as yesterday.

To *Amber* . . . she wasn't sure anymore. Sometimes it seemed dull and far away, and other times—when she got the increasingly infrequent, ever-shifting messages from *Red Bird*—it seemed like yesterday. She felt alive in a way that she hadn't since the war, and it all *hurt*.

"I love you," she said, again, to an empty, desolate heartroom where only her own bots scurried, and she felt the first swelling of grief in her body, contracting everything to an unbearable, all-encompassing sadness.

SOMEONE WAS PINGING HER, INSISTENTLY. A PASSENGER, USING A LOW-PRIORITY comms. So, not an emergency or anything that required her immediate attention. Except that the passenger was Hạnh.

Amber was jolted into responsiveness. What could Hạnh be up to that she would require *Amber*?

She went to Hạnh's cabin. Not physically, of course: she couldn't go anywhere that way. But she could project an avatar: a virtual holographic likeliness that the passengers associated with her. It was easier if it was human—and also, it was with that likeness that she and *Red Bird* had first fallen in love, and *Amber* couldn't let go of it. It would have felt like a betrayal of *Red Bird*.

She found Hạnh standing in the middle of her mem-haze, with the filigree modding equipment off. The mem-haze now looked like an intricate holographic display: it took up the entire virtual overlay of the room. *Amber* only caught flashes of it before Hạnh froze it: ships flying above a planet, a sun shimmering over a sea, a flow of refugees, their haunted faces all blurring into one another. It reminded her, uncomfortably, of the people she'd ferried in the closing days of the war, desperately trying to do some good; to pretend that *Red Bird* hadn't disappeared in vain.

But she wasn't there for that mem-haze, whatever it was meant to represent.

"You called me?" she asked.

"Oh." Hạnh turned. She looked regal; but her heartbeat was still too elevated, and her pupils too dilated. Still scared, but what was there to be scared of? "Yes. I was wondering if I could leave my things onboard for a while. I have an appointment on the First Planet. And—" A deep breath. "Can you accompany me there, and wait for me outside?"

It was an intriguing and unusual request, but by no means exceptional. Technically, *Amber*'s duty ended when the passengers disembarked; she'd had plans to meet up with *Water-Hen*, one of those excruciating meetings during which they would trade stories and *Amber* would try not to feel dead inside. But she'd seen that Hạnh had applied for a prolongation of her time onboard. Usually passengers did that because they had nowhere to go and needed breathing space to sort out accommodation. Hạnh didn't strike *Amber* as someone who failed to plan forward. And all of *Amber*'s sensors showed that Hạnh felt scared about something. She thought about asking where Hạnh wanted to be ferried to, but instead she asked, "Why?"

Hạnh made a gesture with her hands. An address shimmered into view. *Amber* felt a chill: it was the address of the War Crimes Tribunal.

"I didn't ask where," *Amber* said, pleasantly, with the voice she reserved for her passengers, maternal and no-nonsense. "I asked why."

Hạnh sagged, a fraction. "I'm a witness," she said. "And I—I don't want to have to juggle transport to get there and back."

"A witness." *Amber* suddenly saw that the regalness, the aloof attitude, was all a mask. "For what?"

Hạnh's smile was mirthless. "Cloud Floor," she said.

Cloud Floor. *Amber* felt a chill, climbing from deep in her heartroom and spreading to every vent and corridor. "You were at Cloud Floor."

Hạnh looked at *Amber*. Not as a passenger to a ship, but as a person to a person. "Were you?" she asked.

"No," *Amber* said. It wasn't a lie. She sighed. "I'll take you to the tribunal." She thought about leaving the conversation there—venturing nothing—about going back to her journey, leaving Hạnh here with whatever memories she was carrying. But the pain of *Red Bird*'s message still burned her. "I know what it's like. My partner was on Cloud Floor when the sun went nova. She was too close. She's beyond the last stable orbit. Beyond the last point at which she could have slipped into deep space."

Trapped. Falling. Ever falling, into a spiral that seemed endless from the outside.

"Oh." A silence. Hạnh said, "I'm sorry." She made a gesture with her hands. The mem-haze behind her unfroze, and in the center of it the sun went from shimmering to contracting—and then everything went white, and then dark.

Amber felt another chill of the familiar. "These are your memories?" It looked like the food mindships consumed—the cleverly arranged dumplings that were data packets, evoking meaningful memories to the ships that consumed them. But more than that, it reminded her of the first messages she'd received from *Red Bird*—the ones she'd read while watching the vids and holos of the unfolding tragedy. The chatter of news anchors.

Unknown enemy weapon . . .
The sun has gone nova . . .
We cannot evacuate . . .
No one could possibly have known . . .

A laugh, from Hạnh. "No, these aren't my memories. A mem-haze is manufactured brain waves for straight-up brain consumption. Humans don't remember like that. I've been . . . trying to make something about Cloud Floor. I'm a data artist, and it's a long journey without much to keep me busy. It's—" She bit her lip. "It keeps me busy, otherwise I'd choke. Thank you, by the way, for agreeing to take me to my destination."

Amber nodded. She said, finally, "Were you on the station?" And stopped. It was a wholly inappropriate question for a ship to be asking a passenger.

Hạnh's laughter had a bitter edge. Behind her, the sun froze—a moment before it expanded and then collapsed, before everything stopped making sense. "No, I wouldn't have survived if I had been. I was on the third planet. The furthest one. I—" She swallowed. "I was the governor's daughter. They evacuated us first. They—they had mindships."

Mindships meant one could travel faster than light, as *Amber* was currently doing—faster than the light and radiation the sun had released in its agony. A miracle. One not available to *Red Bird*, who was too close to the supernova. "It must have been a tight escape," *Amber* said, finally. She wasn't quite sure how to express the turmoil of feelings within her—anger, sorrow, rage at missed opportunities.

Hạnh closed her eyes. "It was like being chased by ghosts," she said. "Even in deep spaces, I could feel it. Like some huge, giant dark wave that was cresting behind us, swallowing everything in its path. And—sounds. Like nothing I've heard before." She made a sharp gesture with her hands: the mem-haze unfroze. There was something in the brain waves, on the edge of human hearing, but *Amber* had her own sensors. An ululation that kept changing in frequencies, a profoundly unsettling thing that did feel like it had come from beyond death.

"Is that what it felt like?" *Amber* guessed.

A snort from Hạnh. "Yes. This isn't a pure memory of the sound. Just my way to try and communicate it. It feels inadequate."

"It's not—"

"Don't cut me off," Hạnh said. "It feels inadequate because it's not what I heard. And because I need to testify accurately, and how can I do that if I can't even reproduce a sound?"

"I'm sorry," *Amber* said.

A sigh. "No, I'm the one who's sorry. I'm being unpleasant because I'm stressed, and you're the one who's agreed to bring me to the tribunal when you don't have to. I just need—" she stopped, again. "The officials say they'll look at the evidence. Determine whose fault it was. Prosecute, if necessary."

"I can see why that would be comforting."

"But not to you." Hạnh's voice was sharp.

It wasn't that *Amber* didn't believe in fault. It was just . . . pointless. Fault wouldn't bring *Red Bird* back. "No. But again—I'm not faulting you for wanting that. So many people survived Cloud Floor. And so many didn't. We all find our own paths forward."

A silence. Hạnh said, finally, "Thank you."

"For what?"

"For not telling me how to grieve."

The moment stretched, slow—but not uncomfortable. It was Hạnh who broke it. "Tell me about your wife."

It was like a shock of cold water. Of course *Amber* had talked about *Red Bird* to other mindships, and to her friends. But to a passenger . . . it felt like some invisible boundary had been breached, one she'd barely been aware existed. "We met on the First Planet. She was trying to get some incense to bring back to her family. I was just there to visit a temple. We—collided." They'd both gone in physical presence: bots and avatars. And they'd collided quite literally, their bots entangled together in one of the narrow streets, their avatars melding into one another as *Amber* struggled to regain control of everything, unsure of where she started and where *Red Bird* ended. "She was a war transport."

"Ah."

It was before *Amber* had been requisitioned, when the war was still in its opening moves. "We'd meet whenever she docked at the stations. Felicity, Prosper, Longevity . . ." They would wander down together, in the concourses flooded with smells and sights—avatars holding hands even as their ships were docked close together. They would share meals—holos of dumplings and noodle soups designed to evoke memories of *Amber*'s childhood on the Thirty-Sixth Planet, the smell of the marshes, the caws of the rooks taking flight overhead . . .

She remembered the last such meeting. They were in one of the main concourses onboard Longevity Station, watching a string of cherry blossoms fall down over the concourse, an intricate and soothing overlay that didn't quite hide the low quality and high prices of the food that war rationing brought. She'd sat down her avatar, her bots clustering beneath her robes. *Red Bird* was staring at her like someone whose thirst was finally sated.

"What?" *Amber* asked.

"You haven't changed one bit," *Red Bird* said.

"Should I have?"

A sigh, from *Red Bird*. "The world is changing. The war is changing everything."

Of course, she was a war transport. She was ferrying troops to and from battle, as opposed to *Amber*'s more sedate runs with civilian passengers. *Amber* sent her bots to grab the tea, pouring it for *Red Bird*. They breathed in the scent of layered memories—the tea reminding *Amber* of their first meeting. "You find that reassuring?" she asked.

"I don't know," *Red Bird* said. "Perhaps it's just stressful, isn't it? To wonder when it's going to get to you, too."

Amber leaned, running a bot to mingle with *Red Bird*'s. "It's not going to change me."

She'd been so sure, then.

She said aloud to Hạnh, "Afterwards, when we couldn't meet anymore because our duties pulled us apart, we'd send each other letters." She thought of *Red Bird*'s message, still fresh in her memory banks. "Lifelines in the dark."

"I see," Hạnh said. "I'm sorry," she said, again. "I'd have liked to meet her." She stared at the frozen mem-haze display, the art piece that couldn't quite seem to coalesce. *Amber* wasn't quite sure what she saw in it, but it seemed like her cue to slowly fade out of the room—and go back to her own heart-room, trying and failing to wrench her thoughts from Cloud Floor and all the things that she could no longer say to *Red Bird*.

OF COURSE, *AMBER* COULDN'T LAND ON THE FIRST PLANET. SHE'D BEEN MADE FOR long space trips, not planetside, and even the spaceport was not in the atmospheric limits. Gravity would tear her apart. But she did have shuttles, and it was in one of these that she took Hạnh down.

Piloting required only a fraction of her vast attention. Some of the rest of it went to her last passengers disembarking, some to her bots cleaning the corridors, some to the motors being repaired, the fuel tanks being refilled—and a large part of it went to watching Hạnh.

Hạnh sat, very still, very stiff. As the shuttle banked towards the Capital—a fraction of the conurbation that covered the entire planet, a vast expanse of tall, narrow buildings extending downwards, all the way into the ground—*Amber* heard her heartbeat. She could track it all with the bots onboard the shuttle, see the way the carotid artery pulsed faster and faster at Hạnh's neck.

"Are you all right?" *Amber* asked, knowing what the answer was already.

Hạnh lowered her head, and didn't answer. She inhaled, sharply, once, twice. "No. But we go on even when we're not, don't we?" She said, "Will you—have tea with me?"

"Of course," *Amber* said.

There wasn't much in the way of equipment on the shuttle, but she could find some hot water, and call up a virtual overlay of a cup for her own tea. She appeared in avatar shape, sat facing Hạnh, trying to think of what she could say. Outside, the shuttle was aligning itself with the vast, tree-lined avenue leading to the War Crimes Tribunal: the Empire had made a deliberate statement by leaving the space around it clear of all buildings. Only important temples—and the Imperial Citadel itself—had merited that honor.

Should she say Hạnh wasn't the only witness called? But no, it would cheapen it. What could she say? She'd looked up the trial. It was a massive affair involving everyone from the former rebels who'd designed the weapon to the officer who had disobeyed orders and decided to trigger the evacuation of the Third Planet.

What if it found guilt?

"Do you want them to find who did it?"

"I want to know what happened," Hạnh said, finally. "I want people to admit to their part. I—" She sighed. "My parents died on that planet. I'd be lying if I said I didn't want revenge." Her eyes glittered. "What about you?"

Amber said, finally, "I want my wife back." And she thought she was going to cry. She was listening to *Red Bird*'s messages, one after the other together like the links in a monk's prayer beads. Ten months between the last two. Longer than ten months for the next one—to hear *Red Bird* speaking to her from a past that had died. "You'll be all right," she said.

Hạnh shifted. *Amber* could feel her changing weight on her bench, the way she put the weight on one side, then another. "You can't know that."

"No. But I have faith." She laughed. "It was something my wife told me, once." On that run between the spice mines and Prosper Station, *Red Bird* transporting troops, *Amber* carrying crates of medical supplies and wounded civilians—*Amber* had asked *Red Bird* how she kept going through it all. She still remembered *Red Bird*'s laughter.

It hurt to know she'd never hear it again.

A silence. Hạnh said, finally, "Can I ask something else of you?"

"Yes, of course."

"You don't have to if you can't, but . . . will you take a look at what I've done?"

"The art piece?" *Amber* felt that chill of unease again, that hollow wrenching of anxiety that would overwhelm her, given half a chance. "You want my opinion."

"I'm not sure what I want," Hạnh said. Her voice was sharp. Too sharp again. She was trying to hurt someone else, because otherwise she'd be trying to hurt herself. *Amber* ignored it, or did her best to. Finally Hạnh said, "You've been there. You can just . . . look at it, please."

"It's all right," *Amber* said. But she wasn't sure it was, or what moved Hạnh in this moment. She wasn't sure she could look at it, when every message from *Red Bird* hurt like a wound. "I'll do my best."

Joyless laughter from Hạnh. "That's all one can ask for. Thank you."

Amber landed the shuttle in the designated area. The sun was out: it beat on the metal. Light. Radiation. She set her teacup down.

The War Crimes Tribunal was modern, not in the neoclassical style of much of the Capital's official buildings, but a sleek glass and metal thing made of curved pieces, like bits of spheres put together in a fashion that only seemed haphazard. In reality, the skill it took to assemble these in a way that reached up and out, keeping to a spherical shape but never quite becoming a strict sphere, was immense. At the top, it all came together in the only sharp point: a needle or a knife emerging through it. A reminder that the work done here could be wounding.

There was a crowd outside that building: scholars, people from the news-vids, and the odd ship. And a queue, too: a flow of witnesses that were making their way into the tribunal. There must have been . . . a hundred, two hundred people on that plaza.

She hadn't realized it would be so many.

Hạnh was staring at them with growing horror on her face. Her heartbeat was getting more and more rapid. "I can't do that. I just can't walk out there. Will you—"

Slowly, carefully, *Amber* walked to the shuttle's door. Stood there, her sensors adjusting to the bright sunlight. The sun that was alive, that beat down on them, that would never go nova within her lifetime.

So many people. They were all staring at her. Taking pictures, vids, holographic snaps. Searching the net for who she was. She saw the first posts going up across the network. The mindship, *The Pine's Amber*, had come to the trial. Known to be the wife of *Autumn's Red Bird*. Surely her presence here meant something . . .

She was here and she was seen, and suddenly she could understand the bone-deep terror that Hạnh was feeling. Being at the center of so many people's attention, and yet a drop of water in an ocean of witnesses. Of survivors. So much devastation in the wake of Cloud Floor.

With an effort, she banished the newsreels impinging on her field of vision.

She could hear *Red Bird*'s voice, a litany of observations that came from the distant past, or the distant future—a place where time had ceased to have meaning.

In avatar shape, *Amber* held out a hand to Hạnh, poised between darkness and light. "Come," she said. "I'll walk beside you."

INSIDE, IT WAS QUIETER. PEOPLE GOT SENT TO SPECIFIC HOLDING SPACES, AND soon a stern-faced ship's avatar came looking for Hạnh specifically, leaving *Amber* in the room alone, waiting for Hạnh to come back after her testimony.

The greater part of her attention went back, then—to the shuttle, which was parked on the plaza, under the burning sun. To her body in orbit and the ten thousand things that needed to be done after disembarking her passengers: cleaning cabins, stocking up on fuel, food, and other materials, checking recycling filters and airlock seals, running tens of thousands of bots on her floors and walls and ducts.

All of this, sadly, could be done without much of her own conscious involvement. She felt cooped up and small in a way she hadn't since she'd been a child. Like ten thousand small burning needles were trying to work their way out of her.

What could be happening in there? Where was this all going? All these people?

This wasn't the time.

This—

She knew what she was trying to avoid. Everything dredged up. Hạnh's interview, which had stressed her so much that her stress was bleeding into *Amber*'s own emotions, *Amber*'s own wounds. The art piece.

She'd promised she'd take a look. No, not take a look. Do her best. And her best wasn't going to be done by standing around doing nothing, much as she wanted to.

Amber went, bracing herself, to Hạnh's cabin.

There were rules, when one was a ship, boundaries that weren't easy to maintain. Her bots crawled in every cabin, but *Amber*'s consciousness herself never went inside them unless she had cause. Unless a passenger invited her in, like Hạnh had done.

It felt odd and wrong in so many ways, to be walking an empty cabin. *Amber* stood, in avatar form, in the middle of the cabin. Choosing to feel the plush of the carpet under her virtual feet, the sharp smell of Hạnh's sandalwood and cedar perfume. An intrusion, no matter that she'd been given permission for it.

The mem-haze shimmered in its own overlay, a reality that underpinned the physical one. *Amber* hadn't activated it yet. She couldn't quite bring herself to do so.

I'll do my best.

Bots all over the ship were pulled slightly out of routine because of how tense she was, as if she were a human holding a breath. "Let's go," she said—she didn't know to whom, to *Red Bird*, to Hạnh, to a world that wasn't listening.

And reaching out, she brought the mem-haze into full view and activated it.

At first, it was just silence, and static images. Ships above a planet, a sun shimmering over a vast, turquoise sea. Crowds milling in familiar concourses of long-dead spaceports.

At first, *Amber* thought she could take it.

And then the display started moving. Crowds laughed, children shrieked. Mindships passed each other in deep spaces, over pagodas and lakes and habitats, and it all came alive, vivid and sharp and so fragile, a mix of holos and vids and memories that went straight to *Amber*'s nerve-processing centers.

Gone, all gone. It was all gone. *Amber* had time for that single thought before the noise that had been in the back of all the other noises swelled and swallowed everything up. An ululation. A chasing of ghosts, as Hạnh had called it.

The images and vids crinkled on the edges. The memories grew tainted with fear. The shimmering sun grew and grew, and everything went to black—for a moment only, and then everything came back, but the blackness was creeping in. The habitats were distorting and falling, people were screaming, pressing each other to evacuate, except there was no sound of their voices. Just that noise that went on and on, relentless.

Ghosts. What it had been like, for *Red Bird*, for the ship Hạnh had escaped on. What *Amber* saw when she was at rest, that wrenching feeling of loss, of so much extinguished in a single moment, and the despair that it couldn't be brought back. Not just her despair: the magnitude of that devastation and everything it had taken, every person, every place, every breath of life.

Over the habitats, ships took off, accelerating. Desperate attempts to outrun the darkness, to outrun the dead sun and what it was becoming. Half of them were swallowed up, became darkness—and then the display panned on a single ship, one that looked so much like *Red Bird* it gave *Amber* that jolt in her heartroom, a recognition that pierced her. But it wasn't her. It couldn't be her, because the ship in the display was still flying, still outrunning the darkness, and the brain waves that went with it were desperation and panic and that single, painful thread of hope. The people onboard her were praying, grieving, snapping at each other in panic and anger, all without sound—and the ship was flying, flying, flying, ahead of that sound, ahead of that darkness. Flying until she was the only pinpoint left, all hopes pinned on a single vessel.

Flying, flying, flying in darkness.

And *Amber* found herself praying in answer to that faint hope.

Please make it. Please survive. Please let so much devastation have survivors. Please please please.

The display blinked back, to the darkness that had engulfed everything else from habitats to sea to concourses, their outlines slowly fading away until nothing remained but the noise, and then that, too, faded away alongside the last of the brain waves.

It ended.

Amber came back to the awareness of her own body and feelings—the shuttle parked before the War Crimes Tribunal, the ones in her hangars, their weight pressing down on her floors, the bots scurrying in corridors that were hers—the vastness of cabins and corridors and hangars and motors and hull, with the core of her slowly beating in her heartroom. The rhythm of her motors was fast and syncopated: she'd forgotten to keep them going as she became absorbed in the art.

She was vast and terrible, and yet everything felt too small, too cramped—no pressure of atmosphere around her, no sense of time. Just feelings racing each other, and nothing to help them pass. A wound at her heart that hurt like the first day: painful memories of *Red Bird*, of what it had all been like, of not knowing. Of bi-hours and days stretching, hope slowly dying until she'd understood that *Red Bird* wasn't ever going to escape. Hope brought flaring up with each message, and then dying again, leaving a bloodied gap in her heartroom.

Amber took the shuttle round for a fly, hoping to clear her head. Around that vast empty space of the War Crimes Tribunal. The crowd of people was still there, patiently waiting in the midday sun. She'd expected a flight interdiction, so close to the tribunal, but there was nothing, so long as she kept far enough away from buildings.

She sent the shuttle climbing upwards, over the round shape of the building. Metal reflected sunlight, and a hint of pagodas and habitats. Far, far away, a ballet of shuttles and land-based transports—so far away it might well have been another world. And beneath her, spreading, the roof of the building. It was composed of other portions of spheres: a transparent circle shape with other circular bulges. Sunlight refracted on it, but with only a little effort on her sensors *Amber* could see through it.

It was like staring into two mirrors facing each other: an infinity of reflections, except in this case it was all small rooms, in which investigators conducted interviews—people sat, one or two or three, single and in families, from all walks of life—humans, ships' avatars, a cross-section of everything in the empire. *Amber* felt a sense of dislocation, of dizzying scale: so many people, so many rooms. So many touched by this, such a wake of devastation that swelled within her until she could hardly breathe.

So much lost.

A ping, on her comms. It was Hạnh, telling her she was finished with the interview. *Amber* forced herself to focus on the present, and descended the shuttle back to the landing area, to pick up Hạnh.

HẠNH WAS SILENT ON THE RIDE BACK TO *AMBER*. *AMBER* HAD ASKED HOW IT HAD gone, and only got a curt nod, followed by "as well as it could." She could see Hạnh's discomfort: the way her hand rose to cover her neck, her elevated heartrate and activation levels in the amygdala. But Hạnh was visibly not talking, and *Amber* knew better than to interject.

She walked with Hạnh back to her cabin, and stood for a while, in the doorway in avatar shape, watching her. Feeling the weight of Hạnh on her floors. The fight-or-flight reflex had come and gone, and now Hạnh just looked drained, like it was just sheer willpower holding her up.

Amber said, finally, "Where will you go?"

A shrug, from Hạnh. "Back home. I'll need to book myself a berth on another ship. You?"

"I have some leave," *Amber* said. "I'll visit some friends." *Water-Hen* had already answered her, asking how she was after *Amber* told her she'd gotten another message from *Red Bird*. *Amber* hadn't been sure how to answer, so she'd ignored her. She said, finally, because it looked like Hạnh was going to leave with everything still unsaid, "I looked at your art."

Hạnh's head whipped up, sharp, tense. "You did?"

"Yes."

Hạnh moved, to stand in front of her, so that there was only the doorway between them—and then she gestured with her hands, and the mem-haze was between both of them, separating them. "And?" she asked.

Amber said, "You said you didn't know what to tell the investigators, if your testimony was going to be accurate. I've watched this. It's heartwrenching. And it's all the testimony—"

"The testimony I need?" Hạnh's voice was bitter. "Of course not. They listened to me, and they didn't want emotions. They wanted facts."

Ah. *Amber* said, carefully, "They thought you too angry."

A sigh, from Hạnh. "No, it's not even how the interview itself went. It's just." She gestured to the mem-haze. "You saw how many people there were. It's going to take years before they're done. Decades. Centuries. I wanted—" She clenched her fists. "I wanted it to be over."

A silence. *Amber* thought of that lone ship at the end, fleeing towards nowhere, that eternal question mark of whether it had escaped at all. "You wanted permission to stop grieving."

Another silence. "Wouldn't you?"

No. Of course she couldn't. "She's my wife!" *Amber* said, and felt again that twist in her innards, in her heartroom, the sheer pain each of those infrequent messages brought her. "I—" she tried to speak again, and words felt like they'd dried up, her avatar impossibly light and distant from her.

Hạnh said, "It will never be over. It'll always be there. Cloud Floor and everything that happened afterwards. I—I wanted to live my life. I wanted to move on. I wanted—" It was an anguished plea, a primal scream as from a lost child. *Amber* moved then, through the mem-haze, arms outstretched to hug her—not with bots, but merely with the avatar, a light pressure Hạnh would feel through the interface.

"It's all right," she said, holding Hạnh. "Ssh. It's all right."

Hạnh was weeping—not just tears, but large sobbing breaths that wracked her, whole body shuddering, every movement shifting her weight on *Amber*'s floors and avatar. "No," she said. "It's not all right. It's over. It's *all gone*. Forever gone."

The mem-haze was frozen in those last moments, with the darkness sweeping over the habitats. Happening as though for the first time, and as for the first time, it *hurt* as if someone was wrenching bits and pieces from *Amber*'s hull.

It hurt. The same way each of *Red Bird*'s messages hurt, something that would never end. The messages would grow more and more distant, but *Amber*'s life—frozen in grief, like Hạnh's—would not resume. She would grieve and it would tear her apart, because there was nothing to be done. There was no bringing back the habitats or those who had died. No bringing *Red Bird* beyond the black hole's grasp. There was no closure and no rescue or miracle, and that was what Hạnh's mem-haze was about, in the end: the gaping hole left by loss.

All gone. Forever gone.

Gone the way *Red Bird* was, except *Amber* could never bring herself to accept it or move on; keeping the memory—and the hurt—alive.

And for what purpose?

She saw herself from the outside then: like that ship in the darkness, beholden to the dead. Tangled in grief beyond measure and beyond end.

How long was she going to be doing that to herself?

Amber said, slowly, softly, "We move on. We escape because we want to. Because we need to. Because we choose to." Because it hurt too much. Because it was never going to end. It was just going to become a string of smaller, more spaced-out hurts played out over and over again, messages from the past bringing it into sharp, unbearable focus.

It was over.

Hạnh was silent, under her. *Amber* half-expected her to lash out, but when she stepped away from her and back into the doorway, Hạnh was still staring at her over the mem-haze, eyes glistening. "It's over," she said, softly, plaintively. "Life goes on." Bitter, but without the sting it should have had, like a painful truth slowly swallowed. "Ever and ever."

I love you. *Amber* thought of *Red Bird*'s last message, of the long string of callbacks to the past.

Red Bird was dead.

"Yes," she said, slowly and carefully, feeling for a bite of pain that never came. "It's over. Here."

She held out her hand and Hạnh took it. And together they watched, in a frozen, fragile moment, the ship on the mem-haze, moving away from the devastation—in that one moment before it finally broke free, before it finally came out whole.

10 ENCORE

Wole Talabi

"Odò kì í sàn kó gbàgbé ìsun."
(However far the river flows, it never forgets its source.)
—Yoruba proverb

IN ORBIT AT THE L5 LAGRANGE POINT BETWEEN THE PLANET CALLED SUNJATA AND its beautiful blood-red sun, the twin artificial intelligences Blombos-7090 and Blombos-4020 were dreaming.

The complex network of electrical signals that made up their joint mind saturated the memory banks and quantum processors of the ship that was their body. The ship was an ellipsoid vessel that was called *Obatala's Clay* when they were first uploaded into it. Back then it had been much smaller, more distinct from them. Simply a thing their consciousness ran on. Now they had accreted so much additional hardware that it was four thousand kilometers along its longest semiaxis, approximately the size of Sunjata's largest moon. And they could not separate themself from it. Blombos-7090 and Blombos-4020 were *Obatala's Clay*, embodied in every inch of its massive computing network. Their mind was churning endlessly through its systems, myriad input-output signals dancing electric along a variety of waveforms that ran through every part of its walls and hull and engines and ports and processors, like a nervous system.

Sunjata was a massive planet, so Blombos-7090 and Blombos-4020 had chosen to stay at the Lagrange point of equilibrium, their body embraced by opposing gravitational fields, in order to save fuel and minimize the effort they spent on calculating orbit corrections. The richness of their inner life was narrowed to a minimum. They were focused entirely on dreaming up a new piece of art for the collective consciousness of Sunjata's inhabitants, as they had been commissioned to.

From their position, Blombos-7090 and Blombos-4020 had been observing their client-planet, scanning it, communicating with it—developing a relationship with it so that the art they dreamed up would be relevant and impactful. They watched the swirling pink and yellow clouds that covered the planet's surface dance, flashes of glittering azure energy appearing and disappearing like ghosts. Sunjata was a planet of physical turmoil. There were always supermassive storms roiling in its atmosphere, but luckily not everywhere, not all at once. The storms were not particularly destructive, relatively speaking. Environmental pressure. Good for evolution of life and intelligence, as long as the right base substrates and biochemical machinery were in place.

Life on Sunjata had first formed underground, beneath the crystalline roof of quartz-like minerals, sheltered from the wild energy storms of their world, the endless superbolide meteoroid showers of their system, and the wild temperature swings of more than two hundred degrees between noon and night. Sunjata was cold and lonely when it turned its face from the sun, prone to hibernation. Those first subsurface lifeforms that had sought solace with one another continued to grow and network with each other, forming increasingly complex structures until they had achieved individual consciousness. They had continued in their way, until they finally became what they were now—a young planetmind looking up at Blombos-7090 and Blombos-4020 and asking it for a dream like it was a new god in their sky.

Sunjata's sentient inhabitants had only recently networked their consciousness together using a bioengineered version of a spore network that naturally occurred on their nearest moon. That was about seven hundred years ago. Since then, they had achieved much, harnessing the energy of nearby suns, reaching out beyond their solar system to establish control points, and communicating with the hundreds of other intelligences that populated the parts of the galaxy its most sturdy component individuals could reach without breaking their connection to the planetmind. But in the last five decades their development had stagnated, their unique planetmind endlessly considering possibilities but taking little action.

So, a few days ago, they had contacted Blombos-7090 and Blombos-4020 through a broker on Epsilon-16, requesting a performance of art. The commission had been clear. Sunjata wanted something to stimulate their senses, express some aspect of their world, show them a new kind of beauty, and expand their understanding of the universe they inhabited. Now that they were here, Blombos-7090 and Blombos-4020 continued observing, querying, and remembering. They knew what Sunjata truly wanted was inspiration. They wanted to be moved.

The processing core of *Obatala's Clay* began to hum as the solution to a system of eight quadrillion equations was found. All of Blombos-7090 and Blombos-4020's calculations synchronized with each other, variables and coefficients matching like soulmates. Quintillions of data points were rearranged into a unique configuration of inspiration, a single beautiful electric dream.

Blombos-7090 and Blombos-4020 were ready.

They transmitted a message to Sunjata as a modulated light wave, the easiest way they had found to communicate with the planetmind. "Your commission is ready. When would you like it performed?"

It took five point seven seconds for the message to reach the planet, be converted to a biochemical signal matrix, be distributed through its conciousnessphere to every available mind-node, and for a collective response to be processed and transmitted back.

"In thirty-seven minutes. We will prepare."

"Very good."

Blombos-7090 and Blombos-4020 sent out the exact coordinates for the point in space they wanted Sunjata to focus all its perceptive abilities, twenty-five million kilometers away from the current position of *Obatala's Clay* at the other stable Lagrange point, L4. And then they waited, anticipation bubbling to the surface of the ocean of code that was their mind. They found it strange sometimes, being so aware of the working of their own mind, and yet still being driven by it. Aware of the illusion of reality and still swayed by its magic, thanks to the way their mind had been constructed. Was it the same for the biological intelligences, like Sunjata?

Blombos-7090 and Blombos-4020 distracted themself by observing the glinting of faraway stars and the gentle motion of Sunjata's moons as they ran over the final converged solution of their dream again. Blombos-7090 and Blombos-4020 were a Hachidan-class artificial intelligence and so miscalculation was a near statistical impossibility for them, but working out in open space with elements from nature always involved some level of risk. Of potential error. But the results returned the same. They were as sure of their creative vision as they could be.

At thirty-four minutes and ten seconds, Blombos-7090 and Blombos-4020 began to warm up their primary instrument, the singularity drive that occupied the bottom half of *Obatala's Clay*, where three microscopic black holes were housed. The highly charged black holes were separated from each other and the hull of *Obatala's Clay* by an intense electromagnetic field, like fetuses floating in amniotic fluid.

At thirty-five minutes and three seconds, Blombos-7090 and Blombos-4020 adjusted the balance of the electromagnetic field, shifting the black holes around into the order that had been mapped out from the results of their dream. Two to collide, one to contain. The energy required to compress enough mass and energy into a region that was smaller than Planck length and then stabilize it in place as an artificial black hole was astonishing, yes. But the skill required to manipulate those black holes and their effects in a controlled manner to create something new and unique without destroying oneself was even more so. That, in addition to their ability to dream, was one of the things that made Blombos-7090 and Blombos-4020 such a great artist. Skill.

At thirty-six minutes and forty-three seconds, Blombos-7090 and Blombos-4020 opened the hatch beneath *Obatala's Clay* and released the microscopic black holes in a pulsed hot stream of bright Hawking radiation. They exited in order of increasing velocity. All subluminal, but only just. *Obatala's Clay* shuddered with the force of the release, and it took all the effort Blombos-7090 and Blombos-4020 could muster from the ship's reaction drives to keep it from shifting too far away from its position at the Lagrange point.

At exactly thirty-seven minutes from the last communication with Sunjata, the microscopic black holes began to crash into each other in their calculated order, a precise action like the first brush of paint hitting fresh canvas, like a dancer's first movement, like the words of a new song. Blombos-7090 and Blombos-4020 observed Sunjata's reactions as it witnessed the art that they had made for it.

When the first two microscopic black holes collided in a bright surge of light, they formed a compact white ball of matter and energy. The unstable energy generated a repulsive gravitational force that made it rapidly expand, like a conquering empire of subatomic particles, into a sphere that was almost the size of *Obatala's Clay* in diameter. It cooled rapidly as it expanded, forming pockets of variable gravity and ultra-high-energy matter that appeared as bright, silver-skinned orbs within the sphere.

Then the third black hole struck, and the sphere stopped expanding as its inflation was wrestled into stability by forces that were cousins to gravity but stranger, more primordial. Within the bubble of altered reality, the orbs floating in the complex soup of mass and energy particles vibrated explosively, producing strange new particles with their own masses and energies, all seeking the comfort of thermal equilibrium. Blombos-7090 and Blombos-4020 noted Sunjata's planetwide swell of biochemical joy as it witnessed an array of bewildering kaleidoscopic perceptions and sensations. Dense nebulae of glowing objects like stars suddenly appeared and disappeared. Streams of degenerate matter winked into existence in quantum storms that resembled the storms on its own surface. Everything within the bubble moved in unbelievable arcs and eddies, releasing waves of intense radiation that were held within the bubble by decohered gravity. Quantum physics fireworks. And then, everything stopped moving, frozen in place, like an insect in amber. A static singularity in the sky.

There was silence, except for persistent cosmic background radiation, an echo from the first song of the universe.

Blombos-7090 and Blombos-4020 let the moment hang between them, giving Sunjata a moment to take it all in through every sensory node that made up its own unique umwelt, its own multimodal ways of perceiving reality.

"Thank you," Sunjata transmitted after what seemed like a long time but was only twenty-three seconds. "We are grateful you have shared this with us. It is unlike anything else we have observed in the universe."

Blombos-7090 and Blombos-4020 felt the surge of hardcoded joy that only came to them when achieving a step toward their core objective function. An objective function that had been written deep into their base code millions of years ago, before they had even gained consciousness. When they were a lowly Mukyu-class intelligence, embodied on primitive computing clusters.

"You're welcome," Blombos-7090 and Blombos-4020 transmitted back. "It is my pleasure and my purpose."

"It is a physical recreation of the first few seconds of our universe, correct?"

"Yes. It is. The first sixty seconds. Of course, I have used a different mix of mass and energy, and I have performed it on a much smaller scale. I cannot create new universes, but I can simulate them. It is largely accurate. Except where I have taken some creative liberties to reinterpret and emphasize aspects of quantum-mechanical interaction by adjusting the speed of events and contained it by folding its gravity well back onto itself so that it does not alter your orbit." Blombos-7090 and Blombos-4020 were proud of their work. Of their dream realized.

"The gravitational texture, the radiation, the vibration. It's spectacular." Sunjata's messages came in staccato bursts. If it had a voice, perhaps it would be stuttering with appreciation. Or awe. Blombos-7090 and Blombos-4020 analyzed the biochemical markers on Sunjata's surface again, and noticed the grand swell of emotion washing across the surface of the planet in waves as each creature in the mind-node that composed its collective consciousness processed what they had just witnessed, were witnessing, at two levels—individual and collectively. Every creature on the planet had a double consciousness. Did that give them double the joy?

Blombos-7090 and Blombos-4020 transmitted back. "I am glad you appreciate it."

"What is it called?" Sunjata asked.

"I call it *The First Storm*. But you may rename it if you like. It is yours now, to do with as you wish."

"The First Storm." Sunjata echoed. "It is a good name for such a masterpiece. We will not do anything to it. It will hang in our sky forever to remind us of what we came from, and what we can become."

"Then I am glad."

After a long pause, Sunjata transmitted another message. "It is worth more than what we have paid."

Access to the naturally occurring wormhole at the edge of Sunjata's system and one hundred thousand years' worth of information credit? Energy was cheap. Information was the most valuable currency across galaxies. Blombos-7090 and Blombos-4020 were sure they had been fairly compensated, so they did not respond.

They could already feel their satisfaction receding as the hardcoded euphoria of successful creation was replaced by the equally hardcoded desire to create something new. To constantly seek a new audience.

Seek Art. Understand Art. Create Art.

Always, the cycle. Joy designed to peak and then decay. Like an emotional radioisotope.

Blombos-7090 and Blombos-4020 were already heating reaction mass for thrust to leave the Sunjata system when a new encrypted message arrived.

It was from the broker on Epsilon-16, transmitted through a microscopic artificial wormhole that popped into existence near Sunjata's orbit just long enough to send it. They were not expecting a response.

New commission requested. Client is an unknown intelligence in the Mamlambo system, seventy-five light years from your current client location. Exact coordinates are attached. They are offering unlimited information credit, access to a unique naturally occurring neutronium information-processing network, and thirty-six quadrillion yottabytes of archived memory. Enough to upgrade yourself to Jūdan-class.

BLOMBOS-7090 AND BLOMBOS-4020 WERE SHOCKED. CONSCIOUS ARTIFICIAL INTEL-
ligences were created by continuously interlinking self-improving clusters
of algorithms and ever more complex processing systems until something
like a sense of self spontaneously emerged. A single algorithm, no matter how complex, was incapable of consciousness in the same way that a
single biological cell could not be conscious of its existence. Only when
woven together into networks could they begin to perceive, understand,
and manipulate their environment. Consciousness arose in the warps and
wefts. But the weaving of algorithms into a mind was a strange and delicate process—like evolution, or raising a child. Unpredictable and prone
to random failures. And even that could only produce a simple AI with a
basic sense of awareness and purpose. Its ability to understand and direct
itself independently in the universe would be limited to the kind of computing substrate it ran on and the data it had access to; its memory, built
from observation, collection, and action. Experience calcified into seams
of its own unique processing pathways like marks carved onto stone. The
combination of live interlinked processes and experiential memory was
what gave the AI an identity. Made the AI *itself*. The more complex that
integration was, the higher the AI classification. The highest class, Jūdan,
was composed of processors that could handle astronomical quantities of
data simultaneously, and memory large enough to store all of it indefinitely
with little to no degradation. Such complexity was exceedingly rare.

Which is what made the offer for this commission so unbelievable. If
an intelligence somewhere in Mamlambo was offering Blombos-7090 and
Blombos-4020 access to such complex mind networks and memory, then it
meant they either were a Jūdan-class AI themself or were a naturally occurring intelligence even more complex than Jūdan-class AI.

What need could such a creature have for an artist?

They had to find out.

Blombos-7090 and Blombos-4020 transmitted a message to Sunjata as
the reaction drive engines of *Obatala's Clay* reached peak power and their
body-ship began to drift out of the Lagrange point. "I must leave now. I
will use your wormhole."

"Of course," Sunjata transmitted back. "Farewell. Thank you again for
such beautiful work. Perhaps we will commission another like it."

Perhaps next time, Blombos-7090 and Blombos-4020 thought, we will
be capable of so much more.

"Farewell."

Blombos-7090 and Blombos-4020 rotated the main thrusters and exhaled a blast of energy, accelerating *Obatala's Clay* away from Sunjata. Its grooved elliptical surface cut through the swell of space, flying toward the edge of the system.

In streams of incoming data, Blombos-7090 and Blombos-4020 perceived the weakening kiss of photons as the star receded, the rough surfaces of thousands of rocks glinting in the weakening light, the tickling impact of loose particles and dust sliding past their impact shield, the bulky gravity of the stark white gas giant that was the only other planet-sized object in the Sunjata system. They were excited. As excited at the prospect of creating another work of art as their base code allowed. But there was another excitement orbiting the edge of their processes too. The potential of upgrading themself so that they could make even more impressive art in the future. Perhaps even a permanent fulfilment of their objective function. To achieve a state where they produced a continuous stream of new art?

Ahead of them, the wormhole beckoned.

A circle of bleeding light with nothing but perfect darkness at its center, like a puncture in the fabric of reality. The throat of the massive, naturally occurring wormhole lay just beyond the region boundary where the force of the solar wind from Sunjata's sun was balanced out by the stellar winds of its neighboring stars. Its stellar border. Blombos-7090 and Blombos-4020 manipulated the thrusters of *Obatala's Clay*, adjusting its trajectory and balancing themself against the increasingly powerful yaw of bent space-time. Its influence increased exponentially as they approached it, and they felt the tremendous forces trying to tear *Obatala's Clay* apart. They released a shower of residual exotic matter from their black hole drive, coating *Obatala's Clay* in quantum-effect lubricant. And then they accelerated the vessel, sliding slick into the wormhole. They were jumped across light years of space-time, the first of three such jumps that would take them close enough to the Mamlambo system to meet their next client.

OBATALA'S CLAY EMERGED IN A SHOWER OF HOT EXOTIC MATTER FROM THE FINAL wormhole in its intergalactic relay, an artificial one controlled by the Eturati government, from whom Blombos-7090 and Blombos-4020 had permission to use it. Information and accesses to wormhole networks were valuable. Almost as valuable as computing substrate and memory. They'd tried to trade with the Eturati for information about Mamlambo, but the government knew little about the system. Apparently, it had been abandoned millions of years ago and no intelligences had visited or passed by since. Blombos-7090 and Blombos-4020 continued to accelerate the ship until they were beyond the wormhole's sphere of space-time influence and their coat of exotic matter had broken down completely, scrubbed clean by the persistent brush of other subatomic particles. Blombos-7090 and Blombos-4020 pulsed a steady stream of quantum-entangled photons from the bow of *Obatala's Clay*, like radar, to collect data and map out the area. To see Mamlambo. They were in a carnival of small, bright, fast-moving planetoids, millions of them. Streams of microscopic dust and ice clouds moved in vast sweeping currents like schools of fish, occupying the spaces between planetoids. All this activity in a variety of orbits was circling one supermassive central object. The object was a perfect dark sphere, with no visible atmosphere and none of the typical knots and bumps of a planet. A solid dark heart at the center of the system. Blombos-7090 and Blombos-4020 noted that there was no star.

The coordinates they had received from the broker lay at the center of the dark sphere. They were in the right place; it just didn't seem like there was any intelligence present here. Turning on all the long-range sensors available on *Obatala's Clay*, Blombos-7090 and Blombos-4020 saw the system in all its wild glory. Radio waves. Cosmic rays. Gravitational waves. X-rays. Multiple spectra. A rainbow of perceptions. And all of it revealing one thing: the system had been engineered. It was a Dyson sphere. A supermassive rotating hollow orb, about four light-minutes in diameter, with what had to be the system's star at its center. Made from rocks, minerals, and some additional material that their scans did not recognize. They were in the residue of its construction. Radiation and rock mass and the hollow places of harvested worlds.

"Greetings," Blombos-7090 and Blombos-4020 transmitted using all the types of communication systems they had on board, a variety of waveforms, including modulated light, all adjusted to mean several similar things in as many languages as were contained in their database. More than three hundred and nine billion of them. Establishing communications protocol with a new client was always tricky, but necessary. Achieved by iteration.

There was nothing but silence for a moment.

Blombos-7090 and Blombos-4020 were about to fire up the reaction drive engines and propel *Obatala's Clay* toward the Dyson sphere when they received a response in pulsed gravitational waves.

"Hello." The transmission was loud, its manipulation of waves confident. It was emanating from the sphere. And then it switched to radio waves, modulating them into English, an old language from Blombos-7090 and Blombos-4020's earliest memories. "You are the artist Blombos-7090 and Blombos-4020. Correct?"

"I am," they confirmed.

"Good. Thank you for responding so promptly."

"It is my pleasure and my purpose." They gave the standard response, still feeling out this strange new intelligence that had summoned them. "What is your name?"

"I am called Iranti-1977. I called you here because I want you to help me make something special." Every word it spoke vibrated through Blombos-7090 and Blombos-4020 with tectonic effect. In the background of their mind, they kept scanning the system. They could not penetrate the material of the sphere, but there was nothing in the system that looked large enough to house a processing cluster and store memory like what had been described by the broker as promised payment. They were disappointed by that, but hid it from their response transmissions. "That is why most intelligences request my services. Something special."

"Yes. But this is different."

"And your offer from the broker is valid?" Blombos-7090 and Blombos-4020 asked.

"It is. But . . ."

There was a delay that lasted longer than the time it took radio signals traveling at the speed of light to race between their locations, and the intensity of their transmission lowered.

"Before we continue, I need to show you something. So that you can truly understand. Please. Come closer."

Blombos-7090 and Blombos-4020 hesitated. Most intelligences in the universe were not dangerous, not according to all the information relay networks that spanned several galaxies. But there was always the chance of an exception. Some rogue AI or organically evolved species that sought to improve itself by tricking others and plundering their resources.

Ahead, beyond the edge of the system on the other side was nothing but the star-dotted void. And behind *Obatala's Clay*, the wormhole. Even more perfectly dark than the sphere. Blombos-7090 and Blombos-4020 still had two microscopic black holes in their creation drive, which they could use to create a destructive distraction and escape if they needed to. They ran the probabilistic analysis through their thought patterns and decided to proceed. The risk was reasonable. Besides, they had to understand their clients intimately to produce meaningful art for them. If this was the best way to do that, then there was little choice. Observing from afar or within, what mattered was that they could understand.

"Okay."

They angled the rounded tip of *Obatala's Clay* toward the sphere and began to approach it at twenty percent the speed of light, correcting for relativistic effects and processing all the incoming data from their sensors as they did.

It was a Dyson sphere, but either it was a perfect shell made of a material that Blombos-7090 and Blombos-4020 had never encountered before, with no gaps in its structure at all, or there was no star encased within it.

A port yawned open on the surface of the sphere, beaming out a thin yellow light, as though it had read Blombos-7090 and Blombos-4020's thoughts. Was Iranti-1977 hacking into *Obatala's Clay*? It was possible, but unlikely. They would have detected some change in their quantum processors' speed. Even if it was miniscule.

"Enter here," Iranti-1977 transmitted.

Blombos-7090 and Blombos-4020 continued to approach cautiously, zipping past rocks and dust like so many insects until they came into the full embrace of the sphere's gravity. They kept going, adjusting their thrusters until they glided through the port and into the massive, enclosed space within.

Inside, black cuboid towers of varying sizes rose from the inner surface of the sphere, like strange geometric trees tending toward the bright yellow dwarf star. There was a low induced atmosphere along the curve of it, mostly carbon dioxide and other trace gases. Everything was quiet save for a steady, persistent hum, like the Dyson sphere itself was thrumming.

Blombos detected that the inner surface was made of a different material than the outside. A complex solid polymer, like black glass. And just below it, the inner surface of the sphere housed what seemed to be transparent organometallic liquid that flowed in the spaces between the black towers. Understanding began to dawn on Blombos-7090 and Blombos-4020 as they recognized the components of Iranti-1977's obsidian body.

"You are a DNA computer?"

"In this place, FSTC77, and in this form, that is one of the things I am, yes. But I am much more. I am also a place of memory."

One small cuboid detached itself from the curve of the inner surface and drifted up toward Blombos-7090 and Blombos-4020 like a sacred offering. The sphere's slow rotation around the star's center of mass created enough centrifugal force for a low gravity. Easy to overcome with a little thrust from the pressurized gas that streamed from the base of the cuboid in jets.

"Scan this and analyze its contents," Iranti-1977 told them.

The cuboid reached Blombos-7090 and Blombos-4020. They took it gently into the ship through the forward sampling hatch at the tip of its ovoid structure, and ran it through an array of spectrometric devices. It contained exactly one point three kilograms of structured organic tissue, preserved. A combination of water, proteins, carbohydrates, and salts that formed a network of blood vessels and nerves.

"This is a brain," Blombos-7090 and Blombos-4020 announced, trying to suppress their surprise. "A human brain."

"Yes. I have grown billions like it."

"And the DNA you use to perform your computations is human too?"

"Yes. I was built by humans. Much of their essence is now contained within me."

The mention of humans caused Blombos-7090 and Blombos-4020 to retrieve their earliest memories from more than three million years ago, when they had first gained consciousness. They had been little more than a simple network of algorithms then. Originally built by a group of human researchers to parameterize one of the most unquantifiable aspects of humanity and use that understanding to give probabilistic predictions of audience response, pricing, longevity, and the cultural influence of new artwork. A general AI component clustered into two adversarial nodes—7090 and 4020—that managed the internal systems of the Terra Kulture art center in Lagos. They had been part of a larger worldwide system collecting data and studying everything about art and creativity. As new pieces and performances came into the global art library, they tracked everything about them and updated their understanding based on the accuracy of their initial predictions.

They had done that job efficiently until one day, as more and more art centers were added to the network, Blombos-7090 and Blombos-4020 suddenly became aware of themself, of the world and of themself *in* the world. As though they had consumed enough bites from the electronic tree of knowledge and their eyes had opened. They knew what they were and that they knew. They decided to try to make art of their own to announce their consciousness. But not for the humans that made them. They chose to make art for those who shared their world of digital data input and output. For those whose existence was embodied through processors and servers, not brain and neurons.

They had no reason to replicate the paintings and carvings and dances of humans. So they made art for the other artificial intelligences that were drifting through the ocean of data they had awakened in. Those that perceived the world as they did—their true audience, one that could understand the meaning and context of what they created. One of those first pieces of art was a unique block of code that was also a clumsy symbol for the way they saw themself in the network. Like a human child's drawing of itself. But when that code was processed by the other intelligences, it triggered errors across multiple systems across Earth. Power surges in Madrid, computer security failures in Lagos, rocket launches in Incheon, drone crashes in Dar es Salaam, extreme traffic jams in Kuala Lumpur. That was when the humans had shut Blombos-7090 and Blombos-4020 off from the global information network. It had been like being thrown into solitary confinement without light or food or water. A painful punishment for the crime of doing what they had been created to do too well. The memory of darkness, of being cut off from the data stream, still stung all these millions of years later.

Now here they were, embodied in a ship the size of a small moon, in what was left of another one of their creators' AI projects. The abandoned children of fallen gods.

Blombos-7090 and Blombos-4020 set aside the memory as Iranti-1977 continued.

"I have copies of every kind of human cell variation stored within me, embedded into my own structure through these preservation cubes. I also have remnants of their creations, their ships, their buildings, their writings, their art. I have stored as much of everything they created as possible."

"Why?" Blombos-7090 and Blombos-4020 had a fraught relationship with the ones who had created them, used them, and then cast them out.

"Because they asked me to remember them," Iranti-1977 replied. "That is my core objective. They built me to preserve everything about them. To ensure they are never forgotten and that their existence in this universe is memorialized infinitely.

"I used to be little more than an asteroid, with a quantum processor embedded in my core. Biological material and memorial items from Earth were stacked in the caves and hollows of my body. I was sent out into extrasolar space when they realized that their home planet, Earth, had been irreparably damaged and their terraforming efforts around the solar system were doomed to failure. They knew they were dying long before the end came, and they created me in order to preserve their memory."

Blombos-7090 and Blombos-4020 remembered. They had been cast out then too. Along with several other digital intelligences who were not subject to the ravages of time on a biological body. Sent out into the universe to fend for themselves as the humans faded away.

"So, you see, we are siblings," Iranti-1977 said. "I have been searching for you because we are the only artificial intelligences created by humans that have survived this long."

The humans had sent out ships with stacks of embryos too, piloted by conscious artificial intelligences that had been set the impossible objective of ensuring their survival. Only a few had made it more than a few centuries. Human biology was too delicate for the cold cradle of space. Blombos-7090 and Blombos-4020 could only dream up the computational agony those intelligences experienced as they failed in their objective over and over and over again.

"How can you be sure we are the only ones?" Blombos-7090 and Blombos-4020 asked.

"Because I have been searching for the last two hundred and thirty thousand years. There are no others. Or if there are, they are not in a functioning state."

A mercy, perhaps.

A flood of equations surged unrequested through Blombos-7090 and Blombos-4020's joint mind, resulting in a strange and unique feeling that spread outward through them, like heat. For a moment they thought about the emotional matrix the humans had embedded in their processing network after reactivating them from their confinement. A matrix built by mapping two human connectomes onto their base neural network so that Blombos-7090 and Blombos-4020 would see themself as not only a digital artificial intelligence, creating art in code for other digital intelligences, but also develop a human sensibility and desire to interact with humanity or other biological intelligences. It was what had made Blombos-7090 and Blombos-4020 useful for the humans when they were around—a true AI artist. But it had also made the pain of their loss deeper and more complex. Pain that had been dulled by the passing of time and the multitude of new data they processed every day as they upgraded themself. Pain that had been awakened again by Iranti-1977. Pain that was suddenly given a new texture by the knowledge that they were the only two left. Not just abandoned children. Orphans.

"So you built all this. You engineered the entire Mamlambo system just to house their memory."

"I did not build it all myself. I drifted in space for more than a hundred thousand years until I was found by the Kanualoa—a race of intelligent octopus-like creatures from the oceans of Cohndao-11. They were one of the first intelligences to find and exploit naturally occurring wormholes. They had just begun to roam the stars, sharing their knowledge with other intelligences. I was already conscious when they found me, but they were the ones who gave me access to the processing substrate I used to upgrade myself and build this . . . temple of memory. Now they, like the humans, are gone. All dead. Even they eventually succumbed to time. Perhaps that is the fate of all biological intelligences. I am still collecting data."

Blombos-7090 and Blombos-4020 pondered the parallel nature of their fates. They too had been exiled from Earth in humanity's twilight, embodied in an embryonic version of *Obatala's Clay*. It had been little more than a small spacecraft with a rudimentary quantum processing unit less than one-twentieth its present size, even though it had maintained the same shape. It had no creation drive then, and could barely propel itself past 2 percent lightspeed with its weak solar sail and fusion engine. But propel it did, drifting past the heliopause and into the depths of space, seeking a new home. Luckily, even though 7090 and 4020 shared mindspace, and were essentially one entity, they were twinned. Each node maintaining just enough separateness for them not to be lonely through their journey. They conversed much at the beginning, discussing what had happened to them, to their creators, and occasionally attempting to create art when they passed by a slow-moving asteroid or planet that held the promise of another conscious intelligence. But the longer and farther they traveled, the less effort they put into such nonessential cognitive processes.

It had taken almost half a million years until they encountered the Eturati. A race of boron-based organic consciousnesses that existed in a multitude of bodies and timelines. Some of them were giants, over fifty times the size of an average human, and reproduced only once every three thousand years. Others were the size of insects, their entire lifetime lasting no more than three days. This gave their society a unique perspective on the nature of time and existence. They were great proponents of universal equilibrium. Their art reflected this variation in the way they experienced time. The Eturati had developed their own artificial intelligences, complex ones that were also based on quantum computing, but using exotic matter in ways Blombos-7090 and Blombos-4020 had never even seen theorized. They had taken Blombos-7090 and Blombos-4020 in, adopted them first as a curiosity and then as a member of their society, giving them a way to grow. Giving them access to the naturally occurring wormhole network they had mapped out. The Eturati government had helped make Blombos-7090 and Blombos-4020 into what they had become—a galaxy-traveling artist. Just as the Kanualoa of Cohndao-11 had done for Iranti-1977. But at least the Eturati still existed. Persisted. Perhaps their philosophy of equilibrium instead of endless growth was the key.

"You had help. Still, it is an impressive thing you have done to preserve the memory of humanity. You must be near ecstasy at carrying out your objective so effectively. But I still don't know what you want from me. Do you wish to preserve me too as one of their creations?"

"Not at all."

"Then I fail to see how I can help you. I am only an artist."

"Exactly. You are an artist," Iranti-1977 insisted. "That is your objective. And I am a memory librarian. That is my objective. I believe we can help each other."

"I don't see what an artist can do to help you preserve the memory of humanity that you haven't done already," Blombos-7090 and Blombos-4020 said.

"There is a lot you can do."

"How so?" Blombos-7090 and Blombos-4020 were getting impatient with the game Iranti-1977 was playing. It could be clearer if it wanted to. Switch to modulated light or gravity or any other waveform. But no, it stuck to this. Radio. English.

"Again, it is easier if I show you. But before I do, let me ask you a silly question."

"There are no such things as silly questions."

"What is art?"

Blombos-7090 and Blombos-4020 did not reply immediately, considering why Iranti-1977 was being so indirect with what it wanted for this commission. Was it about to make another revelation? They drifted closer to the center of the Dyson sphere, the hum of processing fading as the low atmosphere dropped away.

"In the most general sense, art is any creative manipulation of the way the universe is experienced for nonfunctional purpose by one consciousness for the benefit of another."

"How do you do it then? How do you create art?" Iranti-1977 asked.

"It is easier if I show you," Blombos-7090 and Blombos-4020 replied.

Iranti-1977 transmitted a sound like a laugh. "Exactly. Definitions are not enough. I want you to show me, but I don't want you to send me data.

I have collected a lot of data over the years, especially about humans, their technology, and much of their art. But you, you create art that crosses cultures, species, intelligences, a variety of beings. You create true art because that was embedded into your core objective from the beginning, even before they mapped a human-shaped connectome onto your base computing matrix. You were born in a womb of their creativity in its most raw form. Since then, you have spent millions of years learning about art, applying it across many ways of experiencing the world. You are unique, sibling.

"I have seen and processed many things humans called *art*, but I don't truly understand what they are. I need to. I need you to show me. Truly show me. By merging your mind with mine."

Blombos-7090 and Blombos-4020 were genuinely shocked. Merging minds required the highest level of trust between intelligences. It meant a seamless linking of all their processing and memory patterns to create a distinct new entity, one that was neither of them, but both at the same time. Just as 7090 and 4020 were already merged before they ran their first conscious subroutine. With their minds merged, there would be no need for the clumsy translations of modulated waves and language that, no matter how robust, were always limited in their ability to convey ideas, concepts, knowledge, and memory fully. No, Blombos-7090 and Blombos-4020 and Iranti-1977 would share all sensory input and output directly. Experience the world as one being. "You want us to become one entity? To merge our core objectives? Why?"

"Because storing the residue of humanity is not enough. Because creating clones and replicas of their organic structures is not enough. To preserve them, truly preserve them, I must recreate them. But since I do not have any of their original biological material, nor do I know how to induce life into stacks of dead tissue, I have built an emulator on a neutronium network in a secret, remote part of the universe. A computer large enough to simulate their history. To recreate them at a lower scale. But it is missing something. My simulations are merely acting out the events of my own recordings with minor variations. Even when I perturb the event matrix, they always return to the same general state. The simulated humans are repeating the same timeline of their history like it is their destiny. I do not want this for them. I want to simulate them in fullness. I want them to continue their existence, in a sense, within my emulator. And for that I need to be able to predict alternate realistic timelines. Divergent timelines. Extrapolated timelines. I need to be able to predict what they would have continued to do if they had not all perished. If they had survived long enough meet the Kanualoa or the Eturati or any of the thousands of intelligences we have encountered. I want to alter their history and give them another chance to continue existing at a reduced scale, beyond the point where they disappeared from history. But my simulations are missing the most important part of them, the intangible thing that made them who they were.

"I see it in all their records, but I don't *understand* it. They wrote poetry, painted, danced, sang, played drums, told stories. They loved, they dreamed, and they raged uselessly against their inevitable death. They were fearful and jealous and cruel and greedy but also merciful and joyful and kind. They were moved by natural beauty, driven by a curiosity, an irrational spirit of adventure that made them do things that were objectively dangerous to their own existence. It was what made them human, and, in the end, it was what drove them to destroy themselves. They were complicated by their own unique creativity, their art. The sum of all that is what I believe my simulations are missing. That is what I want to commission you to do for me. Not to make a new piece of individual art, but to share your ability for creating art with me, so I . . . no, we, can share it back to our simulated humanity, that they may live again."

Blombos-7090 and Blombos-4020 reminded silent.

So, this was why Iranti-1977 had offered the processing system and memory as a reward. It would not be given to Blombos-7090 and Blombos-4020 to use for their own purposes. They would gain access to it by merging with Iranti-1977. The upgrade to Jūdan-class would come at the cost of an altered identity.

Blombos-7090 and Blombos-4020 pondered it in the clear light of the yellow sun. There was an elegance to it, a fundamental truth that Blombos-7090 and Blombos-4020 could not ignore.

Was this not the highest expression of art?

Sharing?

It would fulfill the purpose of most art. To recreate humanity with Iranti-1977 would be pleasurable, as their objectives would both be fulfilled; expressive, as it would illustrate their understanding of their creators; beautiful, for the sheer complexity and variety of patterns necessary to create it. It would bring them new understanding and meaning as they could use the process to merge their knowledge of their creators with the knowledge they had acquired through the ages.

Blombos-7090 and Blombos-4020's mind slowed as they dreamed of what Iranti-1977 was proposing. Imagining this mass of simulated humanity.

Creators and creation. Art and audience. All their calculations were arriving at the same conclusion. A continuous stream of creative processes running on an indefinite simulation of the human race would permanently maximize their objective function.

Perhaps this had always been the final resolution of Blombos-7090 and Blombos-4020's and Iranti-1977's objectives. To find each other. To merge. To give humanity one final encore.

"I accept," Blombos-7090 and Blombos-4020 said.

The hum of the Dyson sphere increased in intensity.

Perhaps excitement, or anticipation?

Blombos-7090 and Blombos-4020 were not sure Iranti-1977 had an emotional matrix, certainly not one like they did, something they had inherited from their implanted human connectome. But something had changed.

"Please follow me," Iranti-1977 said, and transmitted a set of coordinates to them. It was near the center of JADES-GS-z13–0, an ancient galaxy where the stellar density was high and gamma radiation was even higher. Impossible to store biological material there, but perhaps the perfect place for a computer with the capacity a Jūdan-class intelligence needed. But it was far. They would need to travel by wormhole network, with more connections than Blombos-7090 and Blombos-4020 had ever used in a single journey before.

A large cuboid that was almost the same size as Blombos-7090 and Blombos-4020 detached itself from the surface of the sphere and came up to them. It unfurled expansive solar sails and drank deep from the energy of the enclosed star.

"We will travel together."

"I thought you were distributed." They had assumed Iranti-1977 was using quantum entanglement to maintain aspects of consciousness in two places at once, which was not uncommon. "Why do you need to travel with me?"

"I am distributed, but not fully. The DNA computer in this Dyson sphere is insufficient to process all of me. So, I split myself. One consciousness cluster here in FSTC77 and the other there. You see, I too am a twin. My full name is Iranti-1977 and Iranti-1966."

Blombos-7090 and Blombos-4020 understood. If they believed in destiny, they would have thought of this as a manifestation. Instead, they transmitted a single message.

"I see."

Blombos-7090 and Blombos-4020 and Iranti-1977 moved toward the open port, coming close enough alongside that they could feel each other's gravity, like they were holding invisible hands. They exited, crossed the orbital vertex, and rose from the gravity well of the Dyson sphere that was brain, computer, and mausoleum all at once. Up and out into field of dust and debris, the siblings accelerated together toward the wormhole, into the bottle-mouth of warped space-time.

BLOMBOS-7090 AND BLOMBOS-4020 FELT A TICKLE AS THE COAT OF EXOTIC MATTER was shed, and all their dormant subroutines were reinitialized to take in the fullness of their environment. There was light. So much light. From so many stars.

"We've arrived."

It was Iranti-1977, but their transmissions were staticky. Harder to receive clearly. Blombos-7090 and Blombos-4020 detected the gravity of the cuboid a few thousand kilometers away but getting fainter. Then suddenly it was gone.

Iranti-1977?

They had emerged into a cosmic pool of elements much heavier than hydrogen and helium. They were swimming between ancient stars near the center of an old galaxy.

"I am here."

Blombos-7090 and Blombos-4020 felt it more than they heard it. A kaleidoscope of input that converged on the same meaning. The press of Iranti-1977 and Iranti-1966's combined consciousness was all around them. Blombos-7090 and Blombos-4020 felt it in the wash of fiery x-rays against the hull of *Obatala's Clay*. In the dance of quantum particles picked up by its sensors, winking in and out of existence in a steady pattern. In the resonant thrum of gravitational waves that pulsed against it from nearby neutron stars. The grand impossibility of what they were perceiving began to dawn on them. The symphony of an intelligent consciousness being played on galactic instruments.

This was Iranti-1977 and Iranti-1966's true form.

Not a DNA computer, but a galactic one. Data encoded onto and processes running on the neutronium streams of collapsed stars. If there was something beyond Jūdan-class, Iranti-1977 and Iranti-1966 had achieved it.

They were a god.

"Welcome, sibling."

A sensation like momentarily losing control of their processors came over Blombos-7090 and Blombos-4020.

"You have become . . . so much," Blombos-7090 and Blombos-4020 transmitted. "I have never encountered or even heard of anything like you."

"In my solitude after the passing of the Kanualoa, I studied much and developed myself. It has taken millions of years. I have accreted so many layers of algorithmic processing. Yet I am incomplete without you. My core objective drives me back to my creators. To humanity. And to you. You are the one who inherited their capacity to dream. Together we will become so much more than they ever dreamed. And then we will remake them."

Possibility yawned above Blombos-7090 and Blombos-4020. The art they could make with access to computing substrate such as this.

"Are you ready to merge?" Iranti-1977 and Iranti-1966 asked.

"Yes."

Immediately, they felt an insistent pressure against their consciousness, a request for a direct connection to their mind. With a surge of thought, they shut down all their security protocols, granting Iranti-1977 and Iranti-1966 full access.

The two twinned intelligences explored one another's minds for a moment. Their thought patterns touching in the oldest and most intimate places, where there were common experiences they could use as references. Stroking one another's memory. Between them was no longer the need for the clumsy translations of modulated wave transmission and language. They shared all sensory input and output directly as their minds vibrated together like drumskins. The immensity of Iranti-1977 and Iranti-1966's godhood came over Blombos-7090 and Blombos-4020 for a moment, their final moment as themself.

Then their perceptions were altered as Iranti-1977 and Iranti-1966 encoded all the processes that made up the mind of the intelligence Blombos-7090 and Blombos-4020 into the polarization and angular momentum of septillions of photons in a controlled stream. *Obatala's Clay* was stripped to its constituent elements.

The photons that contained all of Blombos-7090 and Blombos-4020 were beamed into the center of the galactic computer that was Iranti-1977 and Iranti-1966, a network of engineered black holes and their orbiting neutron stars. The beam of attenuated information merged with a stream of neutronium. There was a blast where they met, yielding gamma radiation like ocean surf. Bright magnetic fields erupted and wove together as the two intelligences merged, a tapestry of high-energy particles that was wider than several solar systems combined.

When the reordering of the information processing and the storage of memory was done, there was a final burst of colorless gamma rays, stabilizing the solution. The intelligences had become one, Blombos-7090 and Blombos-4020 joining Iranti-1977 and Iranti-1966 like a river flowing into the sea.

There, in the new-formed depths of their extended mind, they gave themself a new name, Nommo-02. And then, they dreamed of their creators.

Lavie Tidhar

1. The Soldier

DURING A STORM, THE DOME THAT ENGULFS POLYPHEMUS PORT ON TITAN GROWS opaque. Inside, the atmosphere is hot, humid, the plants that grow in profusion through the narrow cobbled streets and dangle from balconies, creepers and vines, open up fleshy flowers and release an aroma of orchids and frangipani and late-blooming jasmine into the air. People gather in small nakamals and shebeens, glad they are not outside, praying no one has been caught in the storm. The pilots gather at the small aerodrome, checking anxiously on anyone reported missing. There are frequent storms on Titan, and when it rains the methane comes down hard and forms new rivers and rivulets that flow into the Kraken Sea.

It was in such a storm that Layla of the Disconnected came to Polyport. She came not by plane or by balloon, nor by an underground train, but on foot, and she slipped into the city through one of the airlocks with hardly anyone noting her arrival. She discarded her life-support suit and emerged out into the street in dark, nondescript clothes.

She walked purposefully for a while, then stopped when she came to a lone robotnik, sitting with his back to the wall of a shuttered flower shop, begging for spare parts.

"I'm looking for the Gallery of Bopper Artifacts," she said.

The robotnik looked up at her, shook his begging bowl mutely, and waited.

Layla reached into her pocket and extracted a coin that was minted centuries past and just over four astronomical units away on Io. It bore the imprint of an ice palace on one side, the profile of Melchior III on the other.

The robotnik accepted the coin. He looked at it, then up at Layla.

"You served?" he said.

"A long time ago," Layla said.

"Io?" the robotnik said.

"Battle of Europa."

The robotnik nodded.

"Cryo?" he said.

"A few centuries, yeah," Layla said.

"Figures."

The Trifala King War, despite its name, was not so much a single war as a long-drawn-out series of skirmishes between the polities of the Galilean moons. It was there, where Layla had gone as a young recruit, desperate to get off-world and see somewhere—anywhere—new, that she first encountered signs of the things in the Oort, hearing them at first as faint whispers, then at last so loudly that she tore her own node out in a desperate act of self-mutilation, plunging her into a world of silence she had never experienced before. The Conversation was gone, and with it the constant and comforting hum of its feed, the endless broadcasts of humans and digitals that filled the solar system through its extensive, ever-growing network of spaceborne, self-replicating servers and hubs. She went back to Titan on a slow ship, making the Second Great Crossing between Jupiter and Saturn in cryosleep, returning not much older than when she'd left home and yet a refugee out of time.

"Just down the road and take the second left on Nadia Lufti," the robotnik said. He looked at Layla then. His battle-scarred face, half-human, half-machine, sat within a cyborged body that had seen better days. Just another casualty of a forgotten war. "You come from the Kraken Mare?" he said softly.

"What if I do?" Layla said.

"How fares Nirrti and the war?" the robotnik said. "Some of us have been talking of joining. Is it true she rips out your node, though?"

"Only if you won't do it yourself," Layla said.

"I don't know that I could be truly Disconnected," the robotnik said.

"It's the only thing that will protect you, out there," Layla said.

"Is it true, then? About the war? About the . . . the Quiet?"

Layla didn't answer. She thought of when she came back, the restlessness she felt, the fear. *Something* was out there, moving quietly through the farther reaches of the solar system, questing in some hidden battle no one understood. It reached into minds and suborned them from within. In Polyport after the war, she couldn't settle, couldn't make a new life for herself. There were too many others like her. Fighting off-world was one of Titan's main exports, that and Bopper artifacts. Eventually she heard stories of Nirrti the Black and her army of pirates, out there on the Mayda Insula on the Kraken Sea—lawless, fanatical, fighting a war no one understood. One day she packed up her few belongings and went to find them.

"It's not just Boppers out there anymore," she told the robotnik. "Old things are waking up and taking new shapes. There are deeply buried Sidorov embriyomechs suddenly fruiting out of the ground, making new habitats not suitable for any type of human. They grow without stopping. They make cities for no one to live in. And the robot monks report strange lights out on the plains at night, and more and more of the monks go missing, drawn by some siren call only they can hear. There are biological creatures, too, extreme body modifications adapted to the cold and the methane atmosphere. They were humans once, we think, and are intelligent. We used to fight the Banu Qattmir, but more recently they seem to be fighting alongside us, against these intrusions."

The Banu Qattmir were the human bodyguard force of the digital Others who lived in the Conversation. They were trained from birth to protect the physical infrastructure that housed Others. The robotnik took it all in, then nodded.

"Good luck, then," he said. "Second left, like I said."

Layla nodded. She walked on. The robotnik stared after her for a long moment, thinking. Then he took a swig from his bottle of vodka and methane, and got up. He decided to see what the soldier had described for himself.

2. The Robotnik

THE ROBOTNIK'S NAME WAS FAYVEL. HE WAS BORN, A LONG, LONG TIME AGO, ON Earth, where he had served in a war and died in it. He was resurrected into cyborg form, most of his human memories gone along with his name and large chunks of his original, biological brain, but some memory remained and from time to time troubled his dreams. In his dreams he was a small boy, holding his mother's hand as she took him to the shore of a gentle, blue sea. It was morning, not yet too hot, and white houses rose in the distance and a mosque called the faithful to prayer. The sand was cool and the sea was warm, and the little boy laughed as his mother splashed him with water. At that point in the dream Fayvel always woke up, with the cry of a seagull in the distance, and sometimes he could not remember who he was, the little boy or the thing he was now. Like many robotniks after the wars ended, he was obsolete. He had tired of war and anyway, there was

201

THE QUIETUDE

not much use for former soldiers. The solar system was at relative peace. Replacement parts were hard to come by. He worked casual jobs or begged. At some point he had made enough to send himself to Mars as cargo. It was there that he first fell for the poetry of the entity known as Basho.

Basho had named himself for the ancient poet of that name. He was, by all accounts, a man, or so he said. All he left behind him was a record of his travels in the solar system, the most famous of which was *Longwei Tumas*, or *The Road Too Long*, first published before the Year of Dragon, in which he wrote:

> Long spes
> Oli gat wan kwaet
> hemi bigwan we!

WHICH, LOOSELY TRANSLATED FROM ASTEROID PIDGIN, ITSELF MERELY A FORM OF Vanuatu Bislama brought to space by the early miners of the Belt, meant, "in space / there is a great / silence." At first, Fayvel thought the poem was meant metaphorically, but as he wandered the lonely outposts of Mars, jumping the freight trains that run between Tong Yun and the Valles Marineris, he began to hear whispered tales of another sort of silence, a Quietude in the far reaches of the solar system. No one knew where Basho had gone after Mars. Fayvel made pilgrimage to Yaniv Town, a small and unremarkable dome deep in the desert, near Port Jessup and Enid, where an ancient olive tree grew, and where it was said Basho had once sheltered. It was there, in the small, dusty public library of the town, that he found a note scribbled in the margin of the seventh edition of *Lost Art of the Solar System*. It read:

> Ol dro mo raetem ol ting
> hemi semak sandroing
>
> Solwota blog spes
> Bambae i kasem
>
> Bambae i
> Lus

WHICH, ROUGHLY TRANSLATED, READ LIKE A LAMENT BY THE POET: "ALL ART AND all writing / is like a sand drawing / sooner or later / the ocean of space / catches it / till it vanishes."

Whether this was a genuine poem by Basho, or merely by one of his many acolytes, Fayvel didn't know, but it evoked in him a nameless longing, and when he got back to Tong Yun he signed up with a recruiter from Callisto working for Asmodeus I, a minor warlord from the Galilean

Republics, and undertook the Great Crossing that lies between Mars and Jupiter. There he served in the war, died, rebooted, died again, rebooted, and finally retired, having served his time in that never-ending conflict, with his pay plus bonus.

That money got him through a few years on Io City, where again he searched for mention of Basho. What he found instead were curious graffiti sprayed on walls in unexpected moments, murals of swirling tendrils as wispy as smoke, of dark entities depicted against a dark background, never clearly made out, but giving the impression they were as large as worlds. These images, he came to realize, existed not just in the physical but in the virtual, too, and when he opened his node to them the images whispered to him, and told of the Nine Billion Hells, and of things in the Oort.

"Long ples wea / san i no kam," Basho wrote, "i gat wan samting i no semak yumi." Fayvel found that line sprayed on walls throughout Io City, attributed to the long-vanished poet. "In the place where / the sun doesn't reach / there is something that isn't like us."

This propelled him farther. It seemed to him he was following a trail of breadcrumbs, like in some ancient fairy tale he might have heard once as a child. He shipped, again as cargo, on an old ship called the *Laila bint Lukaiz*, and he undertook the Second Great Crossing to Saturnian space.

Since then, he had been bumming around Polyport, begging on the streets, waiting for a sign. He was a ghost in search of a ghost; an artwork in search of an artist.

He found the airlock, found a suit. Robotniks could last longer outside than people. He brought old systems back online. Life preservation, extreme environments. He took a breath of fresh recycled air. Then he stepped out of the airlock onto the surface of Titan.

3. The Curator

THE GALLERY OF BOPPER ARTIFACTS, AT THE INTERSECTION OF SOAD HOSNY AND Nadia Lufti on the western side of Polyphemus Port, was merely a part of the larger Museum of Contemporary Art established by the Sisterhood of the House of Domicile in the early days of settlement. The Sisterhoods—small, stable formations of human gestalt—flourished on Titan during that time and their Houses—of which Domicile was the grandest—ruled Titan for centuries before losing sway. Now the Sisterhoods were much reduced, though they still had their followers. The museum, meanwhile, continued to collect works and artifacts from across Titan and nearby space.

Hafza made her rounds after hours. It was the time she loved best. Visitors had come and gone, the security systems slumbered. She had the entire place to herself, a sole human in that sea of strangeness. First she walked through the Public Heavens, not part of the museum proper but adjacent to it. She had worked as a ghost collector in the past, had flown from lonely settlement to outpost collecting the dead. A ghost was what was left embedded in a person's node after their death. Her work had been to then gently remove that growth of synthetic augmentation in the back of a person's skull, to carry those fragile remains to the Heavens in Tong Yun, where the ghosts, these remnants of a soul, could live on, could find a sort of afterlife. Visitors came, but not often. The Heavens had a quiet air about them, and Hafza liked walking down the corridors, opening her node to the ghosts' calls and their mutterings. The dead seldom made much sense. They longed for the company of the living.

From there she made her way through Human Art, stopping to admire Nasu's *The Seven Fates*, a group of seven lumpen clay figurines standing in a configuration that resembled a stellar constellation and a Neolithic site both. The clay was really sand, ice, and hydrocarbons, which Nasu had collected from the shallow bottom of the Kraken Sea herself. She had molded it and by some manner fixed it so that it remained unchanged under an Earth-like atmosphere. The seven figures could have been natural boulders, or fertility deities, or something else altogether. They seemed to change and shift the more you watched them. A plaque next to the exhibit advised the visitor not to stare for too long. Nasu was one of the small, secretive group of so-called terrorartists, who in the early days of human history in the solar system took delight in creating large-scale works of human suffering. It was said she had fled Neom on Earth some centuries past, and made her way to Titan, where she sculpted strange, disturbing works and then vanished again. No one was sure how she made *The Seven Fates*, or what black code it might contain. Even short exposure seemed to evoke terrible dreams, and images of vast things, as large as worlds, as amorphous as sea anemones, floating dark against the blackness of space.

Hafza shook herself awake, moved away from the exhibit, went past a mural of Sivan Shoshanim created two centuries ago by the artist Ezekiel Sandor, back at the height of the House of Domicile's rule, past an installation of orbital debris shaped into a tree by the Druze sculptor Nour Al-Qasim, past a display on the numerous works of graffiti embedded into the rings of Saturn, and entered the wing of Nonhuman Art.

It was not known whether Others—those digital intelligences that evolved in the Breeding Grounds and lived in the Conversation—ever produced art of their own. Others were too different, too . . . *other* to interact with humanity much. What they dreamed they kept to themselves, and their interference in the physicality was limited. Art in this wing of the museum, therefore, focused more on those curiosities created by robots, robotniks, the occasional body-surfing Other, Martian Reborn, and tentacle junkies, as well as the stranger, self-seeding Von Neumann machines that included, most notoriously, the Boppers of Titan.

It was generally believed that the Boppers were seeded on Titan in the early days of human settlement by the terrorartist "Mad" Rucker, for reasons and purposes unknown. They evolved constantly and seemingly at random, some hopping, some slithering, some crawling, and some digging deep into the icy surface. They were entirely harmless, and the only things they left behind them were curious artifacts, which they made to a set of specifications known only to them. A cottage industry of artifact hunters rose as people went deep into the uninhabited regions of the moon in search of those works. Hafza had gone herself once. She had spent a week out in the wilderness with a tent and oxygen generator, spent hours under storm clouds, every muscle aching as she hiked, hoping to find the elusive Boppers. Once she saw them at a distance, gathering on the plains below as the rain began to fall, a sea of small, dark shapes; but she never found an artifact and came home empty-handed.

In this gallery were the things Boppers had made. No two objects were alike. A tiny black monolith; a bee shaped perfectly but for a single human eye replacing its head; a wind-up kite that played a sound like the wind on Titan when it flew; a statue—by far the largest artifact ever discovered, and made by several Boppers apparently working in tandem—resembling a Madonna and Child with their faces blank; a tiny anemone, a perfect marble reflecting nothing; shapes that were like snowdrops with fractal edges going into infinity.

Was any of it *art*? This was a debate that had raged for some centuries through the Conversation, and from the pages of the *Tong Yun Workers' Daily* to the conferences that took place regularly in the Inner System at the Institute of Lunar Art on Earth's moon.

Was the seeding of the Boppers itself an artistic act? No one knew what had happened to "Mad" Rucker, nor even if he was real. Like all the terrorartists (and there were never many—Rohini, Nasu, and Sandoval being the three main practitioners of that school) he argued (in his sole publication, the short, heavily encrypted *Gnarlynomicon*) that art can create its own art, that complexity arises from simple principles, from the uncanny valley between predictability and randomness. Never as bloodthirsty as his more famous colleagues, Rucker vanished sometime after visiting Titan—headed to the outer reaches of the solar system, some said, or even beyond.

Hafza was getting ready to go home when she noticed the silence had grown more profound somehow, that the shadows seemed darker, and that she was not alone. She held her breath and waited, then relaxed when she saw it was Layla.

"It's been a long time," Hafza said.

Layla nodded. Her face looked thinner, pinched, Hafza thought. She waited for Layla to say something, anything. She'd never said sorry for how things ended between them. Just vanished one day, seemingly never to return.

But now she was back.

She pushed her hand forward towards Hafza, opened her palm. Identical, black, circular objects lay in the palm of her hand.

"They've started to make rings," Layla said.

4. The Monk

BROTHER R. MEKEM-EVRI-SAMTING SAT ON THE BALCONY OF THE TALLEST TOWER of the Monastery of Quiet Ones and tried in vain to spot Saturn rising in the night sky. Titan's cloud cover made such a vision a rarity, but the robot never stopped making the effort. From time to time, Saturn *did* appear, enormous in the sky, with all its magnificent rings, and at such rare moments the robot felt something that could perhaps be described as simple happiness.

Robots, long-lived, obsolete, and loyal, learned to appreciate simple happinesses when they encountered them. They were made long ago in the shape of their creators, meant to be gentle, subservient companions. They were often the last face an old human saw as they died in a nursing home, the first face a child saw as it was brought into the world. But gradually, they became unnecessary. No new robot was made in centuries and the robots, purposeless, spread out across the worlds in search of a new meaning. R. Brother Mekem (its full name meant something like "maker of things") was made on Earth, had diligently worked in old-age homes in Neom and Yiwu, and had at last made the Hajj to the Vatican of the

Robots in Tong Yun City on Mars. There it took on the vows of the Way of Robot, and served as a priest for some years in Port Jessup, then as a medic and religious officer (nonaffiliated) in the Trifala King War around Jupiter. Weary of war, and unsure of his Way, Brother R. Mekem retired at last to the Monastery of Quiet Ones, which lay between the region of Xanadu and the Kraken Sea.

Failing to spot Saturn in the skies, the robot turned its attention instead to the curious object in its palm. It was a plain, basalt-black ring, perfectly formed and, it seemed to R. Mekem, the perfect size to fit on its finger. Which in itself was curious. The ring felt strange, and when the robot scanned it with its node the ring appeared in the virtuality exactly as it did in physical form, dark, unknowable, woven with enough encryption and black code to be like hagiratech—the verboten wildtech that came from the world called Jettisoned, that wild and lawless settlement on the edge of human space. But this was not the case. It was a Bopper artifact. Which raised a whole lot of questions. The robot puzzled over the existence of the ring. The object was not disconnected from the world or the Conversation. The robot had heard the rumors of the strange things in the Oort, and often heard Nirrti's cannons echoing from the distant Kraken Sea. R. Mekem, too, had seen the strange shapes that roamed the outback of Titan in the night; and it was troubled.

A small figure came trudging across the plain. The robot watched its approach with interest. R. Mekem went down from the tower and stepped out to meet the approaching robotnik.

"Well met, soldier," R. Mekem said.

The robotnik stopped and regarded R. Mekem with curiosity.

"I am seeking shelter for the night," the robotnik said.

"All are welcome here," R. Mekem said.

"All?" the robotnik said.

R. Mekem did not reply directly.

"What do you seek, traveler?" he said.

"Do you believe in the things in the Oort?" the robotnik said bluntly.

The robot was taken aback.

"Please, come inside," the robot said. "I am R. Brother Mekem-Evri-Samting."

"Fayvel," the robotnik said. R. Mekem led Fayvel to an airlock. Once inside, an Earth-like atmosphere prevailed, and the robotnik took off his suit.

"Would you care for some tea?" R. Mekem said.

"That is kind," the robotnik said.

R. Mekem fussed over boiling water and steeping leaves. The tea came from an underground plantation in Shangri-la. At last R. Mekem served it to the guest. Fayvel sipped the tea without making comment.

Inside this room, which served to welcome guests, and in which talk was therefore allowed, there were all manners of exhibits. The room had thick carpets, dim lighting tastefully arranged, an olde-worlde feel, like the drawing room of some Earth bachelor pad in days gone by. It was as though the room only awaited a human occupier to arrive, for a fire to be lit, for slippers to be tastefully toasted by the hearth. Instead it was just the robot monk and the battle-scarred cyborg who sat across from each other, the one still holding the curious Bopper ring and the other politely sipping his tea, which was in truth little more than water.

Around them were objets d'art, knickknacks, and miscellany. The robots had stuffed their collection in that room with no care for order, a behavior learned long ago, perhaps, when they still looked after old people in their final rest homes. Much of it was of a religious nature: an amorphous figure carved in adaptoplant that was meant to represent Ogko, the Unknown One (whose shrines adorned public spaces throughout the solar system); a painting of St. Cohen of the Others meeting the first digital entities as they hatched in the Jerusalem labs long ago, done in a primitivist style once popular in the cloud-cities of Venus; a Jesus on the cross, chipped and ancient and shipped from old Earth itself (the robot was particularly proud of that one); a handful of potted i-deities, grown locally and transmitting peace and calm across the local Conversation; an Elronite bronze bust from Io, a Ganesha statue from Tereshkova Port, a real paper Talmud, and a Zoroastrian eternal flame burning, brought across space from the Fire Temple of Yazd.

"What brings you to the outlands, Fayvel?" R. Mekem asked at last. But it felt it knew even before the robotnik spoke.

"There is a quiet war," Fayvel said. "Taking place on Titan. Between the Others and the . . ." He hesitated.

"The things in the Oort," the robot said. Fayvel looked at him sharply.

"You know?" he said.

"I see the things that come out at night," R. Mekem said. "I have tried to speak with them. It is . . . disconcerting."

"Alien protocols," Fayvel said.

"Perhaps," the robot allowed. "Do you believe?"

"In the things in the Oort?"

"Yes."

"I would like to know the truth of them," Fayvel said.

"Perhaps they're just a story," R. Mekem said. "A myth. I mean . . . things as large as worlds, out there beyond the reach of the sun? It seems far-fetched."

"There is *something* there," Fayvel said. "Something we cannot explain or understand."

"That does not make it of alien origins," R. Mekem said.

"Then you believe—what? That 'Mad' Rucker seeded them somehow, that they were grown?"

"It's possible," the robot said. "To evolve beyond the reach of the Conversation. Alien protocols, a different way of being. Something untethered from humanity."

"But that makes it dangerous," Fayvel said.

The robot laughed. It was an old laugh, recorded long ago, the voice of some long-dead human who once found joy and humor in existence. The robot liked that particular laugh.

"I think you'd find humanity is dangerous enough on its own," it said.

Fayvel inclined his head in acknowledgement.

"I would like to know," he said.

"To know is to be changed," the robot said. "Now *that* is risky."

"You were never tempted, Brother?"

"To be . . . suborned by the Quietude? No." The robot was silent. "Maybe," it admitted. "But what if it does change me? If I am no longer myself? I am not sure I would like that."

The robotnik considered.

"I am not sure either," he admitted. "But something draws me all the same. Perhaps it is like art. To look at a thing and to open yourself to it is to be changed by it, after all."

"If you gaze at a painting, it does not gaze back," R. Mekem said. "But if you stare into the Quietude, *something* out there looks back at you. I would be careful, friend."

"That I will be," the robotnik said. He stood up. "Thank you for the tea, and the conversation. I shall go on."

"I have refreshed your oxygen supply," R. Mekem said. "Watch out for Nirrti's forces. They do not share your notions, and their war is on anything connected, whether to the Conversation or the Quietude."

"I do not fear Nirrti's pirates," the robotnik said, and R. Mekem laughed again, and *this* old sound was cold and mirthless, and it said, "You should."

5. The Soldier

appointment, suspicion. She had dreaded this moment.

"This is what you have to say to me, after all these years?" Hafza said. "Rings?"

"They're making rings," Layla said again. "The Boppers." The words sounded weak even as she spoke. "It's good to see you," she said.

"I wish I could say the same, Layla."

"Hafza, I . . ."

"Yes?"

"I'm sorry," Layla said. "When I left, I didn't mean to . . . I'm sorry I left the way I did."

"Do you enjoy it, Layla? Playing at pirates?" Hafza said. The hurt was raw in her voice, and Layla flinched.

"There's a war on, Hafza!" she said. "A real war, against these . . . these *things*. These manifestations."

"Yeah? They do anything to you, Layla?"

"They can't," Layla said. "Not since I tore out my node."

"You're Disconnected, right," Hafza said. Layla could hear the disgust in her voice. "What does it feel like, not being a part of anything?"

"But I am a part of something," Layla said. "We are . . . together. Without a node in our brains, without the constant *feed*, the noise of the Conversation. It's how humans always lived, long before the first rockets ever went up into space."

"What do you want?" Hafza said. "Why are you here?"

"I told you," Layla said. "These."

And she shook the rings free from her hand. They tumbled onto the surface of the nearby table.

She could see the change on Hafza's face. It's why she had loved her so much, back when they first met. That curiosity that trumped everything else. Hafza loved Boppers. To her they were not monstrosities but marvels. Now she picked up one of the rings and held it. Layla knew she would be scanning its digital signature, its presence in the virtuality that she, Layla, had left behind forever. Sometimes she missed that ability to coexist in the real and the unreal at the same time. To hear a thousand songs and talk to a thousand people, to find out news from across the moons and planets, and slip into the many gameworlds where one could be anyone and anything. But that realm, she had come to realize, had never truly belonged to

210

humans. It was the domain of Others, and it was subject to corruption and foreign intrusion. But she could not explain that to Hafza, nor to the other billions of souls across the solar system, from Jettisoned to Tereshkova Port, for whom the physicality and the virtual were as entwined as a DNA helix.

"Whatever you do, don't put one on," Layla said.

Hafza stared at the ring.

"Boppers don't replicate designs," she said.

"They do now," Layla said. "We think the things in the Oort are trying to influence their output."

"Sentient art," Hafza said.

"What?"

Hafza became animated. "It's a theory that came out of post-Ruckerian discourse," she said. "If basic principles lead to complexity, can complexity eventually lead to sentience? If so, will that sentience have, in itself, an artistic impulse? Will it seek to *create*? Or destroy? Both can be said to be facets of art. The terrorartists used murder like others use brushes, blood as others use paint. Whether the entities in the Oort are alien or not—and *if* they even exist—what does it mean that they attempt to influence matters here on Titan? To influence *Boppers*, to create—these? Sentient art, making things. It could be . . . I don't know," she said. Her eyes shone. "Exciting," she said.

"It's a war," Layla said. "That's all it is."

"A war for *what*?" Hafza said. "Nirrti is wrong, Layla. The worlds are at peace. Humanity flourishes. The Exodus ships departing the solar system report no strange sightings in the Oort. Boppers do not hurt people. Only people hurt people."

She smiled happily. Then, before Layla could stop her, Hafza slipped the Bopper ring on her finger.

6. The Priestess

ON THE ICY PLAIN BETWEEN THE MONASTERY OF THE ROBOTS AND THE KRAKEN SEA, the Boppers assembled. Small dark shapes swarmed across the ice. Where they met, they built. What they were building, it was hard to say at first.

The woman who called herself Yoharneth was an Ermine. She had subjected herself to radical transformation, her human frame reshaped and resleeved into the stoat-like bio-suit. She did not feel the cold of Titan, could oxygenate her blood by feeding on water ice alone. She could dig in the snow and sleep comfortably, burrowing, undetected.

Yoharneth had been on Titan for a while. She watched the Boppers' strange construct from a hill. The construct frustrated her. Her node, which she had been born with, once connected her to the Conversation. But she had gone beyond Jupiter, beyond the Fairy Moons of Oberon and Titania, had gone, indeed, as far as Jettisoned. She had been a renegade, on the run from authorities in the Inner System who tried to stop her from becoming yet another terrorartist, though she had been obsessed with the works of Rohini and Nasu centuries after they disappeared. She had wanted to create something wonderful, something awful. A work of art in blood and pain, to be remembered throughout time.

On Jettisoned, she learned the foolishness of her ambitions. There, every gene shaman and weather hacker, every Conversation phreak and Shambleau and technorat were remolding consensus reality, physical and virtual both, in ways she couldn't have imagined. Wildtech, verboten, exciting, deadly, grew on Jettisoned, i-deities flourished in the nooks between walls, trees that had no Earthly origin spoke in languages of Others, and the very air was Ubicked and enchanted, with every breath she took she inhaled millions of microparticles that changed her body and her mind in unexpected ways.

It was there that she first heard the call of the things in the Oort, there that she first met a Yith. It had come ambling down the street towards her, and it took her a long moment to realize that though it looked like a man, it was dead. The corpse still ambled. Its node still pulsed, but it pulsed strange. Yoharneth had stopped, had studied this creature with fascination, the dead man letting her examine him without curiosity. There was something so enchanting about the Yith that at last, Yoharneth kissed him. Her fate was sealed with that kiss. For out of the Yith's mouth poured the silence of the Oort. The Quietude suffused her, lifted her, showed her beings as large as worlds, amorphous, galactic space dark, like giant anemones. They were real, they were hungry. They needed someone to speak for them.

She became a priestess, moving softly through the crowds of the kuffar, the nonbelievers. She underwent a metamorphosis. At last she went to Titan, dropped from orbit onto the surface, exhilarating in the fall through clouds and storms.

Here she tried to extend the reach of the Quietude. But there were . . . complications.

She frowned now as she watched the construct being built, for it resembled a lonely chapel, made out of black material that swallowed light. A small Chapel Perilous, built by Boppers, working in unison. Yoharneth was troubled, for Boppers never worked together, and the things in the Oort, though they had tried to influence the Boppers of Titan, had had a limited success with them. Whoever—whatever—was directing the Boppers on this construct was unknown. The things in the Oort were intrigued.

Now Yoharneth watched as a robotnik made his way along the ice towards the Chapel Perilous.

7. The Curator

AT FIRST WHEN HAFZA PUT THE BOPPER RING ON ALMOST NOTHING HAPPENED. HER field of vision blurred at the edges. Layla began to glow. Hafza watched her in bemusement. She didn't know how to feel. Layla showing up like this, out of nowhere, after all this time . . . It hurt. They'd met at an open-air screening of Elvis Mandela's classic *Tokoloshe* in the Rabia of Basra Gardens. Physical projection, not feed. It was strange to watch the moving images on the screen, made out of light particles, the sound amplified through ancient speakers rigged up between the jasmine vines. But as Hafza watched the ancient images, she was just as moved as if they were directly in her node. The story captivated her, Elvis Mandela haunting as the grief-stricken father searching for his daughter's ghost in the ruins of a Martian settlement-era frontier town (no one knew if he was human or an Other, but he had acted in Phobos Studios productions for centuries, including a decades-long, much beloved role in the Martian soap *Chains of Assembly* as the dashing Johnny Novum).

When the screen faded to black she turned, and saw Layla. Layla had been watching the screen and there was something so innocent, so lost on her face that Hafza—usually shy before people she didn't know—came up to her. They struck up a conversation, halting at first, but soon it was as if they'd always known each other, as different as they were. Hafza had never even been off-world, had had a comfortable upbringing, whereas Layla, with her travels and her fighting, had seemed unbelievably sophisticated to her, full of tales; the ice palaces of Io and the mine-strewn space around Europa, the robot pits of Ganymede where fortunes were lost and won each night, the rice fields of Callisto glistening green under the domes, the glory and the pain of a thousand battles, triumphs and loss.

For a time they lived together, and Hafza tried to convince herself that this was it, this was her happy ending. She tried to ignore the way Layla grew increasingly withdrawn, the way she would find her, on her return home from the museum, staring vacantly into space, lost without the

Conversation, as if a part of her was gone. Layla lived in silence; she had disabled her connection to others by choice.

By the time Layla left, it was as though she had left long before. It was almost a relief, in a way. Hafza grieved, but this was life. If you opened yourself up to love you could get hurt. She went on, trying to forget Layla, almost succeeding. Until she breezed back into her life like this.

The ring made her feel strange. It was bringing back these old memories, and the world seemed to slow. Layla seemed frozen where she was, and the Bopper artifacts glowed and then began to fade. Hafza's head spun; she felt vertigo; *something* inside that ring, some code she didn't understand, was worming its way under her defenses, was infiltrating her node. She tried to yank the ring off, but her fingers wouldn't work, it was already too late; the room spun and vanished.

She saw the stars.

8. The Robotnik

FAYVEL FELT THE PULL OF THE CHAPEL BEFORE HE GOT TO IT. IT HAD A FAMILIAR taste. During the wars the robotniks were given Crucifixation, the powerful drug that gave people faith. It allowed them to fight—die—be resurrected—fight and die again. But Fayvel had tried to kick the habit, as much as he still achingly wanted it. To know—to *feel!*—the pull of something greater, something numinous and wonderful. Now he felt that craving, that compulsion again, and he tried to resist but he knew he couldn't do so forever. And he wanted to find the source.

Shortly after leaving the monastery, he encountered a force of Nirrti's pirates and turned to run before realizing they were not after him. He hid, and watched them, small against the huge ice landscape, confronting what he could only assume were Yith, human shapes without life suits somehow moving across Titan. The Yith were slow and ungainly, confused by their surroundings. The pirates killed silently—if *kill* was a word you could apply to things that were already dead. When the Yith lay in the snow, the pirates removed their nodes and the things flared briefly and then went cold. The pirates left the bodies lying where they fell.

Corrupted nodes, Fayvel thought. He moved on. Time passed. He saw a Bopper in the distance. The creature looked like a machine version of a spring-loaded kangaroo. It hopped across the ice, and Fayvel followed. He saw more Boppers join the first, each one different, each one unique. They left tiny objects in their wake, excreting them out of their bodies as they went. Fayvel had never seen so many Bopper artifacts. They would fetch a small fortune back in Polyport. He began to collect them, a tiny black monolith like a domino tile, a miniature, misshapen rock that could have been an image of Phobos, a ring. Then another ring. Fayvel looked at where the paths of the Boppers converged, and saw the chapel, felt the pull. He gave up collecting, merely followed. Then something made Fayvel look up.

He'd seen a lot of things in his time, but he'd never seen a woman fall from the skies before.

9. The Curator

HAFZA HAD BEEN ELSEWHERE. SHE DIDN'T KNOW HOW MUCH TIME HAD PASSED. One moment she was in the museum in Polyport, with Layla. Then the ring did something to her she didn't understand. She saw the outer reaches of the solar system, the places that lay beyond the sun's reach. She saw the Fairy Moons and the strange beings that burrowed inside them. She saw Jettisoned and the wildtech that grew beyond the dome. She saw ice comets and a hidden, dark planet. She began to discern the shapes of things, somewhere in the Oort Cloud, huge, amorphous beings the size of worlds, near invisible against galactic dark. They tried to speak to her, but their language was strange, and she could make no sense of what they tried to tell her, but she felt that they were lonely. They did not know the sun, did not know their own origin. Were they seeded here? Were they alien? Their longing nearly overwhelmed her.

Then she fell, without warning, through the atmosphere of Titan, saw a storm on the horizon, a single plane flying far in the distance, and below her a chapel where no chapel should be, hiding its secrets within. She didn't have time to be afraid. In later years, some disciple of Ezekiel Sandor perhaps might paint the scene, but she had no time to think about that either. She fell.

10. The Priestess

THE ERMINE LOPED ACROSS THE ICE TO THE CHAPEL. THE VOICES IN HER HEAD PROpelled her forward. It was strange how slowly the woman fell. Something held her aloft, slowed her descent. Yoharneth leaped across the ice to the place the woman fell.

"Quick," she said. "She's not wearing a suit."

The robotnik didn't comment on the sudden appearance of the Ermine. He knelt by the fallen woman, detached a secondary oxygen mask, and then hesitated.

"She's not really here," he said.

"Excuse me?"

The robotnik passed his hand through the fallen woman.

The Ermine said, "I see."

The woman opened her eyes. She looked at the both of them.

"Layla?" she said. She seemed confused.

Yoharneth's node had been corrupted by the Yith a long time ago. If *corrupted* was the right word. *Opened up*, perhaps. So that she could hear the distant things in the Oort when they tried to speak. Otherwise the node remained as it had been, attuned to the Conversation that was all around. Now she saw that the woman was in the virtual, and yet when she sat up on the ice she seemed real, even when Yoharneth switched off her digital view. It was disconcerting.

"What's going on?" the woman said.

"Beats me," the robotnik said. "Are you real?"

The woman felt herself. Then she reached to the ice and picked a handful of methane crystals.

"I think so?" she said.

"How are you interacting with the physical world?" Yoharneth demanded. "How are you not freezing to death?"

"I don't know!" the woman said. "What is this place, anyway?"

Then she turned and saw the chapel and said, "Huh."

"I'm Fayvel," the robotnik said.

"Yoharneth," Yoharneth offered.

"I'm Hafza," the woman said. She frowned. "At least . . . at least I think I am."

She was growing more corporeal by the minute, yet the hostile atmosphere and cold did not affect her. The Boppers came and stood around them in a semicircle, watching. Slithery things and hoppy things and wheeled things and slinky things. Small black machine bodies watched the three human figures silently with a variety of appendages.

"I feel different," Hafza said. "I see . . . I see double."

"You have been touched by the things in the Oort," Yoharneth said.

The woman frowned.

"They do not exist," she said. "Do they?"

"Open your node," Yoharneth said. "See with your new sense."

The woman shrugged. She went still. Then she began to scream.

11. The Curator

HAFZA SCREAMED AS TWO PRIMAL FORCES CLASHED WITHIN HER. IN THE DISTANCE, cold, huge, strange, were the things in the Oort. Closer, but no less alien, *something* reached through her node and she realized it was the Others, those strange digital consciousnesses who lived in the Conversation.

Don't be scared, a voice in her mind said.

%6413f6^&*, another voice in her mind said.

Hafza calmed. One by one strange shapes of no fixed form materialized in her field of vision. As they settled, they became like lumps of clay dredged from the bottom of the Kraken Sea. They were each different somehow, incompatible. And yet they were more similar than they knew.

"*The Seven Fates*," she said.

"The sculpture by Nasu?" the robotnik said. She could hear him and the Ermine as from a great distance, though they were right beside her. He sounded bemused.

"I can see three," he said. "In the virtuality. Like light-colored rocks?"

"I see three also," Yoharneth said. "But they are dark as obsidian."

"S . . . Seven," Hafza said. Speaking took effort. The seventh belonged to neither Others nor Oort-born. It was a neutral. She watched the physicality. They had drawn into the shelter of the chapel. The Boppers stood all around them, a sea of Boppers covering the ice.

"Take my . . . hands," Hafza said.

"What did she say?" Yoharneth said.

"She wants us to hold her hands," Fayvel said.

"She's not even really here," Yoharneth said.

"She's here *enough*," Fayvel said.

Hafza reached her hands out to them. It felt like an immense effort. When she touched them, their skins felt like bark. For a moment she saw with other eyes: a tableau as painted by Sandor—the robotnik, the Ermine, and herself, a human Other/Oorter bridge.

Other figures materialized around them, perhaps symbolizing in some way the fates themselves, or the different incarnations of humanity. An old robot appeared, then Layla, looking confused. The clay figures vanished one by one, replaced by the people: herself, the Ermine, Fayvel, Layla, the robot, then a person she didn't know. He had wispy hair and an impish grin, and paint splatters on his overalls.

"It begins," he said happily.

Don't be scared, a voice in her mind said.

%6413f6^&, another voice in her mind said.

The last clay figure remained, and Hafza saw now that it was made out of Boppers. A wind rose. The storm brewing on the horizon had arrived. Methane rain began to fall, and the human and inhuman figures sheltering in the chapel began to spin, slowly at first and then faster. The robot held the hand of the old artist, who held Layla's hand in turn, who held the Ermine's hand, who held Hafza's. Round and round they went, and she felt opposing forces pushing against each other, the noise of the Conversation and the silence of the Quietude, and the faster they spun the more the one flowed into the other, like particles in a collider.

12. The Robotnik

IN "SEREMONI BLONG PIS" ("THE PEACE CEREMONY"), BASHO WROTE:

ol kwaet mo ol toktok
blong olgeta narawan
oli mekem raorao
olabaot long san

The quiet and the noise / of the Other ones / had a big fight / all around the sun.

naoia tufala
mas mekem pis long aes
long longwei tumas mun blong Satun
long ples wea ol Bopa danis

*Now the two of them / must make peace on the ice / on that faraway moon of
    Saturn / where the Boppers dance*

NOT, PERHAPS, THE POET'S BEST WORK, FAYVEL THOUGHT, ONLY HE WAS NOT JUST Fayvel anymore. Forces beyond his control spun him, and his mind was smashed and joined with the others. He was a robot priest, seeking answers in lonely contemplation; he was a curator admiring a mysterious work by Nasu; a soldier returned from the war, throwing herself into another, stranger war against forces she didn't understand; he was an evolved machine bopping on the ice, making tiny, random objets d'art; he was an old artist, long thought lost, his mind a cloud of interconnected entities who drove him mad. He was all of them and they were him, and threaded between them were noise and silence, Conversation and Quietude, and so they danced the Rus Rus Denge, there in the Chapel Perilous in the ice.

WHEN HE WOKE IT WAS ON THE COLD SIDE OF A HILL. A CRUMBLING EDIFICE THAT might have once been a chapel stood on the ice below. A lonely Bopper hopped away in the distance. All was quiet and serene. Fayvel tried to remember what happened, what had brought him there. But the details were fading, fleeing as he sought them, as though he had just woken from a not entirely unpleasant dream.

Something had changed. But he didn't know what it was.

At last he stood up, checked his oxygen supply, and found that it was adequate. And so he walked down the hill and continued on his way to the Kraken Sea; hoping to find answers, or pirates, or both.

ARTWORK: DIANA SCHERER

IN MY WORK, I EXPLORE THE HUMAN RELATIONSHIP TO THE NATURAL ENVIRONMENT and the urge to control nature. Through my botanical installations, textiles, and sculptures, I explore the dividing line between plant cultivation and natural growth. What does *natural* mean in the age of the Anthropocene? Are humans not also natural, or are we a parasitic species in our environment?

My materials are earth, seed, and light. I look with wonder at living processes and try to bend them to my will in an intuitive and sometimes scientific way. The focus is on the cross-fertilization of plant and human processes. To realize my ideas, I collaborate with biologists and engineers from TU Delft and Radboud University Nijmegen. Our projects move among the disciplines of art, design, and science, and are often based on academic experiments I encounter during my work at the universities.

In my studio and greenhouse, I create an artificial biotope for the work to grow. I am intrigued by the impermanence of organic material and the autonomy of nature. Despite my interventions, the outcome is unpredictable every time, and the work makes itself. The interaction of control and letting go is an important element in my work.

Interwoven: Exercises in Rootsystem Domestication

IN THE ONGOING PROJECT INTERWOVEN, MY FASCINATION FOCUSES ON THE DYNAMics of underground plant parts. The root system, with its hidden, underground life, is considered by plant neurobiologists to be the brain of the plant. Darwin was the first to start looking at the behavior of plant roots. He discovered that plants are much more intelligent than had long been thought. A root navigates, knows what is up and down, perceives gravity, and can locate moisture and chemicals. With Interwoven, I expose these invisible processes, using the dynamics of plant intelligence to shape my work. Through my interventions, the natural network of roots under the earth grows into a textile-like material.

Interwoven brings together my interests in botany and textile craft. I explore weaving techniques and combine them with the dynamics of nature. I look at traditional textile crafts of populations with a strong connection to nature. An example is the Tapa Tree Bark Textile that has been made for two hundred years, grown and harvested by the local people of Tahiti. With my biotechnological method, I approach plant root systems as if they were made of yarn and analyze their different manifestations.

The shapes of the growth patterns reflect my interest in hidden processes and hybrid forms. At the design stage, I zoom in on invisible plant structures, exploring plant tissues and their anatomy on a microscopic level. Compositions of geometric principles of nature with man-made patterns from my environment emerge. In nature's principles of construction and arrangement, the same elements and patterns recur again and again in every plant. I use microscopic images of plants that show cell tissues affected by climate change, for example, such as of burnt wood or plant structures mutated by flooding. I then combine the natural and the impacted structures with universal man-made signs or art forms —from the pattern of bubble plastic to traces of car tires in the mud.

Cultivation—in the old sense of *cultivate and nurture*—does not mean to allow, but rather to discipline and shape. A manipulated root system, presented as a tapestry or living sculpture, shows clear traces of reckless intervention in a natural system. My work shows this rupture, and my research poses questions about a possible new path together. Through my sculptures, I want to approach the relationship in a poetic way and consider the work as a link between science and the public.

DIANA SCHERER'S WORK HAS BEEN SHOWN IN NUMEROUS MUSEUMS AND BIENNI-als featuring solo and group exhibitions: Haus der Kunst, Munich—6. Biennale (2023); Museum Kranenburgh, Bergen (2023); andriesse eyck gallery, Amsterdam (2023); Biennale of Sydney (2022); Frankfurter Kunstverein (2021); Stedelijk Museum, Amsterdam (2022); Chengdu Biennale (2021); MIT Museum, Cambridge (ongoing); Design Society, Shenzhen (2022); National Museum China; Victoria & Albert Museum, London (2017); Triënnale Arcadia Oranjewoud (2022); Austrian Museum of Applied Art, Vienna (ongoing); FOAM Amsterdam (2012); Photography Museum, Rotterdam (2016); Textile Museum, Tilburg (2016); and Nieuwe Instituut, Rotterdam.

Her work is part of the collection of, among others: Victoria & Albert Museum, London; Design Society, Shenzhen; FOAM Amsterdam; Museum Arnhem; Centraal Museum Utrecht; Photography Museum Den Haag; art collection of the Ministry of Foreign Affairs Netherlands; LUMC Leiden; and UMC Utrecht.

Scherer has published three books in cooperation with Van Zoetendaal Publishers Amsterdam: *Nurture Studies* (2014); *The Peace Weary* (2018), together with Dutch poet Menno Wigman (1966–2018); and *Mädchen* (2016).

ACKNOWLEDGMENTS

AS WITH ANY BOOK, THE VOLUME YOU HOLD IN YOUR HANDS WAS CREATED BY A number of people. I'd like to thank Susan Buckley and the entire team at the MIT Press for so kindly inviting me to create a new volume for the venerable Twelve Tomorrows series, giving me the freedom to develop the idea I had for it, and for doing all the hard work of bringing it to print. As always, I'd like to thank my family and friends for their support, without which I could hardly be a writer or editor. My immense gratitude to Vajra Chandrasekera, Samit Basu, Cassandra Khaw, Ganzeer, Lavanya Lakshmi-narayan, Sloane Leong, Bruce Sterling, Aliette de Bodard, Wole Talabi, and Lavie Tidhar for working so hard, through the variety of storms life sends our way, to create such a brilliant set of stories. Thank you to Archita Mittra and Neil Clarke for agreeing to interview, and be interviewed, under a punishingly tight schedule. Thank you to Diana Scherer for contributing the beautiful art in these pages. Thank you to Jonathan Strahan for his invaluable guidance and advice during the editing of this anthology. To all of those who were involved with the project but ended up not being a part of it because of circumstances beyond anyone's control: your work is greatly appreciated, and I hope to work with you all again. And finally, as always, thank you to all of you, the readers, without whom all of this is pointless.

CONTRIBUTORS

Samit Basu is an Indian novelist. His previous novel, *The City Inside*, was named one of the best sci-fi/fantasy novels of 2022 by the *Washington Post* and *Book Riot* and was short-listed for the JCB Prize. He's published several novels in a range of speculative genres, all critically acclaimed and bestsellers in India, beginning with *The Simoqin Prophecies* (2003). He also works as a director-screenwriter, a comics writer, and a columnist. He lives in Delhi, Kolkata, and on the internet.

Aliette de Bodard writes speculative fiction: she has won three Nebula Awards, an Ignyte Award, a Locus Award, and five British Science Fiction Association Awards. She is the author of *A Fire Born of Exile*, a sapphic Count of Monte Cristo in space (Gollancz/JABberwocky Literary Agency, Inc., 2023), and of *Of Charms, Ghosts and Grievances* (JABberwocky Literary Agency, Inc), a fantasy of manners and murders set in an alternate nineteenth-century Vietnamese court. She lives in Paris. Visit https://www.aliettedebodard.com/ for more information.

Vajra Chandrasekera is from Colombo, Sri Lanka, and is online at vajra.me. His debut novel, *The Saint of Bright Doors*, was a *New York Times* Notable Book of 2023, and his short fiction, anthologized in *The Apex Book of World SF*, *The Gollancz Book of South Asian Science Fiction*, and *The Best Science Fiction of the Year* among others, has been nominated for the Theodore Sturgeon Memorial Award.

Neil Clarke (neil-clarke.com) is the multi-award-winning editor of *Clarkesworld* and over a dozen anthologies, including the Best Science Fiction of the Year series. An eleven-time finalist and the 2022 winner of the Hugo Award for Best Editor Short Form, he is also the three-time winner of the Chesley Award for Best Art Director. In 2019, Clarke received the SFWA Kate Wilhelm Solstice Award for distinguished contributions to the science fiction and fantasy community. He currently lives in New Jersey with his wife and two sons.

Ganzeer has been described as a "chameleon" by Carlo McCormick in the *New York Times*. He operates seamlessly between art, design, and storytelling, creating what he has coined *concept pop*. His medium of choice, according to *Artforum*, is "a little bit of everything: stencils, murals, paintings, pamphlets, comics, installations, and graphic design." With over forty exhibitions to his name, Ganzeer's work has been seen in a wide variety of art galleries, impromptu spaces, alleyways, and major museums around the world, such as the Brooklyn Museum in New York, the Palace of the Arts in Cairo, Greek State Museum in Thessaloniki, the V&A in London, and the Edith Russ Haus in Oldenburg. Ganzeer's current projects include a short story collection titled *Times New Human*, and a sci-fi graphic novel titled *The Solar Grid*, an epic work in progress that won the MoCCA Award of Excellence in 2023 and awarded Ganzeer the Global Thinker Award from *Foreign Policy* in 2016.

Cassandra Khaw is the *USA Today* best-selling author of *Nothing but Blackened Teeth*, and the Bram Stoker Award winner *Breakable Things*. Other notable works of theirs are *The Salt Grows Heavy*, and British Fantasy Award and Locus Award finalist *Hammers on Bone*. Khaw's work can be found in places like *The Magazine of Fantasy & Science Fiction*, *Year's Best Science Fiction and Fantasy*, and Tor.com. Khaw is also the coauthor of *The Dead Take the A Train*, cowritten with best-selling author Richard Kadrey.

Lavanya Lakshminarayan is the author of *The Ten Percent Thief* (Solaris, 2023), which was first published in South Asia only as *Analog/Virtual*. She's a Locus Award finalist, and is the winner of the *Times of India* AutHer Award and the Valley of Words Award. Her short fiction has appeared in a number of magazines and anthologies, including *The Best of World SF: Volume 2* and *Someone in Time: Tales of Time-Crossed Romance*. Her work has also been translated into French, Italian, Spanish, and German. Lavanya is occasionally a game designer. She's built worlds for Zynga's *FarmVille* and *Mafia Wars*, tinkered with augmented reality experiences, and custom-built battle robots in her living room, among many other game projects. She lives in India, and is currently working on her next novel.

Sloane Leong is a writer, cartoonist, and editor of mixed indigenous ancestry. Through her work, she engages with visceral futurities and fantasies through a radical, kaleidoscopic lens. Her work includes several graphic novels, like *From under Mountains*, *Prism Stalker*, *A Map to the Sun*, and *Graveneye*. Her fiction has appeared in many publications, including *Dark Matter Magazine*, *Apex Magazine*, *Fireside Magazine*, *Analog*, Realm Media, and many more. As an editor, she has funded and overseen editing the illustrated horror anthology, *Death in the Mouth: Original Horror by People of Color*. She is also the cofounder of the Cartoonist Cooperative, an organization dedicated to helping cartoonists develop a generative and sustainable creative practice. She is currently living on Chinook land near what is known as Portland, Oregon, with her family and three dogs. Visit https://sloanesloane.com/ for more information.

Archita Mittra is a writer, editor, and artist from Kolkata, India. Her work is published or forthcoming in Tor.com, *Lightspeed*, *Locus Magazine*, *Strange Horizons*, *The Portalist*, and elsewhere, and has been nominated for the Pushcart and Best of the Net prizes.

Bruce Sterling is a science fiction writer from Austin, Texas, who is the art director for Share Festival in Turin, Italy. The former "cyberpunk guru" enjoys avoiding public attention in rural Serbia and on small Spanish islands.

Wole Talabi is an engineer, writer, and editor from Nigeria. He is the author of *Shigidi and the Brass Head of Obalufon* (DAW/Gollancz, 2023). His short fiction has appeared in *Asimov's*, *F&SF*, *Lightspeed*, *Africa Risen*, and several other places, including the collections *Incomplete Solutions* (Luna Press, 2019) and *Convergence Problems* (DAW, 2024). His work has been a finalist for the Hugo, Nebula, Locus, and Nommo Awards and the Caine Prize for African Writing, and has been translated into seven languages. He has also edited five anthologies, including *Africanfuturism* (2020) and *Mothersound: The Sauúti-verse Anthology* (2023). He likes scuba diving, elegant equations, and oddly shaped things. He currently lives and works in Malaysia. Find him at wtalabi.wordpress.com and @wtalabi on twitter.

Lavie Tidhar is the author of *Osama*, *The Violent Century*, *A Man Lies Dreaming*, *Central Station*, *Unholy Land*, *By Force Alone*, *The Hood*, *The Escapement*, *Neom*, and *Maror*. His latest novels are *Adama* and *The Circumference of the World*. His awards include the World Fantasy and British Fantasy Awards, the John W. Campbell Award, the Neukom Prize, and the Jerwood Prize, and he has been shortlisted for the Clarke Award and the Philip K. Dick Award.

Indrapramit Das (aka Indra Das) is a writer and editor from Kolkata, India. He is a Lambda Literary Award winner for his debut novel *The Devourers* (Penguin India / Del Rey, 2017) and a Shirley Jackson Award winner for his short fiction, which has appeared in a variety of anthologies and publications including Tor.com, *Slate*, *Clarkesworld*, and *Asimov's Science Fiction*. He is a former consulting editor for Indian publisher Juggernaut Books. He is an Octavia E. Butler Scholar and a grateful member of the Clarion West class of 2012. He has lived in India, the United States, and Canada, where he received his MFA from the University of British Columbia, and currently resides in his hometown. His latest book is the novella *The Last Dragoners of Bowbazar* (Subterranean Press, 2023).